STEEL WITCHES

Working as a private investigator in Cambridge, Tom Fletcher receives an enigmatic message from his missing father. Somehow, he seems to be connected to the murder of a young physics student who was working in a hostess bar. As a massive storm begins to batter the low-lying fen country, Tom's enquiries throw up questions: how is a high-tech American company involved in an officially-suppressed story from the Second World War? Where is the long-disused USAF base, and who were the haunting, haunted sisters who play such a part in the drama that is still reaching out to claim Tom Fletcher?

STEEL WITCHES

STEEL WITCHES

by

Patrick Lennon

Magna Large Print Books
Long Preston, North Yorkshire,
BD23 4ND, England.

British Library Cataloguing in Publication Data.

Lennon, Patrick
    Steel witches.

A catalogue record of this book is
available from the British Library

ISBN   978-0-7505-3090-3

First published in Great Britain in 2008 by Hodder & Stoughton Ltd.

Published in Large Print 2009 by arrangement with
Hodder & Stoughton Ltd.

Magna Large Print is an imprint of Library Magna Books Ltd.

Printed and bound in Great Britain by
T.J. (International) Ltd., Cornwall, PL28 8RW

Acknowledgements

I owe thanks to quite a few people who have helped with this book. To Nick Sayers and Anne Clarke for their diligence on the editorial side; Lucie Whitehouse and Julia Churchill for all their agenting; the kind people at the library in Henley for all their electricity; Chris Williams and June Ford for advice on witch-hunting and weather. For past and present support, also Hilary Johnson, Tina Arnold, Barbara Ostrop; and, for all their encouragement, Julia and James Alexander Gordon.

He bought us like animals, Granny said.

He arrived one night, in the town up there by the sea. The town knew what he wanted, and they paid him to go away. He counted the coins and he said, 'But where will I find what I want?'

They said, 'Down there, sir, you'll find plenty.' They always hated us.

So in the morning he came here and he had a black hat, a grey horse, but he was very pale, Granny said. He came across the fields with his three helpers walking behind, and in our little village here a woman came out and offered to take his horse. He hit her with his whip so she lost an eye.

People came to the doors – there were three doors in the village – and it was all silent except for the chickens, Granny said. Then everyone understood, and the women began to run. His helpers went after them into the fields, and the grass was flicking where they brought them down. Our village men came out in the street, but he wheeled his horse round and caught one of them with a hoof. The horse was blowing steam, all the brass clinking and flashing in the sun. Then his helpers brought the women back, all roped up in a line.

Our men shouted, 'Who are you?'
He said, 'You know who I am.'
'What you wanting from us?'
The man looked down and smiled.
'I want your witches.'

Monday Morning

Tom Fletcher got the call at 5.52 a.m., with snow tumbling in furry chunks past the streetlamp outside the window. He was just leaving, dressed for running and not expecting a call, but he got to the desk phone in two seconds, give or take. Maybe that surprised the caller, because nobody answered at first. No caller ID on the screen, but Fletcher could hear someone on the line; breathing near the mouthpiece and then road noise in the background.

He shrugged and went to put the phone down.

A man's voice said, 'Tom?' Fletcher stopped. The voice had changed, grown older, but it was still the voice. 'It's me, Tom.'

'Dad?' The word sounded cold – something he hadn't used for a long time.

The voice said, 'We have to kill him, Tom.' The line crackled.

'Dad, what are you talking about?'

A long pause, traffic noise in the background on the phone line.

'He went to a place, it's west of the old railway line. It's near an old quarry or something. We have to kill him.'

The traffic noise again. The line went dead.

Fletcher looked at the desk phone in his hand, saw the luminous screen shaking a little in the darkened room. He put it down. He switched on

11

the speakers and listened to the conversation again. Then twice more.

A tough call for anyone to receive. For Fletcher, it was more than that. Not just the content – it was the call itself. The first time he'd spoken to his father for eighteen years.

Eighteen years, then he calls me. And he wants me to kill someone?

What's going on?

He locked the door of his apartment without thinking, his mind still absorbing the fact. He went down the stairs without seeing them. Out in Green Street, the cold hit him. He looked around. The sky above the city was iron black, the snow falling vertically in the biggest flakes he'd ever seen. He felt his thoughts settling down, calming.

If I go to that quarry, what am I going to find?

He watched the snow cascading down, past the college lintels, into the river, white disappearing into black. Fletcher filled his lungs with the cold air.

He finally found the place at 8.20 a.m., after looking through the maps and driving through the frozen countryside west of Cambridge. A quarry, west of the railway line, at the end of a minor road in the farmland. It was minus three degrees outside the car, the windscreen spattered with snow and the washer jets nobbled by ice. The sky had lightened from iron to blue steel, and a half-moon was hanging low, waiting to set. The landscape itself looked pretty lunar: massive fields of ploughed earth glinting with frost, winter barley hugging the ground. The road ran beside a series of farmed-over scrapes in the landscape, leading between the shingle banks of an abandoned railway line and the drainage channels of the Great North Fen. On the map there was a site marked as a disused gravel pit – just around the next curve.

The minor road petered out. He expected a rough track next, but it gave way to what looked like an impeccable tarmac surface, mostly snow-covered but neat bruise-blue in places where vehicles had passed. He rounded the corner and stopped.

In front of him was an old metal barrier, buckled in places, dusted with snow that was being powdered into the air by a breeze. Beyond that, just the grey sky. He got out of the car, his parka over his jogging clothes, his running shoes crunching the snow. He took a few steps, right up to the barrier.

This was it, whatever his father was talking about.

The barrier fenced off a massive depression in the landscape. It was a square hole, maybe half a kilometre across and three storeys deep. Its sides were roughly vertical, a series of terraced steps heaped with snow, the wall at the far end strung with the wreckage of some huge machine: a steel frame from which a conveyor belt flapped loose like a flayed pelt.

Fletcher zipped up his parka. His father had spoken to him for the first time in eighteen years, brought him here – why? To kill someone? To see an abandoned quarry – an empty hole in the ground?

The only way down was over the barrier and to the left, along the lip of the pit. In a few metres, there was a ramp of stones and rubble packed together, a long steep slope that a car might just manage, leading down to the floor. The surface down there was a jumble of smaller pits, some solid with ice, others choked with frozen grass and weeds. In places, bits of old equipment lay scattered around – pipes, barrels, oil drums. Down near the foot of the wall below where he was standing, a series of thin steel girders stuck up from the snow, their tips casting jagged shadows.

Something else.

Fletcher leaned over the barrier to see.

Around the girders, the snow had drifted into curves, luminous in the overcast light. At one point, the snow was darker, the tallest girder obscured by a shape. Fletcher felt his heart thump. He leaned over the railing to see more clearly. Then he was running back along the edge of the pit, onto the ramp, going down it as fast as he could manage across the jumbled stones, slipping at the end as the slope met the floor of the quarry. He regained his balance and stood still, the walls rising around him, cutting out any sound from the landscape above, the sky overhead reduced to a metallic oblong. To his right, just under the wall itself, the row of girders stood in their drape of snow.

The shape he'd seen on one of them was a human body, impaled on the metal itself, the jagged end having gone right through him, sticking up a metre into the air and holding the torso just above the ground. Fletcher took the scene in,

14

through the vapour of his own breath. The person was utterly still, wearing a long brown coat dusted with snow, dark trousers, men's city shoes; but, although the body was positioned face up, the face itself was hidden, the head angled back behind the shoulders. Around the body, the snow was completely unmarked. Fletcher looked up to the edge of the pit, the railing just visible twenty metres above. A straight fall, over the barrier, down onto the spike.

'We have to kill him, Tom.'

Is this him? He's already dead.

What did my father have to do with this?

He took out his phone. Then he put it back in his pocket.

Did my father see this happen? Was he involved?

Fletcher took a few steps towards the body, aware that his boots were sinking into the snow, marking the scene. But anyone finding a body like this would approach it, surely? To see if there was anything to be done.

Fletcher kept to one side, where the snow was thinner, circling the body from a few metres away. A freezing wind was blowing down over the walls, whipping his breath away, raising snow from the drifts, flapping the dead man's overcoat. Fletcher saw the face.

A white man, in his late fifties. A big face, wide jaw, grey hair in a military-type crew cut. The eyes were open, fixed up at the edge of the pit, the mouth open too. No movement, no breath visible at all.

Fletcher stepped across the snow, up to the body. The girder had pierced his lower torso, its

15

steel tip jutting up with a shred of dark clothing stuck to it, the coat around the stomach dark with blood, the snow underneath darkened into mauve crystals.

He guessed the man had been dead for a few hours, the limbs still rigid-looking, although the extreme cold and the dusting of snow over everything made it difficult to say.

Who is this man?

Looking at the body, Fletcher realised how big he was – at least two metres tall, big across the shoulders too, and a massive neck stretching out of the coat collar. Wealthy-looking as well, Fletcher decided: the coat was some kind of cashmere; a powerful right hand stretching out of the sleeve had a gold Rolex on the wrist. Fletcher crouched down to look at the time it showed: 8.27. Still working. A mature, left-handed, affluent man, built like a boxer, who looked as if he'd appeared from nowhere, just fell out of the sky in the middle of nowhere, in the middle of the night. Straight onto a girder.

Fell, that's right.

Who is this man? What was he doing here?

Fletcher knew it was time to call the police. But instead of his phone, he took out a biro and lifted the edge of the coat. The blank eyes looked past him. Under the cashmere, a shirt collar around the huge neck, the tie jerked out of line – by the impact, Fletcher guessed. Or by a struggle? Then a navy-coloured suit jacket. Fletcher reached in carefully with the pen. A left-handed man uses his right inside pocket. The almost horizontal position of the body let him slide out what was in

16

there. A wide, thin wallet, flashy alligator skin that opened smoothly. Bank notes visible, gold Amex on one side. On the other, a plastic window with ID visible. Some kind of corporate ID, like a door pass. A photo of the big face, an aggressive grin. A name, Nathan Slade.

Never heard of Nathan Slade.

Looking closer, the name of the company whose doors Nathan Slade used to open.

Jesus.

The Bellman Foundation.

Everyone in Cambridge knew of the Bellman Foundation. A huge American corporation with its European HQ near the Cambridge Science Park. Bellman meant aerospace, military research, armaments.

Fletcher slid the wallet back.

Now he took out his phone and reported finding a dead body, gave the location, gave his name. The operator said,

'Can I call you Tom?'

'Yes, OK, call me Tom.' He told her he'd been jogging out here and just noticed it by chance. Told her it scared the hell out of him, and that was true. Told her everything except that call from his father, the fact his father wanted to kill the guy. He kept that to himself. And the fact he'd seen the dead man's ID.

'Where are you now, Tom?'

'I'm standing right next to him.'

'Have you touched anything?'

'I just looked to see if he was alive.'

'They're on their way. Just stay calm.'

Fletcher ended the call. He stood for a second,

looking down at the man his father told him to find. A smart, left-handed dead man who liked Rolex, Amex, alligator skin. A dead man who worked for an American weapons corporation and fell out of nowhere onto a spike.

He turned to go, then turned back. A left-handed man. His right hand is empty. So what's he got in his left hand?

He crouched down again. Nathan Slade's left hand was curled tight, touching the snow that had partly covered the huge fingers. The wind was rising now, moving the snow around, covering the fingers even more. Fletcher looked closer. Something was there, no mistaking it. Not obvious, but definitely there. Something fluttering in the wind, snaking out across the snow, shining in the dull light.

Fletcher stood up and walked carefully away.

A rich man with a crew cut falls out of the sky, lands on a spike. On his right hand, his watch keeps ticking. And clutched in his left hand, a big fistful of hair.

Not his own hair.

A handful of long, blonde hair.

Close to him, there was a panting sound. He looked round: a chubby Labrador, big leather collar plus name tag, pink watery eyes looking at him for a game. Fletcher looked at the body, back at the dog. From overhead, a woman's voice calling.

'Tilly. Tilly, girl.'

Fletcher said, 'Tilly, go away.'

The dog eyed the body on its spike.

'Go away.'

'Tilly? Where are you?'

'Your dog is down here.'

Up on the barrier, a head leaned over, looked at the situation, recoiled, came back gingerly.

'Tilly, girl. Come back.'

Fletcher watched the animal lumber away up the ramp, the wind flattening its ears. He wondered how long the police would take to get here. Miles outside the city – but still, a dead body. Three, maybe four minutes. One minute was gone already.

Another half a minute went by in getting up the slope, meeting Tilly's owner. A woman in her forties, holding Tilly by the collar now, peering down at the body.

'Is that what I think it is?'

'It's a dead body. A man who must have fallen off the edge here. I was just jogging past–'

'Are the police coming?'

'I've phoned them.' From the south, the rattle of a helicopter. 'That'll be them now.'

The rattle faded, though. Fletcher listened to the dog's panting, watching the snow in front of the barrier. If you brushed the top few inches away, would there be footprints underneath? Whose footprints – those of Nathan Slade, for sure, but who else? The owner of that long blonde hair? Assuming it was a woman, where was *she* now?

And why is my father involved in this?

Why ask me to come here, to kill someone who's already dead?

Did he ask me to come here?

'*He went to a place. It's near an old quarry or something.*'

19

What's near here? We're in the middle of nowhere.

From the direction of the main road, a police siren began wailing, the sound distorted by the wind. The Labrador woman said, 'Thank God.'

He looked around. Empty, snow-covered land on three sides. The brand-new tarmac road running along the edge of the quarry. He followed with his eyes out into the fields beyond. Something was there. A small building: a newly built, single-storey structure of dark wood and even darker glass reflecting back the sky. The road had clearly been built to serve it, but it had no obvious purpose in the farmland. It looked completely out of place there – as out of place as a dead executive with a handful of blonde hair.

The siren noise came closer – sounding like two cars now.

Fletcher said, 'Please wait here for the police.'

'Where are you going?'

'Tell them I'll be straight back.'

He jumped into his car and drove past the woman, her surprised face against the sky.

From a distance, the building looked impressive: low, but with a modern boxiness suited to its construction materials. Was it an office of the Bellman Foundation? Why here, of all places? For confidentiality? Approaching it along the tarmac, though, he realised it was deceptive: the elegant wood and glass surfaces were confined to the front façade, and the sides were simple blockwork painted black. It was an odd mix, as if the building was meant to be seen just from the front.

From the front, or at night.

A place near a quarry – this had to be it.

He pulled up in a large, deserted forecourt with posts at each corner mounting floodlamps and CCTV cameras. Good security – for what?

Fletcher got out and walked up to the glass façade. It was divided centrally by a tinted panel containing a pair of doors that reflected the moon on the horizon. The doors were locked, and an intercom at shoulder height gave no answer when Fletcher pushed the button. He waited half a minute. Cupping a hand over his eyes against the glass, he made out a reception area, with a central desk unstaffed. Above it was a neon sign, unlit but just visible, forming a single word that was hard to decipher in the gloom. It didn't look much like an office. In fact, it looked like some kind of club.

From behind him, he heard the helicopter again, and the car sirens, overlaying each other. He walked around the side of the building, through fresh snow. At the back, he found a service yard, double rear doors to the building open, in the doorway a bulky young man in jeans wringing out a mop, forcing it over a grated drain, steam swirling around him. The youngster glanced up at him, then back at his mop.

Fletcher said, 'Hi.'

'Alright.'

'I never noticed this place before.'

'It's new.'

'You do the cleaning?'

'I've got a mop. What are you, a fucking detective?' From the quarry, the sirens stopped abruptly. 'What's going on over there?'

'I don't know. It's a club, is it?'

21

The man grinned. He went to close the door, going back in.

'Hold on.' Fletcher reached in his pocket, took out a fifty-pound note. First thing he learned as a private investigator: always carry five hundred in cash – minimum. Even if you're jogging. The man eyed the note.

'What you wanting?'

'Tell me about the club.'

'It's called Hunters. What you might call a hostess club. Men come here to sit with girls, buy them drinks. No funny stuff, just that.'

'What kind of men?'

'Rich men, price of the drinks.' Blue eyes on the note. 'Why are the police here?'

'I think something happened last night.'

'Nothing happened last night.'

'You were here?'

'I'm on the door. Security.' Flexing his big hands on the mop.

Fletcher gave him the fifty. 'Did a man come in, late fifties, big guy with a crew cut?'

'Him?' The man smiled. 'You know him?'

'An old friend of mine.'

'Yeah? He paid to get in, only stayed five minutes.'

'So why did he leave?'

The man shrugged. 'Your mate had an argument with one of the girls. Started shouting at her.'

'Now that's typical. No self-control. Shouting what?'

'Something about witches.'

'Witches?'

'Yeah. Scared the girl. We told him to leave.'

22

The helicopter noise came closer, the man trying to see it now, over the building.

'What's going on?'

'Who was the girl?'

'She an old friend of yours too?'

'Did she have blonde hair?'

The boy laughed, stepping back inside, closing one door. 'They've all got blonde hair, mate.'

Fletcher drove back to the quarry. Two police cars were there, parked in a field, and a Land Rover was just pulling up, the spinning blue lights brilliant under the metallic sky. The Labrador woman was explaining something to a uniformed copper. She turned and pointed at Fletcher as he drove up.

Fletcher waited in his car, running the engine to keep warm.

The first time for eighteen years. Then he says we've got to kill someone. And the guy's already dead.

In twenty minutes, the plain-clothes police turned up. It was someone he remembered from his own time in the Cambridge police: DI Franks. Chubby face, red eyes, a big greatcoat tied with a belt. Franks listened to Fletcher's account, scowling at Fletcher's running clothes.

'Jogging? You often come out here?'

'Sometimes,' he lied. 'I noticed this body. I thought, what's going on? I went over to the building there, asked them what they knew. I think the dead man was there last night. You better get over there, get the CCTV from the car park.'

'You telling me what to do? I'm still in the police, you're not.'

23

Franks took some more specifics. Fletcher gave it all – all except the call from his father.

Franks watched him for five seconds. The eyes of the modern police, watery and calculating. Franks said, 'You still living in, where is it, Green Street? I know where to find you, then.' He put a hand on the car door, turned back. 'So tell me, what's it like now?'

'What?'

'Your life now. When you're talking to someone, with no warrant card in your pocket. It must hurt.'

'It's a different set of skills.'

Franks sniffed, then laughed, looked around. 'Hey, what happened to global warming? This is the frigging ice age.'

'Apparently there's a relationship.

'Yeah?' Franks opened the door and clambered up. 'That's the thing with relationships. Sometimes they're globally warm. Sometimes you get frozen out.'

Granny never saw him, of course, but her granny told it to her from her own ma, and the story was years old before that, but it all happened this way, just the way I tell it to you.

Nobody knows where he come from or what authority he had. But all the towns and villages in Norfolk were afraid of him. They say in the south he hanged four women at Thetford and then three in Norwich on his way to the sea. In the villages he drowned five more. Then he came to us.

Back then, there was a pasture next to the village, and his men put up a tent there, as big as one of our houses. Inside the tent it was dark and hot. He sat at the back in a big wood chair. Sun came in through a slit behind him. Noise of his horse in the pasture outside, and his men drinking from kegs. He sat reading a list of the women's names. There were five women in the village back then. He used a feather pen, scratched two of them off. Against the others, Granny said he put his mark: two big lines crossing.

'Bring me now this first one.'

The first one they brought in the tent was named Gussy Salter. She had a man each side of her; she was shaking. She were deaf in one ear, so she turned her head to listen to him. He said,

'Who am I, Gussy?'

'You are the man that hanged the women in the south.'

'Look at me.'

'Then I can't hear you.'

'Look at me.' She looked. 'I am the witchfinder general, placed on this earth for the purpose of uncovering Satan's works. This place here–' and he looked around the tent– 'I have heard this place is full of such works, Gussy Salter. Tell me what happens here at night.'

'I can't hear you. I can't hardly see you.'

He came off his chair and went round by her ear. He was wearing a fine linen shirt and trousers, polished boots. Very pale, a long thin neck, hair combed apart in the middle. He said,

'I think you must be put to the test.'

She made a little crying sound.

'I think you are a witch, Gussy.'

'I am not. God and his angels help me.'

'Indeed.'

25

That's the way Granny told the story.

Fletcher stood behind the tape, watching the activity. The cold wind flattened the parka against his chest. He could see what had happened here – anyone could. Big guy works for Bellman, puts on his suit and goes to the new hostess club. Has a row with one of the women, says something about witches – whatever that means. He scares her, gets thrown out. He waits outside for her, there's some kind of struggle here by the barrier, he grabs her hair, falls or is pushed over the edge. The girl's out there somewhere, presumably, in a panic, or hoping nobody connects her.

A sad little affair.

But why would his father, Jack Fletcher, know about it?

Why would Jack Fletcher want to kill this man?

On the far wall of the quarry, that wrecked conveyor machine had its belt swinging loose in the wind: a long creak, then an impact against the steel frame, then a long echo. Creak, hit and echo: a few seconds between each one. On the fifth impact, Fletcher decided to do what he hadn't done for eighteen years.

He took a route on major roads: freshly gritted, with the snow ploughed away to show the black surface glinting in the haze. The smaller roads on either side, though, were still choked with the overnight fall, and in some cases abandoned vehicles stood at angles. He stopped once, to rub the ice off the screen washers. The morning was beginning to lose its brightness, with a grey spreading from the north that meant more snow in the afternoon.

He put the headlights on and joined the M11 motorway for a stretch, the road reduced to two lanes feeding slowly forward under the darkening sky between earth embankments. It felt like the kind of road that would take Tom Fletcher back to the last time he met his father, in that bedsit off Union Road. The man tapping his ash in the sink.

You're saying you'll never come to see me again?
Not after what you've done.
I never touched her, Tom. You have to believe me.
I don't believe you, Dad.
Someone's radio coming through the wall.
I never touched her.
Then what happened to her?
Street noise. *I can't tell you.*
Goodbye, Dad.

Monday Midday

And this was where his father was now. Wilbur Court – a redbrick two-storey building, tucked away inside a conifer plantation near Madingley. It offered sheltered accommodation, geographically and socially, for older men who couldn't cope in the dynamic, multitasking environment outside. Today, the conifers were luminous with snow in the midday gloom, and the car park was scattered with puddle ice smashed into chunks. The windows were snugly lit, though, behind red curtains, and the reception hall was well heated. It was staffed by a nurse who folded away a Polish newspaper and looked up at him with green eyes. He didn't know her, but he looked at her paper, then back at her and said,

'*Dzień dobry.*'

One useful skill, in the investigation business was a crude grasp of east European languages. The people with information – the nurses, the security guards, the waiting staff – responded when he made the effort.

She said, '*Dzień dobry. Czy mog panu w czymś pomóc?*'

'You lost me after "hello".'

'Want to see someone?'

'My father, Jack Fletcher.'

'Jack? He's not here. He went away this morning, early.'

28

'What time?'

'Around seven. I just started my shift.'

'Did he say where he was going?'

'No. He doesn't say much, your father.'

'How did he leave?'

'He walked out. He had a bag, like a little back-pack.' She frowned. 'I haven't seen you here before.'

'I don't visit.'

'I mean, I've been here two years–'

'I've never visited. We don't speak to each other.'

She looked back at him calmly. She was Polish: generations of men coming in from the snow, saying weird things, had evolved her for this moment. She just said, 'Now it's snowing again.'

Outside, beyond the steamy window glass, more big flakes were drifting past the conifers. Fletcher said,

'I'd like to see his room.' She watched the snow, chin in her hand. He said, '*Prosz* . Please.'

She smiled. 'You got some ID?'

At the end of the first-floor passageway, she unlocked a door, swung it open and stood back. Fletcher didn't know what to expect. Would it be like the bedsit off Union Street? Vodka in the sink?

The door bounced back slightly.

It was a warm, gentle, older guy's space. Smell of furniture spray and soap. A radiator clicking, and grey light coming through the window. The furniture was just an institutional table, wardrobe, armchair and bed; but the table had a cloth and the bed was properly made under a tartan

29

blanket. The floor had a rug placed over carpet tiles. One wall had a shelf lined with paperbacks. No computer, no phone.

'What happens to his post?'

She said, 'It would be on his table. If he had any.'

Fletcher opened the small wardrobe. A few heavy cotton shirts, some army surplus trousers, some socks and pants. Plus a blue scarf he remembered his mother giving his father one Christmas. There was nothing else in Jack Fletcher's room. No calendar, no filing system or notebooks. No pictures or photographs. Nothing that referred to a hostess club or a blonde girl or a dead man in a quarry.

He turned to the nurse. 'Did anything unusual happen here last night?'

'Not that I know. But I only come in at seven, like I said.'

'Who's here overnight?'

'No staff. The men have a helpline they can phone if they need.' She tapped her fingers on the door. 'I got to go back down. Key's in the lock.'

'*Jasne.*'

He heard her walk away to the stairwell. He looked around the room again, couldn't see any reason for staying. He went out into the corridor and locked the door. The wood veneer was dented and the keyhole was scuffed. He knocked on the neighbouring door: same dents and scuffs, but no answer. Turning, he saw the door opposite was ajar, a light on inside. He knocked on that.

'Come in, boy.'

Fletcher pushed the door open.

The same carpet tiles, shelving, furniture – but a different smell: cigarettes, sweat, old shoes. A man in an armchair by the open window, the curtains blowing in, cold air; the snow coming down behind him was the colour of his face in the light of a table lamp. He had a bottle of supermarket beer open beside him, and a stub smouldering in an ashtray. He said,

'So you're the boy. You're the Tom.'

He was a heavy man in his late sixties, older than Jack Fletcher would be. His stomach was pushing against a pale vest, his bare forearms lined with tattoos blackened by age. The man took the fag from the ashtray and held it while he scratched his head with his thumb: stubble around a bald crown. He took a drag and replaced the cigarette.

'Doctor says I got to stop smoking.'

'I think the draught in here might get you first.'

The man smiled, scratching a tattoo. 'I'm John Rossi, friend of your dad.' His skin had red marks, fingernail-sized. His dark eyes moved over Fletcher's chest, his shoulders, then back to Fletcher's eyes. 'Yeah, Jack said you liked to keep fit.'

That amazed Fletcher – that his father knew something about him.

'You know my dad well?'

'As well as anyone. Sorry you can't sit down. Only got one chair.'

'It's OK. Know where my dad is now?'

'No. What did the ice maiden tell you? I heard you talk her language.' He winked.

'She said he went away at seven.'

'He vent avay at seven!' John Rossi mimicked.

31

He scratched his chest, then grinned suddenly, nodding at the floor. 'Hey, right under here is the room she gets changed, into her little uniform. These floor panels are really loose. Could lift one out, make a little peephole. Could do it easy.'

'About my dad–'

'Your dad's a quiet guy. He thinks a lot. Finds it hard to speak, express himself. When he talks, it doesn't come out quite right. Not in order.'

'Is he in some kind of trouble?'

John Rossi took a long drag, shook his head.

'Did something unusual happen last night?'

'Last night? Yeah, you could say unusual. Your dad had a visitor.'

'Who was it?'

'I didn't see him. Heard him, though.'

'Tell me, John. I'm worried about my dad.'

'Yeah? How come you never visited before?'

'We don't keep in touch.'

'You fall out?'

'Yes, we fell out.'

'You angry at him?'

'I used to be angry at him.' Fletcher felt the ease of talking to elderly people, the feeling they'll forget it later. Deceptive, he knew. 'Tell me about this visitor.'

John Rossi scratched his forearms, studying the tattoos. 'I got these in Gibraltar, nineteen sixty. When they were fresh, they were lovely.' He looked up again. 'What about your mother?'

'I'm not in touch with her, either.'

Rossi frowned. 'What happened?'

'You're prying, John.'

'Sometimes you got to talk about it.'

Fletcher could hear the old bedsit again, the traffic and the noise through the wall.

I never touched her, Tom.

Then what happened to her?

'The family broke up when I was fifteen. My mother left. My dad had his problems; in the end he came to live here. I haven't seen my mother since she left. I don't know where she is today.'

'Why'd she leave?'

'I don't know, John.'

'That's tough, boy. I was you, I'd miss her.'

'Yes, John. I miss her.'

'You ever tried to find her?'

'No. But I think she'll come back.'

'I hope she does, boy. Everyone needs a family. People to trust.' Rossi turned to watch the snow-flakes. 'I didn't see the visitor. I heard someone coming down the corridor, about eleven. Sounded like a big, heavy man. Banged on your dad's door, went inside. Couldn't hear what they were saying.'

'You sure, John?'

'Couldn't hear through the door, across the corridor.'

'But you tried?'

'Couldn't hear. But who are the witches?'

'The witches?'

John scratched his neck. Even his throat was criss-crossed with red marks. 'When the big man came out again, last thing he said, closing the door. He said, *She knows about the witches. I'm going to warn her.*'

'What does that mean?'

'That's what he said, then he walked out.' John

shrugged. 'But look, don't worry about your dad. He can take care of himself.'

'How do you know that?'

John turned and looked at the snow outside. 'There's three foot of snow north and west of here. It'll start melting soon, and there'll be rain, too. Heavy rain, I can feel it on my skin. We'll be flooded.'

'You'll be OK up here.'

'But I might have holes in my floor.'

He turned back to Fletcher, angling his head.

Fletcher asked, 'Did my father tell you anything before he left?'

'No.'

'But there's *something*, John, isn't there?'

John Rossi watched Fletcher through the smoke. Then he nodded at the shelf on the other wall. Fletcher turned to see. There were some paperbacks, a guide to living with eczema, a TV magazine. At the end was a thin spine – too thin for a book. Fletcher looked round at John, and John was looking at the snow again.

Fletcher reached out and picked up the item at the end of the shelf It was a simple card folder, slightly dog-eared. He opened it.

Inside was a photograph. It showed a woman in her thirties, wearing a denim dress, bare arms. She was kneeling on an area of grass, against a blue sky, her longish brown hair blowing out a little in the wind, smiling into the camera, eyes narrowed a little in the glare. In front of her, a small boy, not much older than a toddler, squinting too, eyes narrowed under untidy brown hair, his hands clenched, ready to start running, fixing his eyes on a hard pathway on the edge of the picture.

Fletcher was conscious of John Rossi turning back from the window.

'That you in the photo?'

Fletcher nodded.

'Must be your dad's favourite picture. You and your mother, right?'

'Yes.'

In fact, Fletcher remembered something about the moment it was taken – among his earliest memories. It must have been in one of the Cambridge parks – Midsummer Common, probably, or Jesus Green – because he remembered endless grass, blue sky. His mother saying, *Run, Tom.* Running as fast as he could along the hard grey path, everything blurred by speed.

'My dad gave you this?'

'He said to make sure you get it.' There was a silence. 'You going now, Tom?'

'Yes, John. Thanks for looking after this.'

Rossi nodded: no words needed. He glanced at the floor.

Granny say Gussy Salter lasted till dusk. They brought in a wood table and put it in the centre. They made her squat on it, where the sun came in and shone on her. Two men standing at the tent door. He sat in the chair and watched her. In a while, she began to cry, but he wouldn't let her down off the table. She put one hand down to hold herself up, and he make a note of that in a ledger. The sun moved across the wall. He went out to piss, and when he came back, she's pissed herself too, on the table. He inspected it and

35

made a note of that. At three o'clock she began talking to herself, and he wrote down what she said. The sun went behind a cloud. There was a buzzing in the tent. A fly was moving around. Gussy let out a groan, because she knew what it meant.

The witchfinder looked around, looking for the fly. He laughed, Granny said. He called a man in to witness, and the man mumbled out the words. The fly had sat itself on Gussy Salter's hand. When she brushed it away, it came back on her sleeve. He lashed it with his whip and she tumble off the table on to the grass floor and lay still. He stood over her.

'Proof. You called your witch's familiar to you, Gussy. Your messenger to Satan, which I see is in the form of a fly, as they often are. I have seen many such – also bees, wasps, dragonflies I have seen. What name do you give it?' She didn't answer, just lay still on the grass. 'Then I will write a confession that you will sign with your mark.' He snapped his fingers at the man. 'Clean the table, damn. you.'

That's how Granny say it happened.

In the corridor, Fletcher zipped the photo inside his parka. The card folder was slightly too big for the pocket, and he could feel it curving against his rib, pressing in.

He went back over John Rossi's comments. So that's how his father was involved. Nathan Slade came here, banged on this door. Then he went to the club – not for a random confrontation, but to warn a particular hostess about – what exactly? Witches? Then he ended up on a spike.

What's going on?

He unlocked his father's door again, flicked on

the light. John Rossi had said little, but he'd said enough. He'd referred to 'holes in the floor' twice.

Fletcher lifted the rug. He knelt down and looked at the grey-blue carpet tiles. They were old and worn. One of them, by the wardrobe, was curled up in one corner where it butted against the skirting. He went over and lifted it: it came up smoothly. Underneath, he could see John Rossi was right: the floor was made of chipboard panels easily unscrewed. Someone had already removed the screw from this one, and sawed off a corner for quick access. He curled his hand under it and pulled it up. There was a void below: a narrow space between two joists. A scent hit him. He closed his eyes.

It was a metallic oil, suggesting fine machinery. In his mind, it was always associated with an old typewriter his mother had owned, which she kept in the little upstairs room she used as a study. Later, when he joined the police, he learned that a similar oil was used to clean and lubricate handguns. He sat on his haunches, breathing it in, looking at what was down there in the floor space.

Lying on a folded towel was an old British army revolver. The thing was surely fifty, sixty years old, maybe Second World War vintage, its metal scuffed and battered, the scratches lined with grime. Fletcher used a tissue to pick it up, felt its weight, saw the chambers were empty, laid it back down.

Where would Jack Fletcher have obtained such a thing – and, anyway, why would he feel the need? What exactly was he afraid of?

37

Fletcher put the floor panel back.

He locked the door. Opposite, John Rossi had left his own door open to show that he was no longer in his room.

Downstairs, Fletcher returned the key to the nurse. She stopped typing, took a long look at him. She said,

'You OK?'

'Yes. Have you ever seen anyone come to visit my father?'

She frowned, flexing her shoulders. 'I don't think so.'

'Look, if my father phones, if he comes back, will you tell me?'

She nodded, putting his card under her keyboard. 'You were a while up there. You meet Rossi?'

'Mm. You realise he takes a personal interest in you?'

She smiled. She opened a drawer, took out a massive steel knitting needle, the tip filed to a sharp point. She looked at the ceiling. 'I know what he's thinking. He knows what I'm thinking. Which is, he ever tries it, I'll take his eyes out.' She put the needle away. 'That's what I like about this country. Everything under control.'

Outside, the conifers were contoured with snow against the blue-grey sky – but in places the angles of the branches were cutting through.

Fletcher had an important meeting booked for that day. Two people from the security department of the university, looking to appoint a security man. Someone to help guard the dons against the many threats of the modern world. Fletcher just made it back in time, ripped off his running clothes, put on a suit. In the large hallway of his apartment – a space bigger than any of the internal rooms, which he used as the office for Green Street Investigations – he turned the heating up, straightened the client sofa and focused his projector on the white-painted wall. The visitors, when they arrived a few minutes later, listened carefully. One of them, a wide-faced man with cropped grey hair, said almost nothing. The other, a woman around forty with academic clothes but sharp eyes, asked a few questions. Fletcher noticed her eyes moving around the office, over the scuffed arms of the sofa, the map of the world on one wall, the large-detail map of Cambridgeshire on the other.

She said, 'We wanted to visit you in your office, to get a feel for things. The way you do things.'

'As you see, this is it.'

She nodded. 'Some people pitching for this contract have big offices. They have assistants and so on.'

He smiled. She smiled back.

The man said, 'It's true, we've seen people with bigger offices. But we do want someone who is, how can I say this? From *here*. Who knows about Cambridge, the way we–' he spread his hands –'*do* things here. I think you tick the boxes there. Good. It's also important for this person to inter-face constructively with the local police. Hence your background is interesting. You didn't really tell us about that – I'm assuming you still have contacts there?'

Fletcher spread his hands too. For the time being, he left it at that.

He didn't say, *I was a star, a high-flying detective inspector. I thought the police were my family. Then two years ago, over a blistering summer, I discovered some of their family secrets – things going back for years. I paid the price for that. Now the police are wary of me, and I'll never trust them again.*

At the door, the woman said, 'We'd like you to come and see us, have a longer discussion. This week, it could be Wednesday or Thursday.'

'I'm sure one of those will be fine.'

He saw them down the stairwell, out of the street door. Cold air blasting in from Green Street when it opened. They all shook hands, and he watched them walk away through the frozen snow.

He thought, *I really need that business.*

His stomach growled – he hadn't eaten all day, and just across the street he could see the delicatessen's windows misted in an after-lunchtime fug. He went over and bought hot tomato soup in a Styrofoam cup, sipped it watching the TV on the counter showing the regional news. Big views of stranded cars, swollen rivers. Then, bang, a shot of the hostess club – wood and glass against the snowy fields.

He reached over and turned the sound up.

Following the discovery of a man's body in a gravel pit, Cambridge police say they are anxious to speak to a twenty-year-old woman named Daisy Seager.

A shot of a young woman: strong, pretty face. Hard, dark eyes – green, maybe. Long blonde hair.

So that's her, the hostess. Poor kid.

Fletcher watched her through the steam of his soup, felt the stuff warming his stomach.

Daisy Seager is an undergraduate at Felwell College.

Fletcher put his soup down. Had he heard that right? *Felwell College?* The place had a global reputation. It was the only Cambridge college with a laboratory attached to it. It was where the atom was first split in the 1930s.

The presenter was saying that Daisy Seager drove a white Golf – and they gave the registration. Even weirder, Fletcher thought, scribbling it on a paper napkin. Cambridge colleges discourage their undergraduates from having jobs and cars. This girl had both. He looked up.

The police had clearly moved fast. The TV was showing frames from the Hunters CCTV camera. It was a grainy, bluish view of the car park: a corner label reading 00.06.05 a.m. Midnight. The witching hour.

The first frame showed what a slow night it had been for the club: the parking bays less than a quarter full, the cars with their windscreens already opaque with frost, no people visible at all. Then the second frame: a white Golf appearing from one corner, driving right to left across the picture. The side view showed that the ice had been mostly scraped away from the passenger's window, and through the glass someone was clearly visible: a hefty older man in a coat, bunched up in the passenger seat.

The reporter's voice said, 'Police believe the dead man – who has not yet been named – left the club in Miss Seager's car.'

41

Then the car turned towards the camera. The next three frames went quickly, and not much was visible anyway – only the Golf's windscreen, which had been hurriedly cleared of frost; just two long diagonal scrapes connected with a third at eye level, barely enough to see through. Then the car turned onto the tarmac road, and the last shot was of the driver's side – again, the glass more fully cleared, showing a young woman with blonde hair leaning forward to peer through the scrapes she'd made.

00.06.11 a.m.

Six seconds in total. The white Golf must have rolled onto the tarmac road, crunching through the snow, driving the half-minute to the point near the edge of the quarry.

So that's what happened. They left together. One of them – or both of them – even took time to clear the windows.

Finally, a soundbite from DI Franks. He was standing against a brick wall that Fletcher remembered from a briefing room in Parkside police station.

Franks said, 'We need to speak to Daisy urgently as part of our enquiry.' The red eyes blinked. 'This is in her own interests as much as anything else.' The image vanished, then travel news: road closures, train cancellations, snowploughs clearing airport runways.

Fletcher turned the sound back down. He was alone in the shop, the staff washing up in the kitchen, just a few people passing in the street beyond the steam on the windows.

Nathan Slade said he was going to warn her.

42

About what? Witches?

After they threw him out, did he wait outside for Daisy, did she agree to let him in her car, talk it over? Talk what over? And in the Golf – did their tempers snap again? Did she tell him to get out of the car, did he grab her hair, stumble back against the barrier, fall right over? Did he fall accidentally, his hands tightening on the last thing he touched, until that girder caught him through the belly?

That's what the police were asking themselves.

Fletcher was asking himself something else. What exactly were they talking about in that car? He walked back across Green Street, back up to his office.

Some people leave long traces on the Internet, a wake of references. Daisy Seager evidently wasn't one of those people. She was on the news sites, of course: *Police seek student hostess.* Her face, plus stills of the Golf leaving the car park. There was an address for her now – a street in Newnham, a tidy suburb of Cambridge close to Felwell College. And a picture of Felwell itself: the huge 1970s laboratory building rising behind the façade of the original Edwardian college. Daisy's story was getting a lot of coverage – less than the weather, of course, but still, it had momentum. Fletcher thought: wait till the dead man's name comes out – and his place of work. *Arms man in student hostess death plunge:* he could already picture it. But, apart from the news of her apparent disappearance, Daisy Seager had left few traces.

Someone with her name was reviewed acting in

an end-of-term play two years previously, then achieving a record high score in A levels at a county high school, receiving an award as Young Physicist of the Year. The Felwell College site identified her only as president of the salsa dance society. Daisy looked like the perfect under-graduate: working hard, playing hard. So why the hostess job? Was it the cost of student life? Did her need for extra income take her to the club, even on freezing nights?

Nathan Slade had little to show, either. The Bellman Foundation website was a glossy sum-mary of projects ranging from satellites and com-bat aircraft to radar and ground-based weapons systems. Annual turnover twenty-eight billion US dollars. Share price ninety-five US dollars. It named Nathan as Head of Bellman Corporate Affairs, Europe, based at the Cambridge office.

Fletcher thought back to the Rolex, the gold Amex. That seemed like a head of corporate affairs – maybe the kind of man who would want to spend a cold Sunday night in a high-class hostess club. But what took him to Wilbur Court first, for a talk with Jack Fletcher? What the hell were they talking about?

'We have to kill him, Tom.'

Nathan Slade came up on the Internet just once more. His name appeared on a website run by retired personnel from the Royal Air Force – a site promoting reunions and sharing news of past comrades. The highlighted entry was asking for news of a USAF officer stationed in Britain in the 1970s on the USAF airbase at Alconhurst near Cambridge. The officer was remembered by

44

everyone as being especially sociable with his British counterparts. Pilot Officer Nathan Slade. *'What a guy. Literally larger than life. Anyone know where he is now?'*

The same man? The age was right, and there was a Cambridge connection. Maybe Nathan Slade went from the US Air Force into Bellman, ended up being posted back here.

Fletcher printed out the entries, spread them across his desk. The big American executive, ex-US Air Force, late fifties. The beautiful, salsa-loving Young Physicist of the Year, aged twenty. Something happened between them – something that involved Jack Fletcher, made him pick up a phone for the first time in eighteen years.

Fletcher looked back at the news on the computer screen. The weather, still dominating these human stories. It looked as if John Rossi's doomy analysis had been right: the freeze was predicted to last another day. It was set to be followed by a clear burst, then prolonged rain and powerful gales coming in from the east. Satellite images of mainland Europe showed massive swirls of black and grey cloud.

Sometimes you want to see people mapped out like that: not just what's in front of you, but every-thing hidden behind them, all the traces they're really leaving. That usually means talking to the people who know them. He imagined the Bellman people would be well briefed, tight-lipped by now, waiting for the media calls. He looked at Daisy's address again. Daisy would have housemates, friends, dancing partners, maybe a boyfriend somewhere. Everybody wondering why she drove off with a man she met in a hostess club.

Fletcher accessed the electoral roll, checked Daisy's house number. Thirty minutes' walk, but he needed a walk. He put his parka back on and headed down to the street.

Granny said there was trouble in the night. The big house, which is our house today, was used to hold Gussy Salter and the other two women on the list.

Granny say the men were shut in the other two houses. Those houses are gone today, of course. No locks back then, but barrels pushed against the doors, and the witchfinder's men were leaning on them drinking warm ale with poppy seed crumbled in it, the old brew round here. Granny say their eyes got big and dark and their words got slurred together. Our men try to come out and the barrels got pushed over, and the witchfinder's men got knives, big shiny blades under the moon. It all went bad. Two of our men got killed, the others ran off across the grass.

Outside the village there was an old pit, a big hole from digging up clay and making tiles, the old business of the village. The pit's still there today, now it's a lake we call the Deeping. Back then, the bodies of the dead men were weighted down and rolled into the Deeping. They went straight under.

The snow had stopped, but the temperature was falling again as the afternoon progressed. The footprints left by pedestrians were crisping over, and the snow was drooping off the shopfronts in domes and slopes.

He walked through streets which were largely deserted at 4 p.m. In King's Parade, the college

46

battlements glinted against the darkening sky, where a red blur showed the sun getting low beyond the river. He walked through the heart of Cambridge, down Silver Street, between walls where moss and lichen were frosted into metallic shapes. In Laundress Lane, river punts were frozen at the edge of the water. Some ducks had taken refuge in one of them, asleep on their feet. After that, the Mill Pond was silent and glassy black. Leaving the colleges behind, he made his way along the footpath into the area called Coe Fen, where the river fractured across grassland into channels and ditches: the remnants of the massive project of draining the ancient marshes. When the Normans arrived there a thousand years ago, they found huts perched on wooden stilts in a malarial swamp, the inhabitants addicted to opiates brewed from wild poppies. For Fletcher on that winter afternoon, just for a moment, it was perfect: abandoned, silent, a long delta of white against a skyline where the sun was imploding under a band of cloud.

Times like this, Fletcher thought of his parents.

Overhead, two geese flew low in the still air. They called out to each other, twice, with a sound that echoed across the snow.

Monday Evening

Daisy Seager's street in Newnham was a terrace of small Edwardian houses, their miniature front gardens heaped with snow that looked grey in the late afternoon light. At her house, a downstairs lamp was just visible through a gap in the drawn curtains, but there was no other sign of habitation. There was no police presence, but the snow on the pavement was heavily trampled by large shoes. Fletcher rang the doorbell – the old metallic type, echoing somewhere inside. He waited. The doorstep was cold, the wind blowing down the street. In a while he heard the sound of locks opening on an internal door, and then on the front door itself The door opened on a chain. In the gap, he could make out two big eyes at the level of his chest. He said, 'Hello.' No answer. 'My name's Tom Fletcher. I'd like to talk about Daisy.'

The eyes ran over him, then blinked.

'You a journalist?' It sounded hopeful, not defensive.

'I'm interested in Daisy's story, yes.'

'What paper you with?'

'I'm freelance. Am I the first?'

'Yeah. But the police said don't talk to anyone.'

'Are you a housemate?'

'I'm the cleaner.'

The cleaner – *perfect.* 'Any chance I can come in

for a minute? It's freezing.'

'No. I'm alone in this house. I got cleaning to do, ironing.'

'Daisy lives alone?'

'Oh yes. This whole house for herself.'

'Daisy's a lucky student, having a house and a cleaner.'

The eyes crinkled up, the voice laughed cruelly. 'And a nice car. Oh, she's a lucky girl. Yes.' The laughter stopped. 'I spoke to the police. They said the papers offer money. That right?'

Fletcher nodded. He liked cleaners, and he knew he was going to like this one. He reached for his wallet, took out a fifty.

That got him inside the porch.

He was in a cramped space a metre square, the front door closed behind him but another solid door open on a chain in front, the cleaner standing behind that one now. He had to stoop, and it was cold and gloomy, like being in some kind of punishment cell.

He said, 'What's your name?'

She gave a short but complex sound.

'Where're you from?'

'Turkey.'

'You like it here?'

'Chidem. My name's Chidem.'

'You like it, Chidem?'

'Naughty, naughty. *Condescending*.' She gave that laugh again – a jailer's laugh. 'I can't tell you anything about Daisy.'

'She hasn't been back here today?'

'Not since she pushed the man in the big hole.'

'Do you know who he was?'

'Police said, no name yet.'

'This is what I'd like to understand, Chidem. Did Daisy know a big man, short hair, in his fifties, American, well dressed?'

Chidem frowned, a line visible between her eyes through the gap in the door. 'So you know it was Nathan. Crazy old Nathan.'

'How did you know him, Chidem?'

'He lived at the back. The house behind this house.'

'He lived at the back? So they were neighbours?'

'I'm not saying anything more.'

'You mean, they knew each other?'

Chidem made a spitting noise. 'They got talking over the fence last year, autumn. He's almost sixty, she's twenty, get it? He invited her for afternoon tea one Sunday. Then he came round a few times, brought things he cooked her.'

'Cooked?'

'Apple pies, little cupcakes. Too much, you know? He came past very slow a few times on his motorbike. He had a big Harley, noisy.'

'Was he threatening?'

'Just sad, you know? She kept her curtains closed all the time, like he might be watching her.'

'Did they ever have an argument, a confrontation?'

'I never heard of that, no.'

'Was he bringing her things recently?'

'Not for months. That's all I know. Police came here today, described him just like you have.'

'You told them about this?'

50

'Course I told them. Nathan was soft in the head about Daisy. Everyone can see what happened. Last night he went to that club where she sells herself. I saw on TV, they drove off together. You see that? Then there was an argument, she pushed him off the edge, into the hole. Easy.'

He tried to straighten his neck, couldn't quite manage it. He said, 'What do you mean, she sells herself?'

'She's a...' Chidem stopped herself

'What?'

'I got so much ironing to do.'

He passed another fifty through the gap. She looked up at him with calm, wide eyes.

'She's a whore.'

'In the club, they say she just talks to men.'

'How you think she pays for the house, a cleaner, a car? Her clothes, expensive too. She has men here. I wash her sheets. They are like maps–' Chidem raised a blunt finger – 'of all the sin in the world. In my town, a girl like that would be taken to the river and washed clean.'

'I get it. Did you tell the police this?'

'Yes. And they understood me.'

'I see.' His neck was starting to hurt. 'Any idea where she is now?'

'No.'

Just being in the porch was starting to annoy him enormously.

He said, 'Chidem, can I look at her room?'

'No way, no. You might break something. Then I would be blamed.'

'I'll pay for any damage.' The big eyes blinked at him. 'You want a security deposit, right?'

51

It turned out that Chidem was short, with ringlet hair, stunning in a plump way, dressed in a superbly cut trouser suit in a silky material that caught the light – although the sleeves were rolled back, and the trouser cuffs up, as if it fitted a taller woman. He said,

'You must do well, all this ironing.'

She raised a finger to her lips and giggled – a sound even more vicious than her laugh. 'Daisy's.'

'You've been expecting the press, haven't you?'

'What I could tell about Daisy; what I could show you in this house. It's worth thousands. Five or ten thousand.'

'Just give me a taster, Chidem. Then I'll be back for the full interview.'

'You give me a taster.'

He gave her a hundred.

She showed him the downstairs rooms. A tidy kitchen with the smell of ironing, two living rooms with neutral furniture She smiled at him. 'Now upstairs.'

Remembering her comments about sin, he waited till she was halfway up the stairs before following. She slowed down, her rump at the level of his eyes for a second. Then they were on a tiny landing space, Chidem unlocking a door and saying, 'This is where the police spent most time. Just look, don't go in.'

She pushed the door open and flicked on a light switch.

The ceiling lampshade was draped in a piece of red material – some kind of acrylic fur which cast a fleshy light around the room. It had to be on, because the windows had heavy blackout curtains pulled shut. In the centre, a double bed covered in a similar red fur, no pillows. No other furniture at all, but one wall was lined with a floor-to-ceiling mirror.

He looked at Chidem, she raised a neat eyebrow.

He said, 'What goes on in here?'

'What do you think? It's her whoring room. She brings men here.'

'Have you seen these men?'

'No. But what else is this for?'

He wondered about that. The wall opposite the mirror was fitted with two metal hooks, casting long shadows in the red light. On the floor near the window, various types of long women's boots, black gloves. He had to agree that this wasn't the bedroom of a Young Physicist of the Year, but it looked corny, something from a cartoon. As if – he decided – a young physicist with a background in drama tried to dress a room up as a whoring room. Then he thought, yeah, but she does work in a hostess club, she pays the rent alone. She did leave with Nathan Slade in her car. And the police, looking in here, what conclusion were they coming to? *Blonde student vice girl argues over price, pushes arms man into pit, hides in panic?* Was that what happened?

But they weren't arguing over price. They were arguing about witches.

He let Chidem close the door. He said, 'That's not her bedroom, obviously.'

'No, her bedroom's this one. The police were quicker in there. Nothing to see.'

'Let me have a look.'

At first, he thought Chidem was right. The room was neat and orderly, a faint smell of quality perfume, afternoon light through parted curtains which had a view of the back of the house beyond – Nathan's house, apparently. Fletcher went over and watched it for a minute. It was small and neat, identical to this one, no sign of activity at all – just snow heaped along the roofline. He turned to look at the room. There was a double bed with a plain duvet, a simple wardrobe, two chairs and a desk. No books.

'Where's her computer?'

'The police took it.'

'They take anything else?'

'Nothing else to take.'

He nodded. On the wall in front of the desk, some pictures pinned up on a cork board. There was Daisy herself, looking fantastic in a ballgown with a group of other partying students, her hair pinned up, her hard eyes laughing; other pictures of what could be her parents at a barbecue; then a family dog and a pleased-looking pony with a rosette on its bridle. The cork board of the perfect undergraduate, like something from a magazine feature.

Except for the picture at the top, pinned over the others as if a recent addition.

Fletcher studied it. It was a reproduction of an old sketch – a few hundred years old, judging by the clothes. Done in heavy black ink, it showed a woman being interrogated by a man in a tall hat. The woman had a black cat on her knee, its mouth open in a hiss. The man was writing with a quill in a roll of parchment. Underneath, some words handwritten in biro:

He bought us like animals, Granny said.

He asked, 'What does this mean?'
'I don't know.'
'Why does she have this picture?'
'It's just a picture.'
'Is Daisy into witchcraft? Spells and things?'
'I've never heard her talk about that.'
Fletcher thought, what's going on here? Daisy gets to know Nathan Slade, she has a picture of a witch on her wall. He calls her a witch, falls on a spike. Fletcher looked around the cork board again.

In the corner, under the damn horse, there was a photocopied sheet, A4 size, just its corner showing. Fletcher reached out and lifted the pony away. The photocopy underneath was a grainy enlargement, the pixels blown up to a few times their perfect size. He slipped it off the board, the pin tearing one corner.

He swallowed hard, his throat tight.

It was part of a photograph, about half. It showed a small boy against a clear sky, about to run along a path through grass.

'Where did this come from?'
'I never saw it.'
Fletcher held it up in the grey afternoon light. There was no doubt: it was a copy of part of the photo from his father's room. It was the picture of himself, a few years old. Just Tom Fletcher and his path – not his mother, she was cropped out.

55

He looked at his child's face, the determined expression still there in the swirl of dots.

His head was turning like that, in a fractured loop.

Daisy Seager has a picture of me. Does she know who this is?

And where exactly did she get it?

He turned it over: the reverse was blank. He replaced it, not wanting to draw Chidem's attention to it any further.

Downstairs, she said, 'You'll be back, take the full story?'

He zipped up his parka, his mind elsewhere. 'Someone will be back, yes.'

'And they'll pay me for the story?'

'I think so. Make sure you get a good price.'

She smiled and closed the door of the punishment cell on him.

Fletcher breathed in the cold, clean air. Then he walked around the corner, counting the houses along to the one exactly behind Daisy's: the house where Nathan Slade had lived. The front garden was taken up by a huge motorbike under a padded tarpaulin. The house itself was small, but smartly maintained, in a pleasant street. The kind of house that a senior Bellman executive would have? It looked that way. The snow along the short path was heavily trampled, like at Daisy's house. Nobody answered the bell.

Nathan was soft in the head about Daisy, her cleaner said. He brought her apple pie, became maybe a little fixated. What did they talk about before they fell out? Something that involved Jack

Fletcher? Did it get Daisy interested in witches? And what suddenly happened that Nathan had to warn her about?

Granny said the witchfinder spent the night on a feather mattress in his tent. Maybe he found it hard to sleep, she said, thinking of what he was going to do the next day, the two women he was going to work on. She said once, maybe, he came to the door of his tent and watched the house. He put a few poppy seeds in his mouth, chewed them into pulp, thinking. Then went back to his mat. Just his breathing, his scratching, feeling himself, his places. Chewing his seeds, pulping them over, getting himself to sleep.

It was still office hours. Fletcher took out his phone and checked a number. A short burst of bland music, then,

'The Bellman Foundation, good afternoon.'

He asked to speak to someone in Nathan Slade's department. There was a silence, then a long stretch of the music, so long that it clicked back to the start and began again.

'Can I help you?'

The voice was female, moderate American accent, slightly gravelly.

'I'm Tom Fletcher.'

'Well, my name is Mia Tyrone. I work in Mr Slade's department.'

She sounded defensive, wary of being questioned.

'Are you aware Nathan Slade is dead?'

She was silent for a few seconds. 'What's your interest exactly?'

'I'm the person who found the body this morning.'

'And why are you phoning us?'

'I'd like to talk to you about Nathan. About his relationship with Daisy Seager.'

'I'm sorry, I can't possibly discuss that.'

'What if I said that Daisy knows about witches?'

She was quiet for about three seconds. Then, 'Just give me your name again, please.'

When Fletcher told her, she put him on hold for half a minute.

When she came back, something in her voice had changed. It was still husky, but the air of defensiveness had gone.

'Listen, I can't possibly see you today, Mr Fletcher. It's late, and you can maybe imagine the situation here right now with Mr Slade, er, passing away. But in the morning, say nine-thirty?'

Fletcher considered that a good result.

He began the walk back into Cambridge. It was a cold, empty city. The only people around were trying to get cars moving, or scraping ice off pavements, making their way carefully through the crusted snow, shoulders hunched. Grit lorries were moving slowly along the main streets, spattering rock salt, their orange lights spinning off the cleared tarmac. Fletcher stopped and watched one lumber away along Trumpington Street.

You see a picture of yourself on a stranger's cork board, you want to know what's happening.

He watched another lorry turn the corner, the salt bouncing off the kerbstones behind it. The granules made a rushing noise, like a thousand fingerbones tapping the street, searching for what the city was hiding.

They went suddenly still and quiet.

Maybe they found what they were looking for.

Tom Fletcher, holder of a police bravery medal. Thirty-three years of age. Height, six foot two. Brown hair, cut straight across the forehead. Always stubble on his chin. Now, in the dark at 6 p.m., standing outside a house in Alpha Road. The house he'd lived in until the age of fifteen. His old room was up there on the right, near the streetlamp. The lamp was the way he remembered it – except the light was orange now. Back then, it was strawberry-coloured, and it made a humming sound you could hear if you stood right underneath or had the window open in summer.

Next to that, the window of his mother's study. He remembered the room so well, because she kept it locked. She did work in there: her research, she called it. Once or twice he'd been in there – seen piles of books, papers taped on the walls, the typewriter on her desk. He smiled – the smell of that typewriter oil, the old machine totally out of date even back then, but she loved it. On some evenings, sometimes late at night, the click of the keys coming through the wall by his bed as she wrote up the pages of notes that made their way onto the walls, covering them.

He stopped smiling.

The house was all wrong now: a new family living there. There was a burglar alarm blinking, the curtains were new, a car at the kerb that his father could never have afforded. One of the curtains moved slightly, a face looking out at this stranger watching the place.

Fletcher walked down to the river, stood in the half-dark on the footbridge over the weir. The water was loud, pluming over the drop in long white claws.

It was here, right here.

The last time he saw his mother was here, as she walked away across the bridge. Those last few weeks, she was scared of something, distracted; one morning with a bruise on her cheekbone, tears in her eyes. Tom Fletcher always blamed his father for that, always knew his father had done it.

I never touched her, Tom.

So what happened to her?

He walked on, onto the pathway across Jesus Green, following the dark band across the expanse of snow. Maybe, he thought, of all the paths in Cambridge, this was the one in the photo, the one he remembered running on.

He knew that if he ever met his mother again – if he ever had the chance to see her, speak to her – he would ask the question that had been waiting half his life. Why did you leave us like that?

He knew there was another question now, one that felt just as important. *Daisy Seager's a twenty-year-old physics student who seems to entertain men in her spare room. So who gave her a picture of me?*

On the other side of Cambridge, a mile away from his flat, Fletcher crossed the railway bridge on Mill Road. Normally, the electric cables stretching away on either side would be flashing and swaying as trains passed. Tonight, in the freeze, they were silent and ridged with frost.

Over the bridge, Fletcher turned into a narrow street backing onto the railway yards, with a steel gate at the end of the alley crusted with ice. He let himself into a small terraced house and closed the door, feeling the warmth wrap around him. Pipes clicking, the boiler working overtime. He pulled his boots off on the doormat and stepped inside.

What kind of day have you had? Well, I found this American guy impaled on a spike.

Cathleen was in the downstairs room, snapping down the locks on a roller case. She looked up at him and smiled.

'The ice man.'

She was a year younger than him, and her son had just started at university. More than anything, that summed up for Fletcher what her life had been like. He'd met her when his family had broken up – his mother walking away across the footbridge, his father deemed unfit to care for him – and he'd been placed for a short time in a foster home. She was already pregnant then, aged fourteen.

She said, 'Think my case is too heavy?'

He lifted it, still thinking how to tell her what was going on.

'Seems fine. But will your flight be taking off, with this weather?'

'They've cleared the runways at Stansted. This time tomorrow, I'll be warm. Imagine it, warm sunshine.'

Cathleen held an administrative job in one of the colleges; one of the college professors named Don Simons had recently popped up on TV with a series about early religions. He was filming a second series in Crete, and had asked Cathleen to join the team.

She straightened up and pulled her long, coppery hair away from her face. These last two years, fine lines appearing there, by her eyes. He kissed her. He said, 'You going to miss me?'

She twined her hair in one hand, watching him. 'Come upstairs. I'll give you something to remember.'

When he remembered it, he saw a kaleidoscope lit by the arc lamps from the railway yards, fragmented by the frost on the window. Cathleen's smile, the electric light on her thighs, the long bones of her arms stretching around him. Cathleen's warm breath and the way she gasped, enough to melt any ice anywhere. Then it was just warm enough to lie naked, looking at each other, her nipples still sharp in the light, her hair still across her face. Under that, she smiled.

He said, 'What?'

'Come with me. Get a ticket at the airport.'

'You'll be busy, assisting Don Simons.'

'Not all the time. I mean it, come with me. We'll sit on the beach in the evening and look at the sea. Come on – I've seen your diary for the week. It's virtually empty.'

That was true enough. But he rolled onto his back, saw her kneeling above him. He cupped the weight of her breasts in his hands. He said, 'My dad phoned today.'

She stopped still for a moment. 'Your dad?' She reached out and smoothed his face. 'Why?'

He told her about Nathan Slade – kept seeing that handful of blonde hair flickering out across the snow. He told her about Daisy Seager – saw the distorted photo of himself as a child.

She said, 'Where would she get that picture from? From your dad?'

'It's possible. But why would she want it? Why would she enlarge it?'

It was quiet for a while, in the absence of train noise. Then Cathleen said, 'What was your dad really like? I mean, before all the problems.'

'He...' Fletcher had to stop and think. 'He came home once with two grand he'd won on the horses. Him and my mother, they were dancing in the garden, waltzing, laughing. The neighbours' curtains were twitching. Then he lost it again the following week, lost it and another grand too that he owed to someone from a poker game. That's what he was like.'

'You think he was mistreating her, don't you?'

'Those last few weeks, before she left. She was scared, kind of jumpy. He was drinking more and more. I blamed him, yes. There was nobody else to blame.'

'So what are you going to do now?'

'I'm going to find out what's going on.'

They lay without speaking for a while, listening to the sounds of the little house. Then Cathleen said, 'You want to see the village house?'

'Go on, then.'

She reached over to her bedside drawer and

pulled out a plastic wallet. She knelt again with the duvet around her, and smoothed the plastic out on the pillow. In the lights from the rail yard, he saw the outline of the picture, before she turned on the side lamp and reached out to pull the curtains shut. He admired the swing of her breasts for a second. She slapped his face lightly.

'The picture, Tom Fletcher.'

It was a derelict house in a village to the east of Cambridge. A farm labourer's house once, probably, the farm now streamlined by agribusiness. The roof was full of holes and the door was an iron panel. There had been some kind of garden once, but it was a jumble of brambles now, an old beehive just visible. It would take a lot of work, but Fletcher knew they could make it into a good house – a place they could be together. With what was left of his savings, plus what Cathleen had and a mortgage they could barely afford, he knew they could buy it and start on the work this year. On the pillow, in the frosty electric light, the house looked like a mirage.

He folded it away and lay back again, Cathleen beside him, his arms round her. She said,

'It'll be a new start, won't it? Everything new again.'

'Yes.'

'Nothing's going to put that at risk, is it?'

Putting her face against his chest.

He woke when the street door closed. He heard a diesel engine rattling away along the narrow road, her taxi to the airport. The clock said 4.07 a.m., and under it was a scribbled note.

You look like a little boy asleep. But you're not. XXX.

His own breath was making vapour in the light from the yards. He turned to the window and looked through the scratches of frost, down at the silent railway lines. A fox appeared on the far side, nosing the air, eyes glinting in the sodium lamps, then slipped away.

A new start. Together, in the house they were going to build. Nothing was going to put that at risk.

Down on the tracks, he heard the fox bark.

Daisy Seager knew she was somewhere outside. There was a freezing wind blowing across her, and the sound of water from somewhere nearby. When she opened her eyes, though, there was something in her eyelids she thought was ice, and all she could see was dark sky, bands of cloud moving quickly, a blur of red in one corner. She tried to move, but her hands were tied behind her.

From one side of her vision, through the stuff in her eyes, she saw a shape move against the clouds. It was the outline of a man, his head and one shoulder, quite still, looking down at her. She couldn't make out his face, but she could see his jaw was moving.

It hurt her to look at him, the cold racking her neck.

He said nothing, just kept moving his mouth.

She knew this was him. The man old Nathan had warned her about, said was so dangerous. Nathan who cried in the car outside the club, said 'I shouldn't have told you, honey. I shouldn't have told you about the witches.' Putting his hands all over her, in her hair, till she slapped him, told him to get out of the car. She thought she could make it on her own.

So this was the danger, just looking down at her, his jaw still moving.

She realised he was chewing.

Tuesday Morning

The house was freezing. The heating was off, and the water in the shower was so cold it left an ache in Fletcher's skull. The electricity was still working, though – the TV downstairs was reporting an overnight failure in gas supplies across eastern England. Schools were closed for the day, and hospitals were cancelling non-emergency procedures as the state began hoarding its reserves of energy.

Fletcher watched the mayhem with the volume down, dressing in the spare clothes he kept in Cathleen's house: blue shirt, a heavy blue suit that seemed right for his meeting at the Bellman Foundation. He began to knot his tie, stopped.

The TV was flashing him a picture of Nathan Slade, then an image of a smart glass fascia against white fields. The hostess club – then two of the frames from its CCTV: Daisy Seager peering through the scrapes in her windscreen, her white Golf turning out of the car park. Fletcher got the sound up in time to hear

'*...found early this morning in isolated farmland north of Cambridge.*'

A brief shot of a car at the side of a frozen road. A Golf, burned out, the snow around it melted away to show black earth below. Fletcher thought, burn her own car? No way.

The presenter's voice said, 'An appeal for

information comes from the dean of Felwell College, Dr Tania Nile.'

A shot of a smart, tweedy woman speaking in front of a set of iron gates.

'We're very worried now. We just want her safely back with us.' Then they switched to a police press conference. A wide desk in front of a huge moulding of the constabulary crest, rows of reporters visible in front, some cameras already flashing.

On the desk, Fletcher recognised DI Franks, dressed in a suit with crumpled lapels. Next to him, a distressed-looking couple in their late forties being introduced as Daisy's parents, the man holding the wife's hand in support.

Back in the police, Fletcher had attended seminars on the whole subject of how to manage a police press conference in a murder enquiry. How to strike the balance between authority and accessibility, how to make clear requests for public assistance, involving the relatives for impact without making the event mawkish. The acronym was CAM: *Clear, Actionable Memorable.*

Something felt wrong about this from the start. It was partly the way Franks spoke, in the flat, gapped speech of a mid-ranking policeman with something awkward to say.

'We appeal to anyone who knows Daisy outside her regular life at Felwell College, that is to say through her part-time work as a hostess or escort.' There was a definite buzz around the room, increased rate of camera flash. 'We believe the answer to Daisy's present whereabouts may well lie in that sphere.'

The parents looked astonished, as if nobody had told them about this – or maybe they knew, but weren't expecting it to be broadcast. The father turned sideways and stared at Franks as questions came from the room. Franks took the first one with a jab of the finger, something he must really have practised.

The reporter said, 'You're saying her work as an escort; I mean, you're saying there's a sex industry aspect to this?'

Franks considered for a moment. 'We've showed you all some CCTV footage of Daisy and Mr Slade in a car together.' The parents reacted to that, too. Daisy, but *Mr Slade*. 'We don't yet fully understand the nature of Daisy's work as an escort...'

The father said something which the microphone didn't pick up, which Franks ignored after a sideways glance.

'...but it is logical and appropriate to focus on this sphere she is in, where she is in contact with men much older than her, for business purposes. We believe she may be being held against her will.' Then Franks's face jerked sideways as someone shoved him. The camera pulled back to show the father jabbing Franks on the chest, shouting something. The camera flashes went wild, like a strobe system. Then three men in suits jumped up and hid the scuffle from view, leaning over the desk to separate the combatants. The lights went down, so that only the silhouette of the people at the desk could be seen.

The channel went back to the studio, the presenter shuffling his papers, his eyes wide. Then

69

onto the weather.

Clear, Actionable, Memorable.

So they were calling Daisy a vice girl. Someone who picks up older men. Thinking about it, he could see how they *would* want to focus on that. The gossip from the cleaner, the ambiguous nature of her locked front bedroom.

Then the presenter again. 'The fun side of the big freeze.' Shots of snowmen, ice sculptures, kids on sledges.

Fletcher turned it off and knotted his tie.

Daisy Seager not hiding in a panic, scared because she pushed an arms exec over a barrier. But Daisy being held against her will?

Who would do that?

The second day, they started early. The witchfinder's men were pale and their eyes up in their heads, and their hands were shaking when they brought a girl called Matty Flinter into that tent on the pasture.

Matty Flinter was young and the man she was going to marry was killed the night before. When she saw the witchfinder on his chair, she spit at him, and he marked that down in his book. He wiped his face and settled down again. He chewed on some poppy seeds. She waited. The sun from the tent slit was moving along the wall toward her.

I know that sun, the way it moves.

Sometimes I close the shutters upstairs in our house and I say that I am Matty Flinter and I sit in my chair and I wait for the sun through the shutters to move round to me. When the sun touches me, I cry out. My sister says I mustn't; she says I got to live in the real world, not in the old stories. My sister says it

70

probably never happened, she says how could Granny know? But Granny knew because the story come down to her, word for word.

I cry out because, back then, in the tent on the pasture, Matty Plinter cried out. Matty knew what was coming next.

The Bellman site was on a new business estate near the original science park. The largest building in its complex, it was a semicircle of granite and aluminium, built around an ornamental lake. The lobby was warm; after signing in with the receptionist, he waited on a leather bench, the morning papers on a marble coffee table. He glanced through. All of them dominated by the weather situation, with criticism of the government's response. There was a big story from the USA as well: men caught building a primitive bomb using radioactive waste stolen from hospitals. Suspects were being rounded up across three states, observers saying the trial of the decade was on its way.

Daisy Seager was on page two, with more appeals for her return. And Fletcher's name, as well: *a man's body, found by local jogger Tom Fletcher.* Who put that out – the police?

He laid the papers aside and sat watching a plasma screen behind the desk. It was showing a mute video of Bellman people mouthing subtitled testimonials to their employer.

Defence? It's all about people. And the Bellman Foundation has the best.

Fletcher watched the clips run right through and restart. A woman of Chinese descent came

71

round again, her captions saying, *I'm proud to be on the leading edge of global aviation research–*

'Mr Fletcher?'

He stood and turned. 'I'm Tom Fletcher.'

'Well, I'm Mia Tyrone.'

She was late twenties, he guessed, slim and wide-shouldered. She was wearing a sharp grey office suit, a white flannel blouse. She had a neat face, high bones, eyes a green colour like river water. Thin fingers making a tight handshake.

'This'll have to be real quick, Mr Fletcher. I hope I can help you.'

'I hope so too.'

Her office was on the second floor. There was a view of the lake, then the motorway and the snowy fields. A solo office, medium-sized. Someone with a foothold on management, climbing the ladder. Her desk was tidy – a closed laptop, some sheets of A4, blank side up. She sat, looked at him in his chair, touched her neat fingers together, said,

'You're aware Mr Slade's name has been released publicly?'

'I saw the news this morning.'

'Well, Mr Fletcher.' It was starting to feel like an interview. 'I was Mr Slade's second in command. Therefore, I'm looking after some aspects of his work in the present unfortunate situation.' That slightly throaty voice, and an East Coast accent, quite clipped. 'So, what's this about?'

'It's about Nathan Slade and Daisy Seager.'

Mia Tyrone held his eye for a few seconds. 'Why do you care? I mean, you found the body,

OK. But so?'

'I'm a private detective.'

'You're a private detective and you happened to find the body?' She frowned. 'Can I see your badge?'

'My visitor's badge?'

'Your PI badge. You're a private detective. You must be licensed.'

'There's no licensing of private detectives in Britain.'

'No licensing of PIs? In a country where you need a licence for a TV set, or a dog?'

'Televisions and dogs are dangerous things. But I've got a question for you. Daisy knows about witches. What does that mean?'

Mia Tyrone glanced at her watch. 'Well, I can get ready for my next meeting now. I don't know what you're talking about and I'm not going to pursue this conversation any further. You can contact our legal department if you want – though it's unlikely they'll speak to you. That's legal people the world over, isn't it? Sorry.'

'Is it something to do with *witchcraft?*'

'And now you have completely lost me.'

Her hair was brown with a reddish glint inside, like the glass of a medicine bottle, and she ran her fingers through it for a second – annoyance, or grooming? But if she didn't want to discuss this, why let him in here at all?

Fletcher said, 'When I phoned yesterday, I was listening to guitar music until I said that Daisy knows about the witches. And then you agreed to see me. Why?'

'No, no.' She smiled, crinkling her eyes. 'I

73

remember you saying something about a witch, yes. I didn't know what you were talking about, and I don't know now. The reason I asked you in here was because you said something else.'

He thought back through the conversation. He didn't get it. 'What was that?'

'Your *name*, Mr Fletcher. Your own name.'

'My name?'

'Yes. You told me your name, remember? I realised I'd just seen that name written down. I found that interesting and I wanted to ask you about it.'

'Written down where?'

Fletcher began to picture another letter, with his name on it. And indeed, she reached for a sheet of paper on her desk.

She said, 'Yesterday, I had the sad duty of putting together the personal things in Nathan Slade's office. You see what I'm getting at?'

'Not really.'

'You know, the things on the shelves, in the desk drawers. Every office has some kind of personal stuff in it. Then I had to put that together with some personal effects that were brought from Mr Slade's house. It's really sad, someone's life coming down to a cardboard box full of things.'

'Yes, it is sad. Where was my name written down?'

She picked up the piece of paper and looked at it. 'Well, let me be sure this is *you*. I mean, your name's probably quite a common one, isn't it? There must be dozens of people in this city with your name. But tell me, what are your parents' names?'

'Why are you asking me that?'

'Well, to see if this is relevant to you.'

Through the paper, Fletcher could see a heavy dark oblong – not a letter, but an image of some kind. He said,

'My parents' names are Jack and Kate. Jack and Kate Fletcher.'

Just saying that out loud, it sounded strange.

She nodded. Then she passed the sheet over the desk to him.

It was a photocopy of a page from an old-style photo album, the plastic pockets crumpled in lines, all empty except one. That held a photo of a man and a woman standing against an open sky, their arms around each other. The man with a mane of curly hair, a strong nose, laughing. The woman with her face against his shoulder, smiling, eyes closed. Yes, that was Jack and Kate Fletcher. He knew that even without looking at the caption below it in careful looped handwriting.

Jack and Kate Fletcher – Tom Fletcher never there!

He felt his heart thud. Nathan Slade went to see his father on Sunday night, OK. They discussed something; Nathan went off to see Daisy. But how well did Nathan Slade know Jack Fletcher? How well did he know Kate Fletcher? They let him take a photo of them in this private, happy moment?

And how long had he known them both? Were they old friends?

Looking again at the picture, Fletcher thought it dated from around the late eighties – maybe just before his mother walked out.

Tom Fletcher never there – never with them when

75

they met Nathan Slade? Why not?

Or was the picture stolen, or a forgery?

He said, 'What does this mean?'

'I thought you could tell *me*.'

'Let me see the album itself.'

She raised a finger – not aggressively, but in what seemed a mutual caution.

'You shouldn't be seeing *this*, you understand? The album came from Nathan's house.'

Newnham last night – those trampled footsteps in the pavement snow.

'Sounds like they cleared out his house pretty quickly. Come on, show me the album.'

'No. Anyway, most of the pictures in there are planes and motorbikes, not many people at all. That's why I noticed this, when I was flipping through. It stuck in my mind; then you phoned. But weren't you aware of this? Nathan Slade was obviously friends with your family. Well, I'll let you absorb the news. My next meeting starts very shortly. You'll really have to excuse me.'

She made no move to stand up, though, just sat looking at him steadily.

He said, 'What else is in Nathan's cardboard box?'

'What makes you think there's something else that concerns you?'

'I get the feeling you invited me in here to give me a sample, a taster.' He folded the photocopy and put it in his pocket. 'Is there something you want from me?'

She smiled. Even with everything going on in his mind, Fletcher had to note that she was beautiful like that. She said,

'Anything you dig up about the late Nathan Slade. Bring it to me.'

He held her pale green eyes. 'Bring it to you?'

'Yes, Mr Fletcher. Anything about Nathan or the Bellman Foundation. Straight to me.'

'Why?'

She stood up and went to the door, but didn't open it, waited with her fingers on the handle. She was standing close to him, and he caught the scent of her perfume, could see the stitching on her lapel rising and falling as she breathed. She raised her finger again, put it to her lips this time, narrowed her river-coloured eyes.

She said, 'Nathan and the Bellman Foundation. Daisy and Felwell College. Think about it. I want to know what's been happening too.' She opened the door. 'And you *do* want to look in that box.'

The abandoned Cambridge railway line runs from the science park, through the suburbs and miles out into empty farmland. To clear his mind, Fletcher walked a hundred yards along the nearest stretch. Overhead, the sun was just a red disc through hazy cloud. Up close, ice glinted along the old steel tracks and the gravel embankments. A wartime bunker lay in ruins, its weeds frozen into a photo negative.

His mind didn't clear.

Nathan Slade, the creepy man with the Harley, had a longstanding connection with Fletcher's parents – a link which Fletcher himself knew nothing about.

He thought back. Did Slade ever visit the house,

ever appear on family outings? Never. Someone like that – a big American – you would definitely remember. No – they kept him secret. And what really got to him about that photo was its age: around the time his mother left. His mind went back over that year, like fingers touching an old scar in the dark. He remembered again the door to her office, always locked. Once, late one afternoon, he came up the stairs, saw it half open, the typewriter silent.

Why don't I want to remember this?

He closed his eyes against the red haze in the sky.

That room. Dust in the air, everything still. The typewriter's chrome arm glinting. The papers and other things pinned on the wall. He remembered maps, lists of things. The books in the little bookcase.

What did he remember about those, before he heard his mother walk in behind him, put her hand over his eyes and ruffle his hair? She was laughing, but was it a joke? Or was he really not meant to see what was on the bookcase?

He opened his eyes, looked around at the barren embankment. Auto-suggestion, he knew, was a powerful thing. It makes you remember things that were never there, to fit what you're experiencing in the present. But he was sure he remembered the spines of some of the books. One was something about the American Air Force. Another – he was sure now, before his mother's hand closed over his eyes – was a history of the Felwell laboratory.

What had Mia Tyrone just said to him?

'The Bellman Foundation and Felwell College. Think about it.'

They took Matty down to the Deeping. It's still there today, smaller than it was. Back then, Granny said it was a hundred feet across, reeds around the edge eight feet high. The witchfinder's men cut the reeds apart and trampled them down over the bank. It was mid-day, bright and hot. They led Matty Plinter on a rope across the fields. She was wearing a shirt down to her knees and hair was loose over her back. One of the hired men whispered to her to be brave, but the witch-finder saw that and sent him back to the village. When Matty saw the gap in the reeds and the water shining beyond, she stopped and twisted. They took her by the arms, but she was bucking and crying.

Sometimes I go down to the lake and I do that, I buck and twist and scream. My sister says I oughtn't do that. She says that's why the teachers didn't want us at the school, why nobody comes to the house. They think we're strange. I don't care what they think. I go to the Deeping sometimes and I stand on the bank and look in and see myself standing there, and I don't care what anyone think, what they say about us in the town. I like the way I look.

That's where Matty had to stand. The reeds either side were shivering a bit in the breeze, the muttering sound they make. She stopped fighting back, but she was crying and asking them not to do it. The witch-finder read a paper out, all words she didn't under-stand, about his authority and the way he did his trials. When he stop, he asked her if she got questions. She says why are you doing this to us?

He come up close to her. He was white compared to

her, with her tan from the fieldwork. The parting in his hair got sweat along it. He touched her cheek. She closed her eyes, praying under her breath. He said,

'Matty, this is for your own good, my dear. If you are not a witch, you must prove it to us. You need not be afraid. A witch will float, you know that, for the water cannot take her in. If you sink under, it is only a moment of trouble, and then the men will hook you out and you are free. Matty, you understand?'

She didn't answer, praying in a whisper. She felt the men tie her ankles together, like her wrists. One of the men tripped her and she fell on the reeds and she tried to curl up. She felt their hands moving over her, coming under her shirt. Touching her, the way Granny said men do if you let them. Then they lifted her, one man her wrists and the other her legs. last thing she sees is the witchfinder's eyes.

Granny said the old clay pit was so deep, and the water so cold, Matty went down like a stone. Just a shriek, no bubbles. She said the witchfinder and his men came back slowly over the fields. The men found their kegs and took a long drink. The witchfinder went in his tent and picked up his list. He crossed her off – two lines scraped on the page.

Daisy Seager had chosen her house well: less than a five-minute walk to her studies at Felwell College. Presumably her Golf had been just for transport to her evening employment at Hunters. Fletcher parked in her street and made the walk too. Halfway, he could already see Felwell itself: a rambling Edwardian mansion complex rising above the suburban trees.

Felwell – what did he know? Site of the first

80

successful splitting of the atom in world history, sometime back in the mid 1930s – everybody knew that. There'd been a Nobel prize for the scientists, who later shared their skills with the Manhattan Project, which led to the American atom bomb in 1945. The original laboratory was closed now – the basement where the experiments took place was filled in with concrete, according to Cambridge folklore, and sealed with lead. A new physics lab had been constructed behind the old college in the 1970s – a long, functional white block which he started to see between the hedges as he got closer.

The building was sited just beyond Newnham, facing the river where the banks narrowed sharply, the current raising knuckle shapes in the blackwater. A cold wind was tumbling slivers of ice along the towpath, and Fletcher zipped his parka up to the chin. At the big wrought-iron college gates – recognisable from the morning TV news as the place where the dean had expressed her concern – a police constable was standing, banging his gloved hands together, a ski balaclava around his face. Behind him, a laminated poster was fixed:

Have you seen this person?

And a picture of Daisy Seager – it looked like the summer ball photo from her bedroom corkboard. There was a press photographer taking a shot of the scene.

Past that, he could see a rather quaint porters' lodge, a stone courtyard with a round frozen pond, and then the façade of the original college: yellow brick inlaid with ceramic in a Venetian style, fake turrets on its roofline against the clouds, and small plastic spheres, which the architects couldn't have imagined, presumably holding CCTV cameras.

He heard a click behind him.

Two private security guards. Not cheap muscle, but professionals. Clean faces, peaked caps, black uniforms, trousers tucked into boots. One had just extended a folding baton, holding it loose. The other was using a video device to record Fletcher's face.

That man folded the camera in his palm and slid it into his pocket. No expression under the peaked cap, just steady unblinking eyes.

'What you wanting?'

'Impressive security. Is this because of Daisy Seager?'

'What you wanting?'

'I want to see the dean.'

'Porters' lodge, then, please. We'll watch you walk over there. Sir.'

The police constable eyed him as he walked through the gates.

Externally, the porters' lodge was a charming 1900s villa – timber walls, the eaves hung with carved shields, noble human faces, swords and rowing blades. Inside, the Edwardian era vanished. The space was lined with metal, fitted out with a bank of TV monitors, two more efficient-looking guards behind a counter, tracking them all. The counter itself was equipped like a police station: a scanner for taking hand-prints, a face camera, and a unit that looked like an iris recognition system, one of the first Fletcher had seen in public use, though they were spreading fast. And also a dispenser of leaflets about accessibility, with an aerial photo of the college: the white oblong of the new lab dwarfing the old building. Fletcher took a leaflet as he handed his card across.

One of the guards looked at the card and shrugged. 'No appointment? You're wasting your time, boy.'

Behind the man, another of the *Have you seen this person?* posters. Fletcher pointed at it. 'It's to do with this situation.'

'What to do with her?'

'Look.' Fletcher took his card back and wrote on it *Information on Daisy Seager.*

'Send this up to her. She'll see me.'

Waiting is a skill in itself. He stood against the wall by the door, tipping on his heels. He waited half an hour, forty-five minutes.

He said to the counter man, 'Going to thaw.'

'It is.'

'Think it'll flood?'

'Could be.'

'Any news about Daisy Seager?'

'Not that I've heard.'

Up on the wall, beside the poster of Daisy Seager, there was a print of a picture, presumably taken by the CCTV cameras in those plastic domes on the façade. It showed the outline of a man on the towpath, the iron gates visible in one corner, the riverbank trees in the other. Dark footsteps in the snow behind him. Fletcher rocked on his heels again, looked at his watch. An hour now.

His eyes went back to the man in the print. A very pale face, dark beard along the jawline, very dark eyes.

'Who's that in the picture?'

The counter guard looked up at it, then at his console. 'Someone that's been seen walking past a few times. Could be nothing.'

'Or could be something?'

'Man prowling round a college. We don't like that kind of man.'

The phone rang. The guard listened, watching Fletcher, then hung up.

'She'll see you.'

Fletcher signed in, had his fingerprint taken, signed a declaration that he was not carrying smoking materials or a camera. An old-style porter came in to escort him into the college. Fletcher thanked the counter man.

'By the way, is it true the basement here is sealed with lead?'

The man didn't look up from his screen.

'Old stories. Some things last a long time, boy.'

A porter showed him through a series of draughty corridors, up two staircases hung with Victorian paintings of stags and dogs. Gloss paint over un-even plaster, signposts pointing off to places such as *Middle Common Room* and *Tutors' Refectory*. At the end of a landing, the man stopped and knocked on a door covered in blue felt, then held it open.

The room was warm. The floor was rubber tiling – with under-floor heating, Fletcher guessed.

Between bookcases, the walls were hung with fairly important twentieth-century British art: an early Freud nude, he noticed, and some Francis Bacon sketches. A huge window at one end was modern, heat sealing, and beyond it the original leaded windows glittered with frost. Beyond that, the massive white bulk of the modern lab stretched away under the grey sky, its roof studded with vents emitting a fine vapour.

In the centre of the room was a large glass table, and seated behind that was the woman from the TV news, beautifully postured on a leather office chair. She was wearing a tweed suit, looking at Fletcher with her fingers holding his business card. In person, her neatly cut hair was slightly tinted, and her attractive face had an element of toughness. Pearl studs in each ear, no other jewellery. He couldn't see anything in her eyes except contact lenses – the big old soft type. She didn't offer to shake his hand, but she smiled and gestured at a chair across the desk.

'I am Tania Nile, dean to the college. Do have a seat.' She consulted an open desk diary, checked her watch. The morning so far, full of women checking their timepieces. She smiled. 'Just for a minute, though.'

'A pleasure, Dr Nile.'

'Tom Fletcher. I know that name. You were a policeman, weren't you? You helped the dean of All Saints find his son – three or four years ago, was it? I've heard the dean rewarded you with a parking space. And now you're an *investigator.*' She laid the card down. 'Something else I've heard. You're in the running for the university security contract.'

'Discussions are at an early stage.'

'Well, but these things tell me you have at least some credibility. Now, what's this information you have about Daisy?'

'You realise the police are focusing on her hostess work?'

She made a sour face. 'They are indeed. Frankly, I don't like that, the way they're emphasising it.'

'You can see a scandal coming?'

Tania Nile closed her eyes for a second, then had to let her lenses adjust when she opened them. 'Listen. The practice of escorting, hostessing, call it what you will, is increasingly prevalent at Cambridge, as I believe it is at Oxford and elsewhere. Students need money, and they've found a highly efficient way to earn it. It keeps them solvent, leaves time for study. I'm not condoning it, obviously. But if you really want that university contract, Mr Fletcher, it's probably not something you should be digging up. Why are you interested in Daisy, anyway? Has someone hired you?'

He smiled, shook his head. 'I just want to show the university what a skilled investigator I am. This is the perfect opportunity.'

'To impress us with your skills?'

'Exactly. And, by the way, I don't believe the hostess thing is relevant. I mean, it is, in the sense that that's where Nathan Slade went to find Daisy. He must have wanted to talk to her urgently, something that couldn't wait. She didn't want to talk in the club, they had a row, but she let him into her car afterwards. I just don't think the subject of their conversation was hostess work.'

'So what do you think it was?'

'Maybe she knew something important.'

'How dramatic.'

'About the Bellman Foundation.'

Dr Nile took another long look at her diary, made a show of pulling herself back to the conversation in hand. 'Bellman the defence people? What on earth could that be?'

'I don't know. But Nathan Slade worked for them. Could you shed any light?'

'Awfully sorry, no. I actually rather think we'd better leave this to the police. Unless you have any other theories about Daisy? You can share anything with me, Mr Fletcher. Even if it seems outlandish.'

Fletcher knew he was being assessed, the depth of his knowledge probed. He said,

'Is there a connection between Bellman and Felwell College?'

'Really, I have to get on with my morning now.'

Fletcher tried one last time. 'Dr Nile, there's a word that keeps coming up around Daisy Seager.'

'Mm, what's that?'

'*Witches.*'

'*Witches?* How odd.' She frowned, pursed her lips. 'And do you know the significance of that?'

'I don't think I do, no.'

An emotion flashed in Tania's eyes, clear behind all the polymer, then was hidden away with a blink.

'Well, I can put your mind at rest, Mr Fletcher.

87

There's nothing sinister going on at all.'

'But there is *something* going on?'

'Oh, really.' Dr Nile stood up. Her tweed suit was trim and uncrumpled, and she spoke while already leafing through some papers on her desk, already thinking of her next meeting. 'We're a huge lab, but a tiny college here, Mr Fletcher. More like a family. We know each other's little quirks. Daisy has unusual interests in that respect.'

'Unusual interests?'

'I remember her tutor telling me, Daisy has become very interested in Matthew Hopkins.'

'That name is vaguely familiar.'

'Hopkins, the witchfinder general. He flourished in eastern England, mid-seventeenth century. Completely self-appointed, of course. He hanged about two hundred people, then he disappeared.' She looked up and smiled. 'It's just a harmless interest. There are no witches here. Now you'll have to excuse me. Good luck with the university contract – I mean that.'

Behind her, through the heat-sealing glass, the sky was moving with light and shade, the way feeling had just moved in Tania's eyes when Fletcher had said he didn't know the significance of the word *witch*.

That feeling was *relief*.

He thought about that, going back down the stairs and along the draughty corridors, past the Victorian paintings. Dr Nile was understandably worried about the college being exposed as a recruitment centre for the local hostess industry. She was worried about Daisy herself, too – that was natural. But there was something else on the dean's mind – something she'd suspected Fletcher might know about; something that made her break her morning schedule for five minutes.

He zipped up his parka, going across the courtyard.

The third one on the list was a girl named Bessie Weller. Granny said she was tall, like us, and had the things on her skin that we have, things that make people stare if we go outside the yard. Bessie Weller is in our blood.

The witchfinder had her brought inside the tent.

His men all stank of the beer by then, big eyes from the poppy seed. She stood in front of him, lit up by the sun through the tent slit. She was wearing a long blue dress with a sash, long sleeves, and sandals with wood soles. Her hair was tied up under her blue cap. She got big grey eyes. She held her hands together.

My sister says, 'You don't know that, Evie. You don't know the colour of her dress. Granny made that up.' But I know it's true.

I see Bessie Weller standing there. The witchfinder says, 'Don't be afraid.'

'I am not.'

He writes something on his ledger. 'I believe there are marks upon you, Bessie.'

'What marks?'

'The marks of Satan. He often leaves his sign in the form of a mole or freckle.'

'Everyone got moles and freckles.'

He stands up and come close to her. 'It's a hot day, Bessie. You're wearing a long dress, long sleeves.'

89

'This is my dress. It is washed every two weeks.'

He smiles. He touches her neck. His fingers are cold, the nails are long. 'You're warm.'

'You killed Matty Flinter.'

'My trials have authority of king and church.'

'One day you will come to a village and they'll tear you apart, Witchfinder.'

'Take your dress off.'

'I will not.'

'What is under there, Bessie? Are there marks you want to hide?'

'They'll tear you apart. You are the devil.'

'What do you know of devils? Mm?' He pours himself a drink in a clay mug. She's thirsty. He takes a sip, chews some seeds, spits them out. 'It's the dress off, or it's a ducking in the clay pit. Either is a good test of a witch.'

She stands looking at him. She's turning it over in her mind, knowing either way she's close to death. She knows what the witchfinder is thinking. He's thinking she'll choose the ducking; she might drown but they won't see her naked. But she's clever, this Bessie Weller. She knows how to live on, how to haunt the witchfinder, how to stay with him forever, breaking into his dreams, taunting him when he's sick, tormenting him when he's dying.

She decides. She slips her cap off her head and her hair falls loose. She lifts her chin and pulls her dress up over her head and pulls it clear, lets it fall on the turf.

Witchfinder glances up. His mouth opens, trickling spit.

She spreads her hands and lets him see the marks on her body. She turns to the side, then around, lets him *see her back, then her front again. She looks him in the eye. He can't speak. The witchfinder cannot speak.*

Tuesday Afternoon

Fletcher walked out through the gates, where the poster of Daisy was flapping slightly in the wind. The copper was still there, looking glum. Fletcher walked away along the towpath into the open fields beside the college, thinking. The river was fast and swollen, running almost as high as the banks. He watched a tree branch twisting over in midstream, spiralling towards Cambridge itself.

What was under the surface of Felwell College? Something that connected witches, the Bellman Foundation – and even Jack and Kate Fletcher.

The light was still changing: clouds moving across the sun, the last day of cold before the expected thaw. A few small hailstones fell along the river and vanished into the current.

Fletcher turned away, back towards Newnham and his car.

On the edge of his vision, reflected in the water, he saw another shape turn and move. Looking round, Fletcher saw a man about twenty yards ahead, walking along the towpath towards Grantchester, going into the open meadows. Had he been watching Fletcher, or watching the college? The man jogged a few paces. Trying to get away.

Fletcher followed him. He wondered for a second if this was the prowler caught on Felwell CCTV. The height was about right, but this person was wearing an old-style canvas raincoat, billowing out.

The hail came back, heavier this time: big stones tumbling out of the clouds and scattering on the tarmac. A few hit Fletcher in the face and, blinking them out of his eyes, he saw the man start to run in earnest, trying to pick up speed. Fletcher began to run, too, glad of his rubber-soled boots. The few other people along the towpath were hurrying away before the storm: a couple of students on bikes, a walker calling his dog. The hail began streaming across the river and bouncing off the wall at the end of the Felwell grounds.

The man accelerated until he seemed to be running flat out, lank hair streaming back from his head. They rounded the curve in the river and came to the straight running down to Grant-chester: flat meadows, the opposite bank lined with bare oak and willow glinting steel-colour. Suddenly the hail stopped and the sun broke through, and the thousands of stones on the path began steaming in the light, the willows changing colour to luminous green. The man in the rain-coat glanced back – too quickly for Fletcher to see his face clearly – then forced himself on again, his head bobbing furiously, long arms beginning to windmill. Fletcher looked around: they were alone on the long stretch. He started to run seriously, feeling the mix of cold air and vapour, the hail splintering underfoot.

After a few seconds, the sunlight vanished and the landscape looked like a black-and-white photo again. He looked up and saw metallic clouds overhead. There was an electric flash that reflected off the river and lit up the meadows, then the hailstones really came down.

This time they were the size of machine bearings, making the river surface twitch and bursting on the path in smacks of ice, stinging his face where they hit him. Some spilled into his eyes and he raised a sleeve to push them away.

He slowed down and stopped.

The empty pasture stretched out, flickering with hail. The path ahead was clear for hundreds of metres. No passers-by. No man in a raincoat.

A few yards away, on the riverbank, a clump of willow trees leaned into the water, their fronds forming an arch that was bucking in the hail exploding out of the air. Fletcher ran the few paces down to the arch, and looked in. Compared to the mayhem outside, it was a haven: the trailing branches quivering under the impact but keeping most of the hailstones away, a pool of icy water and a muddy beach a few yards wide, a segment of a fallen tree trunk, then the willow canopy behind that. He stepped in. He walked slowly around the piece of tree.

The man was on the other side, huddled in a gash where the wood had been hacked with chainsaws, trying to wriggle himself into the V-shaped cut. The man saw Fletcher and reached under his raincoat, pulled out a knife.

Fletcher stayed quite still.

It was a long bayonet with a jagged edge, a plastic handle – cheap but lethal, its tip quivering and catching the light. From outside, there was another flash of lightning and the ice roared like

94

a turbine, cutting them off from the world. Fletcher and the man stood looking at each other.

He was aged about twenty-five, with skinny wrists and bitten fingers, shadowy eyes and metal studs through his eyebrow and lower lip, his face wet with melting ice. Definitely not the man from Felwell CCTV. Outside the willow fronds, the surface of the river was a violent black, crackling with hail.

Fletcher said, 'Throw the knife in the river.'

The man hesitated. Fletcher kicked his hand, hard. The man yelped and the knife span out across the muddy beach, flopping over like a stranded fish.

'What's your name?'

'Wayne. Wayne Denny.'

'Open your coat, Wayne. What else have you got?'

'Nothing.' The man shrugged his coat off, showing a damp Tshirt over a skinny torso, grimy jeans. The man closed his eyes and panted, 'Don't hurt me. I won't tell anyone.'

'About what?'

'About Daisy.'

'What about her?' No answer, just the panting. 'Look at me.'

The eyes opened: damp and bloodshot.

Fletcher said, 'Who do you think I am?'

The man studied Fletcher. Outside, the river was smoothing out as the hail slackened off – thousands of stones drifting in the water, collecting on the mud beach under the willows, white pixels on the black sediment. The man

95

nodded to himself, thinking, watching Fletcher's face. 'You're not him. I thought you might be him.'

'Who?'

'I'm not saying anything more. Who are you? Copper?'

'I'm not a copper, Wayne, but I could call them right now. Waiting outside a college, carrying a knife.' The blade was still glinting on the stretch of mud. 'Possessing a weapon, assault–'

'You kicked my hand–'

'Threatening behaviour. They'll be all over you, Wayne. You'll be in a remand prison for weeks before you even come to court.' Fletcher doubted that, but Wayne was nervous, chewing the stud in his lip. A few hailstones dripped in from the branches, already melting. 'I could hand you in, Wayne. Or I could–' he looked at the guy's emaciated chest, his thin neck – 'I could buy you lunch. I could buy you lunch and listen to you talking, Wayne. Telling me all about Daisy and this man you thought I was. You choose.'

Wayne thought it over.

Between home ownership, council accommodation and stable private renting, there's a layer of housing that's home to maybe a million people in Britain. It's the layer of cheap hotels and guesthouses and bedsits, and in Cambridgeshire it extends to parks of mobile homes: static caravans connected to drainage and power, rent payable by the week.

Fletcher followed Wayne Denny's directions, taking a turning off the Peterborough road,

96

through a chain-link gate watched by an Alsatian on a rope. Wayne's home was in the second row, the third caravan along. It was cold, with damp on the windows. It had a bed at one end, and a toilet cubicle, then a kitchen space, and, folding out from the wall, a table where Fletcher put down a cardboard box.

Of all the possible lunches, Wayne had insisted on being driven to the Fen Tiger Diner, a roadside snack-van out near Rampton, then to his caravan. Now Wayne opened the box, chuckling. 'That's a real Cambridge dinner, right?'

Slices of eel in batter, claw-shaped wooden forks, wedges of bread and margarine and a carton of scalding tomato soup to dip them in, Styrofoam cups of tea. The box came free with all that.

Wayne bit into an eel fritter and closed his eyes.

Fletcher took a look around the caravan. It was chilly, but it was tidy and pretty clean. No photos or pictures. Just a small TV, a fridge wedged level on bits of cardboard. An electric hotplate, a microwave, then the door of the cubicle, and a concertina wall for giving the bed some privacy. It was linked to the roof by a cobweb.

Fletcher said, 'You get many visitors?'

Wayne shrugged, gulped some tea.

'So tell me about Daisy and this man.'

'No police?'

'Start talking.'

It turned out that Wayne was twenty-six, and took five Clozapine a day for anxiety. It was meant to be four, but he liked the extra one, the way it put a space between him and things. He

97

had a repeat prescription the nurses gave him when they released him from sheltered accommodation back in October. It was a managed release: the council paid the rent on the caravan. 'The problem with the *community*,'Wayne said, 'is all the time on your hands.' That first week in October, he lay on the bed, watching the clouds through the window. Then one morning he tidied up the caravan, put on clean clothes, decided to get busy. 'These days I wake up at six-thirty, seven. Bus goes into Cambridge at eight-twelve. Bus comes back five twenty-eight. Gives me eight hours a day in Cambridge.'

'What do you do?'

'Mostly I go to the library. I do a lot of reading, a lot of research into things.'

'Such as?'

'I like history. I like ceramics–'

'Tell me something about Daisy.'

'Like what?'

'Like how you know anything about her.'

'OK.' Wayne speared some eel with his claw fork, chewed it carefully. 'It was in the library. In October, I'm in there, reading stuff. I see this girl walking past with a book. She had this dark hair and this face. I can't tell you, man. This face.'

Wayne paused.

'Yes, Wayne?'

'I followed her to the counter. She was taking the book out.'

'Are you sure about that? A Felwell physics student, borrowing books from the public library?'

'It was the sort of book they won't have in a college library.'

There was a silence.

Fletcher said, 'You're good at pauses, Wayne. For a man who takes five Clozapine a day.'

Wayne smiled.

'The book?'

'A book about planes, man.'

'What kind of planes?'

'American planes in the Second World War.'

Fletcher laid down his fork. The eel tasted cold and thick in his mouth. He swallowed.

'This was a book about the American Air Force?'

'I suppose they would have American planes in the war, wouldn't they?'

'What was the title?'

'I didn't see it. I was looking at her library card on the counter. That's how I knew her name. Daisy Seager. That did it for me. Daisy, like a flower. Then she left.'

'And you followed her?'

'In a nice way.'

'Back to Felwell?'

He nodded. 'Yeah. After that, I used to take a walk out to Felwell, pass the time. Used to see the girls going in and out. I saw her once.'

'And?'

Wayne looked at the ceiling. 'She smiled at me.'

'You got to know her? Became friendly?'

'Me, I'm the last person she'd be friends with, aren't I? But she smiled at me. It was October the twentieth.'

Fletcher didn't ask what time of day, but Wayne would probably remember. 'What else, Wayne?'

'That's it.'

'Out by the river, you said you wouldn't tell anyone.'

'About all this, about what I've told you. She's missing, isn't she? I heard it on the radio.'

'You know where she is?'

'No.'

'The thing with Daisy, Wayne, is she has these unusual interests.'

'The hostess thing, on the news? I don't know, man. I don't know about that.'

'Have you heard of the Bellman Foundation?'

'You're losing me now.'

'Or Matthew Hopkins, the witchfinder general?'

'You've lost me.'

'So why the knife, Wayne? You thought I was someone else. Who are you afraid of?'

'Someone was stalking her.'

'*You* were stalking her.'

'No. I followed her that once. She smiled at me once. I take an interest in her. I'm like a protector. This other guy, she was afraid of him.'

'Who is he?'

'He's some kind of American.'

A big raindrop slapped the window glass and spread like a skeletal hand.

'How do you know that?'

'I heard him calling to her cat. He had an American accent.'

'Wayne, what are you talking about?'

The caravan roof began to clang with rain. Wayne put his fingers against the window, tracing splatters.

'She had a cat. Tabby, it was. Last week, he took

it off her doorstep. Called it to him, let it rub against his legs. I was watching from across the road. He took it out to the field and cut it up in pieces. He's got this metal thing, it's like a crowbar, but it's sharp at one end. It digs in and cuts. He was kneeling on it, levering it apart. That's why I got the knife, to protect myself, protect Daisy.'

Wayne reached for the sink cupboard, took out a Special Brew and a sheet of caplets. He popped three in his palm and drank them down, his lip stud chinking on the can, then climbed onto the bed and settled against the single pillow. Fletcher said,

'Why would someone chop up a cat?'

'Scare Daisy.'

'It would only scare her if she knows about it. Otherwise it's just a missing cat.'

Wayne shrugged, settling back.

Fletcher said, 'What does he look like?'

'He's pale, dark eyes. Got a bit of beard.'

The man from the Felwell CCTV – it sounded right. Someone prowling around Daisy, trying to scare her. Trying to keep her quiet?

'So he's got an American accent? What else about him? A name?'

'I just saw him that one time. Don't know a name. But he chews a lot.'

'He chews?'

'Noisy bastard, chews gum all the time.' Wayne's eyes were following a raindrop down the window. 'I hope he hasn't got her right now. You think he's got her?'

Fletcher locked the caravan door from outside and

looked around at the other steel boxes stretching away left and right. It was mid-afternoon, but the air was freezing and the rain had ice in it, smacking pellets out of the snow along the pathways. He dropped the key through the window vent and heard it clunk on the floor inside. Wayne was already asleep in there.

Fletcher was in two minds about Wayne. Easy to see him as a sedated loner who defined himself through a woman smiling at him on October the twentieth. On the other hand, the man seemed articulate and observant, kind of watchful. Had he really seen a young, bearded American butchering Daisy's cat?

So Daisy had an American neighbour, and an American stalker too?

How many Americans were there in Newnham?

Fletcher zipped up his coat, listening to the caravan roofs clattering out their lullaby for all the lonely sleepers along the Peterborough road. Then he ran through the rain back to his car.

Fletcher drove at speed, the Audi's blunt nose flipping the ice crystals hanging in the air, smacking them against the windscreen. The radio reception was fractured with static, but he heard the commentators predict another freeze at dusk. And then, the experts agreed, the thaw would start the next day and the real problems would start. The piled snow of the neighbouring counties would melt down into the water table; rain would combine with it, flowing through streams and ditches into the already brimming rivers. The news programmes were full of discussions about flooding. Some advisors were urging people to leave low-lying areas. Someone else was pointing out that, in Cambridgeshire, low-lying areas accommodated seventy per cent of the population.

Fletcher was forced to brake: slowing up behind a row of army trucks loaded with sandbags, a bored soldier lounging in the back of each one. Leading them, a water-authority truck: pump equipment and electric generators lashed down on the trailer, the truck's orange lights revolving across the snow. Fletcher overtook the whole convoy at speed, pulled in again just as an oncoming car flashed its lights a few metres away.

He was heading back to Cambridge. To the central library, to be exact. Big anxieties were building inside him now. You can wait half your life for your father to call you – and the guy sends you to a quarry to find a dead Yank on a spike. You can wait all that time to see your mother again – and you find nothing except the Felwell laboratory and a book on the American Air Force.

The third day, they killed the witches. They killed old Gussie Salter, because a fly came to visit her in the tent. And my ancestor Bessie Weller, because of everything the witchfinder saw on her skin when she let her dress fall. They took them both out into the pasture, behind the tent.

Gussie Salter first.

She was to be hanged. The men had a gallows from an old hawthorn: a half-dead trunk and spiky limb they propped up with a timber post. It wouldn't do for a grown man, but for an old woman like Gussie it worked fine.

Old Gussie didn't know much about it. In the night, the men had passed her some poppy-seed ale, so she was pale but she was calm, not really knowing where she was. They helped her up on a barrel while the witchfinder read his speech from his horse. He said the proof was the witch's familiar, the insect. He said he believed its name was Tinnyticket or Bedderlugs, common names for familiars. He spat out some seeds. Gussie half opened her eyes. But when they kicked the barrel, she was too light and thin for the rope to snap her neck. So she strangled on the end of it, and that took a while. The sounds her throat made went out over the open. Scaring the hares, Granny told us. Her legs were kicking, her tied hands trying to lift up to the knot. In the end her eyeballs ran with blood and her tongue stuck out, Granny said, and the sounds grew less.

The witchfinder twisted in his saddle and spat some seeds and nodded to his men.

Late afternoon, and maroon light glinted off the freezing slush of the pavements, reflecting in the icicles on the college railings. Turning quickly into Lion Yard, Fletcher noticed the fur steaming on a homeless man's dog, and the whitened cobwebs strung across a tub of dead flowers. Springtime coming to Cambridge.

The public library was barely heated, condensation forming on the windows. In the modern history section, the military reference aisle was silent and empty.

Nathan Slade, an American, ex-USAF. That was a fact.

Daisy's stalker, whoever he was – also apparently American, if Wayne Denny could be believed. And Wayne was sure that Daisy had been in here, reading about American planes from the war. What was she looking for? Something already in the public domain, something so mainstream she came to the central library.

Which book?

Looking along the shelves, Fletcher found a dozen books on the American presence in East Anglia during World War Two. He piled them up on a table and leafed through.

He didn't find any quick answers. What he found was another world.

He went back to the three years, from 1942 to 1945, when up to two million Americans were based in Britain. Those stationed in the eastern counties of England were using the flat landscape as a massive aircraft carrier for daylight bombing raids against Germany, while the British hit the same targets by night. In one book, he found a map showing the locations of the now long-abandoned airfields: scores of them, their runways each forming a triangular pattern, like a letter 'A' lying sideways, signed repeatedly across the landscape. The nearest one, at Longstanton, just west of Cambridge, was only a few miles from where he was sitting.

He ran his eyes over the map, the 'A' shapes.

He leafed through the rest of the books. The massive Flying Fortress bombers were aggressively streamlined, heavily armoured, a stylistic forerunner of the huge American automobiles of the 1950s, which would be built from their recycled metal in the same factories. The smaller aircraft – above all, the Mustang fighters – that flew escort cover for the bombers were built from a brightly polished metal that glinted in the sun.

There were photo-essays on the aircrews' activities when not flying: punting in Cambridge, helping with harvest on local farms, demonstrating American sports to mystified civilians on village greens. One book was a study of the way the Americans used to decorate their planes: each aircraft had a good-luck charm painted on the nose. Sometimes this was a cartoon character or a sports star, but usually it took the form of a voluptuous woman: the wife, girlfriend or daydream of the pilot. The book explained that these images were known as 'Nose Art' – a whole Pop Art tradition in itself. Reproduced in the original colours, or just in monochrome snaps taken by the crews, the paintings had a strange presence, a clumsy sensual yearning.

What did Wayne Denny say? *Not the kind of book you'll find in a college library.* Did Wayne *see* Daisy reading this one?

One image, painted across the riveted panels of a Fortress nose cone, showed a girl in a scarlet bathing suit, her full breasts angled up, her face tilted to gaze into the forward machine gunner's Perspex cowling. One slender hand was brushing out a mane of dark hair into the slipstream, the other held an old-style bottle of Coca-Cola, complete with a straw in the neck. Her name – *Sweet Sweet Susie* – was painted in flowing script along the fuselage. Fletcher wondered who she'd been – a real woman, or the artist's own dream girl – and, if real, what had happened to her in the end.

He noticed another example, along the nose of a Mustang fighter: a reclining nude from the rear, long legs tapering to neat buttocks, glancing over her shoulder at the viewer with a slow wink from heavy lashes, one hand reaching up to touch the exhaust vents above her. Her body was painted with dark rivets, as if she was made of stamped metal, and her name – in blocked letters underneath – was *Steel Witch.*

A witch. Just a coincidence? The caption said only, *Pilot and unit unknown.*

He flipped through the book – hundreds of pages of Nose Art. The paintings were sometimes crudely executed, sometimes a professional standard, the names poignant with vanished affection or lust. He closed the book and reached for the next one: Cambridgeshire villagers' reminiscences of the American presence.

'The Americans were like nothing we'd seen before. They were so smart, dashing you might say. People said they were highly paid. Most of us single young women wanted to go out with a Yank – but we knew their reputation, too, for having a girl in every village around the base.'

A footnote: By 1944, *30 per cent of all birth certificates issued in Britain had the father's name left blank.*

He stopped. He closed the book, and reached back for the one with the long section on Nose Art. Something nagged at him; something that had flickered in front of him while flipping through the pages of colour plates. He found the nude from the Mustang again, lined with dark rivets, her wink as artful as sixty-five years ago.

He turned the pages more slowly. After *Steel Witch* was *Western Wonder* – a naked girl firing six-shooter pistols, taking aim along the fuselage of a Liberator bomber, her breasts ending in conical nipples like cannon shells. But what Fletcher remembered seeing was on the next page. It was a grainy photo of the art from the nose of another Mustang. It showed a young woman dressed only in a black shawl, the loose cloth being blown back by the aircraft's flght. One hand pointed forward to the target, the other flourished a magic wand above her head. She had a pale face, dark eyes, black hair flowing behind her, lips parted to cast a spell, those rivets making lines across her body again. Her name was also painted as *Steel Witch*.

Another one?

Two pages later, he found still another Mustang snapshot, another girl – this one with her long legs twined around a broomstick, hooped earrings flashing as she leaned her head back. *Steel Witch*.

A few pages after that, another slightly blurred photo, another Mustang. A woman tied naked to a stake, her face raised to the sky, eyes closed, the hair flowing over her bare and riveted shoulders merging at its tips into stylised flames. The expression on her face was impossible to read, but her name was quite clear: *Steel Witch*.

Fletcher counted eight in total. Eight *Steel Witches* – voluptuous, aggressive, lined with dark rivets like the planes they adorned. All were painted on Mustang fighters, all captioned as *Pilot and unit unknown*.

He closed the book and rested his fingers on the cover.

What could connect English witches with the US Air Force in the war? Maybe this was a series of imaginary young women, idealised by their pilots, just painted for luck. Or were they *real?* Had they lived and breathed?

He looked back at the photos. Although they were grainy – taken hurriedly, maybe – the eight paintings were a real art, displaying a professionalism far above the simple cartoons on the other planes. They had been painted by a serious artist.

He noticed that the book had been published only the previous year, and made a note of the author – *an aviation enthusiast living near Cambridge.* Then he made photocopies of the *Steel Witch* paintings.

The library was cool and quiet. Through the window, in the shopping centre below, he could see the shop grilles coming down.

He thought, *Or am I imagining it? Did Daisy even read this book?*

He thought for a second.

He opened the book at a central page and slipped a twenty-pound note inside. He took it to the counter and showed the page with the money to the librarian.

'Look at this. Someone's used it as a bookmark.'

The librarian shook his head, rummaged in a

109

drawer for an envelope to put the note in. 'The things the public will leave in books. I've seen holiday snaps, pressed flowers.' He scanned the book's barcode, turned to his screen, checked something and wrote a name on the envelope. 'I've seen love letters – sweaty stuff, too. Saw a suicide note last year. Nobody claimed it.'

Fletcher went down the stairs with the Nose Art photocopies zipped inside his parka. Twenty quid poorer, and he had no idea whether the book he remembered from his mother's study had anything to do with USAF Nose Art. But he was absolutely certain of one thing. The name on the screen back there – the last borrower – was Daisy Seager.

From her office in the Bellman Foundation building, Mia Tyrone could see the sun setting beyond the motorway, and orange sunlight just catching the ice in the lake below her window – where the fountain was, just a big frozen claw of water. Then, looking the other way, through a glass partition into Nathan Slade's office. His chair was still there – colossal and leathery, smelling of cigars – but the rest of Nathan had come down to the cardboard box on his desk.

Nathan. The most unpleasant fucking individual she had ever met in her life. Like a big cigar-smoking bear, standing too close to her, throwing her the pieces of work he didn't want to do, coasting to his retirement knowing he had friends high up in the company, men he'd been drinking and swapping Air Force stories with for twenty years. Men who brushed against her, revolted her. Nathan working late that evening last September. Nathan getting up from that chair, coming in here smelling the way he did at the end of a hot day, walking round behind her desk. Cupping that one dry hand under her chin, stroking her neck, so sudden she froze for a second. By the time she reacted it had gone and he was just standing there grinning at her.

She should have reported it, whatever friends he had. Some nights she couldn't sleep because she hated him so much. That's when she started taking an interest in Nathan, in his background and circumstances. Then, when she heard the guy had been found dead in a hole in the ground, she had to stop herself saying: *Yes. That's exactly how he would die.* Right out loud in the office, with all the senior management coming in to paying tributes to him. She hated that: the way they couldn't see, or didn't want to see, the way Nathan really was. The way they scooped all the personal stuff out of his house, made her tape it up in that damn box.

The phone rang.

'Miss Tyrone? Tom Fletcher.'

She watched the last of the sun glinting on the lake ice. Tom Fletcher: a big guy, nice face. Sad blue eyes. Looked like he knew what he was doing. She said,

'You can call me Mia.'

'Mia, I want to see what else is in Nathan's box.' She could see the box, over in Nathan's darkened office. She didn't reply at first.

He said, 'And you can call me Tom.'

She said, 'So you have something to tell me

111

about Nathan?'

'I certainly think we should be talking.'

She said, 'Good lord. You're trying to do a deal.'

'I have to know what else Nathan had about me, Mia.'

'Then...' she thought for a second. 'Then meet me on the corner of Sidney Street and Jesus. Six-thirty – no, seven p.m.'

'And you'll bring what's in the box?'

She felt Nathan's cold hand under her chin. Tom Fletcher – something about him, like he would help her. She had a suspicion of what was really going on around here. If she was right, it was something that would make the Bellman people sorry they'd ever met her, ever let Nathan loose on her.

'Yeah. I'll bring it.'

Tuesday Night

'Notice anything, Tom Fletcher?'

'You've got a very slight tan.'

'Apart from that.'

'Oh, yes. You're naked.'

On the desk in his twilit office, on his phone's screen, Cathleen smiled. She was sitting cross-legged on a Cretan hotel bed, in front of a window filled with black and red clouds, a breeze flicking her hair. The Mediterranean satellite caught all that, and it caught the smile in her voice when she said,

'Don't you wish you were here?'

'What do you think?'

'So get on the plane. It's twenty-six degrees, a warm wind off the sea. I'm working seven hours a day, then I'm all yours.' She shifted on the bed, the fiery light catching the swell of her breasts. 'Hey, what's the matter?'

'Daisy Seager. They found her car burned out. She was being stalked by someone with a sharpened up crowbar. There's a concern she's been abducted. And the dead American, Nathan Slade, had a personal photo album that contained a picture of my parents.'

She recoiled visibly. 'Well. That pretty much kills the atmosphere, doesn't it?'

'Just for now.'

'What kind of photo? A surveillance photo, like

113

he was spying on them?'

'That's the thing – it's a relaxed, personal photo. Just the two of them, about eighteen years ago.'

She stared into the camera. 'Did he know you?'

'I have no memory of him at all. My parents must have kept him some kind of secret.'

'Eighteen years ago? Just when your mother left?'

'Looks like it. And that's on top of the photo that Daisy Seager had of me in her room, the blow-up of me as a kid.'

'Well, she can't have known you, can she? She would have been five years old or something. So she got the photo from somewhere, or someone gave it to her. Hey, is this bringing problems back? Memories?'

She meant something they rarely spoke about any more – the time Fletcher's family broke apart, the weeks leading up to his mother's leaving. From inside Cathleen's hotel room, a phone rang twice, then stopped. She said, 'Suppose I'd better get dressed. The whole production crew, we're out to dinner. And what are you doing tonight, handsome?'

'I'm meeting someone from the Bellman Foundation who wants to discredit Nathan Slade.'

'Some kind of whistleblower?'

'Maybe she is, yes.'

'A *she*. What's her name? Mia – nice name. What's she like?' He had a sudden image of Mia's weird green eyes. 'She seems very focused.'

'Uh-huh. Be careful.'

'Yes, Cathleen. Hey, do you believe in witches?'

114

'Mm, right. That's what men don't understand, Tom Fletcher. We're all witches.' Cathleen twisted round and pulled her window shut, knelt up on the bed to pull it closed. The beauty of Cathleen from behind, with the red sun on her. She held it like that for a second, then slipped off the bed and came over to the phone, put her face close. 'Remember, in the new house which *you* are going to build, *I* am going to be like this all the time.'

Fletcher sat for a while in his office, while the daylight faded altogether. Shop lights from Green Street began to throw jagged shapes across the wall – and some of them looked like the new house, Fletcher thought. Pale and almost not there. He thought of Cathleen in the new house, the old land reclaimed. He would clear the under-growth and put in fruit trees, maybe restore that old beehive. How long do fruit trees take to grow?

Apples, honey, Cathleen.

Then he put the desk lamp on, and the shapes vanished.

He spread some papers across his desk.

First, his visitor's pass from the Bellman Foundation.

Then the leaflet from Felwell College: the Edwardian roof turrets over the legendary sealed basement, and behind that the white bulk of the modern physics lab dwarfing the original build-ing. His question to the dean of Felwell, 'Is there a link between Bellman and Felwell?'

He typed the two names into his computer.

A sponsorship programme, whereby Bellman

invited two Felwell postgraduates each year to spend a semester at a prestige American East Coast University. *Promoting excellence in shared research.*

Strange that the dean of Felwell hadn't mentioned that.

Then a history of nuclear research from a plausible online encyclopaedia. Nuclear fission, the splitting of the atom, first achieved at the Felwell Laboratory in 1938. The Felwell team used large stocks of a crude radioactive material named hadesium. Photo of men in tweed jackets and white aprons, horn-rimmed glasses, pipes, cheerful grins. Nuclear scientists, 1930s style. The Felwell people went on to work with the American Manhattan Project, their expertise helping to develop the technology for the Hiroshima bomb. Other consultants to the project included the Bellman Foundation, the modern-day armaments and aerospace giant.

Hadesium: an element on the periodic table. Silvery in colour. Fissionable, therefore suitable for reactor fuel or weapons. No weapons application is believed to have taken place. Originally produced in some volume at the Felwell Laboratory in Cambridge, England in the early 1930s. Named by its discoverers after Hades, the Greek underworld, due to its hellish properties.

The stocks of hadesium produced at Felwell have never been completely accounted for, due not to loss but to inaccurate record-keeping.

Yes, those cheerful men in aprons didn't look like great record-keepers. These things happen.

Some dodgy references on conspiracy sites.

116

Long analyses of how much hadesium was produced, how much would have been consumed in the 1930s research. Lots of it still around somewhere, apparently. Lots of veiled accusations that the Bellman Foundation were hoarding it for something. Lots of spelling mistakes and dodgy syntax too. That's the thing with the Internet. Someone somewhere slips up, half a million men in basements start spinning stories.

Nineteen-forties' nuclear expertise? Radioactive stuff named after hell? Was that the link between Felwell and Bellman? Or, far more likely, just a post-grad sponsorship programme?

Fletcher closed the screen, spread out other papers. The photocopies of the *Steel Witch* Nose Art. The copy of the photo from Nathan Slade's album – his parents in their last days together. The photo of him aged three, and his mother, on the Cambridge pathway. Daisy Seager had enlarged one corner of this: enlarged just him, Tom Fletcher, against the path and sky. Why?

He folded everything together and locked it in his desk.

He ran through his messages. That was not a long process – business for Green Street Investigations was slow and getting slower. There was at least an email from the university security people, wanting the second meeting to be on Thursday, 3 p.m., and could he confirm? And could he come prepared to discuss his preferred manner of working successfully alongside the Cambridge police?

He confirmed he would be there.

He put on a clean shirt, then his parka. Mia Tyrone was due to meet him in twenty minutes,

117

and through the windows he could see ice crystals flickering in the shop lights. Going down the stairs, he thought, *Yes, I could discuss how to work successfully with the Cambridge police. Don't tell the Cambridge police anything – and never, but never, trust them.*

Should prove to be an interesting meeting.

It was time for Bessie. She'd refused the poppy seed, because she knew what the men would do to her. She'd spent the night locked in the big house – that's our house here today – with a bowl of water taken from the puddles in the street. She had her blue dress back on. The skin was white on her neck and her wrists. Nothing else showing.

The witchfinder read out his paper to her, seated in his saddle. She looked at the sky, it was blue. There was a vein beating in her head and her throat. Granny say it took the witchfinder a while to finish reading the speech. She say all the time, Bessie watched the big clouds inland. When the witchfinder finished, she stepped up to the hawthorn.

'Where are you going, Bessie?'

'I am going for my hanging.'

'No, that is not for you.'

'Not to be hanged?'

'No. You are to be pressed, you witch.'

'Pressed?'

Bessie didn't know what that meant.

Granny say it was an old thing, from the days of the church arguments. They brought out two short planks of wood, put one on the ground there in the street, in the dust, stamped it flat. They made Bessie lie on it, face up. She did that, starting to shake, starting to

118

guess maybe. Her dress got all dust on it. The witch-finder came over on his horse and watched from the shade of the houses.

They put the other plank on top of her. It was fixed just below her chin, so they could see her face. It stretched down her chest and stomach, finished between her legs. It was shaking, she was shaking. She called out, 'Let me hang.'

The witchfinder stroked his horse.

They began the pressing. The men got a spade and shovelled earth into sacks, packed them so one man could hardly carry each one. They laid the first sack on the plank and stood back. Bessie tried to scream, but the weight pressed all the air out of her lungs, just left a screech in her throat. Her hands tried to push the board, couldn't. The second sack just rested next to the first, Granny said. Bessie's fingers raked splinters out of the plank and the noise from her mouth made the horse afraid.

The witchfinder calmed the horse, steadied the brasses on the reins.

Before the third sack went on, Granny said Bessie opened her eyes and fixed them on the witchfinder. He looked back at her, chewing. Then the sack went on top of the others, and Bessie ripped it open with her hands, clawed the earth out, trying to lessen the weight. Just a few handfuls scattered across the street.

The men looked at the witchfinder. He said nothing. It was silent except for the noises Bessie was making and the wind coming across the pasture. This went on for half an hour. One of the men scooped up a handful of water from a puddle, let it fall into Bessie's mouth. She tried to drink. The men looked at their com-mander again. He scratched his crotch, spat some *seeds. Then nodded.*

The last sack didn't kill her. It pressed her down in the dust so she looked to be sinking through the earth, Granny said. Her arms and legs were flailing, the marks on the skin all open to the light. A cloud went over the sun and the wind dropped, and Bessie seemed to be saying something. The man who dripped her the water looked up at the witchfinder, got no answer. So he picked up the spade and swung it once at Bessie's head.

Crows flew off from the house roof.

Darkness, and Cambridge was back in the ice age. The temperature had dropped further, and the air was sparkling with crystals, the lily-shaped spikes on the wall of All Saints' College glinting with fresh ice. Fletcher stamped his feet on the corner of Sidney Street – Sidney and Jesus, as Mia Tyrone had quaintly called it, like an American intersection in this tangle of medieval streets. Despite his rubber-soled boots and the Nordic cunning of his parka design, he was wishing he'd gone to the Bellman offices to collect Mia in his car. But he told himself there was a reason Mia wanted to meet him here. Such as, she wanted to be off the premises when she handed over the other item from Nathan Slade's cardboard box.

Seven o'clock came and went.

Fletcher walked a few yards into All Saints' Passage, looked in the window of the antiquarian map shop. Old maps bought and sold. A special offer on sea charts, for February only. He passed on that. He went back and waited on the corner.

At eight minutes past, a minicab came crawling down Sidney Street, scattering the slush, and pulled up beside him. It was a new saloon with tinted windows, and the back door opened to reveal a single passenger.

'You look kind of cold, Tom.'

Mia Tyrone was wearing a long quilted coat zipped up to her chin, flat boots catching the streetlight. Her hair in a single twist over one shoulder, a leather satchel beside her. Fletcher climbed in and took a seat, unzipped his parka in the sudden warmth, the scent of Mia's perfume over the taxi smell. They looked at each other, the driver looking at them in the mirror. He said to her, 'Do you ever get hungry this time of day?'

'Yes, but I struggle with British food.'

'What about Polish food?'

She tilted her head. 'In *Cambridge?*'

He gave the driver an address. Then he settled back and smiled across at Mia. 'I'd like to show you a project of mine.'

Stan was someone Fletcher knew from years before. Owner of a breakfast stall in the market square, he was a hefty, taciturn Polish guy, early fifties, whose life revolved around recreating his grandmother's cooking. The previous spring, Fletcher had gone shares with him and opened a small restaurant above a printing shop off Mill Road. Stan had twelve big tables with a candle each, two waiters, his niece behind the bar on busy nights. That first summer, there'd been queues down to the pavement, people sitting on the stairs drinking *alkoholowy* while they waited.

121

Even this early on a freezing night, it was a third full. Fletcher's share of the profits from Stan's was paying his rent at present.

Stan came out in his chef's gear and shook Fletcher's hand and raised an eyebrow at seeing Mia rather than Cathleen standing there next to him. But he took her coat with his usual grim smile and showed them to the premium table: in an alcove with a window and a radiator.

'Drinks?'

She said, 'Vodka.'

Fletcher said, *'Oranżada.'*

She was still wearing her office suit, still looking comfortable in it. Her body was neatly angled, wide shoulders, medium breasts. She glanced up at him, the candle showing green lights in her eyes and those two colours in her hair. The drinks came and she looked at him through her glass.

'You're not drinking?'

'Not alcohol. I never have.'

She took a sip, eyeing him.

He said, 'Tell me about yourself, Mia. Where exactly are you from?'

She felt the radiator with one hand, smiling. 'Bowling Green, Virginia. Don't you laugh.'

'I'm not.'

'It's a fine place.'

'I see white fences, a courthouse?' She nodded. 'How do you feel about being here?'

'Ah, the open question, the therapist's favourite. And the snooper's.'

'Does that mean you don't like it here? Or you just don't like Bellman?'

She leaned forward. 'Let me tell you something. Each year, Bellman takes a small number of interns, develops them, sends them abroad to learn the business. The competition's crazy, literally thousands of people for half-a-dozen slots.'

'You are one of those interns?' She nodded. 'This year's intern?'

'This was a year ago.'

'So you're not an intern any more?'

She didn't answer. Stan appeared with a menu, and she unleashed a smile that would live in his brooding East European heart for a while, Fletcher thought. She tapped her vodka glass – almost empty – and glanced at the card. *'Kielbasa.* For two, how about that?'

She watched Stan go, then turned her eyes on Fletcher.

'Bellman – I don't mind you knowing this – Bellman has not been supportive of me.'

'They haven't promoted you?'

The waiter brought a dish of pickles. He was a nineteen-year-old from Gdansk, and he looked at her slightly too long, though Mia's eyes stayed on Fletcher's. She said,

'Have you ever worked for an organisation, then grown to hate them?'

'That describes my relationship with the police.'

'Then you've got some idea how it feels. When I left, I was a star, a local hero. Girl from Bowling Green actually gets somewhere in life. But Bellman grinds people down, humiliates them in subtle ways.'

'What ways?'

'Nathan's kind of ways. Giving you ever more menial work. Cutting you out of things. There's a lot of innuendo, a lot of subtle bullying. They'll start forcing me out soon, I know it.' Her eyes went hard. 'Basically I fucking hate them. I want to screw them up.'

'You're sort of a whistleblower, but you don't have anything to blow the whistle on?'

'I do. This thing with Nathan Slade.' She took a spoonful of *korniszon*. 'You have something on Nathan? I mean, nice place and everything, but I hope I'm not–'

'Wasting your time? I don't think you are. Nathan served in the USAF.'

'Yes, I'm aware. A lot of people in the foundation served in the USAF.'

'Daisy Seager has some unusual interests. One is old English witch trials.'

Mia raised an eyebrow. 'We had one or two of those in New England too.'

'OK. And Daisy's been researching a thing called Nose Art. Which is this.' He got out the photocopies of the Steel Witches and pushed them across.

She examined them. 'A kind of corny, dated soft porn. Why is she into that?'

'She's researching something from the war. *Pilot and unit unknown,* you see? But I think these are images of actual women, a group of eight or more of them.'

She looked at him, then looked at the photocopies a little more. She pushed her cutlery aside and laid the pages across the table.

'They've got these little dots all over them, like

124

moles or something. But look at their faces. Tom, I think you're unobservant. Or maybe you've been looking at the wrong parts. You don't see any similarities between the faces? To me, these four look like the same girl.' She lined them up together. 'And these other four, they're all of another girl, just one. These aren't eight women, they're just *two*. By the way, this gravy is delicious.'

He looked at the Nose Art and thought, Yes, she's right. Two women. He watched Mia carefully slicing the meat. She had squared-off nails that shone under the candle.

'You want the name of my manicurist? Or something else on your mind?'

He looked up. 'Daisy Seager was being followed recently. He's a white American male, late twenties. Any ideas?'

'No.' But he noticed that she glanced at her satchel, that line coming back between her eyes.

'You sure, Mia?'

'Don't grill me, Tom.' She was clearly thinking something over.

'Well, that's what I know about Nathan and Daisy.'

'It's pretty thin.'

'But it's something. Now, what do you have for me? Something else about my family in Nathan's personal stuff?'

'I just have to think about this.'

'We have an agreement, Mia. I want to know what's in there.'

'Look, Tom. Why don't you *ask* your parents?'

Fletcher took a breath. Then he told her. She listened, looking into his eyes, not eating. When he'd finished, she said, 'I see. I'm sorry about all this. I really am.'

'So what have you got for me?'

She took a sip of vodka, watching him. Then she opened the satchel and took something out. It was a black wooden picture frame, book-sized.

She studied it briefly, then handed it across.

The frame held a colour photo. It was a colour picture of an event taking place at an airbase, with a massive American B52 bomber parked in front of a hangar. There were dozens of people milling around the aircraft: men and women in green fatigue uniforms, some civilians too. The civilian clothes were from the 1980s. Stonewashed denim, leggings. There were children of various ages. People were eating ice cream, and the kids were holding balloons. A big banner across the building read *USAF Alconhurst Family Day.*

Fletcher knew that Alconhurst, about twenty miles outside Cambridge, was the largest of the few American bases remaining in Britain. The complex dwarfed the nearby village, which had coexisted with the Americans since the first crude airstrips for Flying Fortresses were laid out there in the war.

In the photo, right under the nose of the B52, a group of people were assembled, the focus of the picture. A souvenir of a happy, sunny day on the base. On the left were a couple in their mid-forties, holding hands and smiling. The woman, with her brown hair in a tidy summer cut, was wearing a dress that Fletcher remembered her wearing: a belted denim shift that made his father whistle. He said,

'These are my parents.'

Fletcher himself wasn't in the photo. He'd never been to USAF Alconhurst in his life.

He thought, *Mum and Dad. The late eighties. Guns'n'Roses on the radio. I was thirteen, fourteen years old. Something changed then, between you and me. I remember. You started going away for an afternoon, a day now and then. Without me. Placing me with friends, then slipping away.*

The B52 nose wheel was massive. On the other side of it was another couple. The man was in green military fatigues – younger than his press photo this week, of course, but unmistakeable. Big Nathan Slade. He had his arm around the waist of a woman also wearing fatigues, with a peaked cap that partly obscured her face, just showing a wide smile. She was a slim, attractive woman, her age hard to assess.

Fletcher said, 'Who's this woman with Nathan Slade?'

'Her name's Cherelle Swanson. Sounds like an old movie starlet, doesn't it? But she used to be a military psychologist with the USAF.'

'How do you know this?'

'I spoke to her on the phone today. Nathan Slade listed her as his next of kin. She's his wife. They separated some years ago, but it sounds like they remained close. She's just flown in from the States to collect his body. The USAF looks after its people, Tom. Especially people who go on to work for Bellman. She's actually staying at the Alconhurst base right now. The Bellman UK president is going over there with Nathan's effects tomorrow.'

Fletcher felt Stan approach, pause, and walk away without speaking.

He kept studying the photo. Between the two couples, someone was standing on the massive undercarriage wheels. A young boy. He looked about ten years old, maybe less. He was wearing trainers, jeans, a plain green T-shirt. He was pale, with jet black hair, his face fixed in a snarling laugh. The woman in fatigues – Cherelle Swanson – had her hand on his shoulder.

Mia said, 'Who's the kid? Is it you? Doesn't really look like you.'

Fletcher touched the photo. 'No, it's not me. I wonder, though. Did Nathan ever mention a family?'

'Never, at least not to me. But then he wouldn't. First I heard he had an ex-wife was when I had to phone her today to make arrangements.'

'But you never heard him in conversation with other people? No reference to a son at all?'

She said, 'No, never. Maybe that's not his son, then.'

'Or maybe he didn't want to talk about him.'

Stan returned and served them some apple *kluski* straight from the iron pan. Fletcher was thinking back to being a kid again, remembering times his parents disappeared for a morning, an afternoon. The more he thought, the more examples he came up with, stretched over those hot summers in the late eighties. At the time, as a boy of thirteen or fourteen, he didn't mind. He didn't know where they went, but he always thought it was something romantic, something between the two of them. But all the while, were they

128

spending time with these people? With the Slade family?

He rubbed his fingers over the stubble on his cheek, looking at the photo of the Fletchers and the Slades.

Yes, the boy looked like Nathan – the shape of the face recognisable even though the kid was making that vicious laugh.

How old would the kid be now? Late twenties? If you aged this face, what would he look like today? Would he still be pale, dark haired? Would he have an American accent? Would he look like the prowler on the Felwell CCTV?

Was Daisy being stalked by Nathan Slade's *son?* Why?

Fletcher turned the photo over, opened up the frame, looked for anything on the back. There was just *Kodak* repeating diagonally, the way it did in those days.

He said, 'Cherelle Swanson is staying at Alconhurst airbase right now? Do you have a number for her?'

'Why?'

'Let's call her. Ask her if she's got a son, where he is right now. Say there's someone who'd like to meet her after all this time. Tomorrow morning.'

Mia took out her phone. A lot of dialling and asking to be put through. Then he could just hear a voice on the other end. It went quiet for a long time when Mia said Tom's name. Then a few more words he didn't catch.

Mia ended the call. 'Cherelle said yes, she's got a son. Doesn't want to talk about it on the phone. But yes, she'll see you tomorrow, explain a few things.'

Mia settled back in her chair, one arm along the radiator, watching him. Her jacket was unbuttoned, the white blouse underneath smoothly filled out. She caught his eye and smiled. 'See, Tom? We're helping each other.' She uncoiled her hair and let it loose.

Leaving the restaurant, they exchanged numbers and shook hands. She got into a taxi, waved at him through the spattered window. He watched the tail-lights getting fainter down Mill Road, then vanishing.

He zipped up his parka and started walking.

The shop fronts were frosted over, but the sky above the city was clear – the stars of the Plough glinting in their angles. Fletcher reached Parker's Piece, the long tarmac pathways stretching across it glinting with ice. His mind went back to that early memory – that long path ahead of him, so long he felt he could never get to the end of it.

'*Run, Tom. Run.*'

Was it this path? Am I walking in the same place now?

In his memory, the path was wide, dark and warm. Tonight, though, it was hard and treacherous.

He came into St Andrew's Street, where the pavements were gritted, the granules tinted orange by the streetlamps.

If the Slade son really has been stalking Daisy – why? Has he abducted her? Is he holding her somewhere? Why? Because she pushed his father off the edge of a quarry? Or because she found something out

130

about Felwell, about Bellman?

In Green Street, ice was crusting the gutters, the lock of his street door sparkly with frost. Halfway up the stairs, he heard his desk phone ringing. Cathleen, maybe, interested in the night's progress. Then why wasn't she calling his mobile?

Opening the door, he stood for a second. He'd left one of the windows ajar to let some fresh air in. The heating was on, and the office smelled clean, the tang of the hallway floor wax with its 1950s scent and the ionised air from the street. The phone kept ringing, its blind form crying out from the plastic cradle on the desk. It was ringing longer than a phone should, than any caller should. He looked at the screen: number withheld. Fletcher thought, this is my father. With the lights still off, he picked it up, said nothing.

'Tom?'

Not his father's voice. A young man's voice. Slightly nasal. American accent. Making 'Tom' rhyme with 'harm.' 'Tom?'

Fletcher said, 'Who's this?'

There was muffled noise on the line: road sounds, wind over open land. Then a noise close to the mouthpiece: some kind of squelching. Fletcher realised: some kind of chewing.

'Tom, I've been calling and calling. You have to see what I do.'

'Who are you?'

The chewing increased, then stopped. 'See what I do, Tom.' Fletcher reached out and closed the window.

'Are you the son of Nathan Slade?'

'I used to hear about you, Tom. How fucking

131

perfect you were.' The chewing suddenly started again, became frantic for a few seconds, then halted. 'You got a map, perfect Tom? There's a place called Wicken Fen. It's a nice place, night like this. There's a place in there where three little rivers meet together. Take a look, see what I do.'

'What's your name?'

'And I promise you something, Tom. I will find her. I'll find her in the end.'

The line went dead. Fletcher made a note of the time: 9.18 p.m. He was in no doubt he'd just spoken to Nathan Slade's son. The chewing, the American accent – that made him the person stalking Daisy Seager.

I will find her in the end – what did that mean? That he didn't know where Daisy Seager was? Then what did he want Fletcher to see?

Fletcher considered for a minute. Then he went back down the stairs, picked up his car from All Saints' College, and drove out of the city, along roads white with frost, the twelve miles to Wicken Fen.

He knew the place slightly – a nature reserve where the original landscape of the fens was maintained. A great place to visit in summer: an old windmill, bulrushes, dog roses in the bracken, heron nesting on the little silt beaches in the riverbanks. Tonight the mill was lit by an oval moon, a wind blasting ice crystals across the deserted access road, the bare trees shuddering in the headlamps until Fletcher shut the lights off and locked the car. Then there was just the crashing sound of the branches, their dim shapes in the scant moonlight. Fletcher clicked on his metal torch and checked his map, holding the paper down in the wind. There was a point, yes, only a few hundred yards ahead but well away from the main path, where three small rivers converged in a triangular-shaped pool.

If not Daisy Seager, who or what the hell was out there?

He walked in that direction, his torch beam swaying over the icy tree roots beside the track. When the path curved, he kept going straight ahead, his feet crushing the frozen turf. He went through a screen of bare hawthorn which shielded the pool from the normal path. If this was a crime scene, he was corrupting it – he knew that. But he wanted to be here before any police.

He shone his torch ahead, caught the dark ribbon of one of the rivers, brimming almost level with the bank. Beyond that, the triangular piece of water, one corner just reflecting the moon. The wind was rising, and the reflection jangled around. Beside it, something was projecting out of the water. Fletcher stopped and trained his torch on it. It looked like a plank of wood, pale against the dark turf beyond. Fletcher stooped to see it better, the bright disc of the torch lighting the plank up, catching the frost in the air. There was something tied to the plank with heavy rope and, lower down, a pale shape spreading across the water. Fletcher recognised the thing on the plank as a pair of human hands, strapped together. They were raised up out of the water and, below them, a long sweep of pale hair floated on the surface, sparkling in places with ice.

Fletcher didn't go any closer. He didn't think there was anything he could do to help here. He knew that Nathan Slade's son had directed him to Daisy Seager's body.

After phoning the police, he stayed quite still where he was, looking at the unmoving body in the torch beam. He was asking himself what exactly Slade had done to her. Tied her to a plank and lowered her into the water? Wasn't there a word for that – ducking? Wasn't that something you would do to a witch?

I love our house. Upstairs there's the big rooms, where Granny used to live. They're empty now and the shutters are closed. In the walls there are timbers with old axe cuts, marks you can put your hand inside. Downstairs there's the kitchen and then there's the bedroom for me and my sister. It's the only room I've ever slept in. The floor is stone and there's a fireplace. Outside, our yard has chickens and the vegetables, the pen for the goats. You stand there with the goats and look back at the house, you can see how old it is. The timbers are filled between with old bricks, small as your hand. The house leans a bit, it's true. One wall looks like a goat's udder.

I remember that summer we had, before the war, before the Americans came and ruined everything. It was hot, we used to lie on the bed at night, me and Sally, waiting to fall asleep. There was this moth that used to visit us at night. He had big eyes and a tight little belly, used to dance around the paraffin lamp. He made me laugh and clap. I said to my sister, 'We got everything, haven't we, Sally? We got the house

and the yard, our fields, we got three pound a month from Granny's will. We got Mr Moth here to dance for us.' I said, 'Why you crying, Sally?'
She said 'I'm eighteen years old.'

Fletcher wasn't under arrest, so he was spared the mechanics: the DNA sample – taken by force if necessary – and the paper coverall suit. He had voluntarily given samples of his clothing because of his presence at the scene, and a statement of how he came to find a woman's body at Wicken Fen, plus his whereabouts over the past forty-eight hours. Now he watched DI Franks scowl back over it, smoothing the paper down with bitten fingers.

Fletcher remembered this particular interview room at Parkside police station. The way the striplight buzzed, the canteen smell coming down through the ceiling, the electric heating that kept the place either sweltering or freezing. Right now, at 1.23 a.m., it was sweltering, and DI Franks gave off a slightly animal smell as he pushed away the statement and started making notes on a jotter pad.

Fletcher had taken the necessary precaution of waking his solicitor, Maureen Hara, and getting her down here too. Maureen sat beside him: a woman in her late thirties with a soothing Irish accent, normally perfectly presented, slightly ruffled tonight. Maureen caught Fletcher's eye, raised an eyebrow, then looked down at her own pad.

Franks stopped writing and glanced up, flicking his pen, wrinkling his nose.

'So who phoned you?'

'I have no idea. I didn't recognise the voice, it was nobody I've ever spoken to before. Male, hard to tell the age. No distinguishing mannerisms.'

'Accent?'

'I didn't notice one.' Misleading, but Fletcher didn't want to focus the police on Nathan Slade's son, whoever he was. He wanted to be ahead of them on this. Franks scowled, making notes.

'*See what I do?* What's that supposed to mean?'

'I don't know.'

'And he gives you the location and you drive out there and bingo.' Franks shook his head. 'Why'd he phone you, Fletcher?'

'My name was in the media as the person who found Nathan Slade. Whoever phoned must be following the case; he doesn't want to phone you direct. He phones me, but he's getting to *you*. He's challenging you. He knows you're closing in on the vice aspect of Daisy's life. I mean, that press conference this morning.'

Franks grimaced. 'The parents didn't cooperate. Upper middle class.'

'Yeah, but you got across what you needed to. Now everyone knows, it's a vice thing.'

Franks sniffed. 'So why have you been going around all these places connected with Daisy Seager? Her house, Felwell, the Bellman place where Nathan Slade worked. What do you think you're doing?'

'Well, it's like this. Business has been slow. I mean, really slow. Not being nasty, but being the one who found Slade in the quarry was a bit of

136

luck for me.' Franks held his eyes, unblinking. 'I had an idea. I thought if I could find Daisy Seager, track her down, I could drum up some interest. You know, *Private detective finds missing student vice girl.* A real coup. Generate some publicity.'

Franks eyed him. Fletcher wondered if Franks *wanted* to believe that, because it made Fletcher seem weak.

Franks tapped his pen on the pad. 'Think carefully. Obstructing an enquiry, perverting the course of justice. if you're lying to me now, this minute, you're risking a prison term. Can you see yourself inside? Ex-copper. You know what they'll do to you in there?' There was a few seconds' pause, measured by the tap of Franks' pen. 'So what did you find out from these people?'

'Well, not much. The cleaner told me Daisy was a prostitute.' He saw a half-smile on Franks' face. 'Felwell, Dr Nile, she told me how Daisy was a star student, though she's worried about the extent of this, er, hostess activity among the student population.' Franks' eyes wrinkled with pleasure. 'Then, at Bellman, the shutters came down. They didn't tell me anything.'

Franks looked at his pad. 'You say you've had dinner with a Bellman person tonight, this Tyrone woman.'

'That's more social than anything else.'

'Lovely. What did you talk about?'

'Our respective childhoods.'

Franks grunted, then shifted in his chair, looking at the solicitor, back at Fletcher. 'Go home, Fletcher. Back to your little flat. Stay there, by the phone.'

'You think he'll call again?'

'If he does, you'll be there, by the phone. Then you pick up the phone to me. OK? And I'll be coming back to you in the hours and days ahead. If I can't find you...' He left it unfinished.

Maureen Hara raised a smooth, ringless hand. 'I've no doubt my client will assist you in every possible way.' Her accent alone calmed the atmosphere in the room. She tucked a strand of black hair behind one ear and looked at Franks with her head on one side. 'All done?'

Franks looked at her. 'Would you like to make use of our coffee machine? There's a new type of whitener they're using now.' The solicitor looked at Fletcher. Franks said, 'Two minutes, literally.'

Fletcher nodded.

When the door closed, Franks settled back. There was a grim smile on his face and a light in his eye that was more than just the fluorescent tube. He said, 'If you *are* bullshitting me, Fletcher, your life will be over in any meaningful sense. You know that.'

'I know. I'll help out, though. Who would do something like that to Daisy Seager?'

Franks smiled. 'She was mixed up in something. This student hostessing thing, we've been watching it for a while. It's time to crack it open. You just sit by your phone, boy. Forget any interest you ever had in Daisy Seager.'

'I was just trying to make a living, Franks.'

The policeman shook his head slowly. 'I had no idea.'

'Of what?'

'How bad things have gone for you.'

138

'There are good months and bad months.'

'Yeah. And now I hear on the grapevine, you're in the frame for this university contract.'

'Well, let's hope so.'

'Yeah, I hope you get it. I don't like to see a man going under.' Franks grinned at the thought. 'Hey, you want me to put in a good word for you? Tell them how well you're working with the police?'

'That would be excellent.'

'Oh, fuck. You really are desperate.' Franks stopped smiling, leaned forward. 'You see this situation, the power I have? I can throw you a lifeline, or I can use the same rope to string you up. So stay in your sad little office, Fletcher. Stay where we can find you.'

In reception, Maureen Hara looked up sleepily from her coffee. 'The whitener's not so good. Now call me a cab, Tom, for the love of God.'

It was after 2 a.m. Up in Fletcher's flat, the rooftops outside the window made a landscape of white and grey frozen angles. He drew the blinds on that and looked at the local news site.

Woman's body linked to missing student. Police have so far declined to comment on reports of unusual circumstances regarding the body.

Unusual circumstances? That meant someone in the police had tipped off the media about the way Daisy was tied up – already positioning the case as vice-related. In fact, thinking of it from their perspective, that seemed understandable – the most obvious route to follow, if you didn't know about Daisy's interest in the artwork of the

139

US Air Force, and Fletcher's parents' friendship with the Slade family.

Where was the Slade boy now?

When Nathan Slade said to Jack Fletcher, *I'm going to warn her* – was it about this danger? About his own son?

And when Jack Fletcher said in that 6 a.m. phone call, *We have to kill him, Tom.* Was he talking about Nathan, the man who was already dead? Or was he really talking about Nathan's son? Was that the reason Jack kept a revolver under the floorboards?

It was less than ten hours until Fletcher's meeting with Cherelle Swanson at Alconhurst. How would she respond to questions like that? *Do you have a son, Cherelle? A Slade junior? Is he here in Cambridge? Because I think he's just murdered a physics student. And, by the way, how come I never met you?*

He flicked to the other news sites – nationally, the Daisy Seager story was getting coverage, its 'unusual circumstances' giving it momentum, but it was being dwarfed by the weather and all the country's resulting transport and energy problems. He noticed too the case in the USA that he'd read about in the reception at Bellman while waiting to meet Mia Tyrone – the failed radiation bomb plot. It was a major event now – their police still rounding up suspects and materials, the President making a televised address to reassure the public. Plenty of graphics on how the men were going to explode their bomb: a core of normal explosives, radioactive waste packed around it. Enough to contaminate half a city. He read through for a minute, then, as if to demonstrate the British problems, the desk lamp failed in a power cut that put the room into darkness, the only light coming from the laptop screen switching to battery. In its brittle light, he found his way into the kitchen and retrieved an old torch and some candles from under the sink.

He lit two of the candles in his office and closed the computer, went to the window and raised the blind. The street was completely dark, but he noticed, in a few other windows, torches and candles being lit, jagged shadows moving against other curtains.

He sat on the windowsill, watching the darkened street, his shadow flickering on the wall.

The American man had a room on the top floor of a small bed and breakfast hotel on the edge of Cambridge. The window looked over a car park, then the gas storage tanks near the river. In three months of living here, he hadn't met another resident. He liked that about this little city: the way anyone could arrive and mix in and not be noticed.

He was leaving soon, though. He had a night candle burning on the dresser, as the power was down, and in its light he was packing up. His things were spread out on the bed. His passport, his British currency in a plastic envelope, the keys to the cheap and anonymous car he'd bought locally, a backpack with bad-weather clothing, hiking boots, packs of the liquorice chewing gum he loved. Then his favourite thing: a heavy crowbar, blackened steel making a big hook at one end, split into two claws which he'd sharpened so they cut like twin knives. He hefted it in his hand, smiling. Remembering the way it made Daisy scream.

Unusual circumstances, they were saying on the news.

Yeah, you could say that. Unusual to get a girl like Daisy who makes a living – who earns herself *money* – from talking to men in a club. Then you get her on her own, encourage her a little, but she just doesn't want to talk. Crazy, really. After the first few words, when she insisted, she kept saying she hadn't killed Nathan Slade.

Just told him to get out of my car, she said. *Told him to get out and get a taxi. Not my fault if he got lost in the dark, fell off the edge.*

Please.

After that, some kind of shock set in, put a hold on her system. He got a bit more out of her, some things he needed to know, but not much. At the end, she was blue and convulsing, ice crystals in her hair and flying from her mouth, like a real witch.

He knew she had the evidence, though.

He knew she had the document that proved what happened back there in the past. It was an old document, he knew that. Old, done on some kind of ancient typewriter. It was around here somewhere, in this city, hidden among the people that Daisy had been talking to. Twenty or thirty pieces of paper so dangerous that he had to find them, had to destroy them. They held the kind of story that could poison the world. He had to stop it spreading. And after that, the person at the root

142

of it all, the person who had first uncovered that story. That person would have to be destroyed as well. Only then would the American be safe.

He felt the twin points of his crowbar and smiled.

Wednesday Morning

The desk phone rang at 7 a.m. Fletcher had it right in his ear, because he was asleep in his clothes on the client sofa. He blinked, listening to the echo around the office. The electricity was back on, and the desk lamp had lit up, the switch left on. He went over and picked the phone up and waited.

'Mr Fletcher?' A woman's voice.

Out in Green Street, he could see lights in the neighbouring windows. Not candle flames, but steady electric squares: all the switches left on when the power failed.

'Mr Fletcher?' OK. He placed the voice. Green eyes, a Polish newspaper, some talk of holes in the ceiling. 'Wilbur Court here. You're a good person, Mr Fletcher.'

'Thanks.'

'I've just started work. Did I wake you?'

'I've been up for hours.'

She paused. 'Your father's back.'

'Where's he been?'

'I don't know. You want to see him?'

'Yes.'

'I think you better be quick.'

He grabbed his keys. Outside, in Green Street, all the forgotten lamps burned on in the half dark.

Wilbur Court looked clean and washed in the first light, the freezing temperatures giving way to almost mild air, the sun blurring red over the conifers dripping off their snow and raising a fine mist from the melting ice in the car park.

Fletcher found the nurse standing in the doorway, waiting. She looked freshly scrubbed too, and very worried.

He said, 'Thanks for calling me.'

She bit her lip. 'He's been up to his room, came straight down. He's gone down there through the trees.' Pointing behind the building. 'You'll need to run.'

The last time he'd been on this path, it was the humid summer he left the police, an evening when he thought he might have the courage to speak to his father again. Today the track was just a line in the softening snow between the plantation trees, running straight through the shadows towards an open field that was dark crossed with white lines like a shred of old cloth. There was a light down there at the edge of the field, Fletcher could see, not the damp smoke you would expect, but bright flames from an accelerant such as petrol. Fletcher ran down under the trees, cold drops smacking him on the face a few times, the ground where the new sun was reaching just beginning to steam. He unzipped his coat and ran faster, jumping over the fallen branches across the path, the red sun flashing in his eyes. At the end of the track he came into a small clearing. The field beyond was beginning to mist up, but right in front of him was a small fire of branches spattering, blue flames, the smell of paraffin. On the other side of that, Jack Fletcher.

Wearing army trousers and a plastic anorak like a young traveller, but there was no doubt it was him. The six-foot-six height, the skinny frame, the slight stoop. The face was deeply lined, though, and the nose Fletcher remembered as sharp was now a thin beak between bright eyes that turned and glinted in the paraffin light. Then Jack Fletcher himself turned and walked away, along the edge of the treeline. Fletcher said, 'Dad.'

Jack looked back, kept walking. Fletcher jogged after him, came level. Eighteen years, and here it was happening on the edge of some stupid field with the smell of paraffin in their mouths.

'Dad.' Fletcher reached out to touch him. Jack shrugged the touch away, walked faster. His hair was still curly, but in long ringlets streaked with grey, spattered with melting snow.

'Dad, what's going on?'

Jack glanced at Fletcher. 'We've got to kill him before he finds her.'

'But she's already dead.'

'What are you talking about?'

'Daisy Seager's dead. She was murdered.'

Jack broke into a run, an awkward rolling motion. On one side of him, the massive field; on the other, the pine woods, each gap in the trees sending a bar of red light across the furrows. Jack looked back, sweat or meltwater running on his face. He shouted, 'Not Daisy Seager.' He smelled of paraffin and sour breath.

Fletcher ran alongside his father, the two of

them jogging through the snow. He said, 'Then who?'

Jack Fletcher wheeled round, suddenly still, his chest heaving, the lines on his forehead forging one deep V-shape. Some birds flew off from the trees, shrieking. Jack said,

'You must realise, Tom. It's your mother.' His breath drifted in the sunlight.

'My mother?'

'The Slade boy hates her, Tom.'

'Why?'

'You must know why. Didn't you ever go into her study?'

'She kept it locked.'

'Because she was working on something. She was researching something. Something to do with the Americans in the war.'

'What exactly?'

Jack Fletcher closed his eyes, shook his head. 'I don't know. I swear to you, I don't know. But I'll do this myself now.' Jack's eyes opened suddenly. 'He'll kill her if he finds her. He'll kill her to wipe out what happened.'

'Why? What did happen?'

For an answer, Jack Fletcher reached into his coat pocket and brought out his old gun. He took a step back and raised it at his son. Fletcher looked into the muzzle: a black disc in the sunlight, smelling of that fine oil. The chambers were loaded now: dark bullet tips visible. The pistol shook for a few seconds, his father's eyes behind it wide and scared. Then the muzzle lowered again, pointed down at the snow. Jack said,

'I don't know what happened. That's the truth.

147

But if you come after me, I'll use this. I don't want you coming after me.'

'OK, Dad. It's OK.'

Jack Fletcher stood looking at him, his chest heaving, damp in the lines on his face.

'Why do you live here, Tom?'

'What do you mean?'

'A man like you, you could go anywhere, do anything. But you stay in Cambridge, running in your straight lines. Why?'

'I think because...' he swallowed. 'I think I've always believed, if I stay here long enough, she'll come back and find me.'

Jack looked into his eyes for a few seconds. Then he said, 'I love her. And I love you. You know that.'

Fletcher watched him walking away along the edge of the trees, through the red bars of sun spilling across the snow. What his father had said stopped him as effectively as an old army bullet. Jack Fletcher wanted to work alone. But Tom Fletcher knew now what had to be done. He had to save his mother's life. Because she had found out something that the Slade boy was desperate to conceal, that made Slade kill Daisy Seager because Daisy had found out too.

When did the danger start?

I have to think about that. If I go back in my head, I see me and Sally as girls. In the house after dark, Granny lit the kitchen lamp and we sat under it, in the circle it makes. Winter was best, with the fire going, the lamp burning, Granny in her chair, us on the floor. That's when she told us the story of the

148

village, what the witchfinder did to us here, why we are the way we are.

Then Granny died, and Sally stopped believing in the story. That was dangerous, but worse was on the way. When the Americans came, they brought the danger with them. A danger more terrible than anything there is in this world. That's why I had to do what I did. To save us.

'He wants to kill your mother?' On the phone screen, back in Fletcher's apartment, Cathleen was dressed for work in a T-shirt and jeans, the window beside her flickering with rain from a grey Mediterranean sky. 'Why?'

Sunlight was pouring into Fletcher's room, showing up fine cracks in the client sofa and dust in the air. 'I can see what happened now... My dad was a friend of Nathan's, my mother spent time with the Slades, overheard something, picked up on something that interested her. She learned something about the Americans in the war, began to look into it.'

'But what was it?'

'In her study, there were books about the Felwell lab, the USAF. Other things I can't remember. There was a map on one wall. There were things on it.'

'What things?'

Fletcher tried to remember. It was just a glimpse, that afternoon, before his mother's fingers closed over his eyes. He saw it for less time than he'd seen the books on the shelf. 'No, I'm imagining it.'

'What?'

149

'Memory is unreliable, that far back.'

'What?'

'It was a map of eastern England, I remember that. A huge map. And on it there were shapes marked in red. Angular shapes, like the capital letter A.'

'She was drawing letters on a map?'

'No, shapes. The letter A, it looks like something seen from above. The runways of an airfield, joining together. Maybe it's a false memory, but now I'm thinking – maybe I've been wrong about her all along. I thought she left because of my father, the way he was treating her. But maybe she left because of this. Because of what she found out.'

'Something about airfields?' On the screen from Crete, there was a knock on the hotel door. Cathleen looked to one side and shouted, 'Just wait.' Then back to Fletcher. 'I'll have to move. So you're obviously going to the police now, tell them about this Slade person.'

'No. Not the police. I don't trust them, they'll get in the way. There are things, you know sometimes, you have to do yourself.'

'But if you know and you don't tell them, what are the consequences? They'll find out and they'll prosecute you. What about us?'

'It'll be OK.'

'Yeah?' She reached out to the phone, her voice hard. 'I've got to go. Give my regards to what's-her-name, Mia.'

The screen went blank. Fletcher took a long breath. He knew how much the idea of the village house meant to Cathleen – to them both. Not the

150

house itself, but having somewhere safe they were going to build together. But – like he told her – there are some things you have to do yourself. Like stop someone killing your mother to cover up a story about the Americans in the war.

He took out the copies of the old Steel Witch artwork. The flowing black hair of the women, the bodies lined with dots. *Pilot and unit unknown.*

It struck him that pilots have to be based somewhere.

Somewhere like an airbase.

He changed into a dark grey suit, pale blue shirt, the darkest tie he could find. He picked up his car keys and slipped the Steel Witches and the photo of the 1980s Alconhurst family day into his parka. If he was going to save his mother, an airbase was the best place to start. Alconhurst airbase, meeting Cherelle Swanson, mother of the Slade boy himself.

The few American bases remaining in Britain have an ambiguous legal status. Technically, their acreage remains part of the United Kingdom, and all events inside the perimeter are subject to UK law. In reality, the space beyond the razor wire is self-governing, with the forces of the British state rarely intervening. They are marked on maps only as crude outlines, with no buildings or access roads identified.

Fletcher waited in a small queue of three cars at the Alconhurst security gate. To left and right, the razor wire perimeter stretched out, taut and shining in the sun. Ahead of him was a fortified

151

gatepost with cameras on stilts, then two steel barriers, each manned by a uniformed guard with an automatic rifle at half-arms. Beyond that was a row of soft-skinned military cars in drab green, then the side of a building clad in blast-proof concrete streaked with damp, steaming a little.

When the cars ahead of Fletcher moved through the barriers, the nearest guard signalled him to move forward and then stop. One of the cameras swivelled to follow. The barriers came down in front and behind. The soldier made a series of hand gestures to the gatepost. The door opened and a woman emerged, in green combat fatigues, holding a slim laptop with a handgrip on the base. She walked up to Fletcher's window, and he slid it down.

She was a tiny woman with Latin skin, and a small, perfect face like a doll's. She had to lean down only slightly to speak into the car. A name tag over her pocket said *Sanchez*.

Fletcher said, 'You're a long way from home.'

She smiled, long eyelashes closing for a moment. Then she said, 'Remove your car keys and place them where I can see.'

Fletcher did so. He was aware that another person in fatigues was moving around the car, holding a mirror on a rod to check underneath. Then the tailgate opened, and someone began looking around in the boot. Fletcher gave Sanchez his name, and explained the purpose of the visit, that it had been agreed with Cherelle Swanson. He showed his passport and driving licence. She nodded, looking at her laptop screen. The

152

hatchback slammed shut. She said,

'A few identity questions, Mr Fletcher. The dates of your service with the British police.'

He told her. She tapped her keyboard.

'The date of your most recent entry to the United States.'

'A week in New York. It was 1998, some time in October.'

She nodded. 'Your present council tax bill?'

'Monthly? It's about a hundred and twelve pounds.'

She nodded again. She showed him the laptop screen. He saw his name and his bill highlighted among rows of other people's, before she moved it away. She said, 'That's good. I'd be worried if you remembered the thirty-eight cents. Too neat.'

'The little ones are called pence.'

She smiled again. She was the smallest, prettiest woman Fletcher had ever met. Also the most intimidating. She handed him a plastic wallet with his name and a photo of himself that must have been taken from the gatehouse.

'Your pass, Mr Fletcher. Ms Swanson is staying in a house in sector three, red side, number nine. Follow the signs. You may use your car, but you must obey the speed restriction. You must not stop unnecessarily. You must not vary your speed, in particular you must not accelerate unduly. Any questions?'

'I think that covers everything.'

She flashed her doll smile and turned away, snapping her laptop shut, making hand signals to the gatehouse. The barrier in front swung up and the armed guard waved Fletcher to move through.

Fletcher picked up the signs to housing sector three and followed them. He didn't vary his speed.

Cherelle Swanson had a background in the USAF, and was here to collect the earthly effects of an ex-pilot with a senior position in the aviation industry. So they'd given her house number nine – a brick and concrete box in a long terrace, up against the perimeter wire and the main road. The front door was made of a blistered Formica material, and lace curtains let Fletcher see only a shadow moving inside when he pushed the flimsy bell. The Formica opened.

'Miss Swanson? Cherelle?'

The woman was a wreck. Not a minimal, washed clean kind of wreck, but a person bubbling with corrosion. He guessed she was in her sixties, but it was hard to say. She was perfectly upright and neatly dressed in a dark woollen housecoat tied with a sash around her waist, but her hair was a yellowish grey, crinkled short and fixed around her head with grips. Her face was the troubling thing – it looked like a mix of sun damage and smoking – and yes, there was the smell of closed-in nicotine seeping around her. The sunlight showed her face was deeply creased – not just around the eyes, but in long furrows across her cheeks and jaw, the skin a dusty white colour flecked with age spots. She raised a hand made of knuckles and long bones, touched her ruined hair and smiled.

He had a weird moment. For a second he thought he'd seen her face before; he thought he remembered her from somewhere else. Maybe he had met the Slades at some point without realising it? Then he understood – of course, the old airbase photo he was carrying: the much younger woman smiling under the peaked cap, her hand on the shoulder of the snarling kid. This was her, twenty years on.

She said, 'Tom? Oh, Tom, it's you.'

Her voice was low and quavering, and when she reached out and touched his face, her yellow fingers close up were musty with tobacco. Her eyes began leaking tears into their creases. A jet flew low overhead, making the house shake, leaving a scent of hot fuel.

He thought, *This is the last time I'm coming onto an American airbase.*

Granny told us how it ended in our village. The corpses were tied together and pulled behind a carthorse across the fields. It made a mess, the stuff from the bodies streaking the earth and the hair snagging in the stubble. At the clay pit, they were cut apart and rolled into the water. Old Gussie went in first. Granny say there were gulls on the surface that all wheeled up, screaming. Then the men took Bessie's body. They stripped her and stood over her. She looked like a handful of straw, Granny said. Crushed up, with bits sticking out.

The men looked at each other. Then they took her wrists and ankles, swung her out into the water. She went in with a splash that caught one man on his face.

'She touched you.'

'She did not.'

They stayed looking into the pit.

155

Behind them, the witchfinder was already riding away quite slowly over the fields.

Cherelle Swanson made him a pot of coffee. 'It's just what I could find in the kitchen, Tom.' She put it on the table in the little front room: a scratched glass jug that looked as if it was recycled from aircraft canopies, holding a black substance popping and steaming in the light.

She said, 'You smoke?'

'No.'

'On the plane, I thought I was going to die. A patch on each arm and all.'

The room was cloudy with cigarettes, though one window was half open. She curled her fingers inside a packet on the table and took one out, lit it with a Zippo that smelled of more jet fuel and clanged shut again.

'I'm sorry about Nathan.' He took out the picture of the Alconhurst family day and laid it on the table. She glanced at it, pouring the liquid. She said,

'So sad, putting someone's affairs in order. Is that the phrase? Putting in order. Taking their things away. Bellman people are coming with the rest of his stuff.' But she didn't pick up the photo.

Fletcher said, 'Cherelle, who are you?'

She touched the grooves on her cheek. 'I'm Miss Kentucky, first runner up, nineteen sixty-three.' She smiled. 'You should have seen me then.'

He looked at her, thought, yes, under there somewhere. Maybe there used to be a beauty.

156

He said, 'How did you know my family?' She swept some ash off the table. 'Cherelle?'

Her eyes were grey around pale centres, and hooded.

'Your father and Nathan. They got on so well.'

'They were friends?' She nodded. 'How did they meet, how did they become friends?'

She shrugged. 'Well, I don't recall. It was so long ago.' She touched her hair with her cigarette hand.

'Do you know where my mother is today?'

'I'm sorry, Tom. I have no idea. We haven't been in touch since your mother – did what she did.' She picked up the photo for the first time, studied it.

'Why did I never meet you?'

'I guess it just never happened.' Her eyes moving across the group under the B52.

'Cherelle, the boy in that photo. Is he your son?'

The shadow of another jet went over the house, rattling the windows.

She said, 'Do you have a child, Tom?'

'No.'

'You married?'

'No.'

'Got a girlfriend?'

'Yes.'

'Making plans?'

'Yes, we're making plans.'

'That's sweet. What do you do?'

'I'm a private detective.'

'Oh my.' She smiled.

'Cherelle, who is this boy? What's his name?'

157

Her face straightened again in its bloated web of lines. 'This is my son. He's called Aspen. My boy is called Aspen.'

'A-s-p-e-n? Aspen Slade? Do you have a current picture of him?'

'You do talk like a cop, Tom. It's kind of off-putting.'

'Sorry, but can I see a picture?'

'Why are you so stressed?' She fished in a handbag on a sideboard and brought out a purse, took out a small laminated photo, passed it across. A man in his twenties, pale, dark haired, a line of beard around the jaw. Dark eyes. The shape of the face, the wide cheekbones, just like the man caught on the Felwell CCTV. Cherelle said, 'Why, Tom?'

'I want to meet him. Where is he right now?'

'Somewhere in the US. He kind of drifts around.'

'Tell me a bit about him.'

'He's unusual. OK, I got to tell you, that's the reason your parents never introduced you to us. It was Aspen. They didn't want him near you.'

Fletcher thought, is that true? How bad *is* he?

Cherelle sipped her coffee. 'Damn, he started me smoking like this.'

'Is there something wrong with him?'

'He ... he's problematic. He was a violent, difficult child. He's been a violent man. He's been in prison, Tom, but that was years ago. He's straightening himself out now.'

'What does he do?'

'He has casual jobs, seasonal stuff.' She smiled. 'He so wanted to join the Air Force, like his dad.

158

He tried two, three times to get in. But he was considered unsuitable. That was a big knock to him, a big knock. He took that very badly.' She lit another cigarette. 'What do you know about him, yourself?'

'I believe he's here in Cambridge.'

She raised her eyebrows, snagging long folds around her eyes.

'Really? What makes you say that?'

There was something about the way Cherelle was asking questions.

'I've just formed that impression. When were you last in touch with him?'

'You're just like a cop, Tom. But I haven't spoken to Aspen for a couple of years. He's not a good son that way. Not like you, huh?' She exhaled the comment with smoke, let it swirl in the air. Outside, the sky was darkening, tall clouds forming with light between them.

'Cherelle, the young woman who was with Nathan the night he died – Daisy Seager. She's dead now.'

'I heard that on the radio. Yeah, she was, like, a call girl.'

'She was interested in something to do with the USAF.'

'The Air Force, wow. Like what?'

'You've heard of Nose Art, obviously? She was researching Nose Art from the war, pictures of girls on Mustang fighters, a group called the Steel Witches. And I think my mother was researching something from the war too.'

Cherelle took a long smoke, breathed it out. 'Researching what?'

159

'I don't know. Something to do with airbases, maybe.'

'Yeah? So why do you think your mother was interested in that?' What did Mia say last night? *The open question, the therapist's favourite. And the snooper's.* True. Cherelle was showing polite interest in an old friend. Or, she was encouraging him to talk, to disclose what he knew. He looked around the room: basic shelves, a dresser with china ornaments that buzzed when the planes went over, a series of framed posters. He said,

'Well, I wanted to ask *you* that. You and Nathan were her friends in the USAF. Surely you discussed it?'

'No, don't think so. Maybe she just liked stuff like that. What else makes you think she was interested in the USAF?'

He lowered his voice. 'Why are you doing this?'

'I...' she stopped and he thought she was formulating another open question. But she just shook her head.

Fletcher said, 'Thanks for seeing me, Cherelle. I'll help you with these.' He stood and picked up their coffee cups.

She looked at him in surprise. 'You don't need to do that.' But he went into the tiny kitchen, clunking the cups down beside the sink. She came and stood by the door, watching him, outlined against the smoky light of the lounge. He took out a business card and wrote on the back, *Camera in the room?*

Held it out to her.

She looked at the words and back at him, communicating nothing.

160

He took another card and wrote, *Aspen will kill my mother. Help me.*

She looked at the words, then up at him.

In her normal voice, she said, 'I'll just wash these cups.'

She leaned close, put her bony hand on his shoulder and stretched up, getting her mouth to his ear, her brittle hair scraping his jaw.

'Your mother started this. Digging up what she did.'

'How do I stop Aspen?'

She whispered, 'Run, Tom. Save yourself.'

The noise of her corrupted throat, hissing. Her breath was cold and smoky. Like a witch, he thought, as he closed the Formica door.

Mia Tyrone clicked off her screen – the news about Daisy Seager being found dead. Unusual circumstances: what exactly did that mean in this country?

She watched the facilities man dragging Nathan's chair out of the next office. It was a struggle, the chrome wheels catching in the doorway, the man having to lift and twist the whole thing clear. But the office was ready for its next occupant now, whoever that was. Another fifty-something ex-pilot, she guessed, like all the rest of them. She pictured herself exposing the Bellman Foundation – humiliating the whole bunch of them.

Her phone rang. An unscheduled meeting with the human resources department, in one hour's time.

Now what's that all about? Nathan Slade and

Daisy Seager?

Fletcher drove back towards Cambridge on the curving tarmac of the A14. In the mirror, he saw clouds massing over the flat horizon behind. They were sprawling and vein-coloured, still lit on the edges by sunshine, dark in the centre. Fletcher saw them several times in the first two miles. That was because, as soon as he left the airbase, a large vehicle swung out of the security area by the gatehouse and began following, keeping three cars behind.

He checked the vehicle again.

He was thinking, *Save myself? From what exactly? Now the USAF themselves want to know how much I know. They want that enough to let me onto an airbase and set up a webcam in the room.*

The American Air Force.

Christ.

And this is them behind me.

The vehicle behind kept pace. It was a huge American pick-up truck, the grille on the front the size of a window in Fletcher's apartment, a big GMC badge level with the roof of Fletcher's Audi. The truck was painted malt green, a military serial number stencilled in white across the bonnet. For following someone on a road in England, it was the least appropriate vehicle imaginable. That was obviously the idea. After another few miles, the driver moved in right behind.

The sky was overcast now, like dusk, and when Fletcher put his sidelights on, the GM driver did the same, the bulbs glinting as the huge nose rolled over the undulations in the road. There was a man's outline behind the wheel. No passenger.

The road became almost empty. Fletcher thought the driver would come level, but at a point in the road where farm tracks appeared between a stand of conifers, the man flashed his lights twice. Fletcher looked ahead along the side of the road, saw a curve of old concrete leading off between the trees. Fletcher thought for a second, then turned in. He saw the green truck wallow in behind him.

The concrete slipway led between conifers that were glistening in the dull light coming off the rain clouds. A few crows wheeled through the air. Then the concrete became more uneven, and up ahead he could see it only lasted another few hundred metres before it met some kind of uneven barrier. The grille still filled his rear vision.

Th American Air Force.

Sod it.

He accelerated, the engine relishing the cold air, the springs yelping. The grille fell away behind, then moved back close to him. In front, at the end of the slipway, he began to make out the barrier: a jumble of concrete with iron girders sticking up at angles. He was going to hit them in about five seconds.

He gave the wheel a tug to the left and felt the car destabilise, then span it around to the right while wrenching up the handbrake. The Audi screeched around in a half circle, spattering debris, then righted itself with a thump that Fletcher felt in his spine. He saw the GMC badge sliding past in a straight line, smoke blasting from the tyres as the driver tried to stop before the girders. He almost made it, one big wheel arch crunching into them, bits of headlamp glass spinning away across the ground.

The crows flapped away overhead.

The pick-up driver reversed. He killed the engine, and climbed down. Fletcher was already out, waiting. They looked at each other through the smoke in the air, the smell of hot tyres.

The man was a stranger: late thirties, wearing green fatigues with shoulder tabs. Medium build, no fat. No headgear, his hair cropped down to blonde stubble flecked with grey. A plain, Nordic face. Big teeth, blue eyes. A tag sewn above a chest pocket read *Lindquist*.

Fletcher said, 'Shame about your truck.'

The man shrugged and put a hand out in greeting.

Fletcher took it. Cool skin, military grip. The man held it for a second, looking into Fletcher's eyes. Then he smiled. He said,

'Major Jerry Lindquist, US Air Force, Internal Advisory.'

'What's that, Military Police?'

Lindquist spread his hands. 'I'm Internal.'

'Sounds like a disorder.'

'Oh, and feels like it sometimes.' He stopped smiling. 'Listen, we need to have a brief discussion.'

'Here?'

'What better place?'

The man pointed out across the fields. In places, more old concrete surfaces were visible, running in lines between tufts of early beet, intersecting in the middle distance. Beyond that, a tall but derelict brick tower stood against the skyline, tree branches growing through massive empty windows, a few crows circling. Fletcher said,

'It's a wartime airfield.'

'Airbase. A US Eighth Army Air Force base from the nineteen forties. It was built as the twin of Alconhurst. Alconhurst survived; this one closed down. They say it's haunted. Pale figures on the runway, all that stuff. But you can drive onto it pretty easy. Just drive on in your cute little car, drive off, no questions asked.' He laughed. 'You think all US airbases are like this? Not the ones that are still alive. Not Alconhurst.'

'So you've got a camera on me here too?'

'Camera?' Lindquist stood watching the birds circling the old control tower. 'We're peaceful people, Mr Fletcher. We seek no quarrel. What's your problem with us?'

'As you know by now, there's someone called Aspen Slade.'

Lindquist rubbed his nose, thinking. 'This would be Nathan and Cherelle's kid?'

'Correct. He's a threat to my family.'

'Yeah?' Lindquist kicked a piece of his head-lamp glass away across the concrete.

'By the way, Cherelle said he tried to join the USAF, but you turned him down for being too weird. But then, you know what Cherelle said, don't you?'

'You want me to check this Aspen out, get his file?'

165

'That would be very helpful.'

'Hey, you want me to share it with you, give you copies, all that? Come on, Fletcher. We both know the real reason you came here.'

'Which is what?'

'Come *on.*' Lindquist kicked another piece of debris. 'You and Daisy Seager.'

'I never met Daisy Seager.'

'Yeah? Let me tell you something. I know what Daisy was up to as well as you do. I know what she was searching for on the Internet.'

'Which is what?'

'Oh, he doesn't know. Daisy was looking for locations of American airbases. Any kind of search like that, sends out an alarm we pick up. We picked her patterns up a couple of months ago.'

'And then Aspen Slade turns up to deal with her. That's interesting.'

'What about your patterns, Fletcher? Your interests? Anything to cause us concern there?'

'Who were the Steel Witches?'

Lindquist squinted up at the clouds. The bars of sunlight between them were thinner, the sky becoming a block of electric grey.

'It's going to flood around here. That's a shame; it's a good piece of country.' Lindquist straightened his tunic, smoothed down the pocket flaps. 'You know what you're doing? You have any understanding at all? You just breached the security of an American military installation.'

'I went to see an old family friend. I had a pass.'

'You lied your way in there and spied on us for your own purposes. You know what happens to

166

people like you? People like you take a fucking trip.'

A small civilian-looking jet was taking off from Alconhurst on the horizon, rising against the towering clouds. Lindquist couldn't possibly have timed the take-off, but it made a point. Fletcher said,

'You're threatening me? What with?'

'There's a thing called extradition, Mr Fletcher. I'll give you an example. We've just moved to extradite a young British guy, know what he did? He hacked into the Pentagon system, left a message on someone's computer saying, *This computer is not secure.* He'll get ninety-five years – state time. Did you see any computers on your duplicitous visit to Alconhurst, Mr Fletcher?'

'Good try. Not a single one.'

'Yes you did, my friend. At the gatehouse, you covertly analysed the screen of a security terminal held by Sergeant First-Class Antonia Sanchez.'

'In fact, she showed it to me.'

'Covert fucking surveillance of a military installation. We can serve papers on you, be through your door in a week. You can fight it, sure you will. But it's going to take you a lot of time and money; your life won't be your own for a year or three. Then you've got to rebuild it, could take another five or ten.'

'I'm a British citizen. This is England.'

'The old ways are changing.'

'Now I'm really scared. You sound like Bob Dylan.'

Lindquist smiled and slapped Fletcher's shoul-

167

der. 'Think about what I've said, the implications for yourself. Forget this whole thing. Take a break, why don't you? Get out there with your girlfriend. Is it Malta or Cyprus, somewhere Greek like that?' He clambered into his pick-up. 'From what I heard, she's getting a good tan.'

Lindquist laughed and waved, started the engine, turned back towards the main road without looking round. Fletcher watched the vehicle rumble away between the wet conifers. The birds circled and landed again, watching him.

He drove back onto the main road. A mile clear of the old airbase, he pulled into a lay-by and called his solicitor, Maureen Hara. When he got through and explained, she was quiet for a few seconds. When she spoke, the Irish calm had a harder edge.

'Last night a murder enquiry, and today extradition to the USA?'

'Can they do it?'

'Under the new treaty – yes, technically. Depends what you did on that airfield.'

'Airbase.'

'Christ, Tom. This could totally screw your life up. That's a legal term I'm using.'

'Plus, I think they're intercepting images being sent to my phone.'

'You have any evidence?'

'They know Cathleen has a tan.'

'Where is she?'

'Crete.'

'Well, it's not such a great guess, is it?'

'This American Air Force man said I should take a holiday abroad.'

168

There was a smooth Irish sigh. Fletcher could almost hear the lips parting and the eyelashes closing.

'Tom, God love you. I think that might be a sound idea.'

Fletcher started the car again. He let it idle, a little capsule of steel and Perspex under the massive electric clouds.

People like Lindquist could take his future away. They would lose their case in the end, but destroy his life in the process.

Fletcher took out the photocopies of the Steel Witches, smoothed them out on the dashboard. The girls' riveted bodies were streamlined, their hair blowing back, the two of them heading into the future.

Pilot and unit unknown.

Fletcher used his phone to look up the author of the Nose Art book. Someone named Charlie Fenner, with a workshop in the farmland west of Cambridge. He put the car in gear and picked up speed, moved back into the road.

Yes, Major Lindquist was powerful. He had access to databases that Fletcher could only guess at. Lindquist didn't know everything, though.

Lindquist didn't know about the buzz of a streetlamp in summer, the click of a typewriter in the next room. The way Kate Fletcher walked out over the footbridge across the weir. Lindquist didn't know that Fletcher had a sudden purpose in life now. To stop Aspen Slade killing his mother.

And Lindquist didn't know that, after nightfall,

Fletcher would see the Steel Witches for himself – would look into their eyes, and begin to understand the power they held over such a disturbed and lonely man as Aspen Slade.

We were the last to suffer the trials, Granny said.

The next village the witchfinder comes to, the people have heard the stories about what he does. They rise against him. They spit and throw stones. The witchfinder wheels his horse around. His men disappear. His horse gets sold for meat in Norwich.

The villagers hoist the witchfinder on a plank and stuff his parchments in his mouth. They heave him into the mill stream and watch him twitch and flail around, pelting him with rubbish. He goes under once, then twice. It's sunset, and someone gets a cobblestone and wades in, dropping it on his chest. People laugh. The witchfinder hisses and goes under. His face is white like fish meat, going down. Bubbles come up to the surface and break. The water is cloudy and hard to see through. Nobody ever saw him again, Granny said.

They dragged. the pond next day, found nothing. Some say he were washed away, drowned. Others say he were a witch himself, and the water gave him up in the night. Granny said she knew the truth: he undid his ropes and swam away downstream, waited till dark and made off in the fields. Started a new life somewhere else: new name, new living. New place, where his face wasn't known.

It was the end of our village, though. What was three houses became just one: our house, that's still here today. The stones of the others are still here, in the yard walls and the outhouse. Our family stayed on,

Granny said. She said we'll always be here, we'll never leave. Then Granny died and it were just the two of us left.

I remember, after the funeral, I said to my sister, I said, 'We'll be old ladies together here, won't we, Sally?'

She didn't answer, though.

In the distance, the Great Ouse river made a black line on the edge of the fields. Close up, Charlie Fenner's workshop was a small metal hangar, block-shaped against the darkened sky. As Fletcher approached, a crust of melting snow slipped off the roof and broke on the ground.

Someone was obviously in there: the shed windows were brightly lit, and there was a noise that made it pointless to knock – a machine tool being used with an abrasive snarl that rose and fell.

Fletcher pushed the door open.

A smell of oil and paint, the echoing whine of that electric motor. A space about the size of a squash court, the ribbed walls lit by floodlamps standing on the floor. There was an old propane heater, three plastic chairs, a long workbench lined with bits of metal and old machinery – each piece with a hanging label. Leaning against it were twisted propeller blades, an old rubber wheel still on a hydraulic arm, a piece of riveted aircraft skin. Tools were stored neatly in brackets, or wrapped in oiled rags.

In the centre of the space, there was a person wearing a boiler suit with a mask over the face, holding an electric sander in halo of metallic

171

dust. The person looked at Fletcher and turned off the motor, then pulled the mask off.

'Yeah?'

She was in her late thirties, with cropped hair tinted red, a wide face, small, very green eyes. She looked terrified.

Fletcher said, 'Are you Charlie Fenner?'

The woman swallowed. 'Yes.'

'I'm Tom Fletcher.'

'Are you the police?'

'No.' For some reason, maybe because she looked so scared, he found himself saying, 'No, I own a Polish restaurant in Cambridge.' It felt good, saying that. Despite everything else in his mind, it gave him an idea for the future. He said, 'Can I ask you something?'

'That kind of depends what it is.'

'What are those things behind you?'

There were three wires above her, each one suspending a pale globular shape, like a magnified water droplet, with the slimmer end uppermost. They were each about two metres long, dented and torn in places, made of a brittle, reflective material that glowed in the electric lamps.

'They're American teardrop tanks,' Charlie Fenner said. 'From World War Two. Extra fuel tanks fitted under fighter aircraft.'

'Like Mustangs?'

'Yes, Mustangs. Extended their range. The pilot would use up the fuel in them, then jettison them. They just came falling down to earth. We still find them in ditches.' She looked back at Fletcher suddenly. 'What do you want?'

'You published a book about Nose Art.'
'Oh, no. Not this.'
'And someone called Daisy Seager read it.'
'Oh, no. *No.*'
She kicked a floor switch and the floodlamps died. In the rainy light through the windows, the three shapes above her seemed to grow paler and larger. She began cleaning her hands with a cloth. She said,
'Did you know Daisy?'
'I never met her. Did you?'
Charlie closed her eyes briefly, didn't reply.
Fletcher said, 'You know she's been murdered?'
'I watch TV, like everyone else. Why have you come here?'
'Because I've just been threatened by the American Air Force. The phrase "Steel Witches" seems to be highly sensitive, which is strange considering it refers to sixty-five years ago.'
Charlie wiped her forehead with a sleeve. 'Well, manage without me.'
Fletcher said, 'I need your help.'
'Sorry. I'm not getting involved in this.'
'Other people are in danger,' Fletcher said. 'Think about that.'
'You look like a reasonable man. Go back to your Polish restaurant.'
He didn't get anything else out of her. As he walked out, leaving the door ajar behind him, he heard the sander starting up again.
He sat in the car for half a minute with the window down. The noise of the sander was low and idling, not the growl of abrasion.
He waited. In another minute, the tool noise

173

died completely, and the only sound was the clunk of heavy raindrops on the car roof. Then the sander came flying out of the door, snaking its black flex over the snow like an electric tadpole. She appeared in the doorway, hands on hips, shaking her head in a way that said *Yes*, very sadly.

Rain was beginning to streak down the windows and tap on the steel walls of the hangar. She fired up the heater and they sat on the chairs. He said it seemed kind of unusual, a woman being interested in this stuff. She said it was therapeutic, taking a crumpled old bit of steel and seeing it restored. It calmed her down when she wasn't teaching metalwork in a secondary school.

'Shouldn't you be in school?'

'The school's closed, no heating.' She smiled, but she looked worried. She kept hooking a length of her tinted hair behind one ear. 'And Nose Art, I just love it. Did you see the press conference? The police have got it all wrong.'

'I think so too. Daisy knew something; she figured something out. Someone in my family knows the same thing. Can you see my concern?'

'Who in your family?'

'My mother.'

She put her hands out to the fire, warmed the palms, then the backs, thinking. She said,

'Look. Daisy came here; we sat in these chairs at this fire. She was very striking as a person, very charismatic. She was interested in my book, the pictures of the Steel Witch planes. She wanted to know where the photos came from.'

'Can you tell me what you told her?'

Charlie did the thing with her hair again. 'I bought them from a collector a few years ago; he said he got them in a bric-a-brac shop back in the eighties. I don't know anything else about them.'

'Why was Daisy interested?'

'She wanted to know who the artist was who painted the planes. I've no idea, obviously.'

'Can the planes be traced?'

'I don't see how. I mean, every American plane had a number stencilled on the tailfin, a unique serial number, but you can't see any of that in the photos. That's it, really. That's all I know.'

'Well, thank you.' Fletcher watched her, the red light from the fire showing a crease between her eyes. He said, 'When I came in just now, you said you didn't want to get involved. Involved in what?'

She said, 'I'm worrying about nothing.'

'What is it?'

'In aviation circles, people talk, they swap rumours.'

'There's a rumour? About what?'

She shrugged. 'Just a story that people tell. About an airbase.'

The steel roof was starting to drum with rain.

'An airbase?'

'They say there was an airbase that disap-peared.'

'Disappeared how?'

'It's just a story. Some people say it was coastal erosion, it just fell into the sea. Other people say it was bulldozed and ploughed under, kept secret because something happened there that had to be covered up. But these are just drinking stories, though. Like those urban myths, only an aviation myth.'

'Then why does it worry you?'

'Daisy had heard it. She asked me about it. I said, "Why does it matter? It's just a story." She said, "No, it's true. It's where the Steel Witches lived."'

'Where they lived? What does that mean?'

'I don't know, but she believed it. I'm sure she believed it.'

'Something had to be covered up? Such as what?'

'Oh, come on, it's a rumour. Daisy was talking about this and about Felwell College, the laboratory there.'

'The laboratory? How is that connected?'

She looked at him. She'd stopped fiddling with her hair by now. 'It's all a rumour. Nothing was covered up, because it never existed.'

'But?'

She leaned forward, her face close to his. She was pretty that close, with the rainy light in the grooves around her eyes. She said, 'You run a restaurant. Don't grill me. Get it?'

He nodded. 'What do you think Daisy did after that?'

'I said, "Try the Aviation Museum. There are historians there, they've got an archive. Maybe they'll turn up something on the Steel Witches. Though I doubt it."'

'Did she try them?'

'I don't know.' Charlie turned her head to look at the drop tanks hanging from the ceiling. 'She said to me, "if the witches could cry, their tears would fall like this." What did she mean by that?'

Wednesday Afternoon

The window of Fletcher's office was half open, and he could hear the sound of the roof dripping, the drainpipes channelling the melting snow.

He looked for information on Aspen Slade; found only newspaper reports from the USA dating back five years. Someone of that name had been arraigned on a charge of homicide, the murder of a young woman found beaten to death on waste ground. Aspen Slade was acquitted due to lack of evidence, but jailed for a year on other charges of carrying a weapon in public. Was this the man who had phoned Fletcher, said, *See what I do?* The man who had tied Daisy Seager to a plank and ducked her?

Why? Because she knew something about Steel Witches?

He made a long call to the Cambridge Aviation Museum – a massive site with its own airfield, outside the city. He spoke to a director, a resident historian, a public relations person. Nobody knew anything about Steel Witches; everybody went cold at the mention of Daisy Seager's name. In the end he got through to an archivist named Tim Redshaw.

Tim was different. Tim insisted he'd never heard of Daisy, stumbled over his words, put the phone down. Tim knew something he didn't want to talk about.

Tim was the man for Fletcher.

The problem now was getting to see him. Maybe drive over there and demand to see him? How effective was that going to be?

Fletcher thought about it, sitting there with the dripping noise outside, while he created a new file on his computer.

It was a summary of what he knew so far: the people he'd spoken to, the places he'd been to. Hunters, the Bellman Foundation, Felwell College, Alconhurst, Charlie Fenner's hangar. He attached a scan of the Steel Witches photos, then a summary from memory of his conversation with Major Jerry Lindquist. He emailed the whole assembly to his solicitor, with a copy backed up on Internet storage, with instructions to open it in the event of either his arrest or other major event.

Then he printed out a copy and put it in an envelope and taped it in a space under his desk. It seemed a sensible precaution. Rumours about vanished airbases are one thing; being threatened with extradition by a real live Internal Advisory man, that was something else.

He thought, this is what you do when you have time to get ready.

It occurred to him, what if you don't have time to get ready?

If there's no time, or if your time comes sooner than you expected.

How would you let the world know what you've found?

He went to the news site again, printed off those CCTV images of Daisy Seager in her white

Golf pulling across the car park at Hunters, her face visible through the two scraped lines on the windscreen, Nathan's bulk in the seat next to her.

What did you talk to the archivist about, Daisy?

He froze the image of her face: pale, concentrating.

And did you leave us something? A sign, a message?

The war didn't change us much at first. Sally wanted to join the women's forces, she went for a medical in the town. The doctor looked at her and called another doctor in to see. They told her to stay working on the land. Then she come back, she slammed the door so the glass cracked.

We took on some acres from the big farm to the east and we grew leeks, onions, cabbage. It all got shipped down south to the depots. We were working fourteen hours a day, going to bed early. We were eating little, but all healthy stuff. We got lean and muscly. A ministry inspector came to check our work. He said it was well run.

The first two years, we could hear the war happening. Planes taking off from the south, vapour trails and twists of smoke. One night, something exploded in our field. Next day we found an engine with a propeller still on it. The army boys took it away on a trailer. They came and talk to us out in the field – their eyes were all over us. I threw one of them a spade and told him to dig or leave.

Nineteen forty-two was different. We knew that south and east there were new aerodromes. There were more planes in the sky, night and day. We could hear them taking off in waves at night. The noise changed

180

with the wind. Then at dawn we saw the trails of smoke from planes coming back.

Beyond our fields, there's a place we've always just called the Open. It's a heath, flat with long grass, plenty of hares, which Granny used to trap. One corner just touches the river. Early summer, we saw trailers carrying bulldozers moving onto the Open. Behind them, there were trucks with stones, then trucks with open backs, carrying men. They all stopped there, on the Open. Before dusk Sally walked over there to see. She said they'd built themselves dozens of tents, and the bulldozers were unloaded, rattling and letting out smoke. She saw them test one out. She said the blade lifted a long slice from the turf, like skinning a pelt. She went down there every evening, watching them.

She said, 'I think they're runways, Evie. They're building runways.' She had a new look in her eyes.

They worked on it round the clock. It took two weeks. The day after they left, Sally spent all day on the leek field, digging. At dusk I went out and found her. She could hardly see what she were digging at.

I said, 'What's the matter?'

She threw the spade away.

Fletcher answered his doorbell.

On the landing, Mia Tyrone was standing under the cupola, looking up through the glass. She turned her head to him. Her hair was wet, long strands hanging either side of her face, a thin coat mottled with damp and moving with shadows from the rain overhead.

He said, 'How long have you been standing there?'

181

'About five minutes. I've been walking around, thinking what to do. Then I decided to come here.'

There was the smell of the old wax ingrained in the floor, and a gutter outside was gasping.

'What's happened, Mia?'

'They fired me.'

To Fletcher, that was not a surprise, and he felt guilty for involving this well-meaning, embittered woman in his search. He got her seated on his client sofa, closed the window on the rain. 'Why exactly?'

'It's been building up for a year. They've been looking for a chance to do this. They said I was a security risk.'

'Whose security?'

'Bellman security. They've given me a legal letter saying I can't discuss any company matters with outside personnel. That means you.'

'How do they know you've spoken to me?'

'I guess they monitored my desk phone. They'll deny it, but I'm sure of that. I've got five days to vacate my apartment – it's a company lease. And they've withdrawn their sponsorship for my visa, so I have to leave the country. I'll go back home, no payout, no testimonial. I may never get another real job again.'

'I'm sure you will–'

'No, you don't understand how it works. There's a database they put people on, they never work again. What will I say to people at home?' She pushed the hair out of her face. 'I've been walking around this stupid town in the rain thinking what to do. Now I know.' Her eyes were suddenly clear in the gloomy light. She raised one of her thin hands and pointed. 'You're going to help me.'

'Help you what?'

'Make them sorry they treated me like this. I need you, because you know the local set-up. You need me, because I'm from inside the Bellman Foundation. People will tell me things.'

'That's not a good idea, Mia. It's not in your interest, believe me.'

'Why not?'

'Daisy Seager was on a list too. A different kind of list. She'd been researching locations of American airbases. You're putting yourself at risk here.'

'Tom, I cannot go home like this and spend the rest of my life in humiliation. I have to fight them. And I can get people to talk. I've got my Bellman business cards, my Bellman ID.'

'I'm sorry, Mia. It won't work.'

'You must want someone to witness all this, Tom. To see what you're seeing, to testify if any-thing happens. You must want that. And I want to screw up the Bellman Foundation. I really do.'

He thought about it, while the rain burst against the window, spreading shadows over the room.

He had a sudden idea that feelings were like different metals. Ambition was like aluminium, maybe, and love was some kind of bronze alloy. Resentment, though, and desire for vengeance – they were the heavy elements of the mind, the fissile material.

He said, 'There are various things I have to tell

you, Mia.'

'Good.' She stood up, went to his chair, leaned forward and kissed him quickly on the cheek with warm lips, her wet hair brushing his face. 'Tell me now.'

He said, 'I'll tell you in the car.' He reminded himself that this was a good idea. The damp on his cheek was evaporating like jet fuel.

'Where are we going?'

'It's raining. Let's go to a museum.'

It took a while to get there – heavy traffic bunching under low clouds, snow from the fields melting onto the road in huge stretches of water that the cars had to spray through like boats. At least it gave them time to talk. Fletcher told her what he'd heard today. He started out being cagey, leaving out pieces that were personal – like the map of airbases he thought he remembered on the wall of his mother's study. After a while, he realised he trusted her. She listened, watching the wet road ahead. She said,

'Felwell College, Bellman and the US Air Force? We're not talking minor organisations here, are we?'

He didn't answer.

She said, 'And they're all afraid of stories about witches?'

'I would say they're touchy. They're very, very touchy. And whatever the real story is, I think maybe Daisy found something here.'

The museum was rising on the horizon, the massive concrete arc of the aircraft hall, its glass frontage throwing electric light out into the late afternoon gloom. By the time they got to the reception hall, the place was closing, the last visitors leaving and clerical staff in suits exiting the turnstiles too. But the receptionist looked at Mia's Bellman ID, raised her eyebrows and phoned straight up to Tim Redshaw. There was a short exchange, then she nodded them through with directions.

Two days later I was out in the yard at dawn, feeding the hens. My sleeves were rolled up. I have the marks that scare people, but I got muscles too. There were big clouds up over the sea, red at the edges. There was a breeze making the shutters click.

The sounds were low at first, coming from the west beyond the Open. They kept building, getting louder when the breeze changed sometimes. I went upstairs, and Sally was already at the window with the shutters open, the breeze touching all Granny's things that shouldn't be touched. I closed it, but she held her side open. I could see what she was watching. Out beyond the farmland, over the Open, silver-coloured planes were coming down out of the sky. They were shiny; the sun was coming off their wings. Sally laughed and clapped.

'Americans, Evie. American planes.'

I went down and walked out in the field to check the onions. Behind me, I could hear that noise building. I thought of all the history Granny taught me – what Sally says is just stories – everything that happened here, the witchfinder, Gussie Salter and Bessie Weller; the reason our skin is like this. The noise became one long growling, and sometimes I saw flashes of light across the fields, when the planes circled close, waiting

185

to land. Some came over so low they blew dust off the earth. I didn't look up. I said, 'It'll never change here. Never.'

They went up a metal stairway to a corridor of administrative rooms at first-floor height. Tim's office was at the end. He was just opening the door, saw Mia and widened his eyes, smiled. Then he saw Fletcher and lost the smile, but by then they were all in the room.

It was a neat space with a window giving a view of the dozens of aircraft on display in the public area, many suspended from the ceiling or tilted at aggressive angles, all casting shadows across the deserted floorspace. Dominating them all was a Flying Fortress, its plexiglass turrets studded with gun barrels.

Fletcher focused on Tim Redshaw sitting across the desk.

The man was early forties, in a neat blue suit with a silky finish, hair parted on one side, an empty stud hole in one earlobe. A child of the 1980s, not quite grown up. He seemed a tidy person: his desk held a lamp, a laptop with its power light on, plus Mia's business card and Fletcher's, both lying in front of him. He pushed his lip onto his teeth with a knuckle. He looked at the cards again, then at Fletcher.

'You phoned earlier. You didn't tell me you were working with Bellman.'

'Sorry, I thought I did. My mistake.'

Tim Redshaw looked at Mia. 'So how can I help?'

Mia said, 'This is a delicate matter. Daisy

186

Seager.' Tim Redshaw bit his lip.

'The girl in the news?'

'She's dead, yes. Our issue is, she was asking around, asking about rumours and old stories to do with airbases, possibly trying to connect them to the Bellman Foundation. Her death is tragic, of course. But we have to tick some boxes, you see.'

Tim Redshaw touched his fringe, said nothing. The gloss in his suit caught the light from the hangar behind him, sliced up by the curves of the aircraft. Then the display hall began to close down: one by one the lamps shutting off, leaving just the jagged shapes of wings against the glass wall of early evening rain. In the gloom, Tim switched on the desk lamp, then spread his fingers on the desk quickly – what people do to show their hands are steady.

'I've done nothing wrong.'

'Of course not. Nobody needs to know about this. This is just to tick the boxes. We'll be gone in a minute.' Mia's voice, with its clipped accent, sounded efficient. Tim Redshaw's eyes flicked around the room. He said, 'Nathan Slade worked for the Bellman Foundation, didn't he?'

Mia said, 'The late Mr Slade, yes.'

'He's dead, Daisy Seager is dead.'

'Did you actually meet Daisy?'

'I've done nothing wrong. Now you come here with some private snooper, muckraker. I could take all of this to the police.'

'I think you should, if that's appropriate.'

'Well, I think I will.'

Fletcher said, 'Did Daisy come here?' Tim Redshaw made no reaction. 'Maybe she asked you about Steel Witches?'

The phrase made Tim Redshaw scowl. His eyes searched the surface of the desk. 'She was persistent. Persuasive. Did she tell anyone about that?'

It was quiet in the office, just the faint buzz of the lamp.

Fletcher said, 'I don't think it matters what happened with you and Daisy. If anything happened. We're just concerned to know what you told her. That's all.'

Tim Redshaw flexed his shoulders. 'And then you stay away from me.'

'Absolutely. There's no need to involve the management here, for example. No need at all.'

Tim touched his fringe. 'Why is this important?'

'It probably isn't. But what did you tell Daisy, anyway?'

'I didn't tell her anything.'

'Not anything?'

'I just showed her the film.'

There was the noise of someone shouting, out in the hangar. Someone saying goodbye, laughing.

Fletcher said, 'What film?'

'In the archive, there's a small piece of film labelled as Steel Witches. I mean, that's what was on the original canister.'

'Where did it come from?'

'It was donated anonymously to the Norfolk County archive in the 1950s. They kept it in a box for forty years, so it deteriorated. They passed it to us in the 1990s. We preserved it and filed it away. That's what we do.'

'What does it show?'

'What do you think it shows? Secret weapons? Something that changed the war?'

Something went through Fletcher's mind. Everybody so touchy about the Steel Witches – was it a code name for something?

But Tim Redshaw just shrugged. 'It shows a baseball game. Well, the end of a baseball game. Why all the fuss about that?'

Fletcher said, 'A baseball game? Where?'

'It looks like a small American airbase – nineteen forty-three, judging by the aircraft. New P51D Mustangs, the prettiest plane ever built. I think the site has only just opened, because the buildings are still being finished. I think the first crews have just arrived. It looks like they're christening the place with a baseball practice. And OK, then something happens.'

'I think we'd like to see it now.'

'I can't just show this to people. You need to write in and apply.'

Mia said, 'Did Daisy do that?'

Tim looked out over the aircraft, maybe remembering his streamlined moments with Daisy Seager.

'Then I never hear from you again?'

'Correct.'

Then he opened a desk drawer and rifled through for a few seconds. He brought out a DVD and opened the laptop on his desk with a software melody.

Mia said, 'Don't you need a cine projector?'

189

Tim said, 'The films are in vacuum storage, everything's copied. Here – see this, then leave me alone.'

He turned the laptop around to show the screen and re-angled the lamp. In the dim light, the Fortress gun barrels out in the hangar snaked their shadows across the desk. Then the screen lit up and the clip started.

Sally worked potatoes till three o'clock. Then I saw her hoe standing in the earth. I went back to the house and heard her washing in the outhouse. She was using the piece of soap from before the war. It smelled like Granny. I went and pushed open the door.

She was naked and her hair was strung all over her face. She had muscles up over her ribs and under her arms, along her shoulders, on her wrists. On her body, her condition didn't show as much as mine. I mean, I could see how someone could love her, desire her. She kicked the door closed.

I said, 'Sally, you're not going over there.'

I heard her washing her hair, making a noise in her throat.

I said, 'I'm coming with you.'

At four o'clock, she came out of the bedroom. She had her dress on, blue and white dots, and her hair was wet, combed out. She put her shoes on and she started walking towards the Open. I went after her, through our fields, past the Deeping. The sun was getting down to the hedges. It was hot.

Sally went into the wheat fields, me twenty yards behind. We walked in the tractor lines so we didn't damage the crop. Down on the Open, I could see the aerodrome. The concrete was bone colour. The planes

190

were lined up outside a hangar. There were men play-
ing a game, swinging at a ball, running and catching.
Sally stopped for a bit, watching them. I came up level
with her. I said, 'Let's go back, Sally.'
She looked at me. The wheat was moving a little.

It was colour film, mid-twentieth century: rich chemicals, slightly grainy, some dark lines and blobs, otherwise clear. A hand-held camera, competently used: a professional assignment, or someone's well-funded hobby. No soundtrack, though. Silent colour.

Redshaw's summary was right: late afternoon, the camera panning slowly across airbase buildings. First a glass-topped control tower, then some barrack buildings with workmen still on the roof, jeeps and tanker trucks beside them. On a concrete runway beyond that, two silver Mustang fighters, their nose cowls removed for engineering, no Nose Art visible at all, the low sun glinting off a silver tailfin.

Fletcher marked that moment in his mind.

In the foreground, there were improvised baseball markers on the turf beside a runway. A group of airmen in off-duty gear: fatigues, some in shorts and vests, one or two bare-chested. All of them young: late teens to mid-twenties. A skinny one with a baseball bat was replaying his game for the camera, explaining his tactics maybe, his mouth moving, going through his stances again, the others laughing, wiping sweat from their faces. The batter finished his account, bowing to the camera. Someone slapped him on the back, tousling his hair. Then someone on the left of the picture pointed over to the right, away from the scene. Some of the men looked over that way, and stared. They called to the other men, and soon everyone was staring at something off to the right. The cameraman got the message, panned slowly round. He had to refocus manually and there was a moment of blur.

To the right of the game, a field of wheat was growing right up to the edge of the concrete apron around the tower. Mature wheat, ears curving under the sun, poppies standing among the stalks. There was a thin double channel running through the crop where a tractor had passed, and two figures were walking along it towards the camera. The film ran on for a few seconds, then the cameraman began walking towards the two people. The other aircrew were walking over there too, some walking past the camera, all making their way up to the edge of the field. The camera-man approached behind them, and they made way for him. He focused on the two figures, and they filled the screen.

'My God.' Mia leaned forward. 'What's this?'

They were two women. They were young, around twenty. They were both remarkably tall, taller even than some of the Americans. One was wearing a neat blue and white dress with short sleeves. The other wore a patched-up boiler suit. They were lean women – not curved like classic Nose-Art girls – but they were stronglooking. The woman in the dress had long, powerful arms. Something about the arms: the skin over the muscles was heavily coloured, full of what looked like dark freckles and moles. The woman in the

192

boiler suit had big hands which she placed slowly on her hips. The skin on her hands was heavily mottled too.

Their faces began to fill the frame.

There, in Tim Redshaw's little office, Fletcher saw the most remarkable faces he'd ever seen. They had wide jaws, thin lips, strong noses with high nostrils, cheekbones that went out at angles. Their skin was pale, and heavily marked with black freckles running in lines and clusters from their foreheads down to their throats. Their hair too was utterly black – not fixed in the set curls of the era, but dead straight on either side of the face and across their shoulders. What was amazing – what clearly fascinated the cameraman too – was their eyes. They were *huge,* the whites creamy in the sunlight, but the irises a bright orange colour with black pupils – the kind sometimes seen on albino people.

Then the scene became crowded. Some of the aircrew entered the frame, clustering around the women. The cameraman's shadow was clearly visible across the turf: a long male figure, elbows raised behind the camera. Nothing happened for a few seconds. Then the woman in the boiler suit looked at the lens. Her face changed a little, and she put her head back. She said something, just a few words. One of the aircrew beside her frowned in puzzlement. His lips moved. Fletcher thought they made the word, *What?*

The screen went blank.

Fletcher looked at Mia, and they both looked at Tim Redshaw.

Redshaw turned the computer around and

193

folded it shut, the click echoing across the room. Fletcher said, 'Does it continue?'

'No. That's it.'

'Where's the rest of it?'

'There is no rest of it. That's all we have.'

Fletcher looked at the blank screen. 'What was happening, exactly?'

Tim shrugged. 'If you think about it, it was pretty common at the time. Local people, isolated communities, they suddenly find an American airbase next door. They're intrigued, they go over to say hello. In this instance, I think the American boys are equally fascinated. Like, *Jeepers, is this what the English are like?*'

'And another point,' Mia said, 'is what language they were speaking. The crewman couldn't understand the woman who spoke.'

'Rural accent, sixty-five years ago. I probably wouldn't understand it myself.' He looked at his watch. 'Hey, time to close up. I'm probably the last one here.'

Fletcher said, 'I need a copy of the film.'

Tim Redshaw ejected the disc and put it back in the case. Then he shook his head. 'That's not what we said. We said you see it, then you go.'

'I need to make a copy.'

Tim Redshaw made a point of locking his desk drawer, flicking his fringe. 'You can only push me around so much.'

Mia raised a hand. 'I'd just like to talk to Mr Redshaw alone for a minute.'

Tim frowned. 'There's nothing else to say. Stop trying to intimidate me.'

She said, 'I'd just like to talk to you, put the

Bellman Foundation point of view.'

'Put it in a letter.'

'Then we would have to mention so many things, copy it to other people. You see what I mean?' Redshaw scowled back at her. She said, 'Mr Fletcher, just give us two minutes, OK?'

Fletcher waited at ground-floor level in the deserted exhibition hall. The space was even bigger in the dark: the colossal glass front running with rain, lit by sodium lamps in the walls outside. Inside, the only lighting was low-level security along the floor near the walls. The aircraft were spread out overhead, like a ghost squadron in flight, their cockpits and gun turrets dark.

He looked back up at Tim Redshaw's office. Was Mia still acting the role of Bellman executive, or confessing to Tim that she was a whistleblower, out to avenge a year's humiliation – the failure of small-town dreams? There was no sign of activity through the glass panel in the door. Maybe that meant she was getting somewhere.

He walked across the hangar, looking at the planes. Right in the centre, on the floor, there was a Mustang fighter, the same type he'd just seen in the film clip. *The prettiest plane ever built.* He could see why Tim said that. Even static, it looked full of movement, the lines muscling forward to the nose, the bare metal body pearlescent in the gloom. This example had simple Nose Art painted under the pilot's canopy – a 1940s beach girl; very different from the strange faces he'd just seen in the old film. Were those women in the clip the original steel

195

witches? Their disfiguring moles and freckles shown by the artist as dark rivets across their limbs? Were *they* what his mother was researching in her study – even trying to track down the site of the airbase itself? Why?

He reached out and touched the cold steel and aluminium panels of the Mustang's flank, barely feeling the rivets, the discs almost level with the surface. Was that how their skin would feel?

He saw a movement in the corner of his eye. In turning, he caught the old-fashioned scent of liquorice.

Something hit him in the face – not a blow, but a blast of chemical so caustic that he felt the membranes in his nose tearing. He was blinded, the shapes of the planes breaking up as his eyes filled with water, his lids stinging. He tried to cough it out of his throat, but his mouth flooded with the taste of pepper.

Mace.

Someone had sprayed him with tear gas. He leaned forward, retching for air, with his hands on the aircraft steel, the rivets feeling enormous under his fingers.

'Tom.'

Tom rhymed with *harm*. The voice was coming from close behind him. He guessed someone was squatting on the Mustang wing, close to the cockpit, looking down at him.

'Aspen?' Fletcher could still hardly see – it felt like someone had their fingers in his eyes – and speaking hurt, in his throat and diaphragm.

'Don't turn round, Tom. I don't want to use this again. It can cause respiratory failure, long-term defects.'

Fletcher tried to turn anyway. He felt something move around his throat – a cold narrow band, some kind of metal hook. He raised his fingers to it, and the hook tightened, its holder using leverage and height to exert whatever force he wanted, beginning to crush Fletcher's windpipe.

Fletcher stood still, partly raised off his feet. He heard a chewing noise, a damp squelching. The voice said,

'You want water, Tom? Eyewash?'

'Yeah. Yes.'

'I think there's a first-aid station near where they sell the admissions. A few hours, you'll be OK.'

Fletcher felt blood from his corroded membranes running out of his nose. He said, 'Why are you doing this?'

The metal around his neck pulled a little tighter. He knew Aspen could strangle him quite easily in this position. The chewing went on for a few seconds, then stopped.

'I used to hear all about you, Tom. How fucking perfect you were. Not like me with all my issues, my medication. I used to want to *be* you, Tom.' Fletcher felt the voice come closer to his ear. 'You heard the stories? About the old airbase that disappeared?'

'Rumours.'

'No, it's true, Tom. It's all true. It's out there somewhere. It's where it all started.' The voice came right down to his ear, breathing hot, Aspen working to hold the hook in place. 'There's

197

evidence. Daisy dug it up – she sweet-talked my dad, thought she was being smart. She had the evidence.'

'The film?'

'Fuck the film. It proves nothing. What Daisy had is written evidence, Tom. Somebody listened to the Steel Witches, wrote their testimony down. Because the girls saw what happened there, they saw the danger.'

A new burst of chewing, the hook cutting into Fletcher's throat, lifting him off his heels. He managed to grunt, 'What did they see?'

'There's a kind of poison, Tom. It's a terrible stuff. You can't see it and you can't taste it, but it spreads and infects. It arrived there on the airbase, the planes brought it with them. Daisy had the written testimony of that. I have to destroy that proof, Tom. I have to eliminate it. Powerful forces are operating here, can you understand that?'

'Where is this testimony?'

'She hid it. She gave it to someone, someone she trusted. Daisy didn't talk much – and that's funny, isn't it? But she told me enough. She said it was in the last place anyone would look. The last place on earth. You got any idea where that is?'

'I don't know what you're talking about–'

'You sure?' The voice came down to his ear again. 'When I find it, Tom, I'll destroy it. And then I'm going out there to the old airbase. I'll kill Kate Fletcher too. Because you know what she did? She was the first one to find the airbase, to find out what happened. She knows everything. She spreads the story like a poison, you understand?' Fletcher began to twist, felt the metal hook choke him back. 'She's there, Tom. Daisy told me. Kate Fletcher's there, on the old airbase, where everything started.'

'She's on the airbase?'

'But with what she knows she'll never be safe. Never. You want to save her? Find the airbase and stop me. You against me, Tom. The perfect boy against the kid with the medication and the societal issues. But I am going to kill her, Tom.' The hook loosened, then tightened again. 'Just try and stop me.' The hook came free, and Fletcher made a grab behind him, trying to catch it. He saw it through his burning eyes: a crowbar with its curved end glinting, coming down at him through the dark.

After ten minutes, Mia Tyrone knew that Tim Redshaw wasn't going to open that drawer and give her the DVD. The guy tried to flirt at first, asked her out to discuss things further. Then he got annoyed, starting to question her exact position at Bellman, who her line manager was. She felt it was time to move out. As she stood up, the office door exploded inward with a noise that hurt her ears. She jumped back, and saw Tim Redshaw leaping right out of his chair, up against the wall, as the sound echoed out across the hangar.

Tom Fletcher stood in the doorway, blood leaking from his nose and mouth, eyes swollen and half closed, and a huge gash on his forehead spreading a triangle of blood over his cheek. She saw him focus his damaged eyes past her, onto the archivist behind the desk, took the three paces over to him and put his hand out, palm up.

'The disc.'

His voice was damaged and there was a corrosive smell about him, something peppery.

Tim Redshaw got his keys out. There was a slight metallic chiming before he unlocked the desk drawer.

'Does it hurt?'

Cathleen had just called from Crete. She was staring at him, but he thought he looked OK: eyes losing their swelling now, and seven quick stitches from a Polish doctor he knew in Burleigh Street who also checked how bad his concussion was and threw him some Slavic painkillers that were making his entire head buzz.

'He did it by paraffin lamp, there's another power cut here.'

'And I thought the candles were just you being romantic. Making up for this morning.'

He had two burning on the desk, shadows flickering around his office, Green Street dark outside, pattering with soft rain. On the screen, there were droplets on her window too. He could make out that she had a sheet wrapped around her torso, her bare legs curled on the bed. He saw her extend and flex her toes.

'Er, Cathleen, are you wearing any knickers?'

She began to slide her feet apart.

'Cathleen, I think you better put some clothes on.'

'That's very unlike you. Why?'

'Because I think the United States Air Force are intercepting my phone.'

There was a call box at the end of the darkened street – stepping inside it was like going back in time, walking into a smell straight from the late 1970s. A handful of change got him through to her hotel, though. A crackly line. If the Americans were bugging this, at least they'd have to make an effort – and there were no visual treats.

After listening, she said, 'You're telling me Slade got away? He walked out?'

'I was unconscious. The guy just disappeared. The best I could do was get the film clip. Thing is, I can't focus properly to look at it now. My vision's still blurred.'

'So how did you get to the doctor?'

'Mia Tyrone drove me in my car.'

'And where is she now?'

'I don't know, home I suppose.'

'OK. So what the hell did they have on this airbase? Something to do with poison? What poison?'

An idea began forming in Fletcher's mind. What kind of poison would involve the Felwell laboratory, the Bellman Foundation and a wartime American airbase?

Cathleen said, 'Tom, you OK?'

He put the idea aside. 'Yeah, I'm OK. All I can see is that Aspen Slade is obsessed with keeping these events quiet. He's found out that when Daisy was sweet-talking Nathan Slade, she picked up on something and dug around. Somewhere she got hold of this written testimony from

201

the girls in the film. He wants to destroy that. Then there's my mother, the first person to discover what happened. He said she's there on the base, she's actually there.'

'But where is it? There must be dozens of old airbases – how are you going to find the right one?'

'I'll find it. You see what this means?'

She was quiet for a long time: just the buzz of the phone line, the drip of rain on the battered plastic of the call box, a police siren echoing over to the west.

'Do you really want this, Tom?'

'Yes. When I find the airbase, I've got the chance of seeing my mother again.'

'Well, yes. But what if...' The rain was getting heavier. 'What if Aspen Slade gets there first?'

Fletcher tried to rest his eyes, sitting on the client sofa in the dark, listening to the rain. In his mind he saw a series of images: the beehive in the ruined garden of the village house, waiting for him to restore it. Then, for some reason, Mia Tyrone's eyes close to his when she was looking at his head wound – her hands holding his face like a lover. The colour of her eyes, something he'd never seen before.

Outside, there was thunder across the rooftops.

He saw that glimpse of Aspen Slade's crowbar in the museum lights.

His mother's map, the myriad A-shapes outlined in red. He thought, How will I find her? How will I find the right airbase?

He saw Major Lindquist's face looking out at

the old control tower, the crows circling.

Could it be?

He opened his eyes.

He made his way through the rain to All Saints, got into his car and drove carefully to start with, through the blacked-out streets, his headlamps fingering over the dark façades of the colleges, lit only by a deformed moon. With his still-blurred vision and the flickering rain, he went slowly until he came to the edge of the city, entering a stretch of utter darkness. He followed the road west more quickly, gaining speed, ploughing through the flooded patches, feeling the wheels lift up at one point and shiver as they found tarmac again. He passed the sign for *USAF Alconhurst* and slowed down slightly, watching the road on the right. A large aircraft came over low, its lights blinking across the road for a second. Then in his headlamps he saw the concrete slipway, turned onto the other side of the road and doubled back into it: the edge of the abandoned airbase where Lindquist had pulled him over in the morning. He drove along the old runway, around the debris barrier where broken-off bits of Lindquist's truck were still lying. He came onto a stretch of old runway, the Audi's suspension twitching the car around, bits of stone flying up around him until he hit a patch of ploughed field where he knew the wheels would just get stuck. He got out and made his way over that and onto the next runway, his steel torch in one hand. A few hundred yards ahead, where the moon was hanging behind a band of cloud, he saw the outline of the old control tower, the tree branches sprouting around it.

Close up, it was built of small bricks running with mould and plant growth. There was a single doorway with the stubs of old hinges casting shadows in the torchlight. He stood on the threshold.

'Kate?'

The upper floors had collapsed downward, leaving a jumble of masonry and beams around the ash tree that had sprouted up through it. Moonlight just touching the upper branches through the old controller's windows.

'Kate Fletcher?'

Apart from the rubble, there were some newspapers, an old bicycle, some syringe needles glinting orange in the damp.

Walking back to the car, he thought of the map on her study wall, her interest in the Felwell laboratory. Kate Fletcher learned something about an airbase, a poison brought by the Americans that had to be kept quiet. Aspen saying 'powerful forces operating'.

Fletcher's idea came back to him – an idea about the nature of that poison, the reason everyone was so nervous about it. Was that the real reason she left? The reason she was waiting to be found again?

Starting the engine, he thought, Yes, she's out there. On another airbase.

In the early hours, he tried playing the DVD again on his laptop. The part he wanted to focus on was the glimpse of the Mustangs on the runway, the sun flashing off a tailfin. He was sure that if he could isolate that, he could decipher the serial number of the plane, then trace its location through whatever official records existed. But the film was so faint, and his eyes still so damaged, that he couldn't see properly.

He closed his eyes in the dark. He wanted a few hours' sleep, let his eyes recover, then take a run, get some air on them, look at the film again. He'd arranged to meet Mia Tyrone at her apartment the next day to examine it properly. He hadn't mentioned that to Cathleen – no need to. He had to admit, something about Mia he liked, the way she talked, the way she moved her hands.

Outside the window, a gutter was overflowing with a constant tapping, even louder than the rain itself. That repeated impact reminded him of – what? The click of a typewriter's keys, Kate Fletcher typing up her research. Then a younger Kate Fletcher, kneeling on the grass by one of the Cambridge paths, her big smile.

Run, Tom.

He could still see the path, a grey line leading into the future. Still feel it under his feet.

Aspen Slade stood in the dark, his face against the cold glass of his boarding-house window, watching the water drops running down close to his eye. He was smiling, thinking ahead. The storms were coming soon. He could feel them coming over the horizon, the biggest storms this country would ever see, hitting the east coast of England.

Aspen was feeling fine. He liked storms – big violent things. He wasn't worried about Tom

205

Fletcher any more, either. That was a great idea he'd had, there in the museum.

Aspen laughed. He had his best ideas that way, at the moment of inflicting violence. Inflicting, that was just analyst's talk, not the right word. More like *sharing* – sharing the violence inside him, letting someone else have a piece. There was a girl once, in a bar, who called him a halfwit. Other people smirked and looked away. He shared some violence with her later on, yes. Right in that moment, he'd had the idea – *halfwit*. That meant half a brain, right? That's what he left her with.

He went to the mirror over his sink and pulled the little lamp cord. The power was back, and the tube blinked on. He began trimming his beard. A cool idea, yes. Letting Tom Fletcher try to find the place.

The storms were going to break *there*. Just perfect. It had to be *there*, where everything started. Kate Fletcher was out there, Daisy said to him before she died. And Kate would be there, he knew that; he could feel it. Kate Fletcher, the one who started this, then tried to run away when she realised what she'd uncovered. She'd uncovered the most poisonous secret of all. She knew too much, talked too much.

Aspen always wanted a mission. Wanted to join the Air Force, be a big shot in the Bellman thing. The Air Force didn't want him, didn't appreciate him. He had a mission now, though, and he knew they would appreciate this, the way he was executing his mission. They would be impressed.

First, find that manuscript that recorded

everything that happened. It was around here somewhere. Somewhere, the last place anyone would look, Daisy said. Where was that going to be?

Got to find it. Destroy the old manuscript, then get out there and find Kate Fletcher. Kill her, and the discovery of the old poison would be erased, the danger it presented would fade away.

Aspen trimmed carefully, making the dark line sharper against his pale skin.

After that, we didn't see much of the Americans for a while. We heard them, though. They took off in the mornings, usually after dawn. Sally and me were often out in the fields or the yard, and the planes would come over us, still climbing. Sometimes if I looked up, I could see the pilots inside. Sometimes they looked down at us. If they did, Sally would always wave.

Later, I saw they'd painted something on their planes. Each one had a picture of a woman, done in bright colours. I never got a close look.

Can I tell you about the Americans? I mean, I know careless talk costs lives, but this is just us, and I can trust you. The thing about the Americans, I couldn't understand what they were doing. They took off one by one, flew out over the sea. If it wasn't cloudy I could see sunlight flashing off their wings, them all waiting for each other, forming up. I could hear the engines if the wind was right. Then they moved off, up the coast. They came back after a couple of hours, but still together, all in formation. And they never lost anyone, you see what I mean? Nine would go out and nine would come back, every time. Like they were

207

practising something. This went on a few weeks, into the summer, all this practising. As if they were getting ready for something. As if they were waiting for something to arrive.

Thursday Morning

The apartment which Mia Tyrone would shortly have to vacate was on the top floor of a modernist block near the Cambridge Botanical Gardens. Outside, the building was all slab-sided wood and concrete, and at the back were balconies with a view over the trees to the tropical hot-houses, glinting in the rain like chunks of green quartz.

The cool, wet air was good for Fletcher's eyes, his head. He touched his stitches for a second, and the bruised line on his throat where Aspen Slade's crowbar had cut in. Then he went back inside, closing the door on the 7 a.m. rain.

Inside, there was a large open room with dark wooden floor and light walls. Mia was wearing black jeans, a pearl-coloured polo-neck jersey with the cuffs rolled over her wrists, her hair gathered loosely on one side. She was sitting at a long dining table with her laptop, a printer, a stack of maps Fletcher had brought, and a national newspaper. The paper's front page was dominated by weather-related stories – and the radiation bomb case in the USA. Fletcher had already read that carefully. Daisy Seager took a section at the foot.

Police probe Cambridge hostess trade.

Mia asked, 'How long before the police pull you in again?'

'Not long.' He turned the paper over. 'OK. Something poisonous arrived on an airbase in nineteen forty-three. Now Aspen's going back there to kill my mother because she knows what that was. Her map showed eastern England, I remember that. And the film clip was donated to the Norfolk County archive, remember. So let's find this vanished airbase.'

On the wall, mottled by shadows of the rain, they taped up a large map of eastern England, the scale going down to minor roads. Next to that, Fletcher taped a print from an aviation website, showing the location of wartime airfields in the same counties. He highlighted the bases in red on the bigger map.

They stood back and looked at them. Of the eleven US bases that officially existed, one was still in use at Alconhurst. Six others had been converted into civilian airstrips. The remaining four were shown on the map as *Disused,* their runways clearly marked, still roughly forming the old A-shape, though the straight lines were broken up in places by new roads and buildings, and partly lost to intensive farming elsewhere.

'The point is,' he turned to Mia, 'they're all still there. None of the old bases has *disappeared.*'

'So it's a base that never officially existed. And then it disappeared.'

He heard the scepticism in her voice. He said, 'Come on, let's look at the film clip again.'

Mia loaded up Tim Redshaw's DVD, froze the film where the light flashed off the Mustangs beyond the control tower. Things got tricky, because the sun shining off the metal almost

210

obscured the serial number painted there. In the end, though, they produced a reasonably legible image of the aircraft's unique code: 41-13728. Or was it 729?

Either way, Mia printed that and pinned it up on the wall too. Then things got even trickier. They went to the Internet, and looked through the various sites dedicated to USAF aircraft markings. Thanks to the obsessive dedication of enthusiasts, it was sometimes possible to trace a serial number to a plane's unit and service history in the war. Sometimes, but evidently not in all cases. Not in the case of Mustang 41-13728, or even 729. The numbers didn't appear on any of the lists.

Mia looked at the print on the wall. 'Are we reading it wrong?'

'The numbers are clear enough. That *is* the serial. It's just not on the list. Which means the lists are incomplete. Either that, or the plane changed serial number.'

'Great.' Mia sat back. She brought up the film clip again, and watched it with her chin in her cupped hand. 'We need an aviation expert, someone who knows how to trace this stuff. I think we can rule out our friend Tim Redshaw from the museum.'

Fletcher took out his spare phone – one not registered to his name – and dialled a number. The line rang for a while and, when it was answered, there was no voice, just the drumming of rain on a metal roof and the creaking of wires. He said,

'Charlie?'

The drumming echoed along the line.

'Charlie Fenner? It's Tom Fletcher.'

'I don't want to talk to you any more.' Her voice was faint over the background noises.

'Just two things, Charlie. Did Daisy Seager give you a document to look after?'

'A document? No.'

'Or a package, a computer file or something?'

'No. Why?'

'Somebody's looking for it, and you may be in danger.'

'But I'm leaving. I'm going to France for a week.'

'That's a good idea. But second thing, I've been to the museum...' Silence at Charlie's end. 'They've got a piece of film, Charlie. It's in a canister labelled Steel Witches. I've seen it.'

The wires creaked, those old drop tanks moving in the draught.

'I...' She paused. 'What does it show?'

'An airbase, a baseball game, two local women.'

'Planes?'

'Two Mustangs.'

She caught her breath. 'Do they have Nose Art?'

'No. But I'm trying to trace them.'

'You won't trace them. Nobody's ever traced them.' Charlie made a clicking sound in her throat, thinking. 'Runways?'

'Yes, there were runways. It was an airbase.'

'But what were they made of? The material?'

'A greyish material. Probably concrete.'

'That's what I heard.'

'Charlie, is there more you haven't told me?'

'Just rumours. Looks like concrete? You sure? You see, that's the thing.'

'The runways?'

'Why lay concrete runways for light aircraft like the Mustangs? Fighter bases were just strips of flat grass; at the most they'd have some steel mesh overlaid to reduce pitting. No, if you build a concrete runway, it's because you're expecting something heavy. Something big.'

'A big aircraft? A transport plane?'

'Transport, could be. Bringing something in. Or a bomber, taking something out.'

'You know about this, don't you, Charlie?' No answer, just the workshop echoes. 'I have to find the airbase. I have to. I've got the serial numbers of one of the planes. Help me trace them.'

'I'm going to France.'

'Do you want to see the film, Charlie?'

Rain noise, the balcony window full of dark clouds. He saw Mia turn a floor lamp on, throwing creamy light around the room, then sit back at the table, playing the film clip again, frowning into the screen.

Charlie said, 'You've actually got the film?'

'I've got it, I've watched it a dozen times. You want to see it?'

That clicking in Charlie's throat. 'I don't want you coming here.'

'Hold on.' Fletcher covered the phone, turned to Mia. 'Charlie knows something. She doesn't want us going there, but I don't want her coming here to your flat. Aspen may be looking for her; thinks she's got this document he wants.'

She nodded, watching the film clip. 'Well, that's

thoughtful. I suggest the Succulent House.'

'The what?'

She looked at him. 'Say that again.'

'What?'

She watched his face. 'Interesting, the way you say that. Your lips purse up then release, like on the film clip, the aircrew man. *What?*'

'You said something about succulent.'

'The Succulent House. The big glasshouse in the Botanical Gardens. You can see it from the window there.'

Back on the phone, Charlie agreed: the Succulent House. 'I'll drive in now. Show me the film, I'll do what I can to help trace the planes.'

Fletcher said, 'You've got an idea where the airbase is, Charlie, haven't you? Tell me, I'm looking at the map.'

'I'll be there in an hour.'

Finishing the call, he watched Mia still replaying the film clip to herself, twining the ends of her hair between her fingers. The floor lamp cut out for a second, then came on again. Fletcher had a dull ache at the back of his skull, and the stitches on his head were sore. He went out on the balcony and looked through the rain at the botanical greenhouses. Their lights flickered for a few seconds too.

He thought, *Charlie Fenner knows. Or at least, she's heard rumours. Rumours about that airbase — where it is, and what was going on there.*

He breathed in the cool air, going back over it in his mind. Why build an airbase with concrete runways, keep it off the official records, then destroy it? Because it was built for a bomber

214

plane? What kind of bomber was that?

The rain worsened, blowing onto the balcony itself, big cold drops that burst on the modernist cladding. He ignored it, thinking back over what he knew.

Oh, Christ. Is *that* what they were doing?

He went back inside.

Mia looked up from the screen.

'You look like you've seen a ghost, Tom.'

He sat opposite her at the table. 'Aspen Slade was rejected by the USAF. Now he's trying to impress them, to show how good he really is, by suppressing something.'

She looked at him, back at the screen, then folded it flat.

'Which is?'

'How about this? In nineteen forty-three, the British and the US Air Force built a secret airbase in England equipped with heavy-duty runways. They had a team of fighter aircraft stationed there too, equipped with those new long-range fuel tanks, the teardrop tanks. They were preparing to escort a bomber. They were preparing to use a radiation weapon.'

'That's not really possible, is it? The atom bomb was nineteen forty-five. It wasn't even tested till, what, the middle of that year?'

'I don't mean the atom bomb. The old Felwell laboratory had big stocks of an early radioactive material called hadesium. The records have never been explained, it looks like some went missing.'

'*Did* some go missing? Or are you the kind of man who believes Internet rumours?'

'It's *possible* some went missing. The point is,

215

everyone's touchy about this. Felwell are touchy, Bellman fired you because you were talking to me, the USAF want me to take a long holiday and forget about this.'

'Forget about what?' She flexed her shoulders, her breasts moving smoothly under the wool. 'What?'

'Imagine if Felwell and the Bellman Foundation got together to make something off the record, something unofficial. There's a crude type of weapon, the dirty bomb. You've seen on the news, people are being rounded up in the US right now for trying to make one. It's just radioactive material wrapped around a normal explosive bomb. It simply blows radiation over a wide area.'

'An unofficial dirty bomb?'

'Just think about it. The materials existed. Stocks of hadesium from Felwell College, shipped out to this airbase. Plus any kind of large conventional bomb. It could have been done easily. The long-range fighters were there to escort the bomber, maybe the first use of the drop tanks, the element of surprise.'

She tapped her fingers on the lid of her computer. 'But why?'

'Depends where they were planning to drop it. Could have been on Berlin, to irradiate the leadership. It was a way to force a close to the war in Europe, without the need for invading the mainland. Can you see that happening?'

'I can sort of see the logic. But I've never in my life heard of such a thing being even discussed or suggested.'

'But they must have thought about it. They

216

couldn't have had all this radioactive material, knowing what it could do, and *not* thought about doing it.'

She nodded slowly. 'Do you see a little flaw in your theory? Like, they didn't actually do it.'

'But they were planning to, that's the point. Then they abandoned the plan for some reason and bulldozed the airfield.'

Mia frowned, her green eyes darkening. 'So why give up the plan?'

'Plans change. Maybe objections were raised.'

'I don't know, Tom. It's an idea, but it's based on rumours, isn't it? You need things like photographs, testimony–'

'That's just it. Aspen's obsessed with finding this document, some kind of testimony that the local girls dictated. It proves what happened. Maybe they witnessed it, saw the bomber arriving–'

'Tom, the film. They were planning to use a radical new weapon, and they filmed themselves playing baseball?'

'So they were waiting for the weapon to arrive. They probably didn't know what they were waiting for.'

'And this is what your mother found out, this plan?'

He nodded. He thought – *This could be. The thing she picked up in conversation with her USAF friends, the thing she dug into. The thing that meant she had to leave.*

He stood up, putting his own laptop into its rucksack. 'I'm going to show the film to Charlie Fenner, see if she can help. You want to come?'

217

Mia seemed in two minds. She looked through the window at the botanical greenhouses, then opened her screen again. 'No, a new face won't help. And there's something about this film that's getting to me. Like, we haven't really understood it properly. Something's happening on that airbase that's hard to put a finger on.'

At nights we sat on the step with all the lights off. There were moths out in the reeds by the Deeping. I said, 'Sally, you won't ever leave here, will you?'

The moon came up.

Later, a car came into the yard. It was an American Jeep with two men in. We sat still and looked at them and they looked at us. I knew where our gun was hid – the old shotgun under the loose board behind us in the corridor. I knew how to lift the board and pull it out with one hand. I reached back and put my hand there.

The men got out. We could see in the moonlight, they were in uniform and their hair was shiny. One of them reached in the back and started something up. It was a record player, not a gramophone but electrical. I never heard music like that before. It was slow, with a beat inside it. One man come over and put his hand out to Sally.

I knew for a fact Sally couldn't dance. Or at least I never saw her do it. But she took his hand and they started. She settled into it. The yard were full of moths, looking for a light. There was a tiny light inside the Jeep, the moon on the record spinning round. Maybe they found that. Sally and the man moved around slowly, in all the moths.

The other man sat next to me. He took out a

cigarette and offered me one. I said no. He lit his with a petrol lighter. He said, 'Goddamn moths.'

I said, 'They dance for us.'

He looked at me. He said, 'You been a bit lonely here?'

He didn't try to touch me. We sat and watched Sally and the other man, together. The record finished. The two men clapped, and she laughed and bowed. Moths all round her.

Suddenly, it changed. The two men stood still and saluted. On the edge of the yard, there was a red point of light. I saw it glow and get dim. Someone was smoking a cigar, watching the group of us.

I knew who it was. I had my own ideas about him, I had them from the moment I first saw him. I had my ideas about why he was here, and the danger he brought with him.

When I looked again, the cigar was gone.

Mia said, 'Don't go just yet. Look at this.'

She turned the screen so he could see it, and played the clip again. The rich colours of the 1940s lit up and glowed. He saw the skinny baseball player finishing his silent anecdote. She slowed it down for him, said,

'What's really going on in this clip?'

He watched the screen for a few seconds. 'Well, the aircrew notice something over to the right. Must be the two women approaching across the field.'

'Not very impressive security, on a secret air-base preparing for a radiation weapon.'

He had to admit that was true.

She said, 'Then what?'

219

'The cameraman turns to see what they're seeing.'

'How does he turn?' She paused the clip as the camera began to focus on the two women.

'It's very smooth, the way he does it. It's professional.'

'It's on a stand. The camera's on a tripod, not hand-held.'

He thought about it. 'OK, and so?'

'Now what happens?'

'Now he takes the camera off the stand, or he lifts the stand and walks with it.'

'Correct. He walks with it on the stand, because he wants to use the stand again shortly.'

'So it's a lightweight stand, easy to carry – why are we talking about this?'

'Come on, Tom. What's *really* happening on that airfield? Think.'

She replayed it. The baseball players, the warm afternoon, the flash of sun off the Mustang tailfin before the camera focused on the women in the field. Fletcher said, 'Now the cameraman starts walking over there, where the aircrew are starting to cluster on the edge of the field. He comes up behind the other men and they look round at him.'

'Why?'

'He probably says something like, "Let the camera through."'

Mia shook her head. 'Look at their expressions. They make way because of who he is, not because he's got a camera. They *have* to let him through, don't they?'

Fletcher leaned forward. She was right. The

way the men parted for the cameraman, they were deferring to him. 'So he's an officer. He's their superior.'

'Definitely. He's superior to them all. And now?'

'They make way for him and he gets a clear shot of the two women. I think he uses the stand again here, he starts focusing on them.'

'What are the women doing?'

'They're looking at the camera.'

'Sure?'

Fletcher said, 'Replay it. OK, they're not looking at the camera. Slightly to the left of the camera.'

'So who are they looking at?' She paused the clip.

'They're looking at the *cameraman*. He's stepped aside from the camera.'

The clip ran on at half speed. Mia said, 'This is the juicy bit. There's a few seconds' pause, then the girl in the boiler suit speaks. What does she say?'

Fletcher reran it three times, watching the woman speak. Her pale, heavily freckled skin and her dark hair. Her lips moving silently. He said,

'You're saying you can understand that?'

'Maybe some of it. She's speaking slowly. You can see her using vowel sounds which open the lips, see? Then the lips close for the consonants. Here...' She paused on the frame of the girl finishing her brief phrase. 'Look at the way the lips press together, then spring apart. The mouth becomes a little wider. Do it yourself.'

He tried. '*Pa*. Or possibly *Ba*. A word with a *Pa*

221

or *Ba* sound at the start.' He let the clip run to the end. 'Look at this crewman on the left. He hears what she says, he looks really puzzled, he says something – and that's easy to read, in fact. He says, *"What?"*'

'Why does he say that?'

'Because he can't understand her accent.'

Mia said, 'Maybe. It could be *"What?"* meaning *"What the hell did she say?"* But maybe the reverse is true. Maybe he *did* understand the words she said, despite her accent. But he's puzzled *because* he understands her. Because what she says surprises him, or makes no sense to him. He says *"What?"* in the sense of *"What the hell did she mean by that?"*' She settled back and flexed her shoulders. The long pull of her hair was gathered beside her neck and down over her chest, its deep colour against the creamy wool, two dark colours in the strands. 'Think *before* that, Tom. That little pause before she makes her remark. Why the pause?'

'She's looking at the cameraman.'

'More than that. I bet she's *listening* to the cameraman. He steps aside from the camera, leaves it running on the tripod, and says something to them. It's obvious. He says something, then the girl replies to him – and it's the reply that's so mystifying for the crewman on the left. But what does the cameraman say? Imagine it's *you* on that afternoon, and those two women walk up to you. What would you say?'

'I'd say, "Get off my airbase".'

'What if you wanted to impress the locals?'

Fletcher thought about it. 'I'd introduce myself.

I'd say, "I'm Commander Joe Smith", or whatever.'

'Yes, you'd try to show how important you are. You're a man.'

'Thanks.'

'Sure. But the woman in the boiler suit doesn't look very impressed. She stares at you and says something-something-something *back*. And your men are wondering what exactly is going on.'

He could see what she meant. The cameraman was the commanding officer on the new airbase, maybe using his cine camera to take some souvenir footage of the first day on base, something to show the folks after the war. Not something you would expect from an officer preparing his base for the first-ever use of radiation weapons. And there *was* something puzzling about that exchange between him and the weird-looking local women.

Fletcher said, 'It's interesting. I'd like to know what that woman really is saying. What we need is a lip-reader.' He picked up his phone again and clicked through the numbers. Mia said,

'You have one on tap?'

He nodded, making a note of an email address, passing it across to her. She looked at it.

'Kristina Mittanescu? Who is this?'

'She's Romanian. Remember their leader, Ceauescu? His speeches went on for five hours. Kristina's job was to sit behind one-way glass and watch the audience with binoculars, lip-read any comments they made, report any sarcasm.'

For once, Mia looked surprised. 'So what's she doing in Britain?'

Fletcher checked his watch. 'Times change. Ceauescu was shot by his own army, Kristina lost her job. Now she's a speech therapist for the NHS. She still does lip-reading, though. The police use her all the time to decipher CCTV. Sometimes all you've got is a piece of surveillance film, you want to know what's being said. If you isolate that piece of film and email it to her, she might make sense of it.'

'OK. And you know what else I'm going to do? I'm going to summarise everything I know and post it somewhere secure – the film, everything. Plus your hypothesis on the radiation bomb, such as it is. I'll store what we know so far.'

He left her with the electric glow around her, the balcony door creaking slightly as the wind blasted rain against it. He thought, yes, that's the right thing to do. Leave something as evidence. It's just that Daisy Seager didn't have time to leave us anything.

In the street, he zipped his parka against the gale.

Did she?

Fletcher started off into Bateman Street. The rain was bouncing off the walls of the school buildings along the road, forming gullies along the pavement. If this kept up, the flooding would come pretty soon.

The Botanic Gardens looked completely empty, just rain drifting across the pathways through the lawns, the fountain spattering sideways in the breeze. Beyond a stand of bamboo, the greenhouses rose against the slate-coloured sky. He found one with 'Succulent House' on a nameplate above the door, and went in.

It was warm and damp. Smell of paraffin from the heaters. A big space, crowded with vegetation; heavy tropical palms around the door and then, further inside, the glass walls completely lined with a species of giant cactus. The plants were up to three metres tall, the spines glinting in the shadow and light of the rivulets coursing down the windows.

Fletcher waited. He walked right through the greenhouse, breathing the leafy, damp smell. He watched a speckled bug moving along the bark of a tropical vine. He looked at his watch. He hitched his rucksack higher on his shoulder and went out to the doorway. The cold air hit him, the rain making miniature canals now.

He went back into the damp heat and dialled Charlie's workshop. The phone picked up quickly – again, no voice, just the impact of rain and the creaking noise.

'Charlie? I'm already here.' No reply. 'Charlie?'

'You know what, Tom? Your friend Charlie has this really cheap phone.'

'Where is she?'

'How are your eyes, your nose and stuff? You sound OK.'

'Where's Charlie?' Fletcher kicked the door open, then he was out of the greenhouse, running in the rain back past the fountain, towards the entrance, the phone to his ear.

Aspen said, 'Thing is, I've been to everybody now, everybody Daisy talked to about this. Daisy said she hid it in the last place anyone would

225

look. I thought that meant Charlie here would have it hid. But no, she says no, don't you Charlie?'

There was just the sound of creaking.

Fletcher vaulted the turnstile and missed his footing on the wet tarmac the other side – went sprawling over the empty pavement. He got up and retrieved his phone, shook the water off it. Aspen was still talking.

'You figured out where the base is yet? Because I'm going to be there, Tom. Those storms are going to be big, I hear. But we'll have some fun there, Tom. You and me and your damn mother.'

Thursday Afternoon

The sky behind Charlie Fenner's workshop was electric grey, trees on the skyline arching and bucking. There was no other vehicle on the narrow approach road, nobody visible across the entire landscape. The metal door slid open, spattering water which was whipped away by the wind.

Fletcher could see the plastic chairs and the heater inside the doorway, bathed in the pure white light of the floodlamps. The heater was running, and the warmth hit him as he stepped in, the lamps blinding him until he stepped aside, shielding his eyes and squinting past them to the back of the hangar. The three teardrop fuel tanks were hanging in a row from the steel beam, turning slightly on their axes, luminous white. Behind them, Charlie Fenner was suspended by a length of the same steel wire, the cord looped around her neck and twisting it to one side, the heels of her boots a metre from the floor, just touching an overturned toolbox as they moved in the same fractional rhythm – the internal current of the hangar, moving with the pressures on the empty landscape outside.

Fletcher stood looking at her face. There was none of the cartoon stuff – no eyes popping or tongue sticking out. Charlie looked surprised, her eyes narrowed into the corner of the work-

227

shop, her mouth open wide enough to show neat teeth still wet with saliva. Fletcher guessed the wire had snapped the top of the spinal column like a whiplash injury.

He looked around the rest of the workshop. The oddments of aircraft parts, the tools and cables, had been ransacked, everything strewn out onto the floor.

He went outside and called the police, then Mia.

He waited in his car, watching the trees labouring under the rain. Charlie was utterly innocent, a woman with the misfortune to take an interest in military aviation. But, without Charlie, he couldn't see how he was going to find the airbase. He couldn't see how he was going to find his mother.

I was stoking up the fire in the kitchen. The sun was going down. It was the first fire of the autumn. Sally were in the wash house. When she came in, she said, 'There's something inside the door. Is it a letter?'

It was a little printed card. It said:

The English–American Friendship Circle
Invites you to a reception at Hanchton Town Hall
On Sunday 15th September 1942 at 3 p.m.
Our guest speaker, Colonel Harpkin, US Eighth Army Air Force, will give a talk on what it means to come back home.'

I went to the kitchen to throw it in the fire. Sally was quick, she snatched it out my hand and read it. She put it on the rafter next to the clock. Then she stood at the window. She stood there, combing her hair and watching the sky. The clouds were changing colour.

'I came to ask her about planes.'

'Planes?'

'It's an interest of mine.'

The uniformed police who were first on the scene made a note of that, speaking into their radios, their eyes moving all the time to the clouds building over the trees on the horizon. Electric grey light between bands of black.

Fletcher waited in the back of a stationary patrol car, watching the fatality people arrive and enter the workshop, their white coverall suits almost luminous in the stormy light. Once, a copper ducked his head in the car window and asked if Fletcher needed counselling or a spiritual safe space. He declined both, thinking this meant the death was being treated as suicide for the time being. He wondered how long before Franks picked up on it, heard that Fletcher had found his third corpse this week.

He listened to the radio news on his phone, the presenters talking about the weather system building off the east coast. The thing might disperse, or it might build into the worst sea storm the country had ever seen. Then a mention of Daisy Seager: the police saying their inquiry was progressing well.

The car creaked as the door opened and a man slid into the front passenger seat. There was a smell of wet raincoat, stale breath and cigarettes. A big hand went up to the mirror and twisted it to look at Fletcher in the back. Fletcher could see

229

just a pair of reddened eyes and the scowl between them.

'Hello, Franks.'

'You're not untouchable, Fletcher.'

'I've been offered counselling, thanks.'

'Shut up, you cunt.' The red eyes held his, the windows in the car steaming up, cutting them off from the world. 'What happened to your face?'

'I fell down the stairs. My shoes were wet.'

Franks grunted. 'Is this Charlie Fenner person connected with Daisy Seager?'

'Not that I know of.'

It went on for another three minutes. Then Franks' phone rang and he answered it. There was a terse conversation involving yes and no, the voice of a man whose inquiry was progressing slowly. The back of his head was shiny with damp. Franks ended the call and raised his eyes to the mirror again.

'I've got to go. But I'm coming back for you, Fletcher. Go from here to your flat and stay there. If I can't find you, I'll take it as an admission of guilt.' He started to get out, then closed the door again. 'Prison, Fletcher. You know what they'll do to you?' The door opened again and the car creaked.

Fletcher closed his eyes. He knew Franks was right. They would have to bring him in; he would have to disclose what he knew. And then the whole situation would be taken out of his hands, the following hours or days would be spent in a police cell.

He looked at his watch. Three p.m.

Thursday, 3 p.m. His appointment with the

university security people. His chance of building a fresh start. All of that sounded tinny and irrelevant – like a party happening across the street – compared to what Fletcher had to do now.

The most important thing in his life.

Finding the old airbase and finding his mother before Aspen Slade found her. Before Aspen killed her to suppress the story he wanted to conceal.

Aspen killed Charlie, no doubt of that. Killed her because he thought Charlie had something: the voice of the Steel Witches that somebody had listened to and typed out. With Charlie gone, how could the airbase be traced? Was there anything of it left – any of the fragmented A-shape, buried somewhere in the flat land between here and the sea? Maybe it could be traced – if only Daisy Seager had taken time to do what Fletcher had done: summarise everything, post it somewhere safe that other people could see. But Daisy thought she was in control – letting Nathan Slade into her car when he said he'd come to warn her, then throwing him out to let him stumble over the edge of the quarry in the dark. Daisy didn't know that Aspen was waiting on the road ahead. Daisy didn't leave a sign because she didn't think she had to.

He opened his eyes because the door opened again, rain blowing in, the car shifting under him. A uniformed policeman was in the front seat, peering through the mist forming on the windscreen. With a gloved hand, he wiped two horizontal smears through the condensation, making a ragged vision slit. Then he put the engine on

231

and set the hot air to blast. The two smears remained at his eye level, giving a view of Charlie's hangar. He twisted round and said, 'I got stuff for you to sign. Hey. Hey, you. You listening?'

But Fletcher was looking past the copper, at the lines dragged in the windscreen mist, the lines slowly dissolving as the blowers did their work. The kind of lines you have to scrape clean from the outside if the temperature is freezing.

He signed the forms, not really seeing his own signature. He was thinking, *Daisy, you did leave us something. All the time, it was there. It was the last thing you left on this earth, but you knew danger was coming close. You made sure the cameras got your sign in the car park at Hunters on a freezing Sunday night.*

How did he miss it? How did he ever miss that?

I couldn't let her go to the talk alone, so we put dresses on and walked over there across the fields.

In Hanchton, the beach were sealed off with wire and there were pillboxes in the dunes, and sandbags outside the town hall. People in the street were old or very young. They stopped to watch us going past. None of them looked us in the eye. The old grudge, you see. Them knowing what they did to us three hundred years ago, knowing how they sold us to the witchfinder.

The town hall was hot inside. We sat in the back row of chairs. There was dust in the air. There was a wooden stage with the sun coming through behind it. The mayor of Hanchton stood up there; he had his chain on. Fool. He made a speech about history. He said how there were historic links between towns round here and towns in America. Boston and Cambridge and Norfolk were also places in America, he said, started by people from here hundreds of years ago, like they were twins separated by birth. He talked too much, and people started fidgeting. He said now we were welcoming back their descendants, the Americans. Many of them coming back to the land of their ancestors, he said. None more so than his guest, Colonel Harpkin.

Harpkin stood up.

People stopped fidgeting.

He were about thirty. He had a uniform with a brown jacket, cream trousers with a knife edge. He had smooth dark hair combed back, creamy skin and dark eyes. I heard someone in front of us say – 'Rudolph Valentino.' Yes, he was nice-looking. But I had my ideas about him.

He smiled and lit a cigar. He talked friendly, holding each person's eye for a moment, each person in the hall, me and Sally too. He talked about the towns in America, how they were started by our people who wanted to move out there to start new lives. He talked about how many families today in America had little stories about their great-great-something grandparents. He leaned a hand on the back of his chair and talked about himself. He moved his cigar in time with his words, and he tapped it into an ashtray on a stand. Sometimes he stopped and relit the cigar, and nobody moved; everybody watched him. His smoke was curling with the dust in the sun through the window. He said that his family could trace their ancestors back generations, to the people who sailed from England. He said he'd always dreamed about this country, all his life. His heart was full of pride

233

now he was the first of his family to come back here. He'd even bought himself a cine camera to take some memories home again. Then he smiled, and he winked at the people in the front row while he tapped his cigar. He said, just between all of us here today, he had a confession to make. He said he'd done something kind of unmilitary. Something he could be shot for if anyone found out. He stopped and people looked at each other. He said he'd pulled some strings. He'd pulled every string he could, used up all the favours he was owed, to get himself posted here to somewhere near this fine town of Hanchton. He said he felt like he was coming home and, in a way, he was. He said there was a story handed down that his grandfather's grandfather's great-grandfather had said a few words on his deathbed. The old man had said Hanchton, Hanchton over and over again. Then something else, like a little poem. Those words became a family legend, he said.

'I see them dancing. In the water, the air, the earth. I see them dancing, with their eyes upon me.'

I knew it for a fact, then. And I ran right out of the town hall.

Some time after Fletcher phoned her, Mia Tyrone had another call – this one from her parents in Bowling Green, Virginia. She could picture the lawn from their window, the fence, the trees along the avenue – the little world that was proud of her. She pretended everything was fine. She put the phone down before her voice broke.

Then she said out loud, 'Screw Bellman.' Maybe Tom Fletcher was right: they were doing something way back then that would humiliate them today. Maybe Fletcher's mother really did know what it was.

She packed a bag – not a returning-home bag, though. A going-to-an-old-airbase bag, a nailing-the-truth-about-Bellman bag. The more she thought about it, the more she liked the headline. *Bellman built dirty bomb for USAF. First photos of secret airbase.* She charged up her camera and emptied the memory card, tucked it in there.

It was quiet in the flat. She checked her email: no answer from the lip-reader yet. She started to worry, started to think about doing this all on her own.

Close to 4 p.m., there was a knock at the door. She checked it was Fletcher before taking off the chain.

He had his rucksack in one hand and a greasy-looking paper wrap in the other. He had a calm light in his blue eyes, nodding and walking in past her, putting the wrap on the table.

She said,

'What's that?'

'Lunch.' He didn't give it another glance, taking out his laptop and starting it up. She opened the paper thing carefully: circular discs of some fried material, a pale green inner breaking through in places. 'Fried eel.' He began tapping his computer, looking for something. 'It's good if you've had a shock.'

'Finding Charlie like that, must have been a hell of a shock.'

'Charlie was bad enough. But then I realised I'd missed what Daisy was trying to say.'

He turned the screen to her: some frames taken

from a nighttime CCTV camera. She recognised it from the news programmes: the car park of the club where Daisy Seager worked. The little car she was driving, the Golf; amazing anyone could see out of that with just those scrapes across the windshield, the girl's face barely visible through them, then clearer through the side window. Mia said, 'Yes?'

He stood next to her and went back a frame. The windshield full on to the camera, pale eyes in the dark interior.

Fletcher pointed to the windshield with a biro. 'Why would anyone drive off with just those scrapes to see through?'

'She was in a hurry, she didn't have time to do any more.'

'She had time to do the sides. She left the scrapes on the front for a reason.'

'Which is?' Mia took a bite of the eel thing, then put it down.

'What do the scrapes look like?'

'Two lines, one longer than the other, a slight angle. A little connecting bit in the middle. They're scrapes.'

'They're an A-shape. A runway shape.'

'Huh?' She looked at him, saw he was serious.

'Think about it,' he said. 'We've seen shapes like that repeatedly today, looking at the map. The disused airfields, the way the runways get broken up or farmed over. That's what this is. She was leaving a sign, the shape of the remains of the runways at the airbase, something that's just there on the map, not labelled.'

She laughed. Then she went to the map and

looked at the disused bases, the way the runways stopped and started, their angles broken up. She said, 'if it is, where do we look for it? Could be anywhere.'

'Somewhere flat and open.'

'Well, that really narrows it down.'

'You start on the left. I'll start on the right.'

The floor lamp gave a good solid light, showing all the details despite the fading daylight. Mia began scanning up and down the map, where the coast made the bay that the English called The Wash. So many tiny roads, shapes marked on the ground, clumps of trees. In a while, her eyes got used to it, and she moved more quickly, looking for anything with that broken A-shape, her eyes flicking across the quadrants, Tom Fletcher next to her, moving his hand methodically over his part of the map.

She stopped. At a point where the coastline moved east away from the Wash, she curled her fingers over the map and nudged Tom.

'Want to look?'

He took her hand and lifted it away gently. His fingers were warm and stayed on hers until he caught sight of what she'd found. Then he tapped that point on the map.

He said, 'Yes. Could be.'

The shape from Daisy's windscreen was there. You had to believe in it, but it was there. At a point in the county of Norfolk, untouched by other roads, and miles away from the nearest village, a series of dotted lines made those two lines, resting at that angle. To the north, a series of small bays. To the west was a plateau of open

237

country and, to the south, a river curved towards the sea at a small town named Hanchton. Otherwise, there was nothing there – no village name, no farm, no buildings marked at all.

She said, 'You think?'

He ran his finger round it. 'It looks so similar to the scrapes.'

'Would you go out there now, based on this?'

She saw him hesitate. He said, 'We ought to find an older map, see if there was anything marked on there in the past. And an even larger-scale map, to see it close up, see if there's any more detail. It looks like there are no buildings left, no control tower for example. And what's this?'

Moving to the east of the runway, the map showed a roughly circular shape coloured as standing water. A small label below it said simply 'Pit'.

They tried a satellite image service that they thought should give an aerial view of the site.

Sorry – we don't cover this area in detail yet. Check back soon.

Fletcher turned the computer off. 'You'll need a raincoat, Mia. We're going to a shop in All Saints' Passage.'

'What kind of shop – another Romanian snooper?'

'I've never actually been inside. But there's a sign in the window I've noticed.'

She said, 'A sign that says, *Future foretold, your destiny revealed?*'

'No. It says *Old Maps*. They might have something that shows what was there in the past.'

Mia got out her slicker – an army-style rain

cape she kept for English weather. Its canvas felt rough – it even felt rough in her fingers. It felt just right.

They walked into Cambridge. To Fletcher, hands in the pocket of his parka, viewing the town from the fur-fringed circle of his hood, the whole place felt unfamiliar. It wasn't the downpour from a steel-coloured sky, the hiss of traffic and the noise of the gutters, the streetlights burning long before sunset; It was the people: half-running, hands shielding their heads as if the rain was corrosive. Fletcher's parka, though, was water-tight, and Mia's slicker evidently worked. Waiting to cross the street, he looked at her, saw her face under the hood, smiling. She glanced at him and winked.

In the city itself, the gutters were overflowing, broken drainpipes in Sidney Street spewing across the road. All Saints' Passage – a tiny huddle of medieval façades – looked like a village dredged up from the seabed, with green slime oozing water from the walls. The windows of the old map shop window were misted over, but inside it was warm with a dry, papery atmosphere. A bell rang out as they closed the door and looked around. The space was divided into canyons of bookshelves, with counters of old maps and prints stacked between them.

A shopkeeper at an old till scowled in greeting. Fletcher said, 'Norfolk?'

'You'll drip on the stock.'

The man watched while they hung their coats by the door and Mia shook the ends of her hair.

Then he nodded to an aisle at the end of the shop.

They found an open counter with *Norfolk* pinned above it, and began to leaf through the items in there, each of them in a plastic wallet. They were mostly old prints and engravings, priced in shaky ballpoint. Fletcher began to rifle through, reading the title on each one before flicking it down onto the pile. Mia said,

'What exactly are we looking for?'

'Any map of that part of the coast, near Hanchton. Anything old. And don't drip.'

They kept flicking. He found some prints of Norwich Cathedral and an engraving of a Victorian lifeboat rescue.

'How's this?'

She held up an Ordnance Survey map of North Norfolk, dated 1946. One year after the end of the war.

'Thank you, Mia.'

She unfolded it, her nose wrinkling. Fletcher spread it out and compared it to his modern map. The differences were interesting. The 1940s landscape was emptier, the towns smaller and the main roads more jagged. The marshland to the west was not yet fully reclaimed from the sea. There was one similarity, though. Just south of Hanchton, on the empty plateau edged by the river, was the same fragment of A-shape. The same remnant of the runway pattern.

Mia said, 'That means if there was an airbase there, it must have been ploughed under immediately after the war, maybe even during the war. So possibly there *was* a reason to keep it concealed. If, if, if. Know what I mean?'

She took it over to the cash desk.

In front of Fletcher was a solid wall of book spines. Everything was about Norfolk. Norfolk hunting, Norfolk fishing, memoirs of Norfolk sea-farers. On a lower shelf, a history of Norfolk farm-ing. Below that, something called *Pits of Clay.* Gold letters on a cracked cloth spine.

Fletcher turned away, then turned back.

Pits?

What was that on the map, near the runway shape? A *pit.*

He pulled the book out. Published in 1906. A dedication in fountain pen, *Dearest Leo, from your loving Eileen,* and the shop's price in pencil. He turned the pages. It was a history of clay mining in Norfolk, written by a retired engineer. The point was that clay extraction had been an important local industry from medieval times up until the nineteenth century. It was a simple business. Deep pits were hacked into the seams of clay until the walls became unstable. Then those pits were aban-doned, and others were started. An etched map showed mining activity in the eighteenth century – big zones in the south, getting scarcer to the north. Up near Hanchton, there was a tiny shaded area. Another map showed clay mining a hundred years even before that. The tiny shaded area was bigger, and it had a name.

Wytchlandes.

Fletcher began rummaging across the shelves, looking for any book that had old maps of the Hanchton area. All he could find was the memoir of a rural magistrate published in 1870. It in-

241

cluded a spidery chart of the west Norfolk area, showing the region in the author's boyhood. South of Hanchton, there was the outline of an old clay pit – and, next to that, near where the fragment of A-shape was today, the outline of one single building, not served by any roads. The Victorian had labelled it with the name his grandfather used for the place.

Wychland.

So there were people there. Nobody agreed on the spelling – because it was transmitted purely verbally, maybe, and died out from the written records around two hundred years ago. But it had been some kind of community: a few houses, the people digging clay out of the ground for hundreds of years until they dwindled away to ... what? To nothing? Or did they come down to the Steel Witches, the two local girls, maybe thinking the world had forgotten them until that airbase appeared in the fields?

The old pit, the single lonely building. Was that where the Steel Witches lived?

He decided.

Yes, it was. That was where they'd lived, where they'd witnessed whatever the Americans brought onto their airbase – the dangerous truth Kate Fletcher had discovered and that was leading her back there now in the face of the storms, Aspen hunting her down.

At the door, Mia was already in her slicker, waiting under the glare of the shopkeeper. Fletcher showed her the page, his finger on the word, 'Wychland'.

'That's where we're going.'

She nodded. He saw her shiver a little.

In the almost dark streets, the wind was changing direction rapidly, packed with rain which flashed in the city lights like tracer fire. Few people were on the pavements as Fletcher and Mia walked round to the big bookshop in Green Street. Plenty of people were inside there: sheltering in the entrance, staring out.

In the map section, they found an Ordnance Survey map of north Norfolk – the largest scale available. Fletcher unfolded it, the paper getting damp in his hands. It was vastly more detailed than even the map on Mia's wall, showing features down to footpaths and contours. He turned over to the wide stretch of land near Hanchton. Within the map's grid lines, the two stretches of hard surface were clear to see, the same angle and proportion as the scrapes in Daisy's windscreen. They were unlabelled and completely unexplained.

Mia took the edge of the map and straightened it out.

To the east of the runway, that oval shape of standing water, the old clay mine labelled with the one word, *Pit*. Beyond that, the outline in the ground recognisable from the other maps, but now clear as roughly L-shaped, the size of a large house or barn – not current, just an empty contour on the ground. No name or explanation for the feature at all. Mia said, 'And this?'

She ran her nail around a dotted line: a boundary running in a rough oblong to include the water, the building outline and part of the surrounding plain, in all about two square kilometres. A small caption read: *Nature Reserve.*

She said, 'Before we go, I'd really like to know who owns that.'

They folded up the map, took it to the checkout. In the doorway, the final editions of the newspapers all carried satellite images of the weather system building off Norway. It was building up, already forming a grey knot with a dark centre, moving slowly towards eastern England, like a circular sawblade starting to turn.

One paper had given the system a suitable name: the Psychlone.

Fletcher half expected to find a police officer on the door of his flat, but there was only a homeless-looking man standing under the porch, staring out at the rain. Fletcher left him there, walked up the stairs to his own door. Halfway, he stopped and looked back down the stairs.

Mia said, 'What?'

In a low voice, 'I've never seen him around before.'

'So?'

'He could be a police officer. They haven't pulled me in, because they're watching me.'

'One conspiracy too far, Tom.'

Down through the curve of the stairwell, he could see the man's shoulder, slouched against the wall. 'It's what I would do if I was them. I'm sure they're watching me.'

She went on up the stairs. 'He's a homeless guy. Come on. Pack your bag.'

The flat was noisy – the gutters outside, rain thudding on the windows, radiators clicking. He watched Mia peeling her slicker off and pulling some water out of the ends of her hair. Moving his eyes to the desk phone, he saw he'd had a call from the lip-reader, Kristina Mittanescu. He'd almost forgotten that – the odd little exchange on the film clip between the local girl and the base commander. It hadn't struck him as important, but now he'd seen that outline of the building on the map, he wanted to know what the girl was saying.

He called Kristina Mittanescu back.

'That you, Fletcher? You sent me a strange piece of film.'

Kristina's Romanian accent was modulated by years of NHS employment, but it kept the faintly accusing tone that must have terrified the party faithful back in Bucharest.

'Kristina, can you see what the woman's saying?'

'It's difficult. There are five sounds.'

'Is the last of them the word "back"?'

'Probably, possibly. But as for the rest... I'm a lip-reader, you understand, not a mind-reader.' That meant she'd figured it out – her instinct was to keep people guessing. She said, 'It's English, old fashioned and rural. But proper English, not a dialect as such. The first word is "So", that's a safe bet. Next word is actually "ye", meaning you. Then it looks like "have", but she drops the "h", just "ave". "So ye 'ave something back." The missing word – I'm not sure. She makes a "K" sound, then a vowel, then an "M" going into the

245

"B" sound of the next word. It might be "come". The whole thing might be, "So ye 'ave come back." That's about seventy per cent likely. Mind you, in the old days, that's all I needed.'

'"So ye 'ave come back." Thanks, Kristina. It makes no sense at all.'

In the quiet, the gutter began creaking over the sound of the rain. Mia was working at something on his desk computer. She said, '"So ye 'ave come back"? What's that supposed to mean?'

'He's come back. That means the woman recognised the commander, already knew him from somewhere.'

'Such as where?'

'Maybe–' Fletcher struggled – 'maybe he'd been there already, to view the site. Maybe something had happened between them.'

'Yeah, so he walks over in front of the whole base and says hello again? No, I don't think he'd ever set eyes on her before.'

'So what *does* she mean?'

Mia turned to him from the screen.

'Maybe these people could explain. The people who own the land. They're called the Eastern Wildfowl Trust. A charity that owns a number of small nature reserves on your delightful Norfolk Coast.'

'Including this Wychland place?'

'Including one near Hanchton, at least. There's no mention of Wychland, or old runways or houses or whatever. There's no map, either. But I'm sure they're the people to talk to. The Wildfowl Trust is a project sponsored by a number of generous donors who have provided parcels of land. One donor in particular stands out. Can you guess? A prestigious organisation – not a household name, but well known to you and me.'

That made sense. It explained a lot. Fletcher said, 'The Bellman Foundation? They own the land?'

Mia raised an eyebrow. 'Not Bellman. The land up there was donated by Felwell College.' She leaned back, watching him. 'How does that fit our theory?'

Fletcher went through to his bedroom, threw some items into a rucksack. She came and stood in the doorway, watching him. He said, 'We're going, then. We're going to find my mother. She's out there.'

'Right now?'

'Why wait?'

'The police suspect you, Fletcher. They're figuring out you've been misleading them. You think yourself they're watching your door. They know what car you've got and everything. You leave Cambridge, they'll stop you.'

'So I'll change the car.' He closed his rucksack.

She walked over to him, put her hand against his face suddenly. He stopped his rushed packing, looked at her. She smoothed his cheek with her thumb.

'I want us to go to Felwell College now. Ask the dean what she knows about this. It's important to me, get some kind of evidence. Then get a different car and go.'

Fletcher thought for a few seconds. Did it make sense, getting the facts straight before evading the police, going out there? Maybe. And they did need to change the car. He nodded. She kissed him on the cheek, more slowly than the time before.

Then I was out of the hall and walking down the high street towards the beach. There were big clouds over the sea, gulls on the breakwater. I walked to the end of the street and onto the dunes, up to the wire barricade. I went on my knees and took the sand in my hands.

I said, I knew it. I knew who he was, first time I saw him.

I knew it would end bad, but not this bad. Not with Sally fixing her eyes on Colonel Harpkin, making a little sound in her throat when he looked over at her. Not with him saying the words his family kept in their hearts all those years, saying it like a poem. The family handed it down, but they lost the meaning. The stupid bloody family didn't know what it meant; pretty Colonel Harpkin didn't know what it meant, but I knew.

I can see how it happened. The family thought he was talking about angels over his deathbed. Angels from his old home in Hanchton. In a few generations, they imagined him like a saint, in a white sheet, all his white hair combed back, being welcomed into life eternal.

I see it different. I see him twisted on a straw bed, sweating, kinked up with fever. He got big dark eyes and his face is white, all full of veins. He stares at the ceiling and he's seeing water, air, earth. The ducking in water, the hanging in the air, the pressing to death under the sacks of earth. The women be killed at Wychland. Still dancing and watching him.

248

I knew that ancestor was the witchfinder, escaped to America, and his flesh and blood was this Colonel Harpkin, come back to us after three hundred years.

Outside, the homeless man had moved across the street to a shop door, avoiding their eyes. They agreed to walk to Felwell – probably as quick as driving, with the city traffic snarled up in the weather. In the street, the wind had eased, but the rain had settled into a constant downpour which was striking different sounds off the buildings: tapping on glass, drumming off the old streetlamps, a steady thump off car roofs. Mia raised her voice,

'You think the Felwell people will see us?'

'I think the dean will be expecting a visit around now. I remember, speaking to her, she was relieved I didn't know exactly what Daisy was investigating. I think it's possible Daisy was researching an aspect of Felwell College itself. It's like an equation. Felwell land plus the Felwell hadesium. Bellman people plus the US Air Force planes. Maybe the outcome was a kind of private airbase – experimental, off the record. Everyone working together, until something happened and it was cancelled out.'

They walked without speaking for a minute. In the last of the light, they rounded the corner of Garret Hostel Lane, and could see the river ahead between the walls of Trinity and Clare College. They came onto the footbridge and looked along the Backs.

Normally, this view was an image of perfect control over nature: the river between the manicured

249

lawns, the clipped willow trees, the perfect bridges. Today the river seemed about to rise up and take back the city. It was grey-black, moving at many times its normal speed, frothing against the stone embankment. There were long spines of water forming around submerged debris. Mia said,

'Stuff under the surface.'

He turned away. 'Welcome to Cambridge.'

Thursday Night

The towpath leading to Felwell College was alive with people stacking sandbags in a barrier along the riverfront. The college walls were dark, but their spikes glinted with a strong white light from inside the courtyard. Fletcher and Mia made it as far as the porter's lodge before being challenged. One of the uniformed guards tried to block their path. Then he recognised Fletcher, looked at Mia, and hesitated. He stood aside.

Behind him, a TV news crew were interviewing a trio of people floodlit against the backdrop of the fishpond. The fountain was working again, releasing a wide arc of water – and maybe the reporter saw that as a handy metaphor, because Fletcher heard her ask, 'Are we ready, now the ice has melted?' at the close of a piece to camera. She turned to the people behind her. The first in the row was Tania Nile, wearing a waxed jacket unzipped to show a sombre black scarf. A sign of mourning for Daisy Seager? Beside her, Fletcher recognised the MP for a Cambridge constituency and a senior officer the county Fire and Rescue Service. The reporter said, 'Miss Nile, your college is in the front line if the Cam breaks its banks. How ready are you?'

Tania Nile smiled sadly and gave a little tilt to her head. 'We've emptied our cellars of the best wines.' She paused while the MP nodded in

251

appreciation. 'But seriously, we're as ready as we can be. We've got five thousand sandbags on the river frontage.' She noticed Fletcher and faltered. She started talking again, and finished her answer, but her eyes moved back to his. When the reporter moved on to the politician, Tania Nile detached herself from the group and came over to Mia and Fletcher, stood for a second looking at them.

Fletcher introduced Mia. Then he said, 'Making a joke about the wine, while you're still wearing that?' Pointing to the scarf.

Tania Nile didn't reply. Behind her, the TV reporter was quizzing the Fire and Rescue woman. The words 'onslaught' and 'deluge' came across under the rain. Tania kept fingering her scarf.

Fletcher said, 'There's a piece of land in Norfolk that used to be owned by the college. Was an airbase built there in nineteen forty-three?'

'This doesn't concern you, Mr Fletcher.'

'What exactly happened there?'

'Whatever you think, you're wrong. You're completely wrong. There's nothing to say, Mr Fletcher. Goodbye.'

There was the noise of generators starting up with a long throaty rattle. Tania shook her head and turned away and walked quickly to the college entrance, slipping through the great wooden doors.

It might have been the TV lights, but Fletcher thought he'd seen tears behind the technology in her eyes.

That night, when we got back from Hanchton, Sally

didn't speak to me. She put the light out and got into bed. I waited for her to speak, but she didn't. In the dark, I went and kneeled by her bedside. I reached and took her hands. They were cool and rough on the insides. I pressed them against my face. She didn't stop me, you see. Fact is, she touched my face with her fingers in the dark, all from my forehead to my neck, feeling everything. I said,

'Sally.'

'Evie.'

She said it like that. Evie. I wouldn't mind being deaf, if they left me that one sound, the way she said it. I slid my head and her fingers went through my hair. I knew she was going to understand. I said,

'Sally. The colonel is a handsome man. He speaks well. But he's come down from the past, he's come back to us here. The colonel's come down from the man who killed them all here, the man who wrecked our village. I know for a fact he is come down from the witchfinder that Granny talked about. We mustn't have anything to do with him, Sally. We know what's in his blood.'

Sally let go my hair, and I thought she were going to see sense. I saw her moving in the dark. I could see her breath. She kneeled on the bed and I thought, it's alright, everything is alright. She understands. She realises too.

She hit me in the face with her open hand, then the back of her hand. I cried. I said, 'Sally, don't hit me again.'

She pushed my face against the bed. There were blood out of my nose onto her sheets. She put her mouth by my ear, holding my head down. She said, 'When you going to understand? Our Granny told us

253

stories. She told us things to make us feel better. All about the way we look, and the way we are.' I got my head free, but Sally got my hair again. She said, 'Why can't you see that, Evie? There's no witchfinder, there never was. There's something wrong with us. We've got a condition. We can get treated.'

She let me go.

I wiped my face with my sleeve and it were wet.

I said, 'Sally, you mustn't say that. We're like this because of our history.'

She lifted me by the back of my nightshirt and thumped me against the wall. She pulled me through the doorway, and I had splinters in my side from the floor. She put me outside the room, in the light from the kitchen stove. She stood looking down at me. Some spit were coming out of her mouth. She were breathing hard and I put my hands over my head. She said, 'What is this place?'

I said, 'It's our house, Sally.'

She put her face close to mine and lifted my chin up. It were very gentle, the way she did it. I could smell her breath, all natural. She moved her mouth against my ear. She said, 'It's a prison here. I'll leave soon.'

I said, 'No, Sally. None of us can leave.'

She smoothed my hair. I could see her hands in the stove light. She said, 'You can grow old here, Evie. You can die here if you want.'

She pushed me away, down on the kitchen floor.

I lay for a bit, watching the stove light. Blue ashes come from burning tree roots and peat. I knew the witchfinder was trying to split us in two, the way he split the village in the old days. That's when I knew I had to do it. It was for Sally's sake as much as mine. I had to do it.

The courtyard TV lamps threw light up into the streaming air and, out on the towpath at the front of the college, the workmen's arc lamps were shining through the rain. They showed that the river had broken its banks along a length of fifty metres and was moving along the other side of the sandbag barrier, making a rushing sound louder than the rain itself. Curious locals were peering over the wall, maybe wondering how long their own homes would last.

Fletcher and Mia walked back into Cambridge. Mia said,

'She knew something.'

'I think we just have to get out there, Mia.'

They walked in silence for a minute, Fletcher thinking of journey in front of them – the drive through flooded country to Norfolk. He thought, *This time tomorrow, will I have found her? Will I see her for the first time in these eighteen years? Will I save her life?*

Fletcher looked back once, then again. On the outskirts of the city, another flood was spilling across the old meadows at Coe Fen, the black surface between the trees ridged with current. They found a way around it, using a small bridge over a flooded channel.

Mia stopped, turned round and leaned her back against the railing. She slid off the hood of her slicker, some water falling against her face. She looked him in the eye. There was a pause while the rain spattered around them. She said, 'You noticed him too?'

Fletcher knew what she meant. Someone was

255

following them. A man had detached himself from the people clustered round the sandbags by the Felwell waterfront, and stayed about thirty metres back, taking the same path along the half-flooded tracks. Fletcher said,

'Is he still there?'

She looked past him. 'I can't see anyone now.'

He looked round. A single lamp was working, glinting off the water but shedding no light into the spaces under the trees. Somewhere in there was the man he'd seen: tall, in a hooded coat, with the hood over his face. He felt Mia's hand on his arm, saw her other hand point.

'There.'

She was right. Under the third tree, a figure was watching them, his hood glistening in the orange streetlamp. Mia said,

'Your police follower?'

There was something about the man, though. Was he carrying something, there at his side? Something that caught the light?

'I think–' he tried to make it out through the rain – 'I think it could be Aspen Slade. Let's get into the light, deal with him there.'

They walked quickly up the incline, into a deserted lane leading past the Fitzwilliam Museum: wet stone walls on either side and streetlamps at the top. Fletcher stopped and looked back. Down at the end of the narrow street, Coe Fen was shiny mauve, with no movement at all. The man had gone. He looked round. Mia had gone too. Where she'd been standing, there was only roof moss drifting on the pavement.

Fletcher unzipped his parka. He could still feel

the bite of the steel hook on his neck, feel the rain coursing over the stitches on his head. He listened. The gutters sounded like animals drinking. The rain was falling with a steady click. Otherwise, the little street was still. Perfectly empty. Nowhere to go. Except...

Leading off from one corner was an alley running between the backs of two college buildings. Fletcher stepped across and looked in. The space was damp and grey, the walls studded with greasy windows and heating pipes, and a series of basement doorways where a faulty lamp was flickering on and off. Halfway along, a small tree was sprouting from a crack in the brickwork, twisting its way up to the sky past an iron drainpipe with a whole section missing, gushing water. Just below it, the man in the hooded coat was walking along the space, looking left and right, hands hanging loose, the pale fingers curling in the dysfunctional light. Nothing in his hands, though. He was checking the doors along the alley, his head swivelling. Fletcher called,

'Aspen.'

The man turned sharply. Fletcher saw a shape behind him: the flared outline of Mia's slicker as she stepped out of a doorway further along, both arms raised, her hand holding what looked like a piece of broken drainpipe. By the time he'd registered that, she was behind the man, the lamp flickering around her. The pipe came down on his head.

It caught him on one side: not a full blow, but enough to put him down on the flagstones, on his knees at first, then on his side. He was still

257

conscious: locking his hands over his head and raising his knees in a defensive posture, rolling sideways with water spinning from his boots. Fletcher saw Mia get another grip on the metal pipe, moving along behind the prone man, keeping her body away from his curled legs. The man moved his arms to see his assailant, and Fletcher caught a glimpse of his face inside the hood. Not a clear glimpse, but enough to make him start running towards them when he saw Mia raising the drainpipe again. The floored man began to struggle up, his knees sliding together. Mia hit him a second time, a blow to the shoulder blades that cracked out along the alley and sent him back down on his front, his hands slapping the pavement. Fletcher shouted for her to stop. By now, looking at the man's bulk under his parka, Fletcher was sure he knew who it was.

Mia didn't stop. She put a boot on the man's neck, over the bulge of the hood, and raised the pipe sideways through the air. Around her, the lamplight was bouncing off the soaked walls, making the stunted tree cast shadows. Fletcher got to Mia and caught hold of her wrist. He saw her eyes turning around to him. They were blank, water running down her face. She dropped the pipe and it clanged away across the pavement. She said,

'He was going to kill me.'

'I don't think so.'

Fletcher knelt down and rolled the man over, pulled the hood away from his face. He was pale, with blood matting the closely cut hair on one side of his head. Fletcher was amazed that Mia had got the better of him, even with the pipe. The man seemed to feel the same way, cursing to himself repeatedly as he began to sit up, then stand, with his hands on his knees for half a minute. Fletcher said to him, 'This is Mia Tyrone. She thought you were Aspen Slade.'

The man said nothing.

Mia said, 'So who is he?'

The man spat noisily and pulled himself upright. Under his parka, he was in civilian clothes – a neat polo shirt and jeans, suede boots. He said, 'My vision. I'm hallucinating.' Then he looked around again. 'Oh, shit. There really is a tree growing out of that wall.'

It was clear that Major Jerry Lindquist of the US Air Force was going to make a full physical recovery.

I knew he would come for her. I mean, she's beautiful and any man would want her. But with him, it was something in his blood.

The first time it happened, I was upstairs at dusk. I was watching the sky over the headland. I heard a car come into the yard. I went to the other window and I looked down through the shutter. It was a Jeep, dark colour. No headlights. He was sitting with one hand on the wheel and one hand over the passenger seat, watching the house. Full uniform. He kept the engine running. Just sitting there, using up petrol. I could smell it was different from our petrol.

I saw her come out of the house and walk over to the Jeep. She was wearing trousers and an old shirt with the sleeves rolled up. Her hair was loose. That's the most beautiful I've ever seen her. She leaned on the windscreen, and I couldn't see his eyes, but I knew he'd be looking at her hands, her arms, under her shirt, everything. I knew she'd be breathing in his petrol, he'd be wondering what her hair would feel like. I could hear them talking over the engine noise, but not the words. I said, 'Don't, Sally.' And I thought she was saying no, because she looked back at the house. Then she slid in the passenger seat, just one movement. Her shirt was white, though the dusk was almost finished. Her white shape in his black car. Then he made it skid round, scared the hens. The Jeep went off somewhere, on the track beside the field. I could hear it for a minute. Then everything was quiet, even the hens too. I went down in the yard with the broom and brushed away the marks his tyres made. They were different from our tractor, because his tyres were new.

When she came back, I pretended to be asleep. My bed was in the kitchen then, since our argument. She came past me without stopping, went in the bedroom and closed the door. I heard her moving about, pouring water from the jug, washing. In a while her lamp went out. I heard the door open and her feet coming through. I felt her putting a blanket over me. I could smell her skin. I didn't know where he'd driven her, but I could smell salt in her hair too. She went back in and closed the door.

I was already thinking it through, how to do it.

Lindquist mopped some of the rain off his face. He said,

'We're all going to Alconhurst now. I got to talk to you two. Talk some sense into you.'

Fletcher said, 'We're busy right now. And the

last time I went to Alconhurst, you were going to extradite me for spying. Talk to us here.'

'I want a doctor to check my head.'

'Get a doctor here.'

'A British doctor? You want to really kill me? Not before I've told you what you need to know.'

'Which is what?'

'This thing with the old airbase.'

'We're just heading there now.'

'Nuh-uh. That won't be necessary. I can solve this whole problem for you. There's been what you might call a misunderstanding. And if you don't come to Alconhurst with me, I can guarantee you won't be going anywhere. I'll shut you both down, right here and now. So what's it to be?'

Lindquist's transport was not the massive green pick-up, but a discreet British-built Ford driven by a silent man wearing the same outfit of polo shirt and jeans. Lindquist sat with him in the front, Fletcher and Mia in the back. The man tried to drive at speed, but the roads were congested with flood defence vehicles – in the end, he pulled out and passed a whole convoy of trucks loaded with sandbags that was blocking the road east. At Alconhurst, they got through the gatehouse system in a fraction of the previous time. By 7.30 p.m. they were seated in what Lindquist described curtly as a Briefing Suite: a big, overheated room from the 1960 with varnished wood planks on the walls, framed photos of aircraft in flight and USAF personnel pursuing leisure activities. There was a long counter with stacks of magazines, a coffee dispenser and a TV. Fletcher

261

and Mia sat on plastic chairs while Lindquist went through to an adjoining room.

Fletcher put the TV on: the Channel 4 news. He kept the sound down in case there was anything worth hearing from the next room. In a minute a uniformed doctor arrived, carrying a case with a red cross on the side, and went in there. Fletcher could hear him asking about symptoms, Lindquist responding. On the screen, a computer animation showed the so-called Psychlone system revolving slowly towards Britain. In the other room, the doctor was saying,

'You got any loss of vision?'

The screen cut to a live broadcast from the east coast, people heaving sandbags under floodlights and nailing plywood over windows, then what looked like a school gym lined with camp beds.

'You got tenderness here?'

The graphic again: the jagged wheel of cloud getting darker as it span.

'Look into the light. Now down.'

The graphics changed to a cross-section of a coastline: the tide coming in, getting higher, then arrows from the weather system coming down and forcing it higher still, the sea spilling up over the graphic land, covering a cluster of graphic houses. It looked easy, but the map was showing a whole range of vulnerable locations along the eastern coast – the Hanchton area included, he noticed.

Fletcher turned the set off. He thought about leaving, just walking out and driving off. How far would he get? As far as the gatehouse? The doctor came through and left without acknowledging anyone. Then Jerry Lindquist came back in, carrying a plastic chair. He put it down in the middle of the room and sat on it back to front. His head wound had been dressed with two surgical plasters, but otherwise he looked like a friendly young priest about to open a Bible class. He looked at Mia. He said,

'Assault on a serving military officer.'

She looked back at him. 'You followed me into an alley at night. I beat the crap out of you. You want either of those facts on your service record?'

He smiled at her slowly, then winced in an exaggerated way. He laced his hands together on the chair back and looked across at Fletcher.

'You want a theory that explains everything?'

'That would be great.'

Lindquist nodded. 'It would be just fine, wouldn't it? If you could just open your eyes and see this whole thing is a misconception, nothing more.'

Fletcher said, 'Look, I have to go.'

Lindquist banged his first on the chair. 'You're going nowhere till you listen to this. Then you walk out, go where you want. Get the idea?' He ran his fingers over his skull, eyes closed, as if listening for sounds inside. Then he opened his eyes and started, his big rabbit teeth catching the light.

'So. I call my theory the "Steel Witch theory". It starts in nineteen forty-two, American airbases begin opening in this country, flying missions to Germany. The major problem with air strikes against Germany is the lack of range of the fighter escorts, you with me? The Mustangs can fly with the bombers halfway, then have to turn back because they don't have the fuel to make it to the target. The bombers get chewed up by German fighters, it's a big problem. Then someone has the idea of fitting external fuel tanks under the fighters' wings.'

'Teardrop tanks,' Fletcher said. 'Use up the fuel, jettison them.'

'Correct. A simple but revolutionary innovation: doubles the fighter's range. A small team of Mustang aircraft is fitted with the prototype teardrop tanks and stationed at an isolated airbase in Norfolk, England. Their task is to evaluate the tanks – do they work, do they affect the plane's stability, so on and so on. The task is rapidly completed and the teardrop tanks put into use. OK so far?'

Mia said, 'So why all the fuss? Aspen Slade is killing people over this?'

'Well, this is exactly the damn issue. Due to the isolated nature of the base, the secret nature of the project, rumours have developed in the years since then. These are false rumours, entirely without foundation.'

'What rumours?'

'You know damn well.' Lindquist raised his voice, then winced. He said more softly, 'You know damn well. For one thing, the land for the base was supplied by Felwell College, Cambridge. Not a surprise, because all these colleges own huge chunks of land, right? I read somewhere you can walk from the east to the west coast in this country and always be on land owned by King's College – that true?'

'I heard that's north to south.'

'Maybe it's diagonal,' Mia said.

'Whatever,' Lindquist waved it away, 'Felwell happened to own the land, Felwell with the atom-splitting thing, so people perceive an agenda there. Plus Felwell never explained where all their hadesium went, so people whisper about that too, like there's a connection.' He laughed. 'Then, and I've got to be honest, things on the base were not well managed. The commander, some New England rich kid, the service used to be full of them. He let things go lax, even got involved with a local woman. What's the phrase you British use? Something "native"?'

'He went native?'

'Went native. Like the bald guy in *Apocalypse Now*. This man painted Nose Art pictures of local witches or something on his planes. It was a mess. Because of that, too, rumours spread after the war, this phrase "Steel Witches", people saying it's a code name for some kind of weapon. Like, you've got this secret code word, you're going to paint it on your fucking plane. Then there's some story about the runway, why was it made of concrete, were they expecting a Flying Fortress, I don't know what else. So stories start to spread that something massive was being planned there.'

Fletcher said, 'Anything you want to tell me about the base itself? Why isn't it recorded on any maps?'

Lindquist shrugged. 'That's not unusual. I could mention half-a-dozen US facilities in this country that opened up and closed down without ever being on any maps. And it was the war, come on.'

'Why were the runways ploughed up?'

'Come *on*. Stop seeing conspiracy. It was a small-scale airbase for light aircraft. They were using a minimal concrete layer, only meant to last a couple of years. The grass just grew up through it. The runways fell to pieces, OK?'

'So why were the aircraft records erased?'

Lindquist laughed, then winced again. 'What have you been doing – *browsing the Internet?* Looking at websites? That is so frigging superficial. You're talking records from sixty-five years ago. The fact is, it would take me *months* to find certain details about who did what in the war, what plane went where. And I work here.'

Mia said, 'Right. So all these things together – you've got the Felwell land, the radioactive stuff, this secret base with a crappy commander, the Nose Art, the runways – they all just add up to false rumours. About what, exactly?'

'This is what upsets me. You see, if you put all this together, and if you're of a suspicious and hostile mindset, you could start to spread a rumour about an unusual kind of bomb.'

Fletcher said, 'I think the term is "dirty bomb".'

Lindquist slammed his hand on the chair back. 'Do not use that phrase. Do not use it. That's a weapon of terrorists, evil men, wrongdoers of all sorts. You've seen the news, how high profile the dirty bomb thing is. We are actively hunting down right now people who are planning such a thing. We must not give them a propaganda tool,

266

something they can throw back at us, say like, you were planning it, getting it ready, but you kept it secret all these years.' He smoothed his head again, closing his eyes at the thought. 'That would be intensely regrettable. People like you – Fletcher, Tyrone – you're kind of credible, articulate, whatever. You start spreading this story, it makes us look bad at a very sensitive time. You have to get that into your head.'

'Like Aspen Slade has got it into his head?'

Lindquist massaged the chair back. 'Oh, Aspen Slade. I checked his file, by the way. He grew up on US airbases, following his parents around. Problems right from a young age. Instability, irrational behaviour. When they were based at Mannheim, in Germany, there was an allegation he assaulted a woman, held her head down in a river. He was nine years old, for God's sake...

When they were posted here, Alconhurst, his behaviour became violent, he ended up in a secure school back in the States. You know, when he left, he repeatedly applied to join the USAF. We repeatedly rejected him. Kept asking for a chance to prove himself, as if we'd give him that. I did some psychology training in officer class; I think I can see what's going on here. I think in his disturbed mind he's got this all twisted up. He knows how that Daisy Seager girl was cooking up some kind of story, his old man Nathan probably told him. He gets it into his head that here's his chance to do us a favour, prove himself, show us how good he is. How he can suppress this rumour – but in his own way. He entered this country on a tourist visa in January, seems to have gone

267

underground, blended right in with the locals. He's a serious fucking embarrassment.'

'Is he?' Fletcher said. 'He thinks there's a document. Some kind of testimony that actually *proves* what happened on that airbase. He's doing a good job so far of tracking down people who know about this. It's almost as if–' and now it came to Fletcher for the first time – 'as if he's working for *you*, really. Is he working for you?'

Lindquist tried to laugh, holding his head. 'A violent and disturbed man like that, working for us? Come on.'

A plane landed outside – two cones of red fire through the rainy glass, making the window rattle. Lindquist waited for the noise to stop. Then he said,

'No, Aspen Slade is not working for us. He is a serious fucking problem for us all and needs to be contained. You two people could help us with that. Or you could remain uninvolved, pursuing your own mistaken illusions, spreading rumours that only help our enemies. I don't think I need to recap on the consequences for you both if you choose not to support us. Fletcher, you face extradition proceedings for your breach of perimeter security. Tyrone, you face … well. Your employment prospects are not, shall we say, bright.' He paused and smoothed his skull again. 'But you can both put that behind you. Clean sheet of paper, that's a useful thing to have.'

'So what do you suggest, Lindquist?'

'I got a proposal.'

Lindquist stayed on his back-to-front chair in the middle of the room, while he outlined his idea. It was a pretty unimaginative idea: that would be the military influence, Fletcher decided. It was also quite unworkable – that was probably the psychology training coming through. Fletcher and Mia listened to the whole thing, then Fletcher asked a couple of questions. Lindquist explained fully, reiterated the benefits. Mia stayed silent. They walked out into the rain. The driver in the jeans and polo shirt pulled right up to the doorway in his unmarked car and drove them back to Cambridge. The wipers smeared away the view of the flood defence trucks still manoeuvring around the city. Nobody spoke.

I used to wonder where he went with her.

On days when the planes hadn't flown, Sally left the fields early and went in the wash house. When I came back, I heard her singing in her throat and I knew she was wringing out her hair. Then I used to stand by the window upstairs until I heard the Jeep. This was July, still light till late. The first few times, I stood there and watched it get dark. Later on, when she came home, she would pass me in my bed in the kitchen. I could smell the sea on her. Next day, there was always sand in the washhouse drain. After a while, I realised where they went.

One day, I left the fields early, myself. I had an idea where to go. I walked two hours, over the fields, going towards the clear sky over the headland. Beyond the woods, a soldier stopped me, but he let me go on. I looked back, and he was watching me.

There's a place where the headland dips in a ravine like a road with steep sides. The walls are slopes of pebbles, grown with gorse and hawthorn. The sea comes in twice a day and there's a little spread of beach at the end, shingle with a bit of sand. You won't find it unless you know it's there.

I used to go there sometimes with Sally, when we were growing up. It was the one place we could take our dresses off and nobody see us, our bodies.

It was just before dusk when I got there. I lay down on top of one of the dunes with my face against the stones. The sea was grey. The breeze was flicking white spit off the waves on the little beach. In a while, I heard an engine on the headland road. I kept my head down, but I could see the Jeep coming down between the walls of pebbles. When it was too narrow, they got out and walked. She laughed when she slipped. He didn't say anything. I saw him stop and cup his hand around his lighter flame, then cigar smoke went blowing back through the ravine. I heard them pass by right underneath me. There was clicking while they trod on the pebbles, then quiet. I looked over the edge of the pebbles, the other side. It were getting to be dusk, and the tide was coming in. There was something out in the sea I noticed, but didn't know what it could be. I was watching the beach, anyway.

They were down there, on the sand. He was undressing her, the long shirt and her skirt all spread out. He still had his uniform on. I saw the red of his cigar while he moved his fingers around her. Her shape on the beach, the dark shapes on her lovely body all open to the air. He was taking his time, looking at her. He said something, but I didn't hear what. I saw her bare legs moving up around him, grabbing him. Her legs were white like the claws you find in the pebbles. I saw the light of his cigar spinning away, then his jacket coming off. I turned my head

270

away and looked at the sea. There was something out there, in the shallows. There were puffs of water breaking the surface, and a big shape moving. I heard Sally down on the beach calling out, saying his name. Then the shape came closer, and I saw it was a whale. It made a rushing sound when it blew water. It were scared; I think I saw its eye rolling at me. For a bit I listened to the whale. The breeze was blowing spray, and the pebbles were wet. I held my hair to stop it blowing out. I looked over the edge again, between the stones. I saw my Sally's face.

Mia Tyrone sat in the dark, just looking at her apartment. There were clouds moving in the sky outside, moonlight shining on the glass buildings of the Botanical Gardens, the glow coming through the rain on her windows, streaking the ceiling.

She was sitting on the floor in one corner, her knees drawn up against herself. On the carpet there was a hand-delivered letter from the Bellman Foundation. It threatened her with legal proceedings if she discussed any aspect of her Bellman service with anyone outside the company. It also confirmed the annulment of her visa and tenancy. Next to it was a bottle of vodka with a third gone, some lime slices and a tray of ice. She pressed the shot glass against her cheek.

She couldn't believe it. All the old guys with crew cuts and Harleys who looked down her blouse for a year and brushed up against her in the lift. They were going to beat her in the end, when she was so close to finding out, to proving something that would make them squirm. The

Bellman-Felwell dirty bomb, their nasty little secret.

How much would Bellman hate that, she thought as she filled her glass and dropped in another lime. Bellman, the guardian of the US military aviation industry. Imagine them opening a newspaper, seeing photos of the airbase itself, photos she could take. She could imagine them writhing behind their big windows with the view of the ornamental lake.

Would they beat her now?

She leaned her cheek on her knees, thinking back over the proposal Lindquist made in the overheated room at Alconhurst. The proposal was for Fletcher to leave everything to the USAF. The Air Force had a team of people, Lindquist said. They were counsellors, a special type of counsellor. They could talk Aspen's language, understand his problems. They were on their way to Norfolk tomorrow to bring him under control, restrain him in the appropriate manner. Any possible threat that Aspen Slade posed to British society would be neutralised. In return, Mia and Fletcher would drop their interest in the old airbase, and their immediate prospects would be improved as far as possible.

As far as possible. Yeah, right.

What amazed her was that Tom Fletcher had thought about the idea, then nodded and shaken hands on the arrangement. Tom Fletcher, with his local knowledge and this thing he had driving him, finding his mother. He just shook hands on it and got in the car. And, just like that, the chance of justifying herself had slipped away.

Unless she went up there on her own? How – in a frigging taxi?

She sat with her hands around her legs, thinking. It was a posture she liked, her limbs blocking the world away from her body. Then her phone rang, and the screen shed its light around her as she picked it up, looked at the caller.

The voice said, 'Want to buy a theory?'

She smiled. 'Tom. Would this be the Steel Witch theory?'

'It's very plausible.'

'Though it leaves a few things out, doesn't it?' She got to her feet and walked across the darkened room to the window. 'Such as, why would Aspen Slade be so obsessed with suppressing a nonexistent story? Strange way to prove himself.'

'Or why would the USAF be so keen to suppress Aspen?'

She looked at the Botanical Gardens through the base of her glass and the rain, swallowing. 'But you, Fletcher, said *yes* to them. You agreed to stay here in Cambridge, let them find Aspen.'

'Yes, because on balance I think Major Lindquist's theory is perfectly reasonable. I have to go now.' She shook her head, made a bitter little laugh. Then he said, 'Hey, Mia, what kind of food do you like?'

She thought. 'I like Polish food.'

'So do I. The way they do vegetables. Really succulent.'

'Uh-huh. Well, goodbye, Tom.'

'About three, Mia.'

'Bye.'

That night, Sally came home late. I pretended to be asleep, again. She filled a bowl in the kitchen; walked past me without stopping. I heard her washing in our bedroom. I heard her stretch out in the bed, move around. Then quiet. I went into the hall and felt along the floorboards. I found the knot hole and I lifted the plank up. I felt the old shotgun under there. I ran my hands along it a few times. There were oil on it and I sniffed it off my fingers. I lifted it out and felt it in my hands. It balanced nice, an old duck shooter from Granny's time, before I was born. I broke it open and felt the cartridges in the breech. That's all the cartridges we had, just them two. They were snug in the dark there, side by side. Just like real sisters should be.

'You can't possibly do this, Tom Fletcher.'

'My mother's there.'

'You don't know that.'

He said, 'I can feel it. I can feel she's there.'

On the grainy screen of Fletcher's anonymous phone, Cathleen was outlined against the sky of a hotel balcony, in a swimsuit at 2 a.m., a breeze moving her coppery hair in the light of a bulk-head lamp. Either the lamp was flickering, or there were flashes of lightning around her. Her hair looked slightly wet. Fletcher thought, if I was there now. I would twist it in my fingers. He said, 'You've been swimming.'

'Oh, the detective. This is Crete, people go swimming.' Flashes of light in the sky. 'You're perverting the course of justice by not disclosing what you know. Tell the police everything. Let them take care of this Aspen Slade, this lunatic.'

'I can't trust them to do it. Only I can do it.'

'On your own?' A second's silence. 'Don't tell me. Don't tell me Mia's going with you.'

'She needs to be there too.'

'Brilliant. Just phone the police. Don't risk everything we've planned for.'

He didn't reply for a few seconds, watching her face on the screen. There was a brief shadow across the balcony, and for a moment he thought there was somebody in her room.

He said, 'I'm going, Cathleen. I have to save my mother's life.'

Fletcher watched the street. It was hard to see much through the rain, with the shop lights off. The dark walls of the buildings led down to a grey liquid surface, the gutters spilling out of control. Right opposite was a souvenir shop, the darkened windows full of little teddy bears on punts and King's College chapels inside snowstorm paperweights. Tonight, the doorway concealed a man in a nylon storm jacket, visible only when he moved and the wet plastic caught the light from the streetlamp further down.

That could be a real homeless man thinking things over, or a shop owner keeping a concerned eye on his stock. Could be.

Fletcher checked his rucksack. Some warm clothes, binoculars, an old battery radio, compass, torch. He lifted his parka off the radiator, pulled it on, breathing its canvas smell. In the chest pocket, the photo of his mother on the pathway began curving over his heart.

In the street outside, he closed the stairwell

entrance, lit only by the constellation of doorbell bulbs. He waited half a minute, his hood down, then stepped out onto the pavement. The rain hit him, and the sound of the drainpipes too. The whole street was awash – oil stains rippling like angel fish in the dark.

The man in the doorway opposite turned and straightened up, his face invisible under the plastic hood. Fletcher saw him make a movement inside his jacket – reaching for a radio, or scratching a bite?

Fletcher hit him hard enough to smack the man's head back against the glass door, fracturing three sudden lines behind his darkened face that echoed for a second until the intruder siren came on. The man slumped down in a sitting posture, and something clattered out onto the floor. Fletcher moved it into the streetlight with his foot. A police Airwave radio set. Not something that a homeless guy would normally possess.

Fletcher looked back, once. No movement, just a strobe light flicking its tongue around the street.

Mia Tyrone shifted the backpack over her arm and tried the door of the Succulent House. It was locked with some bizarre English system: a keyhole off a cathedral, brass cantilevers straight off the *Titanic*. She cleared the water off the glass and shone her pocket torch inside: mist, and cactus spines all swarming with hard-shelled bugs.

Jesus. When this is over, I'm going home.

A blast of rain hit her, smacking off the glass.

She wrapped her slicker round herself and waited. Three a.m. – if that really was what Tom Fletcher had meant.

When I've nailed Bellman, I'm going home. I'll be the girl who got the big story, beat the weird old guys. I'm going to move into that room over the garage. There's a double bed and space for a sitting room, the little bathroom they put in. I'll be something, I'll be some kind of reporter.

She jumped, shone her torch round. Tom Fletcher came out from under the trees. He had his hood down, water running over his face. She wanted to put her arms around him for a second. Over the sound of the wind in the trees, he said, 'Coming to Norfolk?'

'I already packed a bag.'

His car was parked around the corner, and they slammed themselves inside it, rain banging on the roof. She said,

'If we leave now, we'll be there in a couple of hours, right?'

He turned to her, his hand on the starter. 'The police will recognise this car. Anyway, it won't make it onto an airbase – I tried last night, got stuck. I know where we can change it for something different, but that means waiting for daybreak. After that, there's someone I need to meet. Then we'll go.'

Beyond the trees, blue police lights flashed, and the sound of a siren came over the rain on the car roof. She said, 'Daybreak is what, three hours?'

He nodded.

She said, 'I still want evidence.'

'Let's just sit tight.'

Rain banging on the roof.

She said, 'You know, all along Aspen Slade has been looking for something, some testimony of what happened at the airbase.'

'We won't find that now. Daisy hid it from him, that's what makes him angry. He killed her, he killed Charlie Fenner trying to find it. At the aviation museum, Aspen said to me that Daisy had hidden it in the last place on earth anyone would look, something like that. It could be anywhere.'

'The last place on earth?'

Water coursing over the windows, the street-lamps flickering on and off.

She said, 'Think, Tom. Of all the places Daisy could have hidden it. Of all the people she came into contact with. Who would be the last person on earth you would expect to have it?'

She watched him thinking. His stitches were blackening, he was heavily stubbled, he smelled of soap and the damp fur on his parka hood. Typical English guy.

Suddenly he looked at his watch, started the car. He said, 'There was someone who took a great interest in Daisy. I remember at the time, I was in two minds about him.'

'Where's he going to be now?'

'I think he'll be in his caravan.'

I waited for a day when I thought he would come for her. There was a morning, early August, which was warm and bright. It were silent too, no planes. In the morning, I felled a broken tree for the winter. Sally were in the beet field. Early afternoon I pulled the logs back on the tractor. Sally were in the kitchen by then. She looked tired, staring out of the window. I said, 'I'll make you a cup of tea.' She nodded. I made her tea in the old kettle on the stove. I put in half a spoon of sugar, almost the last of the ration. I put in something else too: stuff Granny told us about. I put in seeds from last year's poppies, all ground into powder. The same stuff the witchfinder's men gave to Gussie Salter before they hanged her. I didn't put in a lot, because that gives you visions, Granny always said. Gives you visions or gives you twins, she used to say, always winking at us. But just a little makes you sleepy, wanting your bed. I tasted it. Hot and bitter. I put in all the sugar we had, and put it in front of her. I talked to her about the tree felling, watching her. She put her head on her arms. In the end, she climbed on my bed there in the kitchen and stretched out. I took her boots off and put a blanket over her. I waited till the evening, watching over her. Then I went out, closed the front door, put a note on it. The note said, *Already there.* I made it like her writing, though I doubt he'd ever seen it. Then I started walking.

I had on a duffel coat and trousers, my farm boots. The wind were coming up, blowing the grass flat, blowing out the willow trees along the track. When I got to the headland, the sun was near going down. Big red clouds. The ravine was still clear to see, the beach at the end of it. I could see there were gulls flying circles. I heard them calling, excited. There was something down there they liked.

I walked along the ravine. About halfway, it hit me. The smell hit me. Then I guessed what there was that the gulls wanted. Going further, I could see the shape of it. It was a beached whale, a small one, dead for a *few days. I gagged a bit, but I got to the end. I made myself ready, the way I'd planned. Then I stood on the beach, near the whale, looking at the sea. The tide was out and there were pools in the sand beyond the shingle. The whale was leaking dark stuff into them.*

I had the hood of my duffel coat up.

The way to Peterborough was almost deserted, scattered with collapsed road signs and fallen trees – a few sliced and cleared by county engineers, most still rearing up at jagged angles through the rain.

The caravan park was surrounded by fields that must have flooded since Fletcher's last visit – water stretching away from the car's lights, bobbing with debris. At the gates, the Alsatian's eyes glinted opal, following the Audi's tyres slithering through the mud, then went back to watching a family with torches heaving some stuff into a van: pots and pans, a pram. Maybe they were the last people to leave, because all the other caravans were closed and unlit. He pulled up outside the second one in the third row.

It was pretty much as Fletcher had left it. The curtains were still drawn, and the window where he'd slipped Wayne's keys back in was still ajar. One tyre had gone flat, but nothing else had changed.

He left the car lights on.

The door was locked. When they banged on it, the noise resounded from inside, but there was no answer. Fletcher pushed the window open, and through the stained curtains his torch picked out the microwave, part of the bed, a few beer cans. Nothing else, except a heavy stale odour that Fletcher recognised from his days in the police.

The door gave way on the second kick, the lock clattering on the floor inside. The smell was intense. He stood on the threshold, shining the torch around. Foil strips of Clozapine scattered on the counter, the cupboards emptied out onto the table. He stepped inside. In front of him, a shelf had been left untouched – it held a directory of support services, and a single Christmas card.

In the circle of light, Wayne was stretched out on the floor by the bed, face up, judging by the position of his hands and feet, though it was hard to see his head. His folding table had been ripped from the wall and placed on top of him. On top of that, a large number of plastic sacks of gravel had been arranged in a pyramid. Maybe twelve sacks, Fletcher guessed. There were some deep scratches on the floor which he didn't remember from last time – maybe Wayne's final gestures.

Fletcher felt the skin of his hand – it was fridge cold.

He heard Mia breathing next to him. She said, 'What the hell happened to him?'

'It looks like Aspen's way of trying to get him to talk.'

'How long's he been dead?'

'More than a day.' He looked at her. 'First dead body you've seen?'

'The third.' He looked at her. 'A car smash near my house when I was sixteen. Two people dead.'

'Have you touched anything?'

'No.'

'Let's both keep it that way.'

On the shelf, the lone Christmas card showed two rabbits pulling a laughing snowman on a sleigh. Fletcher leaned his head to read what was written inside.

To Wayne from Mum and Dad. Please keep in touch more.

'He crushed Wayne to death, probably slowly. He knew Wayne was keeping something.'

'Think Wayne gave it up?'

'There just aren't many places to hide something in here.'

'You've been here before. Anything different about it? Tom?'

Fletcher was making for the door.

The space below the caravan was fetid and earthy, the car head-lamps showing bare soil punctured by worm casts. There were a few drinks bottles, a dead mouse. If the flood came, Fletcher thought as he put his gloves on, it would sweep all this clean and lift the caravan away like a boat. Crouching beside the wheel with the flat tyre, he put his hands around the back of it.

'You said, don't touch anything,' Mia reminded him. She was kneeling beside him, watching.

'This is the only thing different about the caravan.'

He ran his gloved fingers over the raised printing on the tyre, feeling the dirt crumble off, until he found what he expected. A long slit with sharp edges, and shreds of the canvas lining brushing his wrist as he probed it. He put a hand inside, and felt nothing at first. Then, jammed against the upper curve, a cylinder shape. He pulled it free and out of the tyre.

They held it in the headlights. It contained a folded wad of papers, bound with string. The light made them look pure white, but they were thin enough to let words be seen through from the other side – made by an old typewriter: black ink; uneven letters almost punching through in places.

They parked ten miles away on a slight rise, screened by ragged hawthorns. The rain began to slacken off to just a few drops on the windows, and the sky was moving with grey clouds. In the dark landscape, blue emergency lights sparkled in places.

Fletcher watched Mia unscrew the jar lid, frowning in concentration. She carefully pulled out the sheets. Stuck to the first one a modern Post-it note, new-looking, with a scribbled note in biro:

Gregory Tilney – The Tower – near Hanchton

Fletcher said, 'Daisy's handwriting? It looks recent.'

Mia spread the other pages on the dashboard under the roof light. They read them together, as the sky grew lighter behind the trees.

When the wind dropped, I heard the Jeep on the track behind me. The engine revved up and it started moving down the ravine and rattling the pebbles around. Then it stopped. I couldn't hear him, but I knew he was walking towards me I heard him shout, 'Sally.'

I put the hood of my duffel coat up. I stood looking out past the whale, to the sea. The light was going quick and the gulls were lifting up and moving off. I heard him on the pebbles right behind. He shouted,

'Damn, Sally, what's that smell? Let's get out of here.'

I just stood looking at the water. I knew he were trying to light a cigar, I could hear his lighter clicking. I turned round and looked at him. He was handsome. His uniform was clean and pressed. He was smiling, trying to see under my hood.

'Sally?'

I said, 'I know who you are.'

He said, 'And you know what I'm going to do with you, honey, when we get off this stinking beach. Come on, let's get in the back of the Jeep, I'll put that smile on your face.'

The gulls were calling, so I had to almost shout.

'I've been waiting for you all my life.'

He said, 'And now I'm here.' Still trying to see me.

I said, 'I know what you did to us back then. Granny told me.'

He started to laugh, but then he stopped. 'Sally, this isn't funny.'

I let my hood fall back.

'Oh Christ,' he said.

Because I undid the coat buttons too and let the wind blow it open. I had nothing on underneath, except the shotgun. I saw him staring at my body, the marks, for half a minute, seeing everything with his witchfinder's eyes. Then he looked at the gun and laughed.

He put his cigar back in his mouth and managed to light it, and he looked at the tip. He was smiling and shaking his head.

He said, 'What do you want, honey? Want a taste of what your sister likes? Let me tell you what she does for me.'

I pointed the gun at him.

'Fuck you doing?' he said.

'Three hundred years. Now you've come back to torture us again.'

'What are you talking about?'

'You won't split us up. We're the last of the village. We can't leave here.'

'Put the gun down, you stupid bitch.'

I didn't get it right. In fact I almost missed him. The gun jerked when I fired the first barrel and I hit his right side, above the waist. I saw a bit of his tunic fly off. He grunted and his body jerked, then he went down on his knees, quite slow, with his hand over the hole. He didn't say anything, he just made that one sound. I put the second barrel at him and tried to shoot, but it jammed. I opened the breech to clear it, but he started to get up. I took the live cartridge out and dropped it. I closed the gun up and held it by the barrel. He was almost on his feet. I swung it at him, I hit him with the stock, over the eye. He stayed standing, but there was blood down his face, pouring on his clean shirt. His cigar was on the pebbles. He moved away from me, along the sand. I followed him, till he came to the whale.

The smell were like drains, meat and fish. Its skin was grey, with holes the gulls had ripped in. The holes were red round the edges, not blood but light coming off the clouds.

He puked a little blood. He was holding his side, he was shaky and breathing bad. He rested back against the whale. He looked at me. I had the sunset behind

285

me, but he could see me. He said,

'You stupid whore. We'll kill you for this. We have things you've never heard of.'

I laughed then. My coat was still open and the sea wind was all over my body. I was excited, I don't mind saying that.

I said, 'You're paying for everything now. You understand that?'

He said, 'You people are sick. You've been here for fucking centuries, breeding with each other.'

I said, 'Welcome back, witchfinder.'

I hit him with the gun butt again, on the side of his head. It made a real echo, going back down the ravine. I hit him so hard the wood snapped, and the stock flew right off onto the sand. He went down again on his side, trying to get under the whale, putting his hands up, trying to pull the gun out of my hands. Where the wood had come off, there was a metal thing like a spike, and I hit him with that in the face again. It stuck there, in his face. I think it was under his jaw bone, because his mouth came open and some teeth came out on the sand. He made a noise that was quite like the whale blowing water. I had to put my foot on his shoulder and work the metal loose. It was like pulling a spade out of wet clay. His hands were flapping, all hitting at my legs. I think that was without his mind working them, because his eyes were closed and he wasn't saying anything. But his body kept going. He got his fingers up under my thigh, grabbing for me, digging in. I still got the marks today, and I will have them till the day they hang me. He touched me right between my legs, which Granny always said men will do if they get a chance, and she was right. Of course, he couldn't smile. I'd already broke his mouth off. But his hands were hot and wet, feeling me inside. For a second I thought his body got me, even when his brain was gone, but I got the gun loose and let him have it again. Down over my head, like chopping the felled tree. His hand fell off me. I kept on going. Most times I swung, I got him. The other times, I hit the whale. The sound was quite the same. This went on for a few minutes, I think, with the sun going down.

When I finished, I was breathing hard. The wind was blowing sweat off me, blowing out my hair. It was getting dark, but I could see he was a mess. The stuff inside his head had come out and there were bits of the whale too, all over the sand, over me and my coat. Stuff was dripping out of my hair too – that was him as well, his witchfinder's brain coming out in the wind.

I never planned to do what I did next, but suddenly I really wanted to. I dropped the gun and I lay down on the sand next to him. I closed my eyes for a minute and got my breath back, listening to the tide. I thought, maybe Sally does it like this – afterwards, lying next to him. I rolled over and kissed him, what was left of him.

Then I jumped up.

First thing I did was take my coat off and weight it with pebbles and walk down to the water. The tide were still out, but I knew by morning it would be in, washing the beach down, and the gulls would be back on the whale. I waded in, just up to my knees because of the currents. I threw my coat as far out as I could. I heard it go under. Then I squatted in the water and washed myself all over. I didn't know water could be that cold. North Sea, August, rubbing it all over me, in my hair too. Then I ran back to the beach and dried *myself on my shirt and put my jersey on, my other clothes too. I were shaking with cold by then, teeth chattering. I had to be fast, because the army patrols along the headland. I felt around and picked up the bits of the gun, the cartridge. I couldn't find his cigar or teeth, but the tide was going to have them anyway. I went back to the Jeep and found a tarpaulin and a raincoat. I wrapped him in that, like a big carpet, with the bits and pieces. I dragged him back to the Jeep, which took time. Years of working the farm helped, though. I put him in the back of the Jeep – where he wanted to get in with Sally. I laughed at that. I put the canvas hood up. No lights on the Jeep, just the moon coming up.*

I really liked the Jeep, the way it drove, though the wheel was on the wrong side. The roads were empty, but there were some army trucks in places. I drove him back to the farm; no trucks near there. All the windows of our house were dark still. I went past, down to the Deeping. I reversed the Jeep up to the edge of the water. I could hear the back tyres pushing the reeds, breaking them down. The moths came out, spinning around. I stopped and put down the canvas, and stood up in the Jeep. I climbed over and rolled him out of the back. He made a splash, quite a low noise. I said a few words, like 'This is where you finish, witchfinder. Hopkins, Harpkin, whatever you call yourself.'

I waited till the moon showed the ripples had all gone. I spat, one last ripple. Then I put the canvas up and drove the Jeep back to a place on the coast where there are cliffs. Once I passed a patrol, and I thought of cutting the engine and letting it coast, then I thought the opposite was better, and I revved the Jeep up and screeched round a corner so they could see I was a real Yank. They didn't follow me. I parked it on a headland and walked back across the fields, keeping close to the hedges. That took two hours. I got home after midnight.

That's what I did. Me, Evie Dunton, on August the third 1943. Nobody else were in it, nobody put me up to it. That's why you, Mr Tilney, had to listen and write everything down. So you know the reasons, that he deserved what happened. You've helped us, you've looked after us. You know the rest already, the big secret.

When I got home? Well, I locked the door, I bolted it. Sally were still sleeping in my bed. I got in, under the blankets. She stirred a bit. I put my arms around her, pulled her close, just the way. it should be. She said, 'God, Evie, I'm having dreams I'm having visions.'

Too much poppy seed in the tea. Gives you visions or gives you twins, Granny said. and Granny was always right.

Fletcher stood outside the car, watching the eastern sky through the trees. It was getting lighter, showing a wide belly of cloud touched with red underneath. Beside him, Mia twisted her hair into a band, holding it down against a breeze bringing a few last raindrops out of the dawn. She snapped the band, turned her face to him. She said,

'Well, it proves what happened.'

'Does it?'

'Absolutely. It gives their names, it shows the airbase really existed. You can match it with the place we saw on the map – Hanchton, then the heath, the airbase, the pool of water, their old house which is just an outline in the ground now. The old Wychland place.'

He said, 'What did she mean at the end, "the big secret"? There's no mention of radiation weapons.'

'These people never heard of radiation. She was describing what she saw – a group of planes at a secret base, training to use drop tanks, obviously getting ready for something. There's the local tragedy of her killing the Colonel Harpkin guy, OK, but that doesn't change what she saw. See what it means?' She held out the modern Post-it note. 'This person she's talking to in the testimony, Mr Tilney. Says he looked after them. Could be he's still there, near Hanchton. Daisy Seager found him. He's the final piece of proof.'

'Living in a tower? What does that mean?'

'Let's go up there and find him.'

'I'm going up there to save my mother's life. That's what matters to me. You notice something about the way Aspen killed those people? Daisy was drowned, Charlie Fenner was hung, Wayne was crushed. That's how the witchfinder did it in the testimony. Aspen must be imitating something he's heard about; it has some kind of significance for him. He's insane.'

A bird started singing. The air was suddenly warm, like spring, and mist was starting to rise from the sodden ground.

'Come on. Let's go.'

He thought of the people who would try to stop him getting to the old airbase. The Cambridge police, whose existing inquiry into Daisy Seager would surely be collapsing now. They wanted him for perverting the course of justice and assault on a police officer. Then the USAF, with their extradition lawyers ready, and maybe even Lindquist's team of specialist counsellors.

They locked the testimony in a case in the boot, got in the car and started up. In the east, where they were going, the clouds were bruised and blood-coloured, burning from inside with a hidden light, and swelling.

Friday Morning

First, they had to change the car. The Audi was a fine vehicle, but Lindquist and Franks had taken a good look at it – and anyway, it wasn't the right car to take into Norfolk. Not with the way the weather news was shaping up.

The radio commentators were explaining breathlessly that the rivers and drains running across Cambridgeshire – towards Norfolk and the sea – were at bursting point One more day of rain would breach them, overwhelming the system of sluices and pumps that kept the low country of East Anglia dry. Added to that would be the weather system building over the North Sea that was forecast to hit land around dawn on Saturday. The way they described it, the thing deserved the media nickname of Psychlone: a barrage of devastating winds, then a complete drop in pressure bringing heavy banks of mist inland off the sea.

He turned the news off when they got to a used-car dealership he knew outside the city, on the edge of a reservoir where the mauve water was flecked with crests. He trusted the staff there to keep the Audi parked for a while, away from the attention of the police.

They took a look around. Only one 4 x 4 was left on sale: a greasy Land Rover with bald tyres.

A Polish kid was vacuuming a saloon in the

yard. Fletcher pointed to the Land Rover, said, '*Dobry samochód?* This car any good?'

The boy shook his head. '*Nie.* I clean the oil from under it every night.' He turned the vacuum off, glanced at Mia. 'You want something to last? Not pretty, but crazy tough.'

He took them round to the mechanics' yard.

Mia said, 'What the hell is that?'

The kid had found them a 1990 Niva Cossack, an ugly Russian-designed Jeep, in a shade of cream the Soviets must have considered the height of taste. No aircon, no CD. Just a long-wave radio, and vinyl seats, and a huge metal tow chain stowed in the back.

Mia said, 'Will this thing make it?'

'I think so.' He looked it over – dented in places, but well-maintained. 'Two years ago, before I left the police, I got to know a man from the city where they built these.'

'Yeah? What was he like?'

'Well, he wasn't pretty. But he was crazy tough.'

At 8.30 a.m., when the salesmen turned up, Fletcher paid cash. They slung their bags on top of the chain in the back and filled it with fuel.

Mia said, 'I'll drive.'

'On the left?'

'I'll get used to it. Last night, you said that after we change the car, there's still one more person you need to meet. So let's go.'

He gave her directions, through villages where groups of army trucks were assembling, some of them towing generator pumps and trailers of sandbags, troops marking out a helicopter landing site. Then they left that behind and drove

293

out into the empty farmland.

In a while, he pointed out a farm track, and Mia rolled the Cossack along it to an isolated steel barn on the edge of a field where a new crop was breaking the surface.

She turned the engine off and they waited. The soil in the field was almost black, the tufts shivering in the breeze, running in lines into the distance. He felt her settle back in the seat, glanced over and saw her with her eyes closed, her strong face relaxed.

She opened her eyes on him. 'Someone's here.'

A black BMW off-roader came level with them and paused. Then it curved round and reversed into the entrance of the barn, just inside the sliding doors. Tinted windows, no occupants visible. Fletcher and Mia climbed down and walked over to it. The wind was blowing drops of water up off the land, blowing Mia's hair out.

Fletcher said, 'Mia, meet Rupe.'

She nodded in greeting.

Rupe nodded back. He said, 'At your service.'

He was a tall man, mid-twenties. A waxed jacket, corduroys and slip-on boots. Tight black gloves.

Rupert Darcy was the reason Fletcher had a parking space in All Saints' College. He had the pallor, the deep eyes and the pouting lips that confirmed his family's claim to descent from Norman aristocracy. Rupe hadn't followed his brothers, though, into banking or the diplomatic service. When Fletcher – in his police days – rescued him from a group of animal rights kidnappers incensed at All Saints' support for a new rat-and-rabbit lab, the boy had formed his own independent business idea.

Fletcher said, 'What have you got for us, Rupe?'

Rupe opened the tailgate. He pulled a large carton to the edge and opened it. He flexed his gloved fingers before removing the contents. They were two polystyrene blocks, one of which he opened, spinning the lid in his hand and stepping back. Fletcher reached in and pulled out the object inside.

Rupe began his sales talk, in his expensive accent. 'HS 2000, Croatian export. No training needed. Just point and squeeze.'

In Britain, handguns are illegal but widely available. Rupert Darcy had found his niche selling the products of East European arms factories to county society – the gentry afraid of the prowlers and the kids from the towns. *Why should they have guns, and not us?* Now he lit a cigarette, and Fletcher felt him watching with his dark eyes.

The pistol was compact and light, made half of metal and half in a roughly moulded plastic. It looked brand new, cheap, almost disposable. Fletcher picked up the magazine from the box and looked at the top cartridge. He said,

'This is a .22.'

'.22 conversion, yeah. They do them in the factory, it's an export regulation thing.'

'I wanted something effective.'

'This is short notice, Mr Fletcher. But what you've got here is a perfect self-defence weapon. Stop anyone at close quarters. Pop them in the head, the bullet bangs around inside the skull. Like stirring a tin of paint. Will that suffice? Go on, load it up. No safety catch. Just squeeze till it clicks, then squeeze again. Have a go.'

Fletcher aimed at a stain high on the corrugated wall, steadied and fired. He felt it twitch a little in his hand with a sound like a fairground rifle, and a flake of blue sky opened up just wide of where he'd intended. Rupe whistled over the echo.

'You'll be deadly. You want them both? Matching pair.' His eyes flicked over to Mia. She took out the second gun and loaded it, aimed at the same mark. She blew a hole in the wall, closer to the target stain than Fletcher's. Rupe raised an eyebrow.

'Trained?'

'Just some range stuff. Saturday mornings.'

'You want spare magazines?'

Mia said, 'No. We'll only need one shot each. As you say, self-defence.'

Fletcher paid Rupe in fifties, five per gun. Rupe picked up the empty polystyrene blocks.

'I'll put these in the recycling, then.'

Mia and Fletcher climbed back in the Cossack. They wrapped one HS gun in a shirt and put it under the driver's seat, the other behind a rag in the dashboard compartment. Mia started the engine. Everything else was turned off – no phones that might triangulate their location, no GPS, and there was no sat nav in the car anyway.

'Are we ready now?'

'We're anonymous and cheaply armed. Let's go.'

Fletcher asked himself for a second if his father was making this same journey – armed not with a Croatian .22 but an archaic piece of British hand artillery, the one he'd pointed at his son before confessing he loved him. Would that old gun even fire if he needed it?

The last they saw of Rupert Darcy, he was grinding his cigarette on a wall and putting the stub in his pocket.

They started out: back on to the main road and east to pick up the A10, the long road from Cambridge to Norfolk. The old Russian engine chanted away to itself efficiently, the chassis dissenting with clicks and groans. He liked the way Mia drove, fingers resting on the wheel rim, hooking her hands inside for a grip. Coming towards them, long lines of traffic heading south out of the flood zone. The fields on either side were full of water bobbing with gulls – and when he looked in the mirror, the view behind showed wide trails of light coming down from clouds against a dark horizon. Up ahead, towards the coast, the sky was now a band of solid blue under a layer of grey. The road straightened towards it: a long straight pathway, taking them into the future. He took out the photo of his mother and himself, smoothed it out. He remembered the enlargement of this that Daisy Seager had pinned on her cork board – his child's face broken into dots and swirls. He still didn't understand why Daisy had done that.

He put it back in his chest pocket, felt it flexing over his heart.

They passed Ely – the cathedral looming up and then dipping behind them under a cover of gulls.

After that, to the west, there was more than just the flooding they'd seen so far. The land was so flat that they could see over to the area called Ouse Washes – a man-made flood plain between two long drains, designed to take surplus water from the channels and protect the surrounding countryside. Today it was bursting through its boundaries in several places – big ovals of water brimming with tree debris, dark against the brown and green fields. Mia slowed down as the traffic grew heavier, and Fletcher used his binoculars, saw in the distance the water surrounding a small town. On the outskirts, a supermarket was half submerged, and in the streets people were already sitting on the roofs of their homes. As the Cossack crawled forward, he twisted round to see two army Chinook helicopters hovering above them, their downdraught forcing waves along the streets. He panned across the horizon. Elsewhere, the wind itself was raising waves – not ripples, but real breakers tipped with white spray. It was before midday, but it looked like dusk.

He noticed a smaller aircraft flying low over the water: an unusual design, some kind of streamlined single-seater, but with no lights blinking.

They had to stop at a point where the water was pouring over the road, waiting while traffic ahead turned round or tried to ford the obstruction. The waiting was a kind of torment, sitting there actually looking at the clouds in the east, knowing Aspen was there or drawing close to there, the place where his mother was.

He looked at Mia. She was focusing, a little groove forming beside her eyes. The strong cheekbones, a couple of freckles on her jaw he hadn't noticed before. He said,

'Let me drive.'

'I'm OK.'

'We've got to keep moving.'

'You see a way past all these cars?'

They were getting jammed in – the four-lane road heaving with vehicles, people coming towards them trying to drive with two wheels up on the grass embankment. He put the window down an inch and heard shouting, horns blaring, screaming, then, from somewhere behind them, what sounded like a gunshot. Then, close up, the deafening wail of a police siren.

A Land Rover with blue lights spinning was forcing a path through the scrum, a megaphone voice saying, 'Turn back, head south', coming right past them. Fletcher saw Mia try to move out across the road, and a clenched fist from the police vehicle slammed on his window glass.

He looked into the face of a sullen constable in a fluorescent jacket. He stayed still, making his face calm, lowering the window. The policeman was scowling into the car, peering around. He said, 'You deaf? The road's closed.' Wet moustache, sour breath.

Mia leaned across. She didn't look like a woman with no visa and a Croatian pistol under her seat. She didn't feel like it either, the curve of her breast against his shoulder, her hair brushing his face.

She said to the copper, 'We could get through this water.'

The man laughed. 'Nobody comes through

here. See that, across the field?' He pointed across at a structure maybe half a mile away: a series of steel gantries surrounded by construction cranes that were rapidly swinging blocks of concrete into position, one of them tipping a load of gravel. It looked like the site of a chemical accident, the same desperation to hold forces back before they spilled out.

Mia said, 'What is it?'

'That's the Denver Sluice. The flood defence for everything beyond here. You understand what that means? It's close to being breached. If it goes, all the washes go out into Norfolk.' He looked from Mia to Fletcher, frowning, something forming in his mind. 'Tell me your names.'

Fletcher felt his heart thump. Then from back in the queue, the noise of a vehicle impact, then shouting, plus a woman screaming. The copper said, 'Wait here, don't go away.' And drove forward towards the incident.

Mia put the Cossack back in gear and moved away from the scrum, lumbering through the flooded road and then out the other side, straight off it and onto the edge of a field.

The whole car lurched, clods of mud spinning high into the air, then she took it onto a narrow road heading east towards a conifer plantation. In a few seconds, the wet trees rose on either side, cutting out what daylight there was. She took the Cossack over a hump in the track, the whole frame creaking as she accelerated down a long straight between the trees. Fletcher said, 'Good driving. I hope he takes his time coming back to look for us.'

'Think he'd been briefed on us?'

'Somewhere in Cambridge there's a copper with a headache. They know I'm missing.'

They stopped just long enough for him to take over the wheel.

Rain began tumbling on the roof.

Friday Afternoon

They took the track through the conifers, Mia tracing a route of roads on the map that would snake across the county to the site of the airbase. Fletcher took a deliberate decision to use the smaller roads. It meant the journey – a map distance of barely sixty miles – would be laborious, but at least they would make it. The old radio was crackling and booming around the cabin, reporting main roads closed or choked with traffic as the population moved around. And the police presence would be heavy.

'We might get there after dark,' he said to Mia, as he steered the Cossack along a rutted track, rising now through the centre of the plantation. The sun had emerged for a few minutes – low and red, sending bars of light between the thinning trees. The car bounced over a lip of land to the edge of the plantation, and he halted.

'The dark is fine by me,' she said. 'Then we won't have to look at this.'

Ahead of them, a wide plain of land was illuminated in the horizontal sweep of sunlight. On the left, it consisted of undulating hills, the land between them full of bronze-coloured floodwater! The hilltops were mostly empty, but in some cases occupied by stranded animals: a few ragged cows, a few sheep being tended by a man throwing bales from a tractor. Another

Chinook helicopter was flying across the land-scape, pausing above a few buildings visible on the higher land, the rotor blades flattening circles out across the flood.

To the right, in the general direction they wanted to take, the land was slightly higher, with a ridge screened by willow and birch leading into the distance away from the main flood. About halfway though, it neared a site where a group of low metal sheds were surrounded by water – and a group of vehicles, suggesting people still present.

Mia showed him the point on the map, tracing a web of minor roads from there up towards the north. She squinted ahead, towards the ridge. Then she said,

'Hey, that little plane's back again.'

He saw what she meant. Overhead, the small grey aircraft appeared over the line of trees along the ridge, climbing a little as it flew over the water. It made only a faint buzz. The red sun caught the underside of its wings as it banked away from them, towards the helicopter. Mia said, 'What's he doing?'

They both watched as the plane approached the Chinook, dangerously close. The helicopter seemed unaware of its presence, concentrating on the last of the hilltop buildings. Something strange happened with the perspective. As the plane passed between the helicopter and the Cossack, the big Chinook dwarfed it. The Chinook *was* huge, of course – longer than a bus – but the plane appeared tiny against it, like a toy. It wobbled badly on the edge of the downdraught from the rotors, then righted itself and circled away over the flood, disappearing to the west.

Mia looked at Fletcher. 'A midget plane?'

He tried to find it with the binoculars, then lowered them. He said, 'A drone aircraft. It's just flying a camera, remotely operated, used for reconnaissance and snooping.'

'Used by who?'

'The police are starting to use them pretty widely. Especially in situations like this, surveying a wide area.'

'Or is it looking for *us?*'

'I don't think so. But if they have our car type and number, they might spot us.'

He turned round in his seat and looked back into the plantation. A single bar of red light was coming through a gap in the trees, but otherwise the track they'd just used was dark and empty. On the opposite horizon, the sun was low enough to touch the line of trees along the ridge, and the metal buildings were casting shadows across the approaching water. He looked at Mia. She was pale, her hair in a pleat tucked inside the collar of her sweater, her knees drawn up on the seat, the ends of her combat trousers tucked into her walking boots. Her eyes were dull in the light through the grimy windows, but when she looked back at him they took on their green tint. He said,

'You still want to go on?'

She nodded slowly. 'Anyone behind us?'

'Nobody visible. Let's drive along the ridge.'

She leaned forward to see along the track under the trees. 'Something's going on down there. Something not nice.'

Mia heard the shots from a hundred metres away: sharp cracks with an echo that wavered in the breeze. The four metal sheds were grouped in a cross shape beside the road, their unpainted metal walls catching the red sun flickering through the branches of the willows. Outside one of them, Mia could see a figure in a white coverall suit, a white hood framing his face, goggles over his eyes.

Beside her, Fletcher kept the old car going, the willow fronds brushing the roof at times, until they came level with the sheds. She saw that the man in the white suit was taking a break, smoking a cigarette.

The shots were louder now, coming a few seconds apart. From the other side of the road, another man in overalls emerged, this one with the hood of his suit lowered. He raised a hand, and she thought he was going to stop them, but he just gestured to them to slow down and waved them towards a piece of wet matting stretched across the tarmac. She glanced at Tom Fletcher hunched over the wheel beside her. He said,

'Disinfectant. Must be an outbreak of animal disease because of the flood. It's not our concern. Let's keep going.' He twisted round in his seat again and looked back along the road. When she glanced in the mirror, she saw just the clouds and the green wall of the conifer plantation – then, something else?

She looked ahead again as the Cossack bumped over the stretch of matting and onto the next stretch of the track along the ridge, past the sheds.

The shooting noises were accelerating. Beech trees were moving in the wind, branches juddering and splintering up the sun. Fletcher wrenched the wheel and turned in behind the final shed, onto a gravelled platform in the shadow of the walls. He pulled in close, hidden from the road, and killed the engine.

She looked around.

Ahead of them, she could see right into the opposite shed. A huge door was slid open, giving a view of the interior. It was dimly lit by a stripe of sunset and ceiling arc lamps. At first she could only see a blur of shapes; then she realised what was happening. Two men in white suits were standing in front of a wall of turkeys – small, stunted animals with colourless feathers and scarlet beaks. The birds were panicking, scrabbling over each other, feathers swirling in the air, screeches echoing out into the open. The men were firing at them with air-driven pistols, working from the nearest animals into the centre of the mass. There was already a mound of corpses behind them, steaming slightly, some wings and beaks still twitching.

She grimaced and looked at Tom Fletcher.

He pointed to the space beyond the shed, a gap before the next building that gave a glimpse of the road coming down from the plantation. A vehicle was moving slowly past the gap: a dark Chrysler Jeep, window tints obscuring the occupants.

'Someone else taking the minor roads,' Tom Fletcher said.

Inside the shed, the shots were coming at a rate of one or two per second, the echoes and the noise of the birds drowning out any other sound. She looked to the side of the next shed, where the Jeep should be appearing in a second. She waited. She saw Tom Fletcher reach forward and unlatch the glove box where his HS pistol was stowed, the flap swinging open. Beyond the trees, the sunset was a jagged rip in the clouds.

The Jeep didn't appear. In a few seconds, she saw it reversing back past the gap between the sheds, wreathed in its own damp exhaust. Then she saw it beyond the last shed, still reversing back to the conifers. In half a minute it reached them and slipped back in between the trees.

The glove-box flap was still swaying.

She said, 'Could be someone who lost their way, didn't like the sound of turkey killing.'

'Could well be.'

'Could be the police?'

He frowned. 'If they were looking for us, they would have come down here. It didn't look like a police vehicle, anyway.' He tapped the wheel. 'Could be Lindquist's counsellors following us.'

'Following, but not stopping us? Why not?'

He slammed the glove box shut. 'Maybe they're hoping we'll do their job for them. Remove the problem of Aspen Slade.'

He started up and took them slowly along the ridge, the sound of the killing faded behind them. She leaned her head against the door and watched Tom Fletcher's hands on the wheel. The sun had gone, and the skyline ahead was a series of wooded hills, stark against a grey sky. She said,

'Would you have shot them?'

'You're joking.'

'You ever killed anyone, Tom?'

'You really are joking. I'm English.'

She closed her eyes and felt the lurching of the chassis through the seat. She imagined herself finding this person, Gregory Tinley, still alive in some old English tower, the man who helped the sisters, looked after them, taking his testimony about what the girl called 'the big secret'. Then, at the airbase, taking the photos that would go with it, the account of her conflict with the Bellman Foundation and this journey across England. She would be vindicated, making a name for herself. If she didn't achieve that, it would kill her.

She opened her eyes when the car lurched out of a pothole, saw a blur of trees, rain starting to fall again. She looked across at Tom Fletcher. He was frowning, steering the Cossack slowly up a grass embankment to get past an abandoned car stuck in a flood across the road. It had been looted – a family's possessions scattered out of suitcases and boxes. After that was a whole convoy of abandoned cars, water up to their wheel arches, no people in sight anywhere. She looked back through the mud-spattered rear glass. Just raindrops, then darkening countryside, and whoever was behind them.

Fletcher kept driving. The rain was blowing in different directions, the roadside trees bucking and twitching in the headlights he had to put on at 3 p.m. The old Russian car felt solid, the springs holding up along the pitted roads, but progress was slow. Twice, they saw the revolving lights of police vehicles against the land ahead, and pulled over until they'd gone.

Once, as the lights stayed illuminating the trees, he drove in behind a barn and they waited there. He killed the engine, and the sound of the wind against the car body took over – thumps and long sighs. The cabin was warm and dark, only the red veins of the instruments. He didn't want to, but he closed his eyes for a second.

He saw Evie and Sally Dunton, working in their fields. He went up to them and tried to touch them, and they looked at him with their faces from the film clip, and smiled the saddest smiles he'd ever seen.

He woke because Mia was touching his face. He looked around. The blue lights had gone and the sky was almost dark, just a halfmoon rising over the trees.

They moved on – slowly. He kept away from major roads and built-up areas, but the country roads they were tracing on the map were frequently blocked by stranded vehicles, or floods so deep that water began surging over the Cossack's grille and they backed away for fear of swamping the engine – finding other, even smaller tracks. On one of them, well after dark, they had to heave the old chain out of the Cossack's boot and use it to drag clear a fallen tree, Fletcher wrapping the links around one end of the trunk and Mia reversing back up the lane, pulling until the splinters that linked it to the stump coiled into a thread and snapped with a shriek.

After that, they passed through a few small villages where the houses were dark or dimly lit.

In the headlights, the buildings had glittering flint walls and pitched roofs of S-shaped tiles, their edges dripping. To their left, a huddle of flint houses stood in darkness. The headlights picked out sandbags in their doorways, plywood shuttering nailed over the windows. One even had a dinghy capsized on the flagstones, roped to the doorway.

And after that, close to midnight, just trees. Something began to happen here. There were umbrellas flailing across the road – some blown inside out, others collapsed. In the headlights, a line of people appeared, crossing the road – wreathed in plastic smocks, heads bowed against the rain. Two more emerged from the trees on the left, each holding a wooden pole that supported a banner between it – some kind of religious emblem – a lamb or a bird, he thought. Others were holding smaller banners, the cloth squares buckling in the wind as they disappeared into the dark field on the other side.

While they were stopped, Fletcher looked at the map. Mia pointed to their position: coming to the end of the straight minor road leading to the Open. Ahead, the road curved, passing only two more features: first a small building marked as 'Shrine' – where he guessed the religious-looking walkers were headed, across the fields – and then a small circular object with no label. After that, the road disappeared into the green space of the old heath, with the remaining airbase formation and the site of the Wychland house on the other side. Total distance to the airbase was around fifteen miles, across rough grassland in the face of a building gale.

Mia said, 'How old is your mother, Tom?'

'She'll be sixty-three this year.'

'And she's going to be up there? In the middle of all this weather?'

He knew what she was thinking. Would Kate Fletcher try to take shelter somewhere?

She tapped the place marked 'Shrine'. 'She might be there. And, by the way, would that place have a tower? Could be Gregory Tilney's there.'

He looked at the trees in the headlights. They were being blown at forty-five degrees, smaller branches starting to fly off.

'Well, it's on the way. Let's take a look.'

They went up a long incline, between dense woodland forming a wall on either side, then crested the rise, made a sharp curve, and coasted down. There was something down there, some kind of light. They came into a wide clearing of trees, the upper branches flattening in the wind. He braked to a halt.

The open space contained a church-type building with a square tower, its stained-glass windows bright with colour from inside. The glow caught the faces and limbs of marble saints in wall niches, shining with rain. The building was surrounded by cars. There were scores of vehicles parked at clumsy angles, some drifting steam from hot engines. No marked police vehicles. All the cars were empty – the only people visible were a few religious marchers straggling through from the fields, heading towards the light. It certainly seemed that plenty of people were looking for shelter here. Could his mother be among them? Was Aspen Slade here, too?

Fletcher squeezed the Cossack into a gap on the edge of the clearing, and cut the engine. Over the clang of the cooling metal, there was the noise of the wind sawing at the trees and rain on the roof as he slipped the HS pistol into his parka.

They climbed down from the Cossack. Over at the foot of the tower, two great entrance doors were open, spilling a pool of light onto some flagstone steps below. When they reached them, there was another sound. It was a constant low rustling, like the sea on a shingle beach. He realised it was coming from the shrine, from the open doorway. They went up towards the light inside. Fletcher felt his heart thumping.

Am I going to find her here?

At the top of the steps, they found the large chapel interior lit by electric chandeliers, throwing yellow light down onto an ornate altar holding a Madonna and child statue encircled by hundreds of candles in red glass tubes. Clustered on their knees around it were a group of nuns in black habits – grey head coverings flowing down across their shoulders. Then, from the altar all the way back to the doorway, people were packed together, kneeling on the open floor with their heads bowed. It was a real mix of people too. Young, elderly, men who were maybe farm workers, couples looking like weekend cottage owners. The storm was uniting them all in fear.

Fletcher and Mia stepped inside. The sound they'd heard was loud now: made up of all the voices in the room chanting in low prayer, echoing off the stone walls. Apart from the electric light, it could have been a scene from five hundred years ago.

He called, 'Kate. Kate Fletcher.'

His voice echoed for a second, then the chanting came back again.

He shouted his mother's name again, and this time people turned in annoyance, then turned back. Kneeling on the flagstones nearby were two young girls – the type known as Goths – dyed black hair, pallid faces, black lipstick, heavy studs through their lips and noses. Dilated pupils, eyelids flickering in the devotional light. One of them stared at him blankly, her hands clasped around a silver cross.

Mia knelt down beside her. 'Have you ever heard of Gregory Tilney? The tower, near Hanchton?'

The girl shook her head, pressed the cross to her forehead and closed her eyes. Fletcher gestured to Mia, *Let's go.* They made their way back through the crowd towards the door.

Then a girl's voice, 'You want old Tilney?'

He looked round – the other Goth had followed them, was standing under one of the chandeliers, the light making her deathly pale.

Mia said, 'Where is he?'

'He lives in an old water tower up on the heath. But it's in the evacuation zone. The police have taken everyone out.'

'The heath? What they call the Open?'

'Old people call it that. Like, old Tilney. Don't go up there. The storm's coming.'

Mia said, 'Where on the heath?'

'On the road, going north. Before this road

stops, there's a track on the right, goes uphill. It's somewhere up there.'

She meant the round shape on the map, then, near the end of the road. Fletcher said, 'Thanks.'

On the steps outside the doorway, where the rain was falling in silver lines, the electric lights flickered for a second, then went out. There was a long gasp from the people back there, as if they'd witnessed something miraculous, then a silence, then the whispered prayers started again.

Back in the car, the only sound was the trees and the rain pummeling off the roof. A few more cars had arrived, blocking them in. Fletcher slammed into gear and reversed out of the courtyard, shunting aside the rear end of a car across the exit. The Cossack's rear door flew up in the impact, then crashed down again. He got them back onto the road, heading north.

Mia said, 'We're going to stop at the water tower, right? I mean, he's there, the man's actually there.'

'I'm not interested in Tilney. I want to get to the airbase, find my mother.'

'Tilney might know where she is exactly. Damn it, she might be there with him.'

He considered for a second. 'Let's just check it. Then we're going up on the heath.'

The road grew narrower, completely black, rising sharply. The circles of headlights showed a road sign left to Hanchton, then screens of bare trees buckling in the wind and, finally, a tattered line of yellow tape strung across the road, flicking wildly up and down. In the centre, a sign

314

weighted with sandbags said, *Evacuation Zone Do Not Enter*, but the Cossack's grille smashed it aside – the tape flailing around the car for a few seconds before whipping off. After that, on the right, there was a gap in the trees paved with a hard surface. He braked with a long slide, reversed back and wrenched the Cossack into it, bouncing through onto a battered surface of old tarmac patched with rubble and stretches of bare ground running with water. It was a track, but only just. There was nothing on either side now, just the blackness of the early hours.

It was so dark, they almost crashed into the thing. Fletcher saw a grey wall loom up between the wipers, slammed on the brakes, and brought the big car to a halt with the headlights spreading across an expanse of wet concrete. They peered up through the windscreen. The water tower was a simple column, extending upwards beyond their lights.

They climbed down. The tower was sheltering them from the worst of the rain, but the wind blasting around the structure made a constant howl. Fletcher shone his torch upward. He could just make out a wider shape at least five storeys above: a circular storage tank on top of this one, jutting out into the dark. Turning the torch off, he thought he saw lights up there, just catching the rain.

'How do we get in?' Mia shouted.

They found it in a few seconds: a steel door set deep into the curved surface, with an intercom button and grille lit by a tiny electric bulb. Mia pushed the button and they waited. She pushed it again. She was pushing it a third time when a voice came crackling through the grille.

'I'm not leaving. I'm not being evacuated.'

The voice of a very elderly man, scared and defensive.

She shouted into the grille, 'Are you Mr Tilney?'

'Bugger off.'

'Is anyone there with you?'

'Nobody here, just me. Who are you? You and the man.'

Fletcher looked round, saw a small camera in a dome on the other side of the doorway. He put his face close to the grille, his eyes on the camera.

'My name's Tom Fletcher. I'm looking for Kate Fletcher.'

A second's pause, then, 'You're wasting your time. There's nobody here.' The old voice was trembling – through age or fear.

Fletcher said, 'Is Aspen Slade here? An American male, late twenties.'

'Never heard of him. What's this about?'

'It's about the Steel Witches.'

The intercom crackled for a while – ten seconds, then twenty, barely audible over the wind. Then the door buzzed and clicked, and – when Fletcher pushed it – opened.

It gave way to a concrete-lined chamber.

Tom and Mia looked at each other, closed the door behind them and looked around. There were two things here: a metal ladder running up through a hatch in the ceiling, and also a lift shaft – an old concertina door sliding across a metal cage.

Mia said, 'This is him. It really is him.'

Fletcher wiped rainwater out of his eyes. 'We've got to make this quick.'

They got in the lift and rolled the door shut. The controls only had two arrows: *Down* and *Up*.

Fletcher pushed *Up*, and the cage creaked into movement.

He stood opposite Mia. Behind her, the concrete was ribbed with half-buried steel girders, slowly going past. She undid her slicker and freed her hair, shook it sideways. She glanced up at him and smiled. The lift stopped and she heaved the door open.

They were in a long corridor lit by dim bulkhead lights. It was cool and surprisingly quiet, the concrete walls blotting out the storm, but overhead there was the muffled rattle of a machine – maybe a generator. The corridor had a series of metal doors leading off, and Fletcher pushed the first one open. It was a simple bathroom, like something off a boat. The next one was a storeroom full of old furniture, the final one a tiny kitchen with a hotplate and sink, tins and packets of food piled up on a counter. At the end of the corridor, there was a steel door slightly ajar, letting a triangle of light spill through. Fletcher pushed it open and they stepped out into the tower itself.

It contained absolutely no water. It was a massive circular space at least eight metres high, lit by hanging lamps, curving ribbed walls punctuated by two long windows filled with thick glass which showed only the bursting rain.

Fletcher stopped dead.

Mia said, 'Oh my God.'

317

In between the windows, a series of artworks done in heavily textured paint on huge canvases. Long murals of farming life, fishermen mending nets, women working on old-fashioned tractors. The style of the painting was clear and chunky, with strong colours and stylised features to the subjects – their bodies, the tools they were using, the landscapes behind them.

Fletcher stood looking at the paintings. He'd seen the style before – and he remembered exactly where, could see it in his mind. The Nose Art of the Steel Witches on the old Mustangs from Wychland airbase. The images inspired by Sally and Evie Dunton.

A man was standing to one side of the murals, under one of the huge windows. He was very elderly, around ninety, maybe – leaning on a stick, his jowly face deeply lined, his eyes barely visible behind big plastic glasses. He was wearing a nifty fisherman's cap, a striped jersey covering a paunch, baggy corduroy trousers, sandals over woollen socks. He certainly looked like an artist.

Fletcher said, 'Mr Tilney?'

The man peered at him through his lenses. 'Who are you? How do you know about the Steel Witches?'

Mia introduced them both. She said, 'Did Daisy Seager come here to see you?'

'Daisy, yes. Such a beauty. She said other people might come.'

'We've read Evie Dunton's testimony. We want to know what happened on the airbase, what the big secret was. Did you paint the Steel Witches on the planes, the Nose Art?'

318

Gregory smoothed his hair down, nodding. 'The Steel Witches. Yes, I painted them. And Evie told me everything, everything that happened. Have you come here to ask about that?'

Mia said, 'Evie said you knew the secret, the big secret.'

Gregory nodded slowly. 'There's some rum in the kitchen, dear. Don't know about you, but I need a drink.'

'We don't have time for this,' Fletcher said. 'I'm going to find Aspen and my mother.'

Mia said, 'Wait, let's hear what happened. It could be relevant to Aspen, to the story he wants to cover up. This may be part of the testimony.'

Fletcher considered. He looked up at the colossal mural, the stylised bodies arched in their labours.

He said, 'Tell us as quickly as you can, please.'

They sat on battered easy chairs around an old paraffin stove, its flame spreading a purple flower on the concrete floor. The wind was audible now, smacking gouts of rain against the glass.

Gregory said, 'This concrete's a foot thick. The foundations go down into the bedrock. I'll see the storm breaking, though. Perfect view at dawn. I don't sleep much these days. More cat-naps than anything. I'm independent, though. I used to be in a home, a place in Hanchton–'

Mia said, 'You were going to tell us about the two sisters.'

'The sisters, yes. Sally and Evie.'

'Did you know them?'

'Oh, yes. I know exactly what happened. We were

the same age, them and me. I was born in Hanchton, nineteen twenty-two.' He shook his head. 'I wasn't the oldest one in the home, though. There was a woman from nineteen ten. They kept her drugged, they used to forge her signature.'

'You knew about the Dunton family?'

'The Duntons, yes. People had lived on that site, oh, for hundreds of years. Evie was right about that. A few families, digging out the clay. Brick- and tile-making, mostly. Cheap stuff. Always stories about the place – witches, that kind of thing. The place had a local name, Wychland. Places like that died out in the nineteenth century. In the end, a hundred years ago, there was only one house left. Just the house and the yard, the couple of fields they had. It should have died out altogether, really. But the grandmother. The granny. God.'

'Did you meet her?'

'Me?' Gregory Tilney wheezed out a laugh, pushed his glasses back up his nose. 'I was a town clerk's son. I was heading for the grammar school. I had art classes, you know. Private art classes, paid for. I was kept away from people like the granny.'

'Why?' Mia asked. 'What was wrong with her?'

'She tried to get out, you see. She wanted to get out. People said that, when she was younger, she tried to study, to become a schoolmistress. This was the nineteenth century, rural Norfolk. It was too big a jump. There was nothing for her in the world but staying on that farm. Her husband, he died quite young, after the daughter was born.'

'How?'

'There was an accident with a shotgun. After that, the granny worked by herself, scratching a living. She had a little money from the husband's will, enough so they didn't freeze in the winter. It was just her and the daughter – the sisters' own mother. The daughter was everything to her.'

Mia said, 'But?'

Gregory looked out at the darkness, the rain cracking against the window glass. 'Oh, the daughter. I never met her, just heard the stories. The granny wanted everything for her, a grammar school, a clerical job. Things she never had. But the daughter stayed on the farm, produced two girls – one springtime, then the next.'

'Who was the father?'

Gregory spread his hands. 'He was just a rumour, too. People said he had something to do with chemicals.'

'Chemicals?'

'People whispered about the children. About their condition. Almost nobody ever went to the farm, but people talked. The girls' skin was bubbled all over, you see.'

'We've seen a film clip of them,' Fletcher said. He stood and turned to the window, impatient.

'Then you know. The skin, the colour of their eyes. The thing was,' Gregory took a sip of the rum and smiled, 'apart from that, they were lovely. People said the mother or the father must have been exposed to chemicals. Some said the father was a soldier who'd had a dose of mustard gas in the war. Others said he was a pesticide salesman who called on the farm, selling them dangerous stuff. Then, later, I heard someone say

321

he was a university man, up here for his holidays two years running. Some Cambridge professor of X-rays or atoms or something.'

Fletcher turned from the window. 'From Felwell College?'

'I heard the name mentioned. But these are all rumours. The fact is, the father was unknown. And then, when the girls were two and three years old, the mother simply disappeared. She killed herself, maybe, at the thought of her future on the farm. Or she went away to Birmingham or London to make money somehow, never came back.'

'So then it was just the girls?'

'The girls and their granny. You see? The granny was forty, forty-five. She sent the girls to a village school at first. But it was a long walk for them, hours, and the other kids were cruel. So the granny kept them at home – probably did a better job than the school. The girls were clever, they spoke real English without too much of an accent – not like some of the families round here; they spoke an old language, half-Saxon. But the Wychland farm was closed off, you see. Closed off from the world. You could do that in those days, if you wanted. You could live in isolation, like I try to here.'

Mia said, 'You know a lot about them, Gregory.'

The old artist smiled. 'As a boy, I'd heard the rumours about that family. The insane family, the girls who never left the yard. When I got older, a teenager as they call it today, I loved art, I used to ride my bike around the countryside, sketching whatever I found. People working in the fields, clouds, everything. One summer, I was about eighteen, it was just before the war. I came over the Open, along by the edge of a field. Through some trees, some willows. There was a dip, a little stone track. It went past a circle of water – strange-looking thing, still but perfectly clean, reeds all round it. Then the house. I saw them, from a distance, working in the yard. They were tall, strong-looking. I realised, this is it. Wychland. The house was amazing – centuries of patching it up, leaning there next to that bit of water. When I got there, there was no sign of them. I shouted through the door, 'Can I sketch your house?' No answer. I heard someone breathing, though. Behind the door.' He looked up suddenly. 'There's nothing there now. It's all gone.'

'What happened to it all?'

'What happened? First, the granny died of TB. Then the Americans came.'

'You knew the Americans, then? You must have, you painted the Nose Art.'

Gregory winced. 'I thought I was helping. I couldn't join the forces, you see. They didn't want me. Shadow on my lung. I worked as a clerk in a munitions factory. I drew some artwork for morale posters. I was trying to help.'

'The Americans?'

'That airfield. We all knew *something* was there, out on the Open. We saw the planes taking off and landing, the shiny little Mustangs.'

Mia said, 'Do you have any idea what was being planned there?'

'It was just an airfield. The Americans were just

boys. They were friendly. I met him, you realise that? I met Colonel Harpkin.'

'You met him? How?'

'He gave a talk in Hanchton, in the town hall. I saw Sally Dunton there, after the talk, when people were mixing. Everyone left a little circle around her, but Harpkin walked over, kissed her freckly hand. Charming bloody Yank. He had a way of talking, of finding things out. I told him I was an artist. He whistled, I remember that. As if he was impressed. He said, "We might give you a call one of these days."'

'They called you in to paint the planes?'

Gregory was thinking, going back in his mind sixty-five years. He lifted a hand, as if he wanted to touch what he was seeing, feel something again. He ran his hand along an invisible surface. He said,

'The Mustangs. Polished steel and aluminium, bright enough to hurt your eyes. The Americans picked me up in a Jeep, blindfolded me, drove me into the base. Inside, they took the blindfold off; there was a row of Mustangs. I wasn't allowed to turn round, look at anything else. They said, "So you're a real artist? We want real art on these planes, the best art. We want witches." That made me stop and think. I knew Wychland was over there, the other side of the Open. I said, "What kind of witches?" They said, "The local kind." I knew what they meant. So I made the witches look like the Dunton sisters, what I remembered of them, that glimpse I once had. I made their moles and freckles match those smooth rivets on the planes. I called them the Steel Witches – I gave them that name.' Gregory smoothed his hand along the aluminium in his mind again, smiling.

Mia said, 'And you know what really happened to Harpkin?'

'The Jeep was found on a road near a cliff. No sign of the colonel.' Gregory took his cap off and smoothed his hands over his skull. His hair was sparse and wispy, like a baby's. 'Their military police sniffed around, asking questions. Not long after that, the base was closed down. Just left and abandoned.'

Mia said, 'The plan was called off; they never used the weapon.' Gregory rolled his eyes behind their big lenses. 'Weapon? What weapon? Have you been listening to those rumours? The aviation enthusiasts, the conspiracy people? Daisy said she'd listened to them, she thought she was uncovering the big untold story of the war. A secret weapon! A secret bomb, yes?' He laughed, spit flecking his chin. 'You think they would build an airbase for a secret bomb and put an idiot like Harpkin in charge? My God, listen to that rain.' It was flying in bursts against the window, a noise like cellophane crackling.

Mia said, 'But the big secret? What was that?'

The electric lamps dipped for a moment. The wind was rising, starting to wail and gasp over the concrete walls.

'She wanted the story to live, you see. She wanted someone to take it away. She told it to me, I wrote it down as fast as I could. The words were coming out, falling all over each other. But I got it all, I think. And I kept it safe.'

Fletcher watched Gregory. Nice old bloke in a jaunty little cap. Complete fantasist too? He said,

'Why did she tell you all this, Gregory? Why make a confession?'

Gregory seemed to sleep for a few seconds, his hands folded on his belly in the light of the paraffin stove. Then he opened his eyes.

'I looked after them. That year – the year after Harpkin disappeared. I helped, I watched over them. After painting the Steel Witches I felt ... not responsible, but worried. I was worried about the sisters. I was fearful.' Gregory shrank back into his chair.

'What made you so fearful?' Mia asked.

'The Americans were still nosing around Harpkin's death. Not their MPs, but their aircrew from other bases. I think they sniffed something wasn't right. Then they came for Evie.'

'Came for her?'

'It was spring nineteen forty-four. It was twilight. I'd been there, helping them mend their wash-house roof. I was walking back over the fields, near that little sunken road down to the farm. I can smell the willow now. Grasshoppers in the heath, too. I saw a Jeep coming along the track, four men holding on when it bounced. They weren't from the Wychland base, because it was long closed, grass was all coming up around the concrete. I think they were from another base, a twin base they'd built further south. But I think they knew what had happened. I think they knew about Evie, what she'd done. They must have found out, heard about the goings-on. The

Jeep went into the yard, right to the door. The door opened. A dark doorway, because of the blackout. It was the darkest space I've ever seen, that doorway. There were voices; I couldn't hear what exactly. Then Evie came out, got into the Jeep, last of the twilight. The men sat on the handrails, her in the middle. I saw her look back at the house, just once. Then they took her away, along the track. The light was almost gone by then.'

'Where did they take her?'

'Into the fields. The engine stopped. I watched, from under the willows. There were poppies close to my face.' Gregory put his hand out to touch the air. 'I heard just one shout, just one. A woman's voice. Not a scream. A shout. From up in the field.'

The paraffin flower around him guttered for a few seconds.

Mia said, 'What did they do to her?'

'It was dark, I couldn't see properly. But I could hear it, the way they were hitting her. I saw shapes, and her shape I think, being pushed from one to the other. Each time, there was the sound, a blow. No sound from her, just that first shout. When it stopped, I heard her talking, I couldn't hear the words. Her voice was low and thick-sounding. I heard their voices, too; young men's voices, that accent. Then they started up the Jeep; I saw their shapes around it. It went back to Wychland. I followed it back down there, got there when they'd gone. She was still in the yard, kneeling. I lit a match. She had blood all over her face. She had teeth missing. She looked at me under those lids, then the match went out. She got to her feet. She was unsteady, but she could walk. She went and opened the door and went inside. I went in after her. She sat in the kitchen; it smelled of earth and grease. Yes, and that smell from burning tree roots, nobody remembers that now. She sat in the dark and faced me and she said something like, 'Write this all down. Don't ask me questions, just write.' She was shaking. It was the beating, obviously. But also, she knew what was coming next.'

For the first time, Fletcher felt the tower move. He saw the mural lift from the wall and settle back, some powdery dust drifting free. He said 'What did come next?'

'She spoke to me all night, changing things, trying to put things as well as she could. When she finished, my writing hand was tired. I put my pen down, I folded the pages. I walked out, away up the track. I took with me what she wanted to save, you see. I took it all with me. The sun was coming up. The red clouds, they must have been a thousand miles wide, right across the horizon. The plane came over about 6 a.m.'

'What plane?'

'A Mustang. Coming up from the south, with the sun behind it. I stopped where I was and turned to look. It had the extra fuel tanks under the wings, the teardrop tanks. And the noise, my God. The Mustang engine, it made a noise like nothing else on earth. Then it cut out. It stayed low. I wondered if the pilot had engine trouble. Maybe he did. Maybe that's why it happened. Maybe.'

'Why what happened? Gregory?'

'It happened a lot, throughout the war. So many planes in the air, loaded with explosives. It was bound to happen.'

'What?'

'The Mustang came straight towards me. Right over the willows, a hundred feet up. I could see all the rivets on the aluminium, the tanks under the wings, vapour streaking out from the exhaust. I could smell it, like meths. It came right overhead, towards Wychland. The farm was quiet, just a little smoke from the chimney, the chickens in the yard. I've wondered so many times what Evie did in those few minutes, between me leaving and the plane coming over. Maybe she dozed a little, felt the sun coming through the shutters. Or maybe, I don't know, maybe she woke Sally and they clung together and they waited for it. The Mustang came so low over the fields, it ripped up the willow fronds. Near the house, the plane lifted up suddenly, becoming lighter.' Gregory made the movement with his hand. 'It *was* lighter, of course. I saw two teardrop tanks spinning down. They were heavy, so they didn't drift, just fell smoothly. Big silver teardrops in the red sky. A hundred gallons in each of those tanks, high-octane stuff. One touched down first, in the onion field beside the house. I saw the gasoline go spraying out, a big plume of fire the size of the house. Then, just a second later, the other one hit the house itself. I saw it go in through the gable, all the bricks flying around after it. There was a tiny moment then. A little fraction of a second. After that, the house became transparent. I could actually see the beams behind the plaster, the outline of the rooms upstairs, the chimney stack folding up. Full of red light. That was only for a second as well. Then it all blew apart.'

Fletcher said, 'They bombed the house? With Sally and Evie inside?'

'As I said, there were a lot of accidents. A pilot with engine failure has to dump his extra fuel before going back to his base. He sees an open field, he jettisons the drop tanks. He makes it back to the base, lands in one piece. Later on, he's horrified to hear that he might have hit a farmhouse, killed two local women. He drives down there. I saw that too. I saw him get out of his Jeep near the willow trees. He stood watching the soldiers arrive from Hanchton. The soldiers couldn't do anything. No hoses to pump water from the Deeping and, anyway, the house was gone. Not a brick or a tile left. Just a shape on the ground, with dirty red flames, oily smoke. I saw the pilot turn away.'

There was rain on the windows and the hiss of the paraffin heater, the generator's hum, and above that the rising howl of the gale flicking over the tower.

If the sisters could weep, their tears would look like this.

Mia said, 'Surely you told people what you'd seen? The beating?'

'No. I stayed quiet over everything I'd seen. Everything. And I don't regret it, no. I think Evie Dunton wanted to go like that. She wanted to take Sally with her. The Americans thought they were being clever, avenging their comrade. But

330

Evie wanted Wychland to live forever. And maybe it will now.' Gregory turned his head against the headrest of his chair, settled it down.

Mia said, 'Is there something else, Mr Tilney? Something you're not telling us?'

Gregory whispered, 'You've tired me out. You've worn me out. I need to sleep now – just one of my catnaps. I'll be awake again when the storm comes in.' He smiled. 'They'll be doing their voodoo in Hanchton now.'

He said nothing else before he fell asleep.

Mia Tyrone ran the taps in Gregory's little bathroom. The water was noisy, freezing cold, perfectly clean. She ran it through her fingers, then lifted her hair and splashed the water over her face, let some run into her mouth. Then she stood for half a minute, her hands on either side of the basin, watching the water drain away, thinking, *Where does that leave the Bellman Foundation? All this time, were they just covering up a nasty little story – an idiot in charge of an airbase, a murder, then the murder of two women?*

Then she thought, *No – the base was ploughed up, the records were erased. All that, because of a local scandal? No way. The bomb story is the real one.*

She felt her camera inside her slicker, went out and down the corridor to the lift. The noise of the wind was coming up through the lift shaft, and the bulkhead lamps were flickering.

'Mia, wait.' She could see Tom Fletcher outlined against the light from the main living space. 'Mia, you'd better wait here.'

'Oh yeah?'

'Stay with Gregory. The storm's really picking up.'

'Gregory will be fine. We'll lock the door on him. He'll sleep through it all. Now I want to get out there, see the airbase.'

'This isn't just about you and the Bellman Foundation, Mia.'

'No? I've been pretty useful up to now.'

'I'm going out there to stop Aspen Slade. He's insane, he's dangerous.'

'So I help you along this far, and that's it?' She was suddenly angry at the man, patronising her after all of this. She said, 'Fuck you, Tom.'

She slammed the cage door shut. Then, even as he tried to open it, she hit the down button. The lift jerked downward, locking the door. She saw him disappear above her, his feet in their muddy walking boots the last thing, outlined against the bars of the cage. Then she was in the half-dark of the lift shaft, a cold wind coming up from below, chilling the damp in her hair.

That calmed her down.

OK. When I get down there, I'll send the lift back up.

The wind got stronger as she neared ground level – until, when she slid open the cage, there was a real gale blowing in through the main door that led into the open. She glimpsed the front of the Cossack out there, a humped white shape, blurred with rain. She turned to slide the cage shut, to let Tom Fletcher come down here so they could start off together. Maybe the guy would be less condescending.

She never closed the door. Close to her, something moved. She caught a sweet, fruity smell that hadn't been in the tower before. She half turned, just as she realised what it was.

Liquorice.

Saturday Morning

At ground level, Fletcher jumped off the steel ladder that ran down through the tower and looked around the entrance area. It was spattered with rain, the big steel external door swinging on its hinges. Otherwise it was empty. The lift cage was still half open. He rammed the door shut and sent it back up to the living space, where he'd left Gregory asleep with a rug over his knees.

What Gregory had said didn't change anything for Fletcher. So Daisy Seager had tracked the old man here, added his story to her knowledge. The man thought he was describing a tragic little event from the war. He didn't realise he'd really witnessed what Felwell College and Bellman had planned for that airbase. Only Kate Fletcher had achieved that level of understanding – and she was out there now.

Fletcher went outside, where they'd parked the Cossack. The wind hit him, but there was nothing else – no Cossack, just the screaming dark. A couple of tyre grooves led off the stone track onto the turf, then disappeared.

He considered, then switched on his phone. Under the bubble of rain, the screen showed a picture just received from Crete: Cathleen sitting tanned and damp on her balcony. It looked like another planet – safe and warm. The message, *Be good.*

He tried Mia's number. No response.

He turned the phone off, taking any trace off the network. He thought for five seconds, then ten. He could feel his tired and sensitised irises adjusting to the dark.

To his left, down the slope towards the shrine, the line of trees was making a seething noise as the wind rose and fell. To his right, the track disappeared beyond the tower, onto the high ground of the Open. He checked his watch. First light was about two hours away. He took a breath.

He closed up his parka, zipping the hood to keep the rain from his neck, then shrugged himself watertight, feeling the weight of the HS pistol shifting in his side pocket. He began walking up the incline, into the dark. After a few metres, the rough surface of the track gave way to wet turf, compressing under his boots. The wind was chopping violently around him – at times ceasing altogether, then gusting again with a force that made him lean into it to avoid being pushed off course.

He came onto an area where nothing was visible – looking round, not even the water tower behind him – and the only noise was the hiss and screech of the wind. There was no horizon, except lines of slanting rain against the blur of a half-moon. He lost all dimensions – the only unchanging contact was the feel of the turf under his boots. He shone his torch onto his compass, saw the needle swing and set. He pointed himself northeast.

He thought, *What's this feeling? It's like....*

He used the torch to check his direction again,

335

and swept it in front of him for obstacles. The cone of light held nothing except rain and grass. The Open was clear and empty, with no sign of any vehicle or any people.

He thought, *It's like I'm happy. I'm going to see my mother again.*

He kept walking.

I'm going to save her.

He couldn't hear anything, and the air in front of him was alive with rain. He was sure he saw the moon, though, somewhere up ahead. And, some time later, below that, the gleam of a red taillight, travelling roughly northeast.

Mia Tyrone was driving slowly, letting the Cossack bounce over the turf. She could feel her heart inside her ribcage – as hard as the wheel bucking her hands. The headlights showed only a sweep of ground, sometimes a patch of gorse or winter bracken. She said,

'I can't even see where I'm going.'

The man in the seat behind her began chewing again: a wet, clicking noise. From the look she'd been able to take at him, she knew he was wearing tourist clothes: jeans, sneakers, a nylon hiking jacket, a woollen army-type hat. She looked in the mirror. One door was badly closed, so the dome light was on. He suddenly took the cap off and wiped his head with his sleeve, then fitted it back on. He made that noise between his teeth again.

He was armed with a crowbar that had twin points filed down sharp – the split tip resting on the back of her seat, just behind her head. Twice already, when the Cossack lurched, she'd felt it on the nape of her neck through her slicker, the cold tugging her warm skin. But the guy wasn't saying anything, just sitting there chewing.

She said, 'Aspen, right?' The man grunted. 'Look, Aspen, there's no need to hurt me. No need at all.'

She saw movement in the mirror as the man jerked his head from side to side, his mouth still working, his pale jaws moving. Then he calmed down again. He actually said something.

'Daisy told me she went there, that tower thing. I figured you'd be along. Amazed you made it. What kind of fucked-up car is this?'

'I'm no threat to you, Aspen.'

'What kind of car?'

'It's something Russian.'

'It's running hot.'

She could see it: the dial pressing into red, the shuddering from under the bonnet just as strong as the buffeting of the wind. A tree branch clanged against the side and tumbled upwards over the roof, making her flinch. She said, 'Where are we going, anyway?'

'Keep driving. Keep watching ahead.' She felt the steel points brushing her neck again. Then Aspen Slade said, 'You're American. Why are you here?'

'I've got this problem with the Bellman Foundation.'

She heard him chew a few times, then swallow. 'Bellman? What do they want out here?'

'Something happened here. There's no point you hurting me, Aspen. Tom Fletcher will be following us.'

'That's kind of the idea. So he comes and sees what I'm going to do. I want him to see, to witness. Go between these bushes now.'

She steered the failing Cossack between two clumps of bracken, their dead fronds bucking in the headlights. She said,

'OK, Aspen. I'm going to tell you something, and you have to understand. I'm telling you, I won't tell anyone about the Steel Witches.'

'Well, that's good of you.'

'I mean it. The testimony you were looking for? It's in the back of this vehicle, in a case.'

'I know. I found it. At the right time, I'm going to destroy it.'

'OK, you do that. That's what this is about, isn't it?'

Aspen didn't answer. She heard him chewing, louder than the boiling noise in the engine. Then she heard him spit, long and fluid, and settle back in the seats, silent.

She said 'OK? I won't reveal what Bellman were planning.'

He was quiet for a while. Then he said, 'Bellman were planning something?'

They went over a ditch or a hole or something, and she almost cracked her head as the car lurched to one side, then righted, the headlights swaying across stunted trees, then just the rain again. She slowed the car down to walking pace. 'The reason they built the Wychland airbase. You think they were building a bomb, right? I think that's possible too. That's what you want to cover up, to impress the USAF, correct? It's OK,

Aspen. I won't reveal any of that. I'll just get on with my life.'

The way the car swayed, she caught sight of him in the mirror back there for a second. He looked puzzled.

He said, 'What are you talking about?'

'About the dirty bomb they were planning here. It's OK, it was a long time ago, anyway. Plenty of different weapons were considered back then; some got ruled out in the end.'

She saw him rise up on the seats, peering over her shoulder to the ground ahead, then flop back.

He said, 'What the fuck are you talking about?'

'I've noted down all the details, I've stored them somewhere safe. If anything happens to me, it'll all become public, if you let me go, I'll forget it. You understand that?'

He was silent. She glanced in the mirror again. He had his head tipped back, was looking at her, puzzled, trying to figure her out.

He said, 'I don't know anything about any dirty bomb.'

'You killed those people in Cambridge to keep the story quiet.'

'Keep it quiet?' He seemed to realise the door was unlocked, and reached out, opened it and slammed it shut. The light went out, putting his face in darkness. 'Something like this won't stay quiet. There is a story, yeah. But what I want to do is wipe it out, not keep it quiet. Hey, this is the start, right here.'

Something was taking shape in the headlights: a patch of grey showing wet against the grassland – cratered with holes and jagged at the edges, but clearly an artificial surface. The Cossack crawled onto it, and the stuff collapsed under one wheel, making the car dip and bounce. The grey ran ahead into the dark, a line about ten metres wide.

Aspen said, 'You know what this is?'

Mia thought she did, It was in about the right place, if they were going northeast across the Open. The few lines on the high-detail map, the twin scrapes in the ice on a car's windshield.

She said, 'It's the old runway. Harpkin's old airbase.'

'What's left of it. Just a few yards of this section, then where the other one joins it. Just keep going.' The tip of his curved steel bar lifted the hair beside her ear, let it fall. 'Don't know about you, but I don't want to walk.'

The car lurched forward, the temperature needle moving close to red. In front of them, the derelict runway gave way completely at times to patches of grass that had reclaimed it, then appeared again in scales that glinted wet in the lights. Under her seat, Mia felt the HS pistol in its shirt wrapping sliding a little, touching her foot. She raised her voice, said,

'Aspen, I'm going to tell you something you have to believe.'

'Yeah?'

'You know I won't tell anyone about this whole thing. And I'm totally sure that Kate Fletcher won't tell anyone either. There's no reason to harm her because of what she knows.'

She glanced back and saw Aspen's shoulders moving with laughter, though he stayed silent. Then he exhaled in a long sigh, ending in a burst of chewing.

'Yeah. She won't tell anyone.'

'She found out by accident; probably some comment your parents dropped. She's innocent.'

'Innocent? I don't think you get it. She's guilty. It's not what she knows. It's who she is. She's the one who started all this, started spreading this sickness. She could stay quiet the rest of her life, it wouldn't help her. It wouldn't help her at all. We're going to meet her now. Hey, you know what? The storm's coming.'

Fletcher checked his direction for the last time. Then he switched the torch off and tried looking around. The only reference he had was the rain spinning a web of lines. A long way ahead, the sky was changing colour – a line of faint red, above a layer of black that must be the headland rising over the sea itself. He began walking towards that red colour. He guessed the distance from the water tower to Wychland was about six miles – and he guessed he was about halfway there now. A lot of guessing, though. He put his hood down and the rain smacked at his face. He kept walking slow progress against the wind chopping from side to side.

Soon now. Soon I'll be there, and my mother will be there – and we'll see each other again. We'll start again, as if this gap never happened.

In the torch beam, he thought the grass was becoming shinier, blades and clumps becoming more distinct. Water fell from his soaked hair into his eyes, and he wiped it away. Time and distance passed – about another mile, he thought. When he looked up, he could see the headland was still black but, above that, the red layer in the sky had spread into a jagged diamond shape.

He stopped.

Above the red, high over the sea, a colossal formation of storm clouds was being illuminated from below. The light showed up a twisted coil of strata filling half the horizon: reddened in its bulging underbelly, then blue-black higher up. The clouds were moving, trailing long veils of rain down across the sunrise. Once, a single vein of lightning snagged down onto the dark horizon itself.

From somewhere to the west – from Hanchton? – a flood siren began to wail – a rising note mounting a step at a time, the sound being snatched away at times by the wind, then coming back higher and stronger.

Close to him, some clumps of dead bracken were taking on colour: skeletal fronds, showing as bronze and gunmetal in the dawn. He brushed against them. Something flashed through his mind, but he started walking again, between them. Beyond that, he found a stretch of old concrete leading a short way ahead, punctured by more bracken and ragged grass. There were craters filled with water glowing red, puckering with rain.

Elsewhere, though, the surface was smooth and grey.

He stopped again, because the thing that had entered his mind was coming back. Behind him, the siren reached its high point and howled its long, insistent warning.

Mia's windscreen was full of the sunrise, and the dark line of the distant headland angling left and right as the Cossack bounced over the potholes. Then the concrete ran out finally: there was just the junction of the two runways, overgrown with stunted trees, then more of the rolling heath, the wheels spinning for a second on the grass before scrabbling forward.

'Why, Aspen? Why do you hate Fletcher's mother so much?'

He said. 'Watch where you're driving.'

She looked ahead again and saw a wide clump of reeds, heavy tips flicking in the wind. She said, 'Is this the round-shaped lake? The Deeping?'

'Looks like it to me.' In the dim light of the mirror, she saw him twist round to look out of the rear. She put a hand down to the gun somewhere under her seat, but he turned back, hefting his steel hook from one hand to the other. 'Where's that Tom Fletcher, anyway? I want him to *be* here. Pull up.'

She stopped the Cossack just before the reeds. Through them, she could see a wide circle of water: dark grey flashing with red where the rain was striking. The wind was twisting the reeds sideways, its force thumping against the car. She turned the engine off to try and let it cool. She turned round in the seat. Aspen Slade was sliding across the back, putting a hand on the door.

She said, 'What's the answer? Why do you hate Kate Fletcher?'

He glanced at her and said, 'Come on, let's take a look at this place. I'll tell you something.' He opened the door an inch, then closed it. 'Oh yeah, and it's got nothing to do with – what did you say? Dirty bombs.' He unlatched the door handle and the wind pulled the whole thing out of his hand, the hinges cracking against the frame, blasting into the car. He looked back at her, still holding his sharpened wrecking bar. He shouted, 'It's in the family.'

Then he grappled the door shut – slam, suddenly less noise. Through the window, she could see him standing on the edge of the rushes, jamming his cap low down on his head. His image was fragmented by water drops writhing on the glass.

She reached down for the gun under the seat and unwrapped it, put it in her slicker pocket. Then she put her hand on the ignition keys, but didn't turn them.

She looked over at Aspen again.

It's in the family?

Fletcher kneeled down and touched the surface of the concrete. It was hard and pitted, chips of stone in the material loose under his fingers. He stood up and ran his boot across it, feeling that roughness even through the thick soles.

He began walking along the runway, looking at it. His boots crushed the plants coming through the cracks, broke the edges off some of the craters. He could see the concrete stretching out ahead: a hard grey line leading northeast through the grass, towards the cloud formation which was darkening the sky and beginning to blot out the emerging sun on the horizon.

A line of white seabirds flew towards him, low

and fast, flashing over his head and then inland. He looked left and right and saw masses of them all along the headland – hundreds of birds, escaping the storm. He began walking more quickly. After a few steps, he began running, jumping over the deepest of the holes in the runway, taking long strides on the clear areas.

He was thinking, *I've been here. I've been here before.*

The keys were still in the Cossack's ignition.

Mia stood near the edge of the Deeping, watching Aspen Slade. He had his back to her, standing on the bank in a gap in the reeds, the bulrush tips being twisted around by the wind.

With the gun under her slicker now, making a slab against her thigh, she felt better. She could shoot him, she could kill or disable him, or just get back in and drive away. What he was saying, though, kept her standing there for now. If Aspen wasn't obsessed with the old bomb, what the hell was he obsessed with? She tried to think back, watching him, feeling the wind dragging at her slicker. Above her, the sky was filling with massive black clouds, domed layers building from the skyline to as high as she could crane her neck, birds flying under that – seagulls flashing white against the electric dark.

She saw Aspen turn to her and shout something, but it was lost in the noise of the wind through the reeds. She stepped in among them, pushing her way through, the heavy tips whipping against her face and arms. She could see the lake behind Aspen – bigger than she'd imagined it, dark water chopping with waves. She stood near the man, feeling the gun under her hand.

Suddenly, the wind dropped. The Deeping smoothed out, and a few torn reed stems tumbling across the water lost momentum and fell onto the surface. The rain drifted in gusts. It was quiet – just the patter of rain, the creak of some reeds leaning together, the faint sound of a siren in the distance.

Aspen didn't look at her, but he said, 'Feel that? The storm surge is coming. When the pressure drops like that. Only lasts a minute, then whammo.' He threw his crowbar into the wet earth, where it stuck upright, the hook glinting. 'See this water? They're all in there. All of them. The women the witchfinder killed. And Colonel Harpkin, he's in there too. He'll be all bones now. Bones and the stars on his uniform.'

She looked at the water, thought she could see a bright point moving under the surface. Just the reflection of a gull whirling overhead.

She said, 'Why does this matter?'

He didn't answer.

'Aspen, why does Harpkin matter? It was just a sad event in the nineteen forties. Things like this happen all the time, all over the world. What's your problem with it? You said something about, "It's in the family."'

Aspen laughed. In the quiet, the sound seemed to bounce out over the water. He bent down and flicked through the wet earth among the reeds, came up with a flat stone. He tossed it in his hand a few times. 'You got to think about that crazy witch, Sally Dunton. You got to think about the way she came together with Harpkin. The descendant of the witches gets fucked by the descendant of the witchfinder. Just think to yourself, what would be the result of that? The fruit?' He flipped the stone out across the water. It bounced twice, spreading rings. 'Damn, I'm losing my touch.'

Mia watched the ripples expand under the needle-points of the rain. 'The fruit? You're saying they had a child? Is that what this is about?'

Aspen spread his hands, his fingers black with earth. 'It's starting. Feel that change in pressure now?'

She could feel *something* in the air. A new breeze was starting to rise, close to the ground, making the reeds quiver again from their roots to their tips. The air was changing temperature too – it felt suddenly cold, and she caught the smell of salt water. She looked up. There were no birds.

Aspen said, 'A child. What would that child be like? Half-witch, half-witchfinder. Imagine a creature like that.'

She pulled her hair out of her face. She said, 'Sally Dunton wasn't a witch. She was a lonely kid with a British skin condition. You get it? Colonel Harpkin wasn't the witchfinder, you understand that? He was just some East Coast charmer they put in charge of an airbase. You have to get this straight in your head.'

Aspen squatted down and felt through the soil again, his white fingers probing the black silt, the breeze ruffling his hair. He said, 'You really sure about that? I think Sally and Harpkin were two elements that have to find each other. Two things that, if you bring them together, cause terrible destruction. I know this. I don't just think it. I can feel it, like I can feel this rock here.' Without standing, he span another stone out onto the water. It sent up a little plume as it sank. 'Like I can feel this metal.' He reached out and rested his fingers on the steel bar planted in the ground. He squinted up at Mia. 'I can feel it in myself. Because it's come through me. Down from Sally Dunton and Colonel Harpkin, straight into me.'

He stood up – his limbs unfolding and straightening, his hand pulling the wrecking bar out of the ground and taking it up with him, holding it at his side. His head tilted back, eyes up to the clouds, his face streaked with rainwater. 'Straight into me, you understand that?'

She took a step away from him, pushing back against the rushes. The siren noise in the distance was being closed off by the rising wind, and the sky was dark – going back into twilight.

She thought, *Fuck. That's it.* She pulled the HS pistol out from under her slicker and pointed it at him. The muzzle collected water straight away: droplets pooling on the dark metal and dripping off. She said, 'Aspen, I'm leaving now. if you try to follow me, I'll shoot you in the head.'

'With that crappy little gun?'

'The slug will bounce around inside your skull, Aspen. Think about that.'

But Aspen was looking up at the clouds, his eyes dilated. He said, 'Where's Tom Fletcher? Where is he?'

'Kneel on the ground, Aspen. Don't move till I've gone.'

Aspen said, 'It's come into me. It's come down into me.'

She looked back at the Cossack – suddenly wanted to be inside it, all that foreign steel. A blast of wind hit her, like a big hand slapping her shoulder. She said, 'How has it come into you?'

He turned his face and shouted, 'Through the blood. Through the bloodline.'

She looked at him, the wind pushing her arm, making the gun barrel waver. She said 'The bloodline? What's that supposed to mean?'

Aspen laughed, ripping his wool hat off. The wind lifted his fringe, rainwater from the reeds around him starting to spray through the air.

She turned to go, then turned back. She said, 'The bloodline? You mean, your father? You mean, Nathan Slade was the child of Sally and Harpkin? *Nathan?*'

In front of her Aspen Slade rocked himself on his knees, his mouth making words she couldn't hear.

Fletcher kept running. He felt the wind coming towards him over the headland, cooling down further and growing stronger – even stronger than it had been before the drop in pressure. The wind was loaded now too, bringing things from the tide-line, looping and swerving over the grass: old plastic kegs, polystyrene floats, panels of wood, even a crabshell spinning close to his face; all tumbling past him, streaming away inland. Watching them go, he saw on the opposite horizon a half-moon shining clear and veined – much brighter than the sun, which was just a red stain now, glowing behind the clouds over the sea.

He stopped at a juncture in the concrete.

It seemed to be the point where the two lanes met, making the crude shape that Daisy Seager had scraped in the ice: the central bar of the old A-shape. It was punctured by small trees fingering up through the surface, overgrown with dead bracken flattening in the wind but, beyond it, a line of cleaner runway extended a few dozen metres across the heath.

Its edges – mottled with grey lichen – were hard against the drenched turf that stretched out into the distance.

The angle fitted a space inside him.

Run, Tom.

His mother's hand on his shoulder. The earliest moment he remembered.

Fletcher knelt for a second, sighted along the grey concrete, took a few breaths. He fumbled in the wet pocket of his parka, pulled out the old photo that his father had kept for him.

Was this it? Was it here, all the time? The same path that back then – thirty years ago – he thought would take him clean into the future?

Was it not one of the Cambridge paths, after all? Not the neat tarmac of Jesus Green or Midsummer Common or Parker's Piece. Was it here?

The blow-up that Daisy Seager had in her room. She wasn't interested in me, my distorted child's face. She wanted what was behind me. It was the *path*. She was enlarging the path, to see if it was a runway.

Why would my mother bring me here?

The gale cracked around him. Some more

debris from the coast came spiraling up the runway: big nodules of seaweed, spinning water from their trails.

Why?

Something kept him kneeling there in the gale, breathing hard, looking at the old concrete. Thinking about summer nights, the buzz of the streetlamp outside the window, his mother in her study, the typewriter clicking, releasing its gun-oil scent. Kate Fletcher hitting the typewriter keys, the click coming through the walls. Old, uneven keys, striking hard.

Hard enough to punch a full stop right through the paper?

The way the paper of Evie Dunton's confession was typed out?

He stood up, walked a few metres further along the surface. In the distance, in the dim light, he thought he could see the pale humped shape of the Cossack, stopped next to a line of reeds. He started running again, going back over everything in his mind. Running along the smooth grey path he thought he remembered – no, the more he thought about it, running under the red-lined – clouds – the path he was *sure* he remembered.

In a minute, getting closer, he saw the Cossack quite clearly, and the reeds being ripped up by the wind, the stalks flattening and twisting apart. He was thinking of something Evie Dunton said right at the end of her testimony. About the big secret.

He thought, *Evie. Oh no, Evie. Did you mean that?*

Mia made it back into the Cossack by putting all her weight on the front door to pull it open. She slid inside and just got her feet in as the wind slammed it shut again, with a bang that hurt her ears. She hoped the car was heavy enough to stay on its wheels – but the springs were already creaking as it leaned from side to side.

She could see Aspen coming back to the car, too, crouching low through the disintegrating reeds, his face twisted by the effort and the force of the gale, spiking the ground with his steel bar to keep a grip. In the end, he made it to the tailgate and she saw him clambering through, folding his arms and legs inside. The vehicle filled with the air pressure, blasting her hair away from her face. Then the wind slammed the tailgate down and it felt suddenly quieter. She could hear Aspen's breathing as he squirmed over onto the back seat, half lying with his legs stretched out, the wrecking bar left back there with the luggage and the tow chain. Aspen coughed and looked up, straight into the mouth of the Croatian pistol she was pointing at him, resting on the back seat, both hands on the grip and two fingers on the trigger. The muzzle was moving – but that was the car rocking, not her hands shaking. She said, 'You're bullshitting me. You're lying.'

He shook his head, getting his breath. He began chewing again, twitching his lower jaw.

She said, 'You're lying, Slade. The age is all wrong. Nathan was aged late fifties. Fifty-eight or something, yeah? He must have been born in nineteen fifty, something like that. Seven years after Harpkin was killed. Nathan can't have been

Sally's son.'

Aspen closed his eyes, chewing. A little trickle of dark spit appeared in one corner of his mouth, and he wiped it away with his fist. He said, 'If we stay here, the truck will flip right over. We'll be crushed or something. We've got to move.'

'There's nowhere else to go. We're on a frigging nature reserve.'

But she felt the Cossack lift up for a second on two wheels, then clump down again, making the gun barrel bounce in her hand.

Aspen said, 'You stupid whore, you're going to fire that piece. You're going to shoot me or shoot yourself.'

'Shut up. Get out of my truck.'

'Let me drive. We can go down the old track, to Wychland. To the old house.'

'There is no house.'

'The place where it was. It's in a dip, the wind will be less.' There was an explosion, and the window glass behind Aspen blew apart. She thought, *Fuck – I've shot him, I've shot right through him –* but her fingers were still loose on the trigger, her palms curled around the grip. Then she realised a tree branch had hit the car – its torn end stuck right through the window, still twisting in the wind.

Aspen was moving under the flakes of glass, brushing them off, like a creature ridding itself of an old brittle skin. Another branch slammed into the door and twisted overhead. She could see the car was going to get torn to pieces around her.

She said, 'Get up here and drive.'

Fletcher saw the Cossack begin to move, its creamy paint luminous against the dark grassland. He saw it turn away from the Deeping and head roughly east.

He kept running after it, ducking his head against the wind, being blown sideways but still following the disappearing white shape of the Cossack, down towards a line of willows in the middle distance. Somewhere down there, he knew, was his mother.

He left behind the pathway he remembered. The weight of that hand on his shoulder, though, he could still feel – even with the wind ramming into him. Thinking what Evie Dunton said about the poppy-seed tea she gave to Sally that afternoon.

Gives you visions or gives you twins.

Mia watched Aspen driving. The man was hunched over the wheel, scowling through the cracked windshield, a few cuts on his face leaking dark blood. She was jammed against the front passenger door, facing him sideways, with the pistol on her knees. Aspen said something to himself, but the wind pouring through the smashed window drowned out his words. She just wanted to get off this open space – tree debris was whirling through the air, and the ground beyond Aspen's profile was starting to spark in places with static. Then she glanced through the windshield and said, 'Oh thank God.'

They were at a dip in the heath, the grass flicking over the edge of a low area that the Cossack lurched down into, Aspen wrenching the

354

nose around to the right, following the depression as it deepened and narrowed into a sunken track dotted with gorse and bracken, rocks under the soil making the wheels twitch and slide. The wind came twisting down into the depression after them, but most of its power was blasting up over the track: some willow trees up at ground level were being shredded, their fronds being stripped off by the gale, one already shorn of its branches. Looking one way, to the sea, the sky was boiling with those dark shapes. The other way, inland, it was almost blue, with a big half-moon just above the lip of the sunken road.

Aspen glanced at her, then ahead. He shouted, 'The poison's come down through the blood, you understand? But not through the father, no. Not through the father.'

She steadied herself with one hand on the dash, one hand holding the pistol at this idiot. 'What are you talking about, Aspen?'

'There's girls in the family. Sally and Evie, the sisters. Only natural, wouldn't it be?'

'What are you talking about?'

'If the Steel Witch, Sally Dunton, gave birth to a daughter.'

'You said—'

'I said she had a child. I never said it was a boy.'

Behind Aspen, the moon seemed to be moving, bouncing along the edge of the heath.

'You're saying Sally had a girl?'

'Girls in the family, I told you. Girls are witches. Everyone knows that.'

The Cossack bucked for a second, swerving up over an obstruction, slithering down after it, ploughing up stuff under the wheels. Looking back, she saw a few bits of old rubble – bricks and timbers, matted with grass.

She looked back at him. She said, 'You mean, your mother?'

Aspen smiled, squinting through the arc of the wiper blades, and he nodded – or maybe it was just the bounce of the wheels.

She said, 'Your mother? Cherelle Swanson was the daughter of Sally and Colonel Harpkin?'

Aspen laughed, fingers loose on the wheel, slowing down because the gully was partly blocked by the trunk of a fallen willow. He said, 'My mother used to say, *What did I do wrong, Aspen?* And at the time, I'm like, I don't know. I'm like, Why do I do these things? Why am I like this?' He chewed violently, his mouth open, peering around through the glass, the willow branches blocking the view. 'I didn't know then, but I know now. It was when we were posted here, I mean here, Britain, to Alconhurst. I was ten years old. That's when I found out.'

'Yeah? What did you find out?'

'Hold on.' Aspen took the Cossack clunking over the trailing branches, long spines flying up and whipping over the roof. Then he braked the car to a halt as the walls of the sunken track gave way to a wider view. 'Hey, look. Just look at this, honey. We're home.'

She looked through the rain bursting on the glass. In front of them, a massive ploughed field was littered with flints, which glimmered in the light from the storm clouds starting to erupt over the coast. Close up, there was a final patch of

356

heath: a roughly square depression containing only a few low shapes of grass, shuddering in the wind.

All that was left of Wychland, the old house.

Mia held on to the door as a blast of the gale came across the field and hit the Cossack, slamming it on its springs. She kept the gun flat on her knees and said over the noise,

'So what did you find out when you were ten years old? Anyway, how could Cherelle be born here? She's an American. How could Cherelle be the daughter?'

Aspen turned and looked at her. He was pale, the blood streaking his face and his hair plastered back behind his ears. He said,

'When I was ten, I found out the truth. That her mother died here in the war. And guess who wanted to adopt her? Who was it that stepped forward to give her a home? An American pilot who was based near here. An American pilot who had a terrible accident with his fuel tanks, his teardrop tanks. Turns out he blew some little British house to pieces. He made up for it by adopting the girl. Him and his wife being a childless couple. A couple who thought they would never have children, then they got this opportunity, bammo. They took the little child, my mother, back to the US, raised her as their own. Did a good job, you got to say. In time, she joined the USAF too. She met Nathan Slade, my father.'

'So she told you about all this, what happened here?' Mia gestured with the gun out at Wychland.

'*She* didn't tell me anything. But I found out.

357

Just as soon as Jack and Kate Fletcher came into my life.' He rested his forehead on the steering wheel and rubbed it there.

'Tom Fletcher's parents? Tom's father was a friend of Nathan. Did he find out about this; did he tell you?'

'Not exactly, no.' Aspen raised his head and banged it on the wheel. Then he turned his face to Mia, chewing silently, his eyes closed. 'It wasn't Tom's father who told me. No.'

Fletcher knew the gale was at its worst when he saw one of the police drone planes. This one had crashed on the grassland near the Deeping, the wings ripped off, the central part being blown across the ground. He watched it go cartwheeling away inland. If it was still transmitting images, they would be spinning wildly – just grass, clouds and moon.

The water of the Deeping itself was thrashing about, spray bursting through the few reeds left standing. Fletcher left it all and kept going, sideways on to the wind. He had to stop after a few metres because the pressure was so great, and he threw himself down on the ground as debris from the beaches came blasting over the surface around him. Through his fingers, he saw an old plastic jerry can spinning over the grass, felt the impact as it struck his back and broke apart – shards of plastic bursting over him like the petals of a brittle flower.

Under all of that, he could still feel the old memory, the hand on his shoulder. He got to his feet and started running again.

Aspen Slade was worried. He pulled the cap back down on his head.

He wanted Tom Fletcher to be there to witness it, but there was no sign of Tom at all. Maybe the guy had been hit by something, all this stuff flying around. And Aspen wasn't sure how long he himself would last – blood in his eyes from the broken car window, making it hard to see much, just the Mia Tyrone woman hanging on the seat there, with that cheap little firearm pointing at him. If the gun didn't go off, the truck would fall to bits anyway.

It was dark outside, like twilight. Almost time now. Kate Fletcher would be here soon, he knew it. And perfect Tom Fletcher would have to be here to see her die.

Where *was* Tom?

Then Aspen decided – this Tyrone woman would do. She would tell him later, for sure. The important thing was for Tom to know the truth.

So he began telling her. About the fine, sunny morning when he was ten. The family accommodation on the base at Alconhurst. The British couple at the door. Cherelle, his mother, expecting them for some reason, a neat dress and makeup, coffee ready. Cherelle and the British woman looking at each other without speaking, for a long time. Standing there, just looking at each other, like searching each other's faces. Nathan and the British man shuffling their feet, going outside to the little yard, sitting in the plastic chairs. From his bedroom upstairs, Aspen could hear them making dull conversation about home towns, holidays, planes, cars. Pointless conversation.

What were the women talking about?

Aspen could see himself still, aged ten, going to the door of the downstairs room where Cherelle and this Kate Fletcher woman were sitting. The door closed, but the smell of coffee and his mother's cigarettes still coming from inside there. And the voices, the women's voices. His mother saying:

'This cannot be true. I cannot believe this.'

'It is, Cherelle. It took me years to put the story together, what really happened. Then years more to find you – searching, going back through the old records. Now I've found you. Look at us, anyone can see it's true. Aren't you happy?'

Cherelle saying nothing for a while. Then, *'How? How did it happen?'*

Aspen silently opening the door an inch. Seeing this Kate Fletcher, this creature from nowhere, holding his mother's hand in her own hands. Aspen listening to the whole story Kate Fletcher had to tell. She was reading some of it, he could tell. Reading off a few pages of paper, done on a typewriter. A long story, starting years ago when a man in a black hat came into a village in England and the women went running out across the fields to escape him, what he wanted to do to them. Aspen listening through that gap in the door, taking in every word. The story trickling into him, drop by drop, spreading into his bloodstream, infecting him.

Making him go, *Oh yeah. That's me now. I hate girls.*

Making him realise who he really was.

Making him the man be was today.

Here in the truck now, he was shouting, trying to yell over the air howling through the broken windows and out again. He dug in his chest pocket and got out the testimony, the cursed typewritten pages Kate Fletcher had brought that sunny morning. Time to destroy them, set himself free. He let the wind have them, the paper whipping out of his fingers and flying out over the grass of Wychland, blasting out there and just disappearing in the air. He laughed, watching them go. He felt better, cleaner, free of some of the poison. He wiped his mouth.

One more step, now.

He knew that killing Kate Fletcher herself would finish it, free him completely.

Mia Tyrone was staring at him. She had one hand on her gun and the other on the door handle beside her, holding on. So Aspen just clicked his own handle and let the wind smash the door open, and he let himself fall out, right out of the truck onto the ground where the wind was so strong it was hard to breathe. He crawled around the back of the truck, and flattened himself up against the shallow wall of the old road. The wind was blasting over him, but this was the least bad place to be right now. He watched the other door open and the Tyrone woman fall out onto the grass and make her way over to him, her hair and her rain cape snapping and twisting out behind her. She made it, and lay on her back near him. She still had the gun in her hand, but she looked dazed.

Then the truck door came right off and flew up

over the roof, a white smear in the storm dusk, staying on his retina. He looked again and saw it bouncing away across the turf, scattering bits of glass. Beyond that, up at the end of the track, he saw that line of willow trees being ripped up, the branches stripped off and the trunks just slamming over, roots flying up in the air. He closed his eyes then, and hoped nothing hit him before he had a chance to finish his work here.

The wind slackened, then rose again, then dropped into a low rush that still brought bits of tree debris over the edge of the embankment above him, but let him sit up, then get to his feet. It felt strange, like standing under low gravity. He saw Mia Tyrone get onto her knees, then stand up as well, facing him.

He breathed in the air. It felt cool and electrically charged, the landscape blasted clean, just for him. The clouds overhead were breaking apart, letting red sunlight through, long rays sweeping across the ground, full of vapour.

It was time, right now. His time. He walked past the woman, out of the lee of the track, past the battered old truck with its smashed windows and one door missing, out into Wychland.

He heard Mia Tyrone shout, 'You're fooling me or fooling yourself.'

He turned to look at her. She had the little gun in her hand again, the sleeve of her cape thrown back to let her use it. He laughed. He said, 'Your friend Gregory, up in his tower with his paintings. He didn't tell you everything, huh? Cherelle and Kate were sisters, twin sisters. The last thing old Evie did on this earth was give them to him, let him save them.'

'But Tom Fletcher met Cherelle last week, at Alconhurst. He met her personally. You saying he didn't recognise his mother's twin sister?'

'Cherelle's changed, honey. Smoking sixty a day for twenty-five years, she's a wreck. Sometimes I don't recognise her myself.' Then he felt a new air pressure in his ears. 'Hey, can't you feel it?'

'What?'

He jumped up onto the raised shape of the old Wychland house, the outline of the walls making scars under the turf. His time had come now. He was back here at the old place, where everything started and everything was going to end. He was going to cure himself, wipe out the source of the infection that had entered him along with Kate Fletcher's story.

He shouted,

'It's started. She's here. Kate Fletcher's here.'

Once the wind dropped, Fletcher found it easier to run. After the Deeping, he came into the sunken track, under the ridge of willows stripped of their foliage, the jagged fronds reaching out as he passed, some of them toppled down into the road itself. He knew Wychland would be ahead, at the end of this track, the way Gregory Tilney had described it. He could see where the Cossack tyres had cut mosaic tiles into the wet ground, and he trampled them, clambering over the splintered branches in his way.

Gives you visions or gives you twins.

He got clear of the last fallen tree, onto an open stretch of the track. Without breaking his stride, he pulled the HS gun out of his parka pocket, then pulled the coat open, shrugged it back off his shoulders while he ran, let it fall off behind him.

Thinking of Cherelle Swanson in her smoky little house at Alconhurst airbase. The woman's face destroyed by worry and toxins.

I thought I knew her. I thought I recognised her.

If I took that face and smoothed it out, made it younger, took away the lines and folds. Would that be my mother?

It could be.

Is Cherelle my mother's twin sister?

Fletcher stopped where the track gave way to an open field. The Cossack was there, what was left of it. The paint was glowing fleshy bronze in the reddish sunlight pouring down between the clouds, the light splintering off the shattered windows. Through the crazed glass, he could see the outlines of two people.

Mia Tyrone saw Tom emerging from behind the Cossack. He was wearing just his combat trousers, still tucked into his boots, a T-shirt streaked with damp. He was lit from above in red, the light jumping off his gun held beside him in one hand, off the water in his hair, the spray his steps were leaving as he came into Wychland's old sunken farmyard and looked around.

She knew that Aspen Slade, standing on the raised grass shape, had seen him too. Aspen turned to him and held out his hands, the light sparkling on the nylon of his hiking jacket. Mia guessed what Aspen was going to say next, from the triumphant look on his face, the way his fingers curled in the light.

Aspen said, 'Welcome, cousin.'

Tom Fletcher stopped. He wiped his free arm over his face, the gun still in the other hand. He looked from Aspen across to Mia herself, then back again. She said,

'He's insane. He says Kate and Cherelle are sisters.'

She watched as Tom Fletcher began to circle around Aspen. The American was trembling, beads of water flicking from his black hair, trying to follow Tom with his eyes.

Aspen said, 'She's here, cousin.'

'Shut up.'

'She's here. Your mother's somewhere around here. She's come because she knows what she's done to me. It's like, there's going to be one last witch trial. She's the last of the witches, and I'm the last witchfinder – and then it'll all be over. She's coming to me now.'

'Shut up, Slade.'

But Mia saw Tom take a quick look behind him, at the track. Then look at the patch of heath on one side, and at the ploughed field on the other side, the scraped up flints catching the white and red light. Beyond the field, on the distant flat headland, the storm clouds were giving way to mountainous walls of vapour. Between that and Wychland there was absolutely nothing – no buildings or trees. No person at all. She saw Tom Fletcher assessing it, the towering sea mist reflected in his blue eyes. Then Tom turned back to Aspen Slade.

Aspen was chewing violently – there was nothing in his mouth, just his jaw clamping up and down, eyes closed, the line of beard along his jaw damp and shiny. Then Tom Fletcher touched the muzzle of his gun against Aspen's cheek. Aspen stopped chewing and opened his eyes, tried to slide them sideways at Fletcher.

Aspen said, 'She's close. I can feel her, almost touch her.'

Tom lowered the gun and stood back. Mia watched his face, but it gave no sign of emotion. He was examining Aspen Slade in a detached way, like a scientist confronted with an unusual sample. He said, 'You're ill. Do you understand that?'

Aspen shook his head, but said nothing. Around him, Mia began noticing things in the raised outline of the old house: bits of debris breaking the surface, not completely grassed over. Close to her foot, a rusted iron spring stuck up from the wet ground.

Suddenly, Aspen said, 'I was fine. I mean, I used to be fine, cousin. I had a few little problems they called behavioural. Nothing that couldn't be ironed out. Then your mother came into my life. She'd been researching, see. She'd been to see Gregory Tilney, typed out the testimony.'

Tom Fletcher remained still, his head on one side. He said, 'If it's true they were sisters – so? Why hate her like this?'

Aspen shook his head violently again. Some droplets hit Mia, and she stepped back away from the two men. Looking at them, she thought maybe they *were* cousins – different builds, different hair, but related in the shape of the face.

Aspen began talking quickly, jabbering his words.

'She came into my life and confused me, Tom. She fucked my mind up. One minute I'm a fun-loving kid growing up on military posts. Innocent. Just a few kinks the doctors were fixing with medication. Next thing this woman comes into our house and I discover all about myself. I'm descended from the witchfinder. Ten years old, and she let him possess me, Tom. I could feel his blood in me, pushing my kid's blood out. He's living inside me now. Look at me. I look like him, don't I? The way that bitch Evie Dunton described him. There's no Aspen the kid any more. No Aspen the little kid, he's gone. There's only the witchfinder. He's made me do the things I've done, Tom. Things you know about, and other things, too. Things nobody knows, maybe never will. I've done it because of him. When the witchfinder gets loose, you can't stop him. And your mother set him loose in me.'

'There is no witchfinder, Slade. It's you and your sickness. You're using some old story to explain yourself, explain away your problems.'

'Why do you think she left you, Tom?' Aspen's eyes glinted, his chin tipped up. 'Hm, cousin?'

Tom Fletcher didn't answer at first, looking at Aspen with the tip of the gun still pressed into his cheek. Then he said, 'My mother discovered a plan to use radiation weapons—'

Aspen laughed silently, his jaw clamping up and down. 'No, no, cousin. No. Now it's you, you're using a story to explain *yourself*, Tom, explain your own fucking problems. There are no secret weapons, no secret plans.' He shook his head again, water flying off. 'I mean, why exactly did she leave you, Tom?'

'She was frightened, maybe she was intimidated—'

'Nobody frightened her. She frightened herself. She left because of the witchfinder, Tom. Don't you see? She could see what was happening to me, how she poisoned me with the story, how the witchfinder was taking me over. I hit her once, I admit that. It was the witchfinder in me, him using my fists. She cried; she was afraid for you. She thought if she stayed, you'd learn the story somehow, she'd infect you too. She tried to keep you safe from her poison. The witch tried to keep you safe.'

'There are no witches. There is no witchfinder.'

Behind Aspen Slade, columns of fog were rolling in off the headland: the tail of the weather system, trailing enough vapour to cover the sun all over again.

Aspen said, 'There is no witchfinder? You need to face reality, Tom. There is Colonel Theodore Harpkin, US Eighth Army Air Force. Born Cambridge, Massachussets, nineteen eleven. Disappeared, presumed drowned, in Norfolk, England, nineteen forty three. I've checked out the Harpkin family, Tom. They've got ponies and servants. They drink fucking *tea*. You know what they're really proud of? They trace themselves back to an Englishman who stepped off the boat in sixteen fifty with no background, no history. Just stepped out of nowhere, they say. They don't know it, but

I know it and now you know it too. He was Matthew Hopkins. He was the old witchfinder.'

'This is all in your mind, Slade.'

'Why do you say that? Look at this evil place. Just look.'

In the distance, the ploughed furrows were already disappearing, converging under a wall of haze.

Aspen said, 'I was so innocent. I was an innocent kid, and this place poisoned me. Look at me now.' He held out his thin fingers. Behind him, the mist was coiling across the field, lit with a faint pink light. 'It's me, it's what I do. But I don't like it, Tom. I hate it, I hate myself like this. I want to be a kid again. Playing around, just a little bit of medication.' He laughed. 'I want to be free of this poison. When I kill her, I'll be free. It'll be soon now. She's almost close enough to touch.'

Mia looked at the advancing wall of fog. The stuff was playing tricks with light and distance – was it halfway across the field now, or closer? And ... was there something else there? She thought there was a dark outline against the haze, moving like a person on foot.

She said, 'Tom.'

She saw Tom stare at it, then stare again, because it flickered and disappeared for a moment. Aspen didn't look, but he said,

'She's here now. I can smell her. She's mine.'

'Don't move.'

Tom held the pistol up against the side of Aspen's head, but kept staring past him to where the figure had been. Mia saw his eyes narrow, desperately searching the wall of glare. She tried to find it again, but the fog was unrolling smoothly, blankly.

She said, 'There's nothing there, nobody there.'

Aspen said, 'She's here – trust me, cousin. And if it's not now, it'll be later. I'll find her in the end. I'll spend my life searching, hunting her down. She'll never get away from me.'

When he stopped speaking, the place was totally silent. The fog was almost on top of them – and, for a second, the shape in the field appeared again, sharper this time. She tried to focus on it. It could be a figure, or just a gap showing the dark earth beyond, a space already being closed down as the vapour rolled over Wychland, thickening and spreading around them.

Mia gasped.

The stuff was freezing cold, making her shudder as it settled in her hair, putting a salt taste in her mouth, stinging her eyes. She blinked and wiped them with her hand. Now Aspen Slade and Tom Fletcher were themselves two outlines in front of her – Tom with an arm raised holding the gun, Aspen thinner, hunched over. She had to keep blinking the damp out of her eyelids. Out of the silence, she heard a man's voice – Tom's voice – shout something. She thought the word was *Kate*.

When she looked again, the fog was too thick to see anything, just a wall of pearl-coloured sheen right in front of her. Then an outline took shape – growing right in front of her eyes – a man's face with a line of beard, the mouth grinning. She realised it was Aspen, but he looked changed –

even paler, his dark eyes wide and blazing. The word sparked into her mind: *witchfinder.* As she took a step back, his clenched fist flew out of the vapour, punching her in the face, hard enough to jolt a flash of light across her vision. She saw the ground sliding up at her out of the glare. She felt fingers under her slicker, feeling across her breasts, her thighs, searching her. She felt the hands close on her pistol and draw it out.

Then nothing, just the grass beside her face. Close up, the blades were jewel-coloured, dripping water into her mouth as she tried to move her limbs.

Fletcher called his mother's name again. There was no answer, no sound at all, not even an echo. The fog was distorting his vision – giving the illusion of space, then a solid wall in front of him. The only real dimensions were the feel of his boots on the turf and the red tint to the mist on the right, where the sun must be. He tried to look around in a full circle. Aspen had gone; Mia too. He thought the figure had come from there: due west, where the sun was. He took a few paces towards the red light, his gun pointing down. There was something ahead, a shape against the redness. He shouted, 'Kate, I'm here.' He felt his heart powering in his chest. He reached out with his free hand, saw his own arm disappear into the blur. He felt something against his fingertips. He definitely felt it – real, after all these years. He stumbled over something – some piece of debris sticking up from the ground, and went down on one knee, keeping the gun away from the person he'd touched.

He felt something cold on the back of his neck, in the cleft at the base of the skull, a metallic stub. He felt a heavy boot trying to press his shoulder blades down. He resisted, and from behind his ear he heard the tinny click of an HS trigger going past the safety stage. Mia's gun.

'Tom. Listen.' Aspen's voice, breathless and trembling. 'Oh, cousin. Kate's here. Your mother's here. She's here right beside us, just a few yards away. I've seen her walking. Just a glimpse, but it's her.'

Fletcher felt the gun muzzle tremble, moving up onto the back of his head. He pressed his body up against the boot, trying to push clear. Aspen said, 'No, don't move, Tom. Don't try to stand up. I'll use this.'

Fletcher felt something fall on his neck, thicker than rain. He realised it was Aspen's saliva.

He closed his eyes, made a decision, took a breath. Then he began to stand up.

Mia got to her knees, then to her feet. The front of her face felt hot and slippery, and when she touched it her hand came away with long streaks of blood on her palm, shining black against the fog around her. Up ahead, there was a reddish tint in the air, and she began walking towards that. The fog parted around her, silently, suspended salt brushing her skin. Her mouth was full of liquid, and something had happened to her hearing, because all she could hear was her own throat as she tried to clear it, magnified hugely. She put her hands on her knees and spat, thought she was going to pass out completely. She stayed like that for a few seconds, getting her breath, the ground around her steaming. When she looked up, the fog was thinning out a little, the red sunlight breaking through and starting to burn it away.

It happened right in front of her – the thing she would always remember, the rest of her life, before she slept. Even with her damaged hearing, she heard a shot. She saw a bright flash, and at the same time a single red burst, exploding upwards through the vapour ahead of her, a wide plume of pink spray and heavier black droplets. Her mind made a connection with the droplets – blood, the same stuff as on her hand – and spinning among them shards of white and grey expanding in a cloud that reached an apex and then curved over, becoming finer and more dispersed. For a second, there was enough of it hanging in the air to form a spectrum, the resurgent light flashing through it and making a rainbow.

A perfect rainbow.

The colours were there and then gone. They collapsed in an instant, leaving no stain in the air. Leaving nothing behind at all.

Gregory,
I want you to take care of these girls. They are Sally's girls. You know who their father is and yes you might think I hate them for that for being born of the witchfinder. If they were boys I would hate them I think. But there must be a fight inside everyone between the innocent and the witchfinder. With these girls I say the innocent has won. When I look at them

I only see Sally.

These girls will need a family. You can do that, you are a man who knows things, you must know people who arrange that. A family or two families. I've heard if twins get split, they live the same lives anyway, they think the same things, they marry the same and have children the same and the children grow up the same. I have heard that. I don't mind you splitting the twins if you have to. Whatever happens out in the world, they'll be taking this place on with them. Wychland will never die now. The old place will always live, despite what the witchfinder has done.

It's time for me and Sally now. I can't live without her and she can't be happy without me. She doesn't know that, but it is true. It is better we go together like this. She won't know, and she won't suffer any pain. She'll just be sleeping.

Gregory Tilney smoothed the old letter, raised it to his lips for a second. Then he folded it and put it on one side. He settled back in his chair, watching through the window as the fog coiled silently around the tower. He closed his eyes again.

Monday Evening

Fletcher rolled his Audi to a halt in the car park of Wilbur Court. He looked around. The tarmac was damp and clean, puddles reflecting the blue, 6-p.m. sky. Up in the building itself, some of the windows were open, the curtains moving in the breeze. Beyond that, the conifers were quivering a little too. Beyond *them*, Fletcher knew, was a hundred miles of flooded land, and then the newly altered coastline – but Wilbur Court was sheltered from all that.

Inside, the reception was unstaffed, just a faint tang of chain-store perfume.

At the top of the stairs, Fletcher looked along the corridor. The shiny rubber floor reflected the line of doorways, some of them open. He stood there, taking it in. There was the sound of old guys' radio, someone crooning a chorus, someone laughing, someone coughing. Fletcher walked along, down to the end. The smell of cleaning fluid and tobacco and laundry drying. The last door, there on the left, was closed. Fletcher knocked. No answer – he tried the handle. It was locked.

'Hey. You, boy.'

John Rossi's door was swinging open.

John was sitting at his place by the window. There was a bottle of cheap beer on the table again, a cigarette in the ashtray. He had a bright T-shirt on, a young man's shirt, but his bare arms were full of 1960s tattoos and those long red scratches.

Fletcher stood in the doorway. He said, 'You didn't get flooded, then, John.'

John Rossi scratched his elbows. 'Rain kept me awake all night. Other places got it worse, though.' He adjusted his smoke. 'You heard about that little place in Norfolk?'

'Hanchton.'

'Yeah, Hanchton. I heard on the news the sea came in and tore it to bits. Picked up the promenade and threw it at the town. Fucking well demolished it.' He looked up at Fletcher suddenly. He was outlined behind veins of smoke against the rich blue sky. He said, 'Some people would say, if that happens, there's a reason.'

Fletcher looked back at him steadily. 'John, is my dad here?'

John Rossi thought about that, tilting the foam inside his beer bottle. 'No, boy.'

'Has he been in touch?'

'Yeah. He's told the management here that he's coming back soon. The ice maiden, she's keeping his room aired. All his stuff still in there, just how you left it.'

Fletcher nodded. 'I remember something about the floor in his room.' John raised an eyebrow, still fascinated by the label on his bottle. 'John, do the management know about that? Or what was under the floor panel?'

Rossi cleared his throat slowly, then took another sip of beer. 'The management don't know sod all, boy.'

'That's good, then.' A bird sang in the trees

outside. 'When you see my dad, can you tell him I was here?'

'I can, Tom. Any message?'

'Tell him I'll be coming to visit.'

John Rossi nodded. 'OK. You're the boy. You're just the way he said.' Scratching his arms. 'I see something different about you now. What happened to your head there? You got stitches?'

'I had an accident.'

'You lost weight too?'

'Maybe a bit.'

'Something else.'

'It's been good to see you again, John.'

'*Do widzenia.* See? I'm learning.'

Major Jerry Lindquist watched the helicopters in the distance sweeping across what was left of the sunset, over what was left of the little English town of Hanchton. The helicopters – a bright yellow British coastguard, then two green British army didn't slow down, didn't alter their course.

His own helicopter transport was in the field behind him, its engines still sending a heat blur up into the cool evening.

Lindquist looked back down at the little round lake, his suede boots on the remnants of the bulrushes. The water was a colour somewhere between aubergine and black, with white crests now the wind was picking up.

Lindquist, with twenty years' service. He'd been to some weird places on this planet. This was the weirdest place of them all.

He was still trying to make sense of what he'd seen the day before. He'd been lying up on the ridge, in the lee of the wrecked willow trees, using binoculars to see what was happening down there. It was blurry, the felled trees getting in the way at times, damp on the lens from the storm. But it was clear what he'd witnessed. First, Tom Fletcher and the Tyrone woman, plus Aspen Slade, having some kind of conversation. Then the fog rolling in, covering them. Then, when that thinned out, three figures moving around in the mist, crossing and recrossing. Hard to see exactly what happened, but looked like Aspen Slade struggling with Fletcher until there was that one shot – and Aspen Slade's whole head just blew apart.

He thought, *I still don't get that. I can see why Fletcher would go for a head shot – but with that little European popgun? To do the damage he did? How did that happen?*

There was no need to explain what they saw next, though – it was clear, as the fog evaporated completely. Tom Fletcher and Mia Tyrone dragging the body on chains behind their ruined truck, over to here at the lake, dragging it right into the water and letting it sink through the haze. It had gone down feet first, because the head was mostly blown away, the skull just an emptied shell.

Well – he had to admit one thing. That solved the problem of Aspen Slade. Aspen, who knew that something significant had happened here back in the war, and was unstable enough to broadcast it around, maybe.

It also kind of solved the problem of Fletcher and Mia Tyrone. Fletcher would keep quiet, for sure. If not because of the threat of extradition, then because of the fact he'd just killed someone and sank the body in a lake. And the Tyrone woman – she was heading straight back to the US. She had no evidence, no proof of anything. Just the same old rumours that had been circulating for years. And she looked pretty shaken by the events of yesterday – terrified of what she'd seen. That would help. Maybe she'd be taken off the blacklist, allowed to get on with her life. She would live quietly, he was confident of that. If not, she was another problem that could be solved.

Yeah, it could work.

So he gave the sign for the transport to start up, saw the rotor blades begin to turn with a whine.

Walking over there, he kept thinking about what he'd seen or thought he'd seen. He had to ask himself – was it Tom Fletcher who shot Slade? Because damn, for a moment it almost looked like there was someone else there too – a fourth figure on the edge of the group in the mist, holding something. Then, bam, the way Slade's head went apart. Some shot. No – that wasn't a .22 at all, no way. The flash and the noise it made, that was some vintage artillery piece. Something military. Maybe some old army pistol he thought. Some big old British revolver brought out of retirement.

He put that out of his mind as the chopper took a low path across the grassland. For a few seconds, they followed the decayed Mustang runway, then they left all that behind in the dusk.

Mia Tyrone was taken from check-in to a sealed office inside the Heathrow building. They went through her papers and held her passport in an ultraviolet screen. They placed her hand on a scanner and put her eye against a machine that captured the web of her retina.

They said, 'You've got a one-way ticket. Why is that?'

'Because I'm never coming back here.'

'Really? Why not?'

'Because I fucking hate it.'

They looked at each other. 'You bought your ticket at the counter and you have no luggage. We have to understand this.'

She said, 'I'm going home. OK?'

'We've checked your name. You work for the Bellman Foundation.'

'Not any more. I left.'

'You have an injury on your face.'

'I fell over.'

They questioned her for another thirty minutes, then shrugged and left.

After that, two women came in and stripped her naked. They went through her clothes with hands in disposable gloves, felt over and inside her body. In the room, there was a mirror on the wall with one edge peeling. She could see shapes moving behind it.

They let her go.

In the departure lounge, she sat watching the sky – what of it was visible, quartered up by the steel lattice of the Heathrow terminal windows. It was deep blue, clouds in one corner filling with sunset.

On the other side of the lounge, above the heads of the waiting passengers, the American Airlines

747 had its nose almost touching the glass. The cables and towers were being pulled away from it, pilots visible up in the cockpit. She was going to get into that thing, have three drinks and try to sleep, her legs tucked up, a pillow clasped over her stomach, the way she always slept on planes.

The way I always sleep anywhere, she thought.

She was going to sleep and wake up in her own country and never come back here. Never.

I was innocent. This place poisoned me.

She closed her eyes for a second, already thinking of sleep. When she opened them, someone was standing sideways between her and the plane, his profile outlined against the silvery light coming off its metal.

She focused.

It was a policeman in an armoured jacket, a peaked cap, a semiautomatic carbine held across his chest, the plane lights glinting off the buckles and clasps on his rig.

The man turned to look at her: white skin with blue veins under the stubble, ice-white eyeballs, the pupils almost black, looking into hers for a second, two seconds. Looking straight into her, seeing everything. One eye closed in a wink.

Then he moved on, continuing his patrol, his colleague just behind him, the two officers progressing slowly away across the lounge, creaking, their heads swivelling left and right.

She sat feeling her heart beating, watching the plane. The loudspeaker called the flight for boarding, and she stood for long minutes, her fingers getting damp on her passport.

She knew, she just knew. She was going to see

him everywhere. He was going to follow her over the Atlantic like his sick ancestor. Wherever she went to find safety, he was going to be behind her.

When the witchfincler gets loose, you can't stop him.

Fletcher looked up as Cathleen slid into the window seat opposite him.

She was tanned, and her hair was lighter, combed out and oiled, her shirt undone three buttons, the light from the streetlamps on Mill Road flooding her face, the freckle inside her left breast. She reached and took his hand in her two hands.

In the kitchen, Stan was singing some gloomy old Polish song about a meadow – Fletcher got that much – and a bull or a bulldozer or something.

Cathleen didn't let go of Fletcher's hands, just sat looking into his eyes. She said, 'You look tired.'

He said, 'Listen. There are some things I have to tell you.'

She lifted one hand, put a finger to his lips, pressed it there. She smiled, with a crease between her eyes, unblinking.

'*You* listen for once, Tom Fletcher. There's one thing I simply have to tell *you*.'

The publishers hope that this book has given you enjoyable reading. Large Print Books are especially designed to be as easy to see and hold as possible. If you wish a complete list of our books please ask at your local library or write directly to:

Magna Large Print Books
Magna House, Long Preston,
Skipton, North Yorkshire.
BD23 4ND

This Large Print Book for the partially sighted, who cannot read normal print, is published under the auspices of

THE ULVERSCROFT FOUNDATION